I0659657

THE

STONEBEARER

By Bucky Montgomery

Book One of the

KINGDOM CONTINENT CHRONICLES

For Legend, Amber, Destiny, Jasmine and Chance
To Jasmine Day Montgomery

Copyright © 1976, © 2014, © 2021 by William V. Montgomery. All Rights Reserved.
ISBN-13: 978-0692327241 (Custom) ISBN-10: 069232724X
buckymontgomery@gmail.com, or 502-322-7895 text only

Gaebryl Dindiane, the Prince of Bursia, trained warrior, explorer, map maker, and philanderer of some reputation, discovers a crashed skycraft one fateful morning and rescues the sole survivor, an aristocratic and mysterious young man, from certain death. From that moment on, his otherwise pre-ordained life changes forever.

As wounds heal, the nameless boy is surprisingly arrogant and uncooperative. Day by day, as Gaebryl faces exponential dangers for this thankless boy's sake, the intrigue and mystery surrounding him increases. Not only are two of the continent's most notorious assassins after him for unknown reasons, but the entire Gharnian army, and other dark and insidious creatures are as well. It takes every skill Gaebryl has to remain but one step ahead of them on their flight back to civilization and safety.

Enlisting the aid of several loyal and unique characters, the boy soon reveals his true identity, a family name shrouded in legend and myth, and an inevitable quest begins to take shape, a quest impossible, pitting this small crew against countless enemies advancing upon them from all sides.

Soon they are racing across the wildest of lands to seek out the legendary Stone of the boy's legendary forefathers, the only hope for a land of kingdoms virtually powerless against the dark militant tide rising against it. For with this Stone, supposedly, comes the absolute power of Destruction by Thought to he who wields it.

Yet, Prince Gaebryl suspects this boy holds more secrets than he is willing to share, and every single day seems to bring about a new discovery about this troubled lad... Gaebryl alone suspects that this boy is not who, or even what he says he is...

...The Stonebearer.

TABLE *of* CONTENTS

*

One

DISCOVERY

Y16 / Y17 Dogmoon Toy II, 512 Age of Tears

1

As the afternoon waned, the prince warrior Gaebryl found the way more difficult than he could have ever imagined. The dense foliage was hearty and ungiving, the ground at his feet precarious and rocky, strewn haphazardly with fragments of the huge gray/blue granite boulders that towered in great piles around him. Hidden under loose stones were pits and caves; often Gaebryl could hear water splashing deep in chasms far below, and hot, steamy geysers erupting, the sounds echoing up from unseen crevasses at his weary feet. And as if this weren't enough, the rockflies were large and hungry and had decided that Gaebryl was to be their lunch; his skin was covered with red welts from their painful bites.

Using a green stained machete, Gaebryl slashed his way through a wall of sticky vines, white sap dripping from the hanging stumps like leaky faucets. He climbed to the near-flat top of a blue granite boulder to evaluate his progress. To his relief, he had made it back to the rim of the Great Edge of Gaaloth. He had come by a roundabout route, through a sliver of a cave, but he was pleased to now be able to map it satisfactorily. By standing on his toes, he could just see a marker he had left on the outermost edge of a jutting rock, two hundred fifty feet west and fifty feet below his present location. Using his compass as a guide, he roughly sketched the boundary of the cliff in a small, black book. Then he matched it to another map he had brought with him; this one old, yellow and rotted, nearly flaking into pieces even as he gently held it. The maps were close in their detail, not identical, but very, very close. He replaced them securely in a rainproof knapsack, feeling very optimistic that he was now on the right course...

He sighed as his mind strayed back to his home, Dindiane, and to the events that were unfortunately unfolding there in his father's great castle city during his absence: his pre-arranged betrothal to a princess of a distant kingdom. Meetings. Arrangements. Plans. Ceremonies. Exchanges of money, land and services. Dowries. Headaches. The last thing Gaebryl wanted at this point in his life was marriage. However, his aging father, Isaial the King, was adamant.

He had heard that his fiancée, the princess of Cissel, Amber Leigh, was very beautiful, which was encouraging at least, taller than most, and as graceful as a wild antelope of the Eaophian plains. He had been told that she was intelligent, clever in conversation, and politically astute, everything that he had been taught to find attractive in a potential partner. But, despite all the nudging and coaxing from his father and his counselors, Gaebryl just wasn't prepared to take that harrowing road just yet. He had too many unrealized plans of his own. His father harped continuously that he would eventually sit on the throne of Bursia, and would need a wife to bear him an heir. Even though Gaebryl was at the burgeoning young age of just twenty five; his father had been married at a much younger nineteen.

"I'll get married as soon as I'm ready," he said aloud, then laughed at himself. "Talking to myself now. I do believe I've been out here too long."

Twenty seven days ago he had stepped away from the last outpost of rural civilization to map this insect and snake infested jungle, leaving his small skycraft Horizon behind, hidden in a secluded spot on a wooded plateau near a small jungle town called Daerooge. He chose this particular corner of the Great Rock Gaaloth not just to explore and map, but to test an intriguing theory of his. According to the deteriorating map he had found stuck between the pages of a Bursian sibyl's thousand year old wine bible a few months previous, he was possibly getting very close to an ancient mahekian city, all but lost to man's written history. It was known as Sweria Taaluu, the City of the Sky. He had never seen it rumored on any other map, nor had any loremaster he questioned have any knowledge of the place, other than vague references in remote children's fables. So far, after twenty seven fly ridden days, and an equal number of mosquito infested nights, he had not come across a single clue regarding Sweria Taaluu, not a bit of road or wall or crumbled foundation. Not even a blessed patch of level ground to calculations were accurate, so he persevered, feeling more than ever that he was drawing very close to *something* now. A few more days were all he needed, to find the mystic city ruins, or to prove that it did not exist there after all.

He paused to drink from his waterpouch. The lemon and herb drink was tart, cool and refreshing on his dry palate. Behind him, the forest loomed: huge, twisted gray barked trees, their broad green leaves waving like fans in the breeze; long, hairy vines looped from the heights, knotting the trees together like giant spiders' webs. Steamy geysers erupted somewhere in the distance with a wet whistle, a constant reminder of the geographical oddity that had created the Great Rock Gaaloth and the year round temperate climate across its southern and central regions. A myriad of animal noises filled the air, birds and insects mostly, but sometimes Gaebryl detected a larger, more sinister throat among the din.

He turned his back to the wall of trees and looked out before him. Where he stood on the southern cliff top of Gaaloth, the ground fell away at his feet, straight down for as far as could be seen, more than four thousand feet at certain points. Several small streams ran out from between the giant tree roots nearby, falling over the precipice and into the misty depths below. From Gaebryl's viewpoint, the vista was breathtaking. sunslit clouds swirled far below, but sometimes the clouds would break and he could see patches of earth, a twisting green river or some other glistening body of distant water. The wind rose in cool drafts, tossing his dark wavy hair and ruffling his loose fitting shirt. Standing on this cliff top, looking out over rugged Galgariah, Gaebryl felt an exhilarating urge to leap off of the stone and soar like an eagle, the wind strong beneath his wishful wings.

With a sigh, he tightened his pack and followed the crumbling rocks down the cliff edge, hacking steadily as he went. Past a thin ridge, his trail led across a natural granite bridge formed by one long narrow boulder, perhaps fifty feet in length, five to ten feet in breadth, lying precariously across a crevasse hundreds of feet deep. Geysers sprayed clouds of boiling steam into the eddy far below. On the other side, he found the undergrowth impervious. He hacked at it until he thought his notched machete was going to break. Around him, the jungle seemed so still that it was nearly anticipatory. There were many dangerous creatures always lurking nearby, he knew, so he was always wary.

His mind went to a young lady he had met in Daerooge just days before he had left on this exploration. Her name had been Aphelia. Quite an astonishing creature, this gypsy girl had not the accustomed modesty or restraint Gaebryl was used to from his usual female courtiers. She had raven hair and eyes like chips of topaz and emeralds reflecting somber moonlight. He had met her on the street at a fair, selling ribbons and fancy fabrics, and had been instantly taken with her sensuality and striking beauty. They spoke for awhile, and she agreed to meet him later at a place they both knew, a tavern in the seedy part of town called the Has Been Inn. Gaebryl went on his way to finish up business he had, but as night came, his mind dwelled continuously on Aphelia, so he left early for the rendezvous, hoping to have a drink or two by himself before she arrived. He was always more sociable and relaxed around the opposite sex after a good, stiff belt.

Aphelia had shown up right on time. She wore a flowing coral and white sun dress with mint green ribbons. Her dark hair with its red highlights, tied up in the marketplace earlier that afternoon, was loose then, flowing down to her hips in shadowy waves, adorned with tiny coral bows and white ribbons. They drank wine together and laughed until the wee hours of the morning. Gaebryl could not remember having a more delightful time. She was a wonderful conversationalist, able to drag him into all topics of debate and discussion. Of course, wine was a notorious tongue loosener. He told her his name, but he never told her who or what he was. Gaebryl had found that people often treated him quite differently when they knew his social status, and he did not want that with Aphelia. Things had been going too well between them to chance it. This was one of those occasions when he treasured rare anonymity.

The rest of the night was a blur: fleeting glimpses of faces, movement and color, and cold laughter, distant and condescending. A sleep so deep that he was unable to dream.

The next morning, Gaebryl awoke on a carpenter's doorstep. He did not remember how he had gotten there, and he had no idea where he was. It wasn't until he felt his empty pockets that he realized what had happened. A bit of something in his drink had put him to sleep, and now this gypsy girl had Gaebryl's purse and all the gold coin he had in it...more than the angry carpenter who kicked Gaebryl off his stoop with a swift boot made in over a year. He had been taken by a female again. When would he ever learn his lesson? They were scheming, conniving villains, the lot of them.

All inquiries concerning Aphelia's whereabouts came up fruitless, as he knew they would. One thing was certain, he would never judge anyone at first glance again, particularly a woman. In his experience, people were never what they seemed.

"Selfish, scheming manipulative wench. Another reason I should not be contemplating marriage!" he growled with a smile. "Women!"

2

Enough daydreaming, he told himself. He struggled through the dense brush, squeezing through as he ascended. As he noisily emerged from the crevasse, hair covered with mud and wet leaves, he heard a sudden noise in the trees nearby. A rowdy flutter. Gaebryl froze, alert and listening. Directly ahead of him, to the northeast, some startled birds had taken suddenly to the air. Gaebryl waited and watched as the colorful jungle fowl circled and landed in the nearby branches overhead. Their cries were anxious and wary, as if something was hunting nearby.

He remembered waking that same morning to a strange sound, something mechanical he had thought at the time, roaring and *whirring* from far off. That was all he could recall after he was fully awake, a whirring sound, like a skycraft's failing turbine. Now, he wondered if that noise had anything to do with the startled birds in the trees above him, still squawking chaotically. He knew that there were no coincidences in the jungle.

Unfortunately, his path continued in that very direction, so keeping a cautious eye and ear, Gaebryl moved onward, chopping at a particularly stout vine that was barring his way, severing it completely.

After a short while, Gaebryl came to a standstill. Near the spot where he estimated the birds had been startled, he came to a sheer wall of rock. It faced the open south, with no trail to either side. He could not head back in hope of circling around, because this had been the only route through. He searched the wall for any possible handholds to help him climb, but the rock was so smooth that it almost seemed unnatural. He began unstrapping his climbing claws...

It was then that he noticed something that he hadn't noticed before. He held his breath, quickly backing away to get a better look. There was some kind of immense carving on the face of the rock! Excitedly, Gaebryl stepped back as far as he was able, craning his neck back to see. There were a series of letters, great, thirty foot letters, carved into the granite, facing the southern sky like an immense welcome sign. They were strange, unknown characters of mahekian descent, mostly covered with a blanket of clinging ivy. Gaebryl was elated. Civilization, ancient and forgotten. He had found it! "It must be," he said. This had to be Sweria Taaluu!

He pulled some rotten foliage away from the stone face and discovered a fissure, ten feet from the ground. Using a dead limb as a makeshift ladder, Gaebryl pulled himself up into the narrow, jagged crack. It was tight, but widened slightly just above his head. Far above, the cloudless blue sky yawned past the lips of the fissure.

Bracing with his legs on either side, he slowly hoisted his way up, first with his legs, then with his arms, over and over. After a half hour of struggling thusly, he reached the top and emerged into a large, open glade. It was here that he made two remarkable discoveries:

The first was an ancient stairwell at the far end of the glade, cut into the natural granite, leading up into the hillside trees. The intricate carvings on the posts and arches were definitely ancient mahekian. Excitedly, Gaebryl stepped through the underbrush, pulling debris from his way as he followed the stairs skyward with his eyes. They led up the hillside to an ancient stone temple, half hidden by forest rot and years of untended foliage. All of the ancient mahekian cities were bordered with temples, which were the gateways to their mystical interiors. Inside the walls, no doubt, were vast treasures, and answers to mysteries, ancient books and scrolls, magick, weapons, potions, medicines, secrets and much more. This was the beginning of a great spiritual and intellectual adventure; Gaebryl felt it in his blood and bones. All great rangers were known for their discoveries: Faabel for the Gharzad Tower; Hymstrey Greer for Eaglesphere, the circular road of the winds; Mine Jabderflure for the lost underwater city of the Altantaris. Now Gaebryl would be credited for the discovery of the lost city of Sweria Taaluu, and just as important, he would make his aging father, Isaial Dindiane, the king of Bursia, very proud of him. Perhaps, he could only hope, this significant discovery would help postpone the wedding to Princess Amber yet another year, politics be damned. His heart leaped, and he cried out, his voice echoing boldly off the cliffs. He had been searching for this lost city for nearly a year.

And then it was at this point that Gaebryl made his second astonishing discovery... He paused in the middle of his victory dance as soon as he noticed it. Beyond the stairwell and to the right, he detected something else much more subtle; a less trained eye might have missed it altogether. There was but the slightest anomaly in the forest. A small tree had been recently severed at a height of about thirty feet, and further into the forest, several more were sheared and broken, as though something from out of the skies had torn through the trees at a terrific speed, slicing through the middle terraces as it crashed to the earth. He climbed up on a tall wall to get a better look, following the probable path of the falling object. He detected nothing at first, and then, between the huge waxy leaves, he spotted a glimpse of red and white, uncommon colors for the Gaalothian forest floor. Red and white on a smooth, wooden surface.

His brow tightened. He was quite sure that it was the hull of a crashed skycraft. It must have been this crashing skycraft that had made the sound, the *whir*, that had aroused him from his sleep that very morning. Someone might still be inside, he was thinking. Someone could be alive, and possibly hurt.

He glanced at the temple as he scrambled over the rocks toward the skycraft crash. More than anything, he wanted to rush up the stairs and find a way through the gates of Sweria Taaluu. But someone may need assistance. The ruins of the City of the Sky would just have to wait. It had been there for thousands of years and would be there for many years to come, so a few more minutes would not matter...

As Gaebryl neared the wreckage, he determined that the crash was indeed recent, as he had assumed, within mere hours. The skycraft was dirty and disgusting, a Bursian make, once very elegant, but modified for fighting, a two man sabotage vehicle used primarily by rogue thieves and scyropirates. He assumed that it was most likely stolen. There were no identifiable markings on it, or if there had been, they had been scoured off or painted over. It was overturned, its contents scattered in the bush around it. There was no sound now, not even the hissing of turbines, which meant that there was a good probability that it had run out of fuel, forcing it to fall from the sky. It was splintered into several pieces, but for the most part, the pear shaped main cabin was intact. Gaebryl decided to initiate his investigation there.

He circled at a safe distance, staying low behind the mossy trees, pausing to watch for movement and to listen for noises. He could see that there was no one in the upper cabin, alive or dead. Except for debris and scattered garbage, it was empty. If there were survivors, somewhere out in the jungle, Gaebryl pitied them, particularly if they were injured in any way. This was not a safe place, especially at night.

Stealthily, Gaebryl advanced upon the broken hull. The thought of an ambush crossed his mind. Or traps. So did the thought of repairing this wreck, finding some fuel close by, and going back after his own, more reliable, skycraft Horizon, near Daerooge.

Cautiously, he knelt to look underneath, and what he saw made him gasp.

The pilot's chair had come unfastened from the hull and was sitting upright in the rocks and vines beneath the skycraft. A large, magnificently colored jungle snake was coiled around someone still strapped in the pilot's chair. Its coiled muscles tightened in rippling knots. The reptile's jaw was unhinged, encircling its mouth around its victim's entire head, up to the neck. From between its sinewy coils, Gaebryl spotted a hand, a small, human hand, grasping weakly, yet desperately, at the muscled body of the snake. The hand quivered weakly, then went limp.

Gaebryl did not waste a second. He seized the snake by the tail and attacked it with his machete. Blood sprayed. The snake, unable to finish its meal, badly wounded and unwilling to fight, finally relinquished its hold on its victim, a young boy, and slithered quickly and desperately into the rocks beneath the ship.

Working quickly, Gaebryl dropped the machete, released the boy from the chair and laid him on the ground in soft ferns. He propped the boy's head up and checked for breath. It was there, faint and sour, having the smell of sickness on it.

"Hey, there," he called, checking the boy's eyes, which rolled up sleepily under the lids. "Can you hear me, boy? Hey!"

The boy stirred and took a weak swing at Gaebryl's face. The blow fell painlessly against his cheek, then the arm dropped, listless.

The boy was gaunt, malnourished, and he burned with fever. His skin was covered with red, blistery blotches, some rising to infected points. There appeared to be no broken bones, but there were cuts and scrapes, and patches of blood on his hands, in his hair, but mostly on his left leg. Gaebryl gingerly peeled back the torn pants on the boy's left calf. There he discovered the main cause of injury: a vicious, infected wound. The leg had been lacerated with a sharp object, deep and razor-thin. It had been jabbed quickly, such as with a knife. The skin around the wound had peeled back and blistered, as if retreating from acidic poison. It was days old, but it was not healing. A thin trail of dark blood ran from it, mixed with the yellowish white flow of infection. The skin around the wound was green, the bruises gray and deep into the muscle, from the knee to the ankle. The veins around the wound were bulging as though they were about to burst.

When Gaebryl laid a finger on the sore leg and the boy moaned and twisted, Gaebryl frowned. The situation was very bad. If he did not die, it was Gaebryl's opinion that the boy would eventually lose his leg.

"Listen to me. Be still. I'm going to try to help you," Gaebryl said. "Drink this." He tilted the boy's head back and trickled some water into his mouth. He expected the boy to choke, but he did not, so Gaebryl gave him more. He took out some medicinal herbs from a thin pouch on his belt and stuck them between the boy's cheek and gums. Fortunately, Gaebryl still had a small vial of ointment called *bachrad* that he had obtained from a physician savant in Daerooge, and he mixed the rest of the herbs into it, then placed the glob onto a strip of clean, dry cloth from his pack. He carefully placed it directly onto the wound. As soon as the cold, oily ointment touched the leg, the boy stiffened and cried out. Gaebryl worked firmly and diligently. He wrapped the strip around the bruised leg several times and tied it loosely, squeezing the ointment against the sore. The boy, fading in and out of consciousness, kicked and grabbed at the dressing, trying to free himself of it.

"Stop that," Gaebryl said softly, holding the boy's hands at the wrists. "Just relax. Rest if you can." He deduced conclusively that the boy had been poisoned with an assassin's blade. He did not know how potent the poison had been, but the dosage seemed deadly enough, although it was inflicted with the cruel intention of making him suffer a few days first before dying. It had all the qualities of a torture poison.

Reluctantly, Gaebryl removed another vial from his pack. It was a generic anti-venom that he always carried, one that worked well enough against most known nerve and bloodstream poisons, if given timely. But, if Gaebryl was wrong, and the boy was not poisoned, the anti-venom would kill him instead.

Gaebryl saw no other choice. He squeezed the boy's mouth open and flicked the lid off the vial with his thumb. He upturned it and several clear drops fell into the boy's mouth. The boy's face tightened repulsively. He tried to expel the bitter liquid with his tongue, but it had already been absorbed into his saliva.

"There you go," Gaebryl said, leaning back against the skycraft hull, for that was all he could do for the moment. Just sit back, watch, and wait. Under the circumstances, his resources were very limited.

Despite the dirt and blood, Gaebryl saw that the boy had the look of some aristocracy to him, and that he was not properly dressed for travel. His tailor made clothes had at one time been fine and expensive. His leather boots were crafted as fine as Gaebryl had ever seen, and he had two small gold loops hanging from both of his ears. His blonde hair and nails were well groomed, but his face was red and suns blistered. His hands were thin and elegant, like a pianist's, nails trimmed; he had certainly never seen hard physical labor before.

The boy's eyes fluttered open and their eyes briefly met for the first time. It appeared as if the boy, despite his injuries and sickness, snarled defiantly at Gaebryl.

Suddenly, the boy began retching.

"That's a good sign," Gaebryl said, turning him to the side. "Maybe you'll live after all."

3

The afternoon passed slowly. A sudden rain came, drenching everything, then, as quickly as it had arrived, it was gone again. The air about them grew thick and steamy, and the damned flies returned with a vengeance.

Gaebryl crawled out from underneath the overturned skycraft. The air was stifling. He continued his search of the area until he was sure that there had been no other passengers aboard. He covered the ground and brush meticulously and found that no tracks led to or from the crash. The boy had been traveling alone. Bizarre, to say the least.

The boy's delirious moaning continued.

Gaebryl frowned. There were no cities or towns within several days of travel, and this boy needed immediate medical treatment. Gaebryl did not like the prospect of amputating the boy's leg himself should it get worse, but that was a decision that would soon need to be made. Something else was dreadfully wrong here, too, something on a broader scale. This boy was certainly no ranger or assassin, although he was traveling alone in the wilds, piloting an assassin's skycraft, and he had been stabbed in the leg by an assassin's poisoned blade, to torture him or to make him talk. If this were so, where was the assassin? If the boy had somehow escaped and stolen the assassin's skycraft, then the assassin's work with this boy remained unfinished. The boy was still alive, and obviously fleeing.

"Not good," Gaebryl mumbled to himself, and he caught himself checking his weapons. He wished that he had brought more.

Again the boy moaned deliriously. His dry heaves continued.

Gaebryl shook his head and cursed aloud. "Looks like I've got my work cut out for me then," he said. He knew that he was going to have to carry this boy back to civilization on his back, across horrible terrain, while eluding any pursuers, possibly professional hunters and killers. Maybe there was just one, maybe there were many. This was not going to be an easy task.

He breathed deeply through his nose and let out an angry snort. There was little doubt that the only reason he was taking this boy back to civilization was to give him a proper burial. How would he get him up into the trees at night? What would they eat? There was not enough food for one in his pack, let alone two, the second one needing constant and crucial nourishment just to stay alive. Gaebryl felt weary and frustrated. And selfishly disappointed.

The temple, he thought. *So damned close...*

"Fine then. One step at a time," he said sternly to himself, looking up at the Westering suns. He noted that there was a stream close by where he could dip the boy, clothes and all, until his fever broke. That was as good a start as any. He could lighten the load. Pack only the essentials. Nature would provide. Then, he would carry the boy back to Daerooge for a doctor.

It wasn't *that* far, he thought, facetiously.

He lifted the boy up in his arms and carried him toward the clearing. "Let's get going, then," he said.

Gaebryl never saw the temples of Sweria Taaluu, City of the Sky, ever again.

Two

THE ASSASSINS

4

Two dark figures crept through the thick underbrush just outside the forest town of Daerooge and paused near the bars of the tall iron fence that encompassed and (supposedly) protected it. It was past midnight and very dark. Inside, they saw tranquil lights flickering from lamps hung on distant posts and porches. It was hot and the air was moist; beads of water gathered and dripped down through levels of leaves to the fertile black earth. The two assassins crouched in the twisted roots of a great knotted banyan tree to reevaluate their situation. Their names were Habad and Tursdah, infamous assassins from the far off land of Bursia, Prince Gaebryl's own distant kingdom. They had been on the hunt for many weeks now, searching diligently for a young boy, a novice traveler of the wilds (at first escorted by an inexperienced crew), who was carrying with him a mysterious stone key of some kind... They did not know the boy's name or where he was from, or what the stone key unlocked. Those things did not concern Habad and Tursdah. They were motivated only by gold and reputation, not politics, and the Gharnian generals who hired them for this particular job were offering an abundance of both upon their successful return. The killing of the boy, as far as the Gharnians were concerned, was of no consequence. That was to be the assassins' prerogative when the time came. The Gharnians only wanted the key.

Since that time, Habad and Tursdah had found the boy, and somehow, lost him again. Now, with Gaebryl in the picture, matters had complicated exponentially.

Habad signaled for them to move closer to the gates with a subtle hand gesture. He was thin, quick, and cautious, now nearly seventy years old, but calculatingly deadly. Tursdah, on the other hand, was a mass of muscled flesh, young, large, and big boned, slower, but very strong. He was just as deadly, but his youth made him boastful and careless at times. This irritated Habad, who had agreed to become his mentor thirteen years before only if Tursdah would listen and obediently learn from him. Often Habad found himself regretting that decision. Tursdah's lust for gratuitous pain and killing had almost gotten them captured on three recent occasions. Habad did not want to end up dangling from the end of a ranger's rope now, not at his age. Retirement was just one good paying job away.

"Damn it, Tursdah, tracks have stopped. They've given us the slip again," Habad said, hissing like a snake as he spoke. His eyes reflected the dim town lights like dried pools of milk. "I told you they wouldn't stop here. I knew it. Gaebryl knows we're hunting them."

"Let's move before it rains again," Tursdah whispered, looking towards the turbulent sky. "We've wasted two days here already. I hate this jungle."

Habad rubbed his nasty nose. "Where do you think then?"

"Anywhere else but here."

"Hush... Guards."

The sound of muffled footsteps came from their left. The assassins became as still as shadows as two armed Daeroogian nightguards, hired police from Tungulin, passed near them just inside the protective fence. They were lean and gaunt for men, but soft and easily broken by the experienced assassins should it come to it. The road that encircled the town, just inside the fence, was patrolled regularly, although Habad and Tursdah could not figure out why. Except for their own presence, there was no real danger for this quaint little mining town, and the iron fence adequately repelled any dangerous wildlife. There was no political significance or great horde of wealth in Daeroogc. *The human animal's paranoia* was it, they had finally decided between them.

Strolling at ease, two helmeted guards entered their patrol station, a small, wide, bullet shaped stone structure near the huge iron gate. Habad and Tursdah curiously watched the guards check in while two others began their semipunctual rounds of the Daeroogian perimeter. It was shift change for the guards, which meant that, for a few minutes, the town's already slack security was even more vulnerable.

When the guards had passed, Habad spoke again. "Hmm... I think Gaebryl will take the boy on to Tungulin, where he can get good medical attention. It's the only place that makes any sense. Gaebryl knows the land between here and there better than most. He'll take the old paths through the Gaalothian Forest and avoid the main roads until he gets closer to the city. That's what I'm thinking."

Tursdah groaned in response. "I'm bored, and I'd love a flask of whiskey. I want to get this over with. The Week of Eleven Trials begins soon in Irisia..."

Habad hissed at him. "You're so damned impatient! You must *think*, sometimes, you ignorant toad! Haven't you learned anything?"

"I learned that I get stiff if I squat too long. My knees ache."

Habad wiped his nose on his scrawny forearm. "Crouching in the slime and muck, waiting, watching, and *thinking* comes with the job, Tursdah. It's made me very rich and you haven't done so bad yourself, tagging along with me. So stop your belly aching."

"We should've had them by now. Hell, Habad, they're on foot. Gaebryl's probably still carrying the boy. We keep falling for his damned woodsman tricks."

Habad held the bloodstained dagger in the air before him and twisted it back and forth, reenacting the cruel technique he had used to inflict the boy's leg wound. "At any rate, the boy should never walk again. I poked him good. We should've kept torturing him that night until he told us where the key was. We shouldn't have stopped."

"We shouldn't have gotten so pissed, either."

"He must've hidden the key somewhere close by, in the woods, maybe. I do admire the little bastard for his cunning escape, though, Tursdah, lame as he was. We should've chained him up better."

"We'll catch him again, Habad."

"Yes, we will."

"And we'll be far less kind the second time around."

"Yes, we will!" Habad responded. "I'll hobble the little maggot at the ankles for stealing our craft. Little *scum...*"

Tursdah groaned. The sound was deep and ominous. "I don't know," he said. "His escape was in fate's hands, Habad. I believe that now. It's no random chance that led Prince Gaebryl Dindiane to this particular boy in this little out-of-the-way forest. It's destiny, his and mine..."

"Distractions!" Habad said. "Don't set your mind on killing Gaebryl, Tursdah. That's not our job! Focus only on the key! The Gharnians are paying us for the key, and that's all. If it requires murder, then yes, so be it. They must have suspected that it might come to that, otherwise they could've hired a handful of trackers and thieves to retrieve it instead of us, renowned as we are," Habad said, smiling with a devilish pride. "This key must be very important to them to be offering so much."

Tursdah shifted his weight from one leg to the other. His dark brown skin, leather rough and hairy, was adorned with thick, crude leather straps and dirty brass circlets with spikes in the center of each, which shimmered slightly when he moved. "Your motive is greed. Mine is infamy. Coming across the prince warrior of Bursia is my destiny," he groaned hungrily, eyes distant. "I have no control of this, Habad. In the grand scheme, the key is incidental. This meeting is meant to be. It is villainy versus royalty. You do understand this?"

Habad sighed. "Your thirst for infamy will be your

downfall, my brother."

A squeaky, clattering cart came down the road and turned toward the busy town inn. The guard near the gate took a sip of tea and waved casually to the driver. They exchanged a few cordial words concerning the inclement weather.

Habad and Tursdah took the opportunity to skirt along the fence line and pause under the shadow of the gate wall. The gateway arch was made of huge fitted stones, covered with mosses and hairy lichens. The stone foundation was old and weatherworn; the black rusty bars were just as ancient, all wrought before written history by the thordians, who were supposedly the original settlers of Daerooge. The assassins froze under the shadow of large ferns; the solemn light cast by a flickering lamp lashed at them through the leaves. A large wild cat, somewhere in the valley to the north of the city let out a long, shrill cry. The crescent shaped blooms of the sensitive catwatcher nightflowers closed at the eerie sound.

Habad wiped his crusty nose on his shoulder, and then he rubbed it in with the palm of his hand. "Here's the plan, then, mate. We'll head north, and fast. No use tracking them. Gaebryl's too good a woodsman. He lost us here, he'll lose us again. We must catch them by surprise..."

"They've got a two day start on us. That means they'll reach Tungulin in less than two more."

"The inn is busy tonight, so there will be plenty of skycrafts in the lot. We'll steal two. Then we'll catch up to them. We'll patrol the incoming roads to Tungulin from this direction, and pay scouts to..."

Immediately, Habad and Tursdah fell silent, fading back further into the shadows. A guard had stirred and was coming toward them, beamer in one hand, keys in the other. The assassins sunk low, toward the ground, eyes squinting into non reflective slits.

"I thought I heard whispers again," the guard said to the other, who was sitting lazily inside the station, nose in a book. He pulled a small handheld blaster from his hip and stepped up to the fence, just feet away from Habad and Tursdah, and peered out over them into the dark forest beyond. The inky blackness was total, a lightless void stretching infinitely in all directions. Only creatures with nocturnal senses far superior to those of civilized beings wandered restlessly and silently under the cover of those dense wooded canopies. "Didn't you hear it that time, Lake?"

"You've been hearing things for two nights in a row, Qan," the other guard replied. "It's just the wind in the trees again, I'm telling you."

"I'm going to have a look for myself this time, just to be sure."

Lake looked up from his reading, peering out the window. "I don't think that's a good idea, Qan," he said. "Not at night. You know better than that."

As Qan stepped up to the black iron gate that separated Daerooge from the savage forest, he flashed his beamer into the running shadows. The air was thick with mosquitoes swarming right outside the gate, as though they knew, like all bad and wild creatures, that they weren't welcome inside. Fumbling with the keys, Qan unlocked the massive deadbolt and stepped out into the darkness.

Lake stood. "Qan..." he said.

It was forbidden by law for any regular Daeroogian citizen to step outside the gate at night for any reason, and the Tungulinian nightguards could only do so under exceptional circumstances, and only with permission from one's superiors. There was an old fireside story about a foolish young Daeroogian watchman who opened the gate one night for whatever reason; some say he was lured by a beautiful woman with white skin and lips the color of roses, with coal black hair, standing alone, barely dressed, outside in the middle of the road. The next morning, many barns and sheds were found broken into, and the livestock had been drained of blood. No one had ever found any clues regarding the whereabouts of the young watchman, only the gate standing wide open the next morning. The fable was appropriately known as "The Foolish Watchman."

Qan, remembering the story, hurriedly locked the gate behind him, then turned and took the beamer out from under his arm, holding it up in a shaky hand. He bravely stepped off the cobblestone road into the summer weeds, moving awkwardly through the knotted undergrowth to where he thought he had heard the clandestine voices. All around him, shadows swayed in the forms of leafy boughs and groping crawlers. The moaning night wind swept upwards into the night sky, pushing the dark clouds westward, end over end. The Gaalothian Forest at night was a murky, foggy marshland with hungry mouths hidden in quiet brambles and tangled roots.

"You all right?" Lake called from the guardhouse, hand on the warning bell.

"Fine," Qan answered from the woods, his voice quivering just a bit. "It was right over here..." He came to the approximate point and paused, listening intently.

He heard no whispers now, but he did hear crickets and other insects, a night bird, occasional water dripping into shallow puddles, and trees rustling in the wind all around him. In the distance, the sound of occasional erupting geysers hissed and sputtered. A chill ran up his spine. It was so dark that he could step on a leopard's tail without even knowing it until it was too late.

Half expecting to feel talons at his throat, Qan held his hand to his neck and looked up at the churning clouds that clothed the starlight from his eyes. Summer lightning lit the sky, and a bellow of thunder rattled the earth beneath his feet.

The two assassins took advantage of this distraction and slipped out from under him, and slithered around the back of a huge tree. Blending with the shadows of the clouds, they lightly scaled the 'impenetrable' iron fence without notice as the thunder rolled away into the distance, leaving Qan alone at the forest's mercy.

"Qan! Do you see anything out there or not?" Lake called

nervously.

As though he could now feel the difference of being left absolutely alone in the forest, Qan grew uneasy, as if he sensed that dark things were creeping in on him from every direction. He turned and dashed up the slippery bank, high stepping comically through the weeds. "No," he hastily answered, stumbling once, and then again, before reaching the gate. With great relief he stepped back inside and locked the gate behind him. He flashed his beamer into the forest for one last check; a score of shining eyes disappeared with a rustle of leaves.

Lake held out Qan's tea for him as he stepped back inside the guardhouse, his face slightly pallid.

"You were right, Lake," Qan said. "Must've been the wind."

"Let's have a smoke," Lake said, handing him his pipe. "Relax awhile. I think you need it."

"You're right. I do."

"We've got Westwatch the rest of the week anyway. Nothing ever happens up in Westwatch."

Qan agreed. "That's a lot of steps on a lot of stairwells to reach!" He took a seat and lit up his pipe, never knowing how close to death he had just been.

5

A messenger came past the same guardstation some time later that night with an urgent note. TOP SECURITY, it read. TWO SKYCRAFTS HAVE BEEN STOLEN AT THE INN AND SQUIRE AXEN FOSTER HAS BEEN MURDERED. NO SUSPECTS AT THIS TIME. URGE CAUTION AND APPROPRIATE ATTENTIVENESS. REPORT ANY UNUSUAL SUSPECTS OR ACTIVITY AT ONCE.

Qan looked pale. "I know Foster," he said. "He was always patrolling the inn. You don't think..."

Lake shrugged, looking at his friend. "I was watching the whole time, Qan. Nothing or no one came through that gate."

"I know what you're going to say, Lake, but I think I better report what I did here tonight." Then he mumbled to himself, "The Foolish Watchman."

6

After leaving the stupid, inept, blind guards at the gate, the two Bursian assassins had slithered secretively into town, up the main hill and into a narrow alley, laying up against the wall of the Has Been Inn. There was enough loud music, singing and dancing inside to camouflage an entire battle. Although they moved with uneasy anxiousness, being heavily and illegally armed, so far, they had gone completely undetected through the center of the town. They were afraid that their luck would not hold out much longer, though, and secrecy was a hunting assassin's greatest asset.

Lightning flashed; thunder followed. A new wind tossed the trees. Rain was imminent.

"By the gods, that whiskey smells good," Tursdah said.

Habad pointed a crooked finger toward the lot where the patrons of the Has Been Inn had anchored their skycrafts. "Never you mind about that right now. I see two guards, one at either end," he said, his voice tapering off as the wind howled noisily over the rain vent on the corner of the building, spinning loose debris around their booted feet. "Might have to kill them if we're ever going to get out of here unnoticed."

One of the nightguards, a burly retired admiral, was making rounds when he came down the platform outside the inn to the steps beside the alleyway and looked into the darkness, toward the assassins. He wiped sweat from his face. It was hot and unbearably humid, even for a midsummer's night. He suddenly felt as though unfriendly eyes were focused upon him and this thought made him shiver. Out of the corner of his eye he thought he saw something cross the road toward the skycraft lot, but when he turned to look, he saw only restless leaves and some papers being tossed about by the humid wind. A few drops of rain began to fall, dotting the porch and ground beyond with big, dark spots. He squinted, but he saw nothing unusual. The other guard over at the skycraft lot, Squire Axen Foster, nodded to him, and he casually waved back. He felt uneasy, but he didn't know why. Hesitantly, he moved on down the ramped stairs and headed to his next station as the rain began to fall in earnest.

Tursdah rubbed his callused hands together and smiled. "Might as well be blind," he said. He adjusted his huge battle axe in its hold on his back. "I hope Gaebryl gives me more sport than these oafs."

Habad squatted, watching the lone guard near the back of the lot, less than thirty feet away. The dolt was biting his fingernails and paying no attention to his job. Habad took a Haas throwing knife from his belt and balanced it lovingly between his fingertips. "He will, my stubborn apprentice, he will. If it's sport you want, you'll get plenty from the great Bursian prince..."

He quickly stood, flicked his wrist in a fluid, graceful manner, then squatted again.

"...I've seen him do mock battle in the Harvest Festival Games at Dindiane. Good fighter. Very quick. Resourceful. Cunning. You'll see."

Tursdah peered over the wall with one big yellow eye and saw the guard futilely attempting to pull Habad's blade from his gushing throat. The man fell limply to the ground without muttering a sound, and quivered for a moment before becoming still. Tursdah looked into the stormy heavens and snorted. "Mock battle? Where's the glory in that? Gaebryl, wherever you are," he swore, spinning a glaring gaze, "Tursdah the Great is coming to show you the Door of the Dark Valley. Prepare yourself for the sweet sleep of infinite death."

Blinding lightning. Bellowing thunder. "Come," Habad said. "Let's get that damn key." The assassins hopped over the rickety fence. They watched the streets for a moment to make sure no one was watching, then they backed two small one man skycrafts into the woods behind some tenant cottages that bordered the Daeroogian livery apartments. Then, as silent as the sullen moon that peeped from behind a purple storm cloud, they shot out into the rainy heavens on a high slope, toward Tungulin, the City of Science and Magick.

Three

TUNGULIN

7

An ember in the coals of the quieted campfire popped, waking Gaebryl from his sleep.

The morning was peaceful. Songbirds were singing somewhere above the translucent blanket of mist that rose from the woodland gully where he had made camp. Nearby, a crystal clear spring bubbled up from the rocks, and it trickled, sparkling, over large, smooth, black creek stones, running down into a noisy brook in the shady hollow to the east. Along with thick flowering ferns and downy green moss, it was as beautiful a forest garden as could be imagined. Great, regal trees seemed to hold up the leafy roof like giant ornate columns of gray and brown, their immense limbs stretching toward the climbing suns like chilled arms and fingers seeking warmth. The sky through the trees was a deep, rich blue, promising a good day of travel ahead.

Gaebryl pulled his blanket aside and stood, stretching. His neck was sore and his back ached from carrying the boy and their two packs for so many miles. How he wished he could have retrieved his skycraft Horizon near Daerooge, but it had just not been safe enough to head in that direction. Gaebryl knew that they were being tracked and hunted; twice he had spied two figures in the distance scouring the trail behind them for clues, and both times he was able to elude them again before being spotted. He had intentionally misled them in the direction of Daerooge, hoping to gain some valuable time and distance.

He stood in a shaft of golden sunlight that had broken through the trees, allowing it to warm his chilled skin. It had been thirteen long days of foot travel and he was weary, but now their destination was close at hand. He was more anxious than ever to finish this burdensome chore and get back to his previous business at Sweria Taaluu.

He washed up in the cold brook, then made a meager breakfast of leftover rabbit, brownberries, and stale corn muffins from his canvas shoulderpack. After he had finished eating a lean portion himself, he went to the foot of an old, gnarly pine tree and gently kicked at something curled up in the flowers between the knotty roots. There was a stirring, then the boy sat up and rubbed his eyes.

"Come on," Gaebryl said to him, helping him to his wobbly feet. The boy looked up at Gaebryl and scowled. "We need to get going."

Gaebryl escorted him to the large flat stone that would serve adequately enough as a breakfast table that morning, and helped him sit. "Try and eat something, Chatterbox."

The boy crossed his arms at the chest and turned away, his nose arrogantly in the air.

"You'll eat. I've no doubt about that," Gaebryl told him. "Now let's have a look at that wound." He knelt and checked the rough bandage behind the boy's left knee. "Hmm. The healing herbs we found have taken a lot of the swelling out, and the bleeding's finally stopped. It looks better today than it did yesterday. Should be fine in another few days."

The boy retracted his leg haughtily, then winced in pain. Gaebryl shook his head. "I always made a point of avoiding children in the city. Now I remember why," he said. He walked away through the ferns, back toward the trail they had been following the day before, a few hundred feet to the north of their camp. "I'm going to have a look around. Try and behave yourself, Chatterbox."

The boy ignored him. Only a week ago the boy's chances for survival had looked grim. Miraculously, the possibility of a complete recovery now seemed imminent. The bachrad and antivenom had saved his leg and possibly his life, but to Gaebryl's chagrin, not a word or gesture of thanks had been given. Ever since the boy had regained consciousness, he had not smiled once, nor attempted to mutter a single word. Gaebryl still did not even know the boy's name.

"Lucky it wasn't a deadlier poison," Gaebryl called over his shoulder as he weaved through the trees, high on the opposite bank of the hollow. "Or I might've been amputating this morning, instead of having another one of these pleasant conversations with Your Highness."

The boy watched Gaebryl disappear into the brush on the far side of the dale, then he hungrily seized the food in his hands and shoved it handful by handful into his mouth. He was so famished, now that his appetite had returned, that he swallowed everything without hardly chewing, not leaving a single morsel. He even went so far as to lick his fingertips and dab for the tiniest crumbs on the surface of the rock. Still, it wasn't enough for him. With all this food rationing, he felt like Gaebryl was starving him, and it made him more cross than ever.

He looked around for any other scraps, and then he poked through Gaebryl's pack for more. All he wanted was some decent food. He found a small bag of dried fruits and nuts and ate them all without pause, then dug for more, but the pack was then empty. The boy scowled. At least Gaebryl had finally left him alone, allowing him some time to think.

He limped back to the spring and filled his belly with clear, refreshing spring water, then wiped his mouth on his silk shirt sleeve. After the ripples stilled, he looked at his reflection in the pool. He was filthy. His mop of goldenrod hair was shaggy and unkempt. He looked at his dirty, torn clothes, his dirty fingernails and muddy shoes, and frowned contemptuously. It was degrading and utterly unthinkable, a person of his stature wallowing in such lowliness. And lapping water like a dog! Abhorrent! As soon as he was physically able, he planned to give Gaebryl the slip. No telling where they were heading, and there were still pressing matters to attend to...

He splashed the cold stream water on his face and neck,

and washed his hands as best he could, wiping them dry on his shirttail.

He practiced putting weight on his bad leg, walking up and down the small bank of the stream as best he could. He stretched and squatted and kicked and twisted, yearning to regain full use of it as soon as possible. It was healing well, but, still, the area immediately surrounding his wound was red, numb and sore. There would surely be a horrible scar there.

"I love this little forest," Gaebryl suddenly said, popping out from the trees a few yards behind him. The boy jumped at the sound of his voice. "Sorry. Didn't mean to jolt you," he said, and then he continued, playfully, "You know, it's said by an old wyzard that used to live near here that strange little people live in this forest. They're called Gaalothians. This forest is named after them. Supposedly, there are thousands of them, living here in their homes built under the roots of the trees. I've been through these woods many times, but I've never seen a trace of them. It's said that these little elves work all night tending these forest gardens, keeping them clean and beautiful, but I just don't know. You didn't see or hear anything while we were sleeping, did you?"

The boy rolled his eyes.

"Me neither." Gaebryl looked at the breakfast table. "Look, you missed a crumb."

The boy looked, but, again, Gaebryl was just aggravating him. The rock was as bare as a bone. The boy frowned, feigning indifference. Gaebryl smiled at him. The only pleasure he could muster on this dreary trip was to aggravate the boy whenever possible.

"Glad to see you have your appetite back, although that's the last of our food, except what we can rustle up along the way. I checked the path ahead and it looks clear enough. If there are no objections, I'd like to be on the way. No? Good."

Gaebryl packed up their belongings. He put out the coals with a few bowls of water, then spent nearly an hour hiding all traces of their having camped there, as he did every morning. It was a meticulous job of digging and burying, raking leaves and sticks by hand, then arranging pieces of debris piece by piece so that every scent and clue was either covered or disguised.

As usual, the boy did not help. Instead, he chose to watch a sparkling silver butterfly flutter about the woods and descend into a small flowering bush. He was surprised to see it snatch up a rain beetle to feed to its carnivorous family, waiting hungrily in the branches nearby.

"Off we go, then," Gaebryl said as he shouldered the two packs. He pulled the boy onto his back with a grunt, slipping his legs into a rough harness he had devised. Already his back ached, and there were many miles to go before they would rest again.

Hours passed on the trail. Gaebryl kept a brisk, steady pace, always wary of the possibility of anyone following them. They crossed paths with other curious travelers on occasion, always with a friendly nod or gesture.

The trail wound down a steep hillside and over a ravine on an old bridge carved from a hollow toudra tree. By the skilled and detailed handiwork of the carvings, Gaebryl knew that mahekians had been the bridge builders, although few mahekians lived in or around Gaaloth anymore. The mahekians were a solemn, hermitlike people, proud, intelligent and fierce if need be, very different from humans. Gaebryl had known many, and liked them in general. As he crossed the mahekian footbridge, echoes of his footsteps reverberated through the dense wooded valley below.

Optimism but mostly boredom prompted Gaebryl to attempt another conversation with the restless boy on his back. He tried speaking in several of the most common languages, but as before, and he had expected it, it was to no avail. After awhile, he gave up and began singing a whimsical Bursian travel song, something that reminded him of his own land so far away:

"Forest o forest, trees o green Alter not thy ancient ways Fill us with thy scent and lore Bursia of the Kingdom of Day!

Home is where'ere our heads doth lay, Our feet shall lead us far away-- Hey! Hey! On the 'morrow! Forest of the Kingdom of Day!

Paths lead us to bubbling brooks, We feast on fruit and honey-o-- Fire at night to sooth our souls, When the day's journey is done-e-o--

Home is where'ere our heads doth lay, Our feet shall lead us far away, Hey! Ho! On the 'morrow-- Forest of the Kingdom of Day!

Dear, mind the cottage 'ere I return, O lady fair of hair silk golden, No danger shall I fear tonight! For her love lay in my heart hidden!

Home is where my heart resides, Paths shall lead back to familiar doors, Some tomorrow-- Forest of the Kingdom of Day!"

When he finished the last word, Gaebryl picked up the pace but fell silent for a long time.

8

For a few hundred yards, the trail ran along the edge of a rocky cliff. Another toudra tree bridge crossed a rushing stream that fell over the edge of the cliff far below, to a deep, crystal clear pool. Gaebryl took the opportunity to rest there on the rocks, plucking a few handfuls of fat blackberries that grew on the rocky ridge. Whippoorwills soared nearby above the cliffs. To the southeast, the hills rolled off into the distance; the nearest ones were spring green, every leaf visible and clear. The furthest hills were pale gray and misty.

Gaebryl dove off the cliff and had a refreshing swim in the icy pool while the boy tried to fill his empty stomach with berries. Gaebryl called for him to join him in the water, but the always modest boy ignored the offer. Gaebryl thought it was just as well.

Soon the suns passed the halfway mark in the sky and began their slow western descent. Gaebryl scaled the higher rocks and basked in the warm sunlight on top a smooth boulder until he was dry. Then, he picked up his load, and, with a grunt and a sigh, he continued on his way.

Varieties of woodland flowers covered the hillsides: yellow, violet, red, and white. Bees busily dashed from blossom to blossom, gathering golden nectar for their nearby hives in the Howling Caves. Even the tiny birds called pipers seemed exceptionally playful as the two marched by. Soon, the single path they had been following for days joined a wider one, a column of stone marking the intersection. There were fresh cart tracks and many footprints on this wider road: men's boots, horses, rramas, dogs, cattle, and an occasional wild animal's foot. Gaebryl could tell the boy was interested in this new development, because he struggled from left to right to try to read the words on the marker.

"Can you please...be still?" Gaebryl said sternly. "I can't hold you if you keep wiggling."

The boy ignored him, craning his neck to read the marker. The print, however, was worn so badly that it was illegible.

"By the gods, boy!" Gaebryl snapped. "It's a road marker! We're almost to Tungulin, about ten more miles as the crow flies... Hey!"

At the word "Tungulin", the boy had kicked himself free from his perch, and he fell to the ground with a painful grunt. He quickly struggled to his feet and did a little dance, limping when his weight was on his left leg. Gaebryl was aghast to see that the lad was actually smiling.

"Did I just hear you say something?" Gaebryl said.

"Tungulin," the boy exclaimed, arms out to the sky. He grasped his hands together, prayerlike. "I made it."

Gaebryl shook his head. "Not yet, but almost," he said. "Finally, some dialogue. I take it that you approve?"

"Yes, yes, a hundred times yes," he answered. "Tungulin was my destination all along."

"You could've asked me, if you were that concerned about where we were going. I would have told you."

"I didn't know who you were for quite a long time, and even when I learned, I wasn't sure if I could trust you," the boy replied, exhibiting his usual arrogant disdain. "You were serving my purposes well enough for the time being, doctoring my wounds, feeding me (although not very well), eluding possible dangers with your fancy woodsman tricks. So, I persevered while I regained my strength."

Gaebryl looked at him, frowning. "You speak Eash pretty good," he said, "but I've never heard your accent. You're not from Galgariah, are you..."

"Yes, well, I am very pleased with this most recent development," the boy interrupted. "Perhaps all is not lost after all. You said ten more miles?"

"Eight to ten."

"Let's be on our way, then, sir. There's not a moment to waste. I'm sure you're as anxious to reach Tungulin as I am."

"Hold on there, Chatterbox. You're a bit commanding for someone your size, aren't you? How about answering a few simple questions for me first? I think I deserve it."

The boy stamped his good foot. "I assure you, there's no time for nonsense!"

"I don't care if you fall to the ground and throw a watergirl's tantrum! I'm tired and sore, and we're not leaving this spot until you explain a few things first," he demanded. "How did you end up way out there in an assassin's skycraft? Why are assassins after you? What is your *name*?"

The boy's hands went to his hips and he scowled.

They stared at each other for a moment before the boy finally spoke. "I knew I shouldn't have said anything," he muttered. He looked at Gaebryl. "I can't tell you," he said.

"You can't tell me? Then we can just sit here until you starve to death. That should take until nightfall with your appetite."

"You don't understand," the boy said. "I didn't say I *won't* tell you, I said I *can't* tell you. More truthfully, I *shouldn't* tell you. Not yet. I can't tell you anything. Not until I'm safely within Tungulinian walls. Only there will it will be safe enough to speak."

The muscles in Gaebryl's neck were knotted tight. "I didn't like you much when you didn't talk, and I like you less now. I should put you over my knee and take a willow branch to your backside for all you've put me through. You're the most ungrateful little tyrant I've ever met."

"Don't let it bother you. You'll understand well enough when we reach Tungulin. Now, please, can we get on with this? I've been traveling for so long."

"There's no excuse for such rude behavior..." Gaebryl started to say, but then he stopped. It was no use. There was no need to encourage this battle of wills. There was plenty of time for all questions to be answered.

He pointed to the south, where the brown trail bent and twisted like a snake over the rolling, wooded hills. "We'll be there by nightfall if we're not *intercepted*," he said. "Otherwise, by tomorrow morning."

The boy stared intently toward the south. He relaxed, leaning back on a tree stump, sighing as he unbuttoned his embroidered blouse at the shoulder. He looked nearly radiant. "Almost there," he said to himself. "I thought this day would never come."

9

Gaebryl had ranged lands far and wide and had seen many strange peoples and strange customs, but, like the boy's clothes and manner, his sharp, eloquent accent was completely unrecognizable. Perhaps he *had* come from far away.

"I'll get you to Tungulin," he said. "I'm familiar with the

castlecity, and I know quite a few people there. My father is good friends with King Vantoo. It's been awhile since I've been there, but we should receive a warm welcome."

The boy stood. "Excellent. Let's depart, then, immediately, sir," he ordered. "I am in haste. The sooner I reach..."

Suddenly, Gaebryl sprang to his feet, gazing down the trail behind them. "They've found us," he said. The boy followed the gaze. With desperate effort, Gaebryl seized the boy under the arms, and pulled him off the trail with him, squatting behind a dense orangeberry thicket. He took his blaster from its holster and charged it. Before the boy could mutter an objection, Gaebryl slapped a palm over his mouth. The boy started to struggle, but froze when two skycrafts whizzed down the trail at full speed, right past the spot where they had just been standing. The sleek one man crafts made little more noise than passing birds. A bit of dust stirred, then settled.

Gaebryl released his grasp and stood. "So, that's who've been after us this whole time. Habad and Tursdah. By the bones of Oziah Aabx..."

"How dare you manhandle me as if I'm some kind of baggage!" the boy spat, jerking away from him. He stomped his foot in anger.

"Habad and Tursdah are *assassins*. Killers. Murderers. They're *hunting* us. Do you understand what I'm saying to you?"

The boy yanked his small pack free from Gaebryl's shoulder and marched back toward the trail, dragging it in the dirt. "Believe me, I know who they are, and I know what they want," he replied arrogantly, keeping an eye in the direction of the assassins. As soon as he stepped onto the trail, he paused only a second to make sure the coast was clear, then he headed south, in the direction Gaebryl had instructed him, toward Tungulin. "My leg seems to have healed up just fine, and so the time has come for us to part ways. Thank you for all you've done," he called. "I hope to reward you fairly one day, should you call on me. If not financially, which I doubt you need, then in recognition. A plaque or something. Now, good day, sir."

Gaebryl watched the boy waddle away. "A plaque?"

"Or something."

"That's it?" Gaebryl spouted. "That's it? No explanations? Nothing?"

The boy continued marching, limping as he walked.

"Hey!" Gaebryl called out.

The boy stopped in his tracks. As if he were being repeatedly inconvenienced, he turned to face the Bursian prince and took a deep breath. "You're a noble and gracious man, Gaebryl Dindiane," he began, patting the beads of sweat from his face and neck with what appeared to be a fine kerchief in bad need of a washing. "There is no doubt that I've traveled with the best of company. The few reports I've gathered regarding your deeds have been favorable, (except for your cavorting with women of ill repute) and respect for you is widespread and growing. I was very fortunate to have you come upon me when you did. Surely luck was with me that day. But here, our paths must divide. You may now go on your way, back to your beloved temple if you desire, or to your fiancée up in Cissel, or wherever else. My path is chosen for me, and I am no longer in need of your services. Thank you for your help. I tell you this in all sincerity. Prosperity to you. Good day, sir."

Gaebryl stared at the boy's back as he hobbled purposefully away. Within a matter of seconds, he had disappeared around the turn.

10

Gaebryl had a seat on a craggy tree stump. He supposed that he should be relieved to get rid of the impudent teen. He had been nothing but a bother, a pest, an itchy blister, a drain, a thorn in his boot, a rash, a relentless ache in the backside.

But he wasn't relieved. He was confused, angry, and

irritated. The obstinate little brat could not march one full day on that bad leg, especially without any water or food. And the assassins were still at large, closer than ever. It wouldn't take them long to realize that they had lost the scent, and turn back around to backtrack for them. Did the boy even have a weapon? None that Gaebryl had seen. And it was wolferine season, too. Without his assistance, Gaebryl knew that the boy would not make it another hour alone.

The ungrateful imp needed to learn a lesson here. Gaebryl was tempted to turn his back, as the boy had suggested, and be on his merry way, just to serve the little devil right.

But, instead, against his better judgment, he shouldered his pack and started reluctantly, angrily, down the trail after him. He planned to keep just out of sight, shadowing him from the trees only to keep an eye on him, until he reached civilization safely. Then, Gaebryl would gather fresh supplies and return to the City of the Sky to resume his explorations.

Once he finds himself in a little trouble we'll see how he welcomes the sight of me, he thought.

11

Evening came. Shadows drew longer, the air cooler. Ahead, the boy started down a long, twisting flight of stone stairs cut out of the hillside bedrock to avoid the longer, more gradual slope generally used for carts and livestock. Gaebryl was off the path, among the trees, knee high in purple clover and ragweed, impressed with the progress the boy had made. He had been more resolute than Gaebryl had given him credit for. The sky became visible to his left as the trees on the mountainside thinned more and more. The path they traveled cut through a crevasse in the protective Subring Mountains that encircled the immense Tungulin valley like a giant wall, and they were now passing down into the other side.

As Gaebryl drew closer, he could now see why the boy kept stopping and staring. Tungulin came into view through the pines. The castlecity shone as bright as a shrine, silver/white and fair, from on top of a solitary mountain base set in the direct center of an immense, circular, bowl shaped valley. It was enormous. No single king or people could claim creation of this architectural monument. Lifetimes upon lifetimes of constant loving architectural labor were to be credited for her massive construction. The main body of the intricate castle stood four or five times the size of the huge toudra trees that lined the lowland forest valley. The highest towers were wreathed in clouds of pearl white; her blue and green flowing banners whipped in the upper winds. Great white birds soared above the trees of the valley below his vista view.

Gaebryl watched the boy continue his slow descent down the stairs, until he came to a wide lip in the trail, offering a magnificent view of the Tungulin valley. Then, as Gaebryl watched, the boy's weak leg wobbled, then appeared to give out. He dropped the walking stick he had been using as his knee buckled, and he fell to the ground.

Gaebryl broke from his cover, bounding over the wall, and he descended down the rocks like a sure footed mountain goat, until he reached the boy's side. "I told you," he said. "Are you hurt?"

The boy frowned when he saw him. "You followed me!" he said, gritting his teeth.

"I knew you couldn't make it the rest of the way on your own," Gaebryl said. "Obviously, I was right."

"Obviously, you don't know me very well, otherwise, you would have left me alone. I can reach Tungulin without any more of your so-called help."

"You ungrateful, egotistical brat! You wouldn't have gone another hundred yards without a pair of crutches!"

"Well, if that's what I have to do to get rid of you, I'll carve a pair..."

The boy stopped in midsentence and his eyes went wide, looking over Gaebryl's right shoulder. "Gaebryl..."

Gaebryl felt his blaster jerk from his holster before he knew what was happening. He sprung around to find the two assassins before him, weapons already drawn and ready. He knew who they were. Their reputations were legendary. "You two..."

"Careless," Habad said, smiling with a mouth that separated his face from ear to ear. "That was much too easy." He backed away, placing Gaebryl's blaster loosely in his twisted belt. Habad was nearly as tall as Gaebryl, but much thinner, sharp bones protruding like horns from his knees, ankles, elbows, and wrists. His skin was a dirty, pale, olive green color, cracked and dry. The scattered tufts of hair on his spotted head were dingy red; the unkempt tangles blew about freely in the mountain updraft. He wore two earrings in each ear and another in his flat nose. As he spoke, his pale yellow forked tongue flicked in and out of his thin white lips, dispensing spit like a sputtering fountain. "You were much easier to track today, after eluding us so well for so long. Too kind to too many passersby along the way today, I'm afraid. They were all too eager to tell us which direction you were heading. Pity, too, because you almost made it..."

Tursdah, the brute, stood silently behind him with a look of perverse reverence on his diseased face. The boy backed away, toward a pile of rocks behind him.

"Habad and Tursdah," Gaebryl said, trying to think, trying to find a way out of this dire situation. "You both look exceptionally well since the last time I saw you, rotting away in shackles in a Bursian jail, I do believe." He stood with his back facing a sheer drop to jagged rocks, far below. The boy was safe for the moment, perched on a boulder to his left, although Habad's beady eyes darted at him time and time again. "What were the charges that time, Habad? Murder and necrophilia again, wasn't it?"

"We escaped from all that," Habad said. "And we left a bloody mess."

"Good for you, Habad," Gaebryl said. The assassins stood directly before him, blocking the trail from which they came. The path to the right, toward Tungulin, was left unguarded.

"Gaebryl Dindiane, we have no quarrel with you," Habad told him, as if reading his mind. He nodded toward Tungulin. "You may be on your way if you so choose."

"They are the ones who hurt me," the boy said obstinately, but it was clear that he was truly frightened of them.

"We'll do much worse this time if you don't give us the damned key," Habad hissed.

Gaebryl glanced up at the boy. *The key*? The boy returned the glance. *What key?*

Habad was watching Gaebryl's expression. "Yes, the *key*. Very special, this key. Didn't he tell you about it? He stayed rather quiet during his brief visit with us, too. That's why he hobbles so."

"I hid it in Tursdah's belt," the boy snapped. "In the back, where his fat head couldn't see it. Then I took it back after you both passed out."

"Sleeping," Habad corrected. "While we were sleeping."

"Sleeping in such a drunken stupor that I spat on you before I left. I call that passed out."

"Ah, yes, well, semantics and interpretations," Habad said, smiling again. "You're right, of course. Forgive me. You were clever enough to escape. Kudos." He looked at Gaebryl. "He stole our skycraft and '*poof*' he was gone. We were quite impressed. And how lucky he was to have made it up over Rock Gaaloth before the fuel ran out. Miracle really."

Tursdah stepped closer. Gaebryl watched the huge brown muscles begin flexing in the giant assassin beast's arms. The evil creature began breathing heavier as he bared his animal fangs. His black eyes were filled with red veins. He leaned forward on his battle axe, gripping it tightly with his four fingered hands. He was barely clothed in thick leathers, fur, and brass, and he wore shrunken heads on the rungs of his spiked brass belt. Gaebryl never took his eyes off of Tursdah for more than a split second.

"Why do you want this key?" he asked them. "What does it unlock?"

Habad's tongue flicked jubilantly. "Who knows for sure? There is a reward for it, you see. It will bring us greater wealth than all our other jobs have ever done, rolled into one. I plan to retire once I receive my reward. Tursdah here, I'm afraid, is driven by other demons. He will go on with the legacy we've built together, I suspect. I have little control over him anymore. So," he said, eyes sharp and businesslike. "Without further ado, the key please."

All eyes turned to the boy.

"Absolutely not," the young man stated unflinchingly. Despite his frail size and stature, he appeared proud and grim, like a mighty general. "It is mine to protect. You'll have to kill me to get it."

"As expected," Habad said, turning to see what Gaebryl's reaction would be.

Gaebryl's countenance was just as resolute. Habad was a worthy opponent himself. Tursdah, on the other hand, was a living, breathing *mountain*. How he could possibly defeat them both without a blaster was incomprehensible. Still, he had no choice. He couldn't let them harm this boy again. "And you'll have to go through me to get to him," he told them.

"So be it," Habad said, shrugging his bony shoulders. He stepped aside to watch the upcoming show. "Tursdah, you may begin."

"So be it," snarled the sweating brute that swayed menacingly behind him. "I told you, Habad. It was destiny all along."

Gaebryl quickly took in the surroundings, analyzing: the nearby saplings, the slope of the ground, the amount of steps to the cliff edge where pebbles might break away underfoot. He moved slowly, circling to the left, arms extending out to his sides.

Sweat trickled down Tursdah's skin like rain over a rock. He flexed his muscles: tensed, relaxed, tensed, relaxed. He began snorting air through his wide nostrils like an angry bull, grinding his yellow teeth together, making a horrible scraping sound.

As the grotesque beast advanced, Gaebryl met him eye to eye. Tursdah lifted the axe, as wide as a shovelplow, with one hand, apparently without any effort whatsoever. Gaebryl stepped to the left, knowing that his razorsword was no match for Tursdah's heavy battleaxe. The beast mirrored the motion, pressing Gaebryl closer to the ledge.

"I would get just as much satisfaction if you leaped off this cliff like a coward," Tursdah told him. "You don't necessarily need to go through all this pain and humiliation first..."

Before Tursdah finished his sentence, Gaebryl dashed at him, pulling a knife from his boot sheath in one quick movement as he rolled. He plunged it full force into the creature's stomach, then danced to the side, just missing the grasp of a huge brown hand.

Habad cheered from the side.

Tursdah looked at the trickle of blood that rolled down his gut to the matted fur of his leather britches, then up at Gaebryl. "You're fast," he said, surprised and amused. "And devious. That's good."

To Gaebryl's astonishment, the blade had done little damage to Tursdah's thick skin. The assassin had turned in time to make the blow glance off to the side.

Habad was laughing. "I swear, I don't think he has any nerve endings at all, that Tursdah."

As Tursdah came toward him, this time moving faster, Gaebryl found the beast's reddened eyes unnerving. They almost had an odd glowing quality to them. The battle axe came up, slashing at him with a speed that Gaebryl would never have believed, barely missing him. Again, the blade, as wide as Gaebryl's shoulders, cut through the air, then again, and again, forcing him backwards too fast to keep his balance. His foot slipped on crumbling rock. He seized a limb of a small tree that grew at the very edge of the precipice, catching himself. One mighty chop sent the tree sailing over the brink. Gaebryl teetered, heels hanging off over the edge.

Meanwhile, Habad had crawled up toward the boy, displaying the poisoned knife that had previously injured him so badly. "Come here, you," he hissed. "You remember this blade, do you not?"

The boy attempted to crawl away backwards, but found himself cornered in the rocks. His eyes were desperate. "Gaebryl!" he cried.

Tursdah was suddenly losing his footing on loose pea gravel, and he slid, almost stumbling. Gaebryl ducked under his outstretched hand, seized the beast's belt, and swung around behind him, clearing the edge of the cliff. With a quick sprint up the rocks and a leap, he knocked Habad's feet out from under him, sending the surprised assassin tumbling down the jagged rocks and into the weeds at the cliff's edge. "Climb higher!" he shouted to the boy.

The boy saw Gaebryl's blaster slip from the Habad's belt, rattling off into the rocks near his feet. "Gaebryl, watch out!" he cried, looking up.

Coming up quickly from behind, Tursdah seized Gaebryl by the ankle and sent him spinning like a ragdoll across the dirt clearing, toward the edge of the cliff. He barely stopped in time, with one leg dangling over.

"Gaebryl!" the boy cried, as an angry Habad started back up the rocks after him. "Help me!"

Gaebryl tried to shout back, but Tursdah kicked him in the side with a brass toed boot, sending him rolling, now both legs now dangling out over the edge of the precipice. He cried out in desperation as he struggled, grasping for anything he could to keep from sliding off.

"Should have jumped," Tursdah said, sneering as he walked over to him. He straddled Gaebryl's head and raised the axe high overhead, intending to split the man right down the middle with one defining blow. "Gaebryl, I am Tursdah the Great, your battle master. It is time for you to pass through the Door of the Dark Valley..."

Gaebryl was quickly losing his grip, and expected to feel Tursdah's huge blade split his spine in two at any second.

Then he heard a sudden cry, and there was a blast that shook his grip loose. He slid, fingernails digging desperately at the rock.

Tursdah wailed above him. He dropped his axe and surged forward, putting a boot within Gaebryl's reach. Gaebryl grabbed a bootstrap just in time to keep from falling over into the abyss. Tursdah then stumbled backwards, unintentionally pulling the prince back up with him. The great beast toppled over onto the ground on his back, howling in a painful rage. From there, Gaebryl could see what had just happened. The boy had somehow retrieved the blaster before Habad could get to it, and with a lucky shot, he had torn a big piece of Tursdah's shoulder off with it. Gaebryl got to his feet and looked down at his mortally wounded opponent.

"Tursdah!" Habad wailed from above. "What have they done to you!?"

Gaebryl quickly lifted the axe by the handle, dragging it toward the cliff. It was even heavier than it looked.

Tursdah saw what was happening and spun over, coming up onto his knees as he howled, dragging his limp left arm in the dirt. With a lunge, he grabbed the huge blade before Gaebryl could get it over the edge, and he held on to it tight. "I'm not done with you yet, prince," he growled.

Habad was boiling. He felt foolish and ashamed at what had happened. He snatched the blaster back from the boy and slapped him hard across the face, sending him to the ground. "You insignificant fool!" he cried. He looked at Tursdah's bloody, wounded shoulder. A white bone protruded from the gnarled meat. Things had gone very wrong. "Enough of this! Let's end it now," he barked to his injured comrade. He pointed Gaebryl's own powerful gun at the boy's face at point blank range and fired. The flash of light was unusually bright. For a moment there was a strange sensation where there was no sound at all, a few seconds of electrified bright white nothingness, then there was a hideous scream... Habad's scream.

"No!" Gaebryl cried. The shot echoed through the hills. Renewed rage and power instantly filled him, like nothing he had ever felt before. With all his might, he jerked the axe from Tursdah's hands, and he slung it out over the edge. It sailed off into the valley below.

Habad was still screaming, as if in absolute terror... Eyes glowing as red as molten lava, Tursdah's maniacal anger metamorphosed into an uncontrollable hatred for this human. He landed a blow to Gaebryl's head with his hammerlike fist, sending the man to the ground hard. His head bounced like a rubber ball on the ground. As he rose, dazed, the assassin swung again, but he was able to duck the blow this time. The monster, off balance, fell forward onto his face, and it sounded as though the bone in his already wounded shoulder shattered with the impact. The beast wailed.

Gaebryl pulled his long, razor-sharp sword from its sheath, straddling the assassin's hairy back, and he seized a handful of hair on his broad, sweaty neck. "And I am done with you!" he cried.

Tursdah howled. He took hold of Gaebryl's right leg and squeezed. The muscle and tissue crushed in his viselike grip, the bones nearly shattering, sending a chill of pain rippling throughout the prince's body. With a cry of anguish, Gaebryl jerked the beast's head to the side and with a tremendous effort, he plunged his sword through the thick hide of Tursdah's neck, and out the other side, all the way up to the jeweled hilt. The beast screamed. Again and again the sword pierced his great throat from behind like a giant pincushion, until there was no doubt left. Tursdah could not survive such a thrashing. For a second, they paused. The outcome was now inevitable. Gaebryl had slain the

Great Tursdah.

His throat filling rapidly with blood, Tursdah squalled pitifully in pain and anger. The thought of defeat by this measly human was infuriating and unacceptable to him, even in the throes of his own death. He was not going to die and rot on this cliff under the eyes of accursed Tungulin. He could not end in such a dishonorable way, not if he had one ounce of strength left in him! Everyone would climb up there to mock him, to watch the vultures peck out his eyes. He would not allow that disgrace to happen. His faltering mind turned to the nearby cliff. He could not speak with his throat shredded to ribbons, but he gurgled a hideous sound that resembled macabre laughter. If they both fell over the cliff, there would be no victor, and no defeated.

"Die! Die, you bastard!" Gaebryl cried, trying to kick himself free from the steely grip that had begun to sever his leg from his body. Sweat, dirt, and blood blurred his vision. His royal robes were filthy, bloody and torn to shreds. He tried to look about the clearing for the boy, but both he and Habad were nowhere to be seen.

Blood spewed everywhere. Barely able to get a breath, Tursdah came to his one hand and knees, and began crawling to the cliff, dragging the prince along beside him. Gaebryl dug his fingers into the dirt. He grabbed a root and held as tight as he could, but Tursdah ripped him away like pulling a loose thread from a cloak.

Tursdah stopped just feet away from the cliff edge, his strength waning. He choked and coughed, trying to grasp at his mutilated neck with his free hand to try to stop the profuse blood flow, but his maimed shoulder prevented him from doing it. He fell forward, whipping Gaebryl against a tree trunk. He coughed up more blood, then with a tremendous effort, he spun over and hung the prince completely out over the edge.

Suddenly, there was no ground under Gaebryl, only a towering drop to a sudden and final destination.

Swinging up, Gaebryl grabbed Tursdah's chain bracelet just as the beast opened his mighty hand, releasing Gaebryl's leg.

Gaebryl swung. His injured leg hit a rock and he screamed in pain.

Tursdah surged forward, shaking his hand back and forth, trying to dislodge Gaebryl from his bracelet.

Gaebryl reached around desperately for any hold: a rock, a root, anything. Tursdah's pallid face came over the edge right above him, cold and red eyed. Various body fluids poured from his face and neck, and out of his mouth and nose, raining down onto Gaebryl.

Tursdah pulled his chest to the edge, his weighted arm dropping over vertically. Gaebryl bounced, but was still able to keep hold. Only a few more inches to crawl before Tursdah would lose balance and they would both leave the precipice, falling to death together.

Gaebryl could not hold onto the chain any longer. His fingers were being cut in two. He began seeing spots of color dancing before his eyes, beautiful colored lights, dazzling and bright. As these lights began to turn into a vivid, warm white, all the pain seemed to seep away, draining down through his body and out the tips of his toes.

Just then, two blaster shots rang out and chips of sharp stone and dust scattered. The sound momentarily jolted Gaebryl back into the world of the living. He shut his eyes to protect them from the shattering debris, and held on with all his might. Tursdah's bloody body quivered and went limp, eyes returning to black for the last time.

Gaebryl struggled to hold on, dangling, but, again, he felt consciousness slowly slipping away.

12

"My name is Feren Den," said the squatty little man who had saved Gaebryl's life. The cart they were in hit a pothole and everything bounced. Gaebryl detected the sound of smooth stone rattling beneath the wooden cart wheels, like an actual paved road, instead of dirt and loose rocks. He knew that they must be nearing the city. He was in shock and could not see very well. Everything was unfocused and vague. He couldn't remember how he had gotten into the cart, nor could he remember how he had gotten back up onto the top of the cliff.

The man was still talking. "I'll bet you think I'm a warrior of some kind, huh? I'm a Tungulin farmer, and proud of it."

From where he lay in the back of the small cart, Gaebryl could only see the farmer's broad back, and the old beagle who sat beside him, eyes intently fixed upon the injured Bursian prince. Gaebryl smelled coal and realized that he was lying in a wagon full of it, black and dusty. He attempted to bend his leg, but bolts of pain stopped him, radiating from his ankle to his hip. As a reminder of the encounter, Tursdah had left four huge black and blue fingerprints outlined on Gaebryl's bare leg. Feeling had returned to his foot, but he was afraid that there could be serious damage to the tendons and ligaments around his knee.

It was at this point that he realized that someone was holding his hand. He turned his head and saw a hazy figure silhouetted in the setting suns sitting beside him. He raised his head and squinted to see. To his complete bewilderment, he saw that it was the boy, alive. Alive and unharmed.

"How..," he started to say, but he became dizzy and had to lay his head back down. The farmer continued talking, though his words sounded slurred and hollow to Gaebryl. He tried to listen, but time seemed to be speeding up and slowing down to him.

"I was on a nearby ridge, collecting some flint and coal for my brother who runs a fire store in the city. I heard a shot and jumped clean out of my britches. I suspected that it came from the lookout, so I grabbed my blastrifle and dashed up the hill, leaving my rrama and cart near the cave where I was mining." The cart hit a rut. Gaebryl cringed. "Then I heard another shot, and somebody cried out, 'No!'"

Gaebryl thought about what he could remember. What had happened. "The first shot is when the boy shot Tursdah in the shoulder..," he mumbled. "The second shot was..." Gaebryl paused long enough to look at the boy again, confused. "When Habad killed you."

The boy's expression, what Gaebryl could see of it, was one of both concern and also utter confusion. Gaebryl could see dirty trails on the boy's cheeks. He had been crying.

The farmer continued on with his story: "I saw something like a big axe fall off the cliff, and a lot of rubble, so I ran faster. I didn't know what to expect. Just then, a dirty red headed man thing, ugliest thing I ever saw, mutant tyberlian maybe, come running down the road right past me, crying like he'd seen a ghost or something. I got to say I ain't never seen fear in a face like that before. I let him go, without a shot fired. I figured he was harmless enough."

Gaebryl did not take his eyes off the boy. "He shot you, point blank. Right in the head. I saw it. He couldn't have missed. He didn't miss. I saw."

The farmer had paused his storytelling for a moment to try and reenact the horrid face of Habad. "When I reached the top, I saw the boy first, standing alone, staring at his hands as if he were somehow amazed by them. Next, I saw the big, nasty fellow, and I saw what he was trying to do to you, so I took me two shots, and, well, it was all over. I just had to pull you up, which wasn't an easy task in itself, and here we are, on the doorstep of Tungulin."

Gaebryl struggled to sit up; the boy aided him. Traffic along the road was moderately active for that hour. Other animal drawn carts and travelers gliding in small industrial and recreational skycraft moved by at various speeds. Shopkeepers and vendors were, for the most part, closing up for the day.

The cart rounded a broad curve that led to the main gate of Tungulin. Eleven tall walls protected the castlecity, with only one wide, heavily guarded entrance in the first, and largest, southernmost outer wall. Feren Den called out to the people ahead to let them pass by as they reached the first grand gate. Everyone seemed to know the old timer and let him pass without question. The six legged rrama pulling their cart did the best she could as she shuffled along, heeding her master's light whip (sound of it, not touch), head bobbing like a bouncing ball. Rramas were not known for their speed, but for their strength and endurance.

"The boy here says that it was a fierce, world renowned assassin up there. Whether there's any reward or not, I reckon I'll be a hero to my own family, at least," the farmer happily said. "I better get my story straight before everyone comes a asking." Then he started his tale again, from the very beginning. "Howdy, there, folks. I bet you think I'm a warrior of some kind, but I'm a Tungulin farmer, and proud of it..."

His beagle barked. The story sounded good to him. Things began getting dark in Gaebryl's eyes.

"Are you going to be alright?" the boy asked him.

Gaebryl nodded. His eyelids were getting too heavy to hold up. "I'm starving, though."

The boy smiled. "I'll prepare a feast for you, I promise."

"I'm going to rest now, for a bit," Gaebryl said, as he fell again into unconsciousness.

The boy gripped Gaebryl's hand tightly. "Hurry on, farmer. Never you mind about getting your story straight right now," he said. "This man cannot die. Get this cart to a doctor straight away. Faster, man!"

Four

EMERGENCY SECRET COUNCIL

13

With nothing but slow burning candles for reading light, the elderly wyzard Dedlin Dane, leaning like a bent twig over his antique, handcarved richmond table, squinted hard at a flake edged page of an old black book, trying diligently to translate the puzzling text. It was written in ancient Heash, certainly not his language of preference or expertise, but finding other scholars to help him with his personal projects had been more difficult as of late. Silk robes of crimson and gold, the colors of the Tungulin hierarchy, hung loosely from his wiry frame, draping at his feet like melted wax. The reading specs on his hooked nose glowed in the warm light, casting dual reflections on the cluttered mantle before him. Except to turn the pages, the only motion in his room was the slight movement of his bright eyes working up and down the handwritten scripture. Around the room, hundreds of other unlit candles sat atop mountains of melted wax that had dripped from the shelves to the floor in beautiful colored fountains. A soft, goose down bed filled one corner, a cabinet full of charts and maps was next to that, an old cedar chest sat beside the door, and an old gray cat with cataracts was folded up on a straw mat in front of a slowly dying chimney fire. Every inch of his study was filled with books, thousands of them: large, small, old, new, thick and thin.

Raising an arthritic finger to his tongue, he tenderly, reverently, turned the yellowed page, careful to not dismember it from its rotted backing, and he pressed it gently into place with his palm. Since midafternoon, Dedlin had been deciphering a series of rare daksas' accounts concerning the dark arts and militant field tactics of the Gharnian nation, specifically regarding emergency field codes and communications. It was old and outdated, but still, possibly, very relevant.

He drained the last few drops of a hazelnut liqueur from his silver chalice and yawned. He was very tired, but he could not yet lie down for the night. The king (great-grandson of the king Dedlin had first served there) had granted his request for audience. More than that, he had summoned Dedlin to Secret Council meeting. It had been a long time since the wyzard had been summoned to Secret Council, and Dedlin found it a bit ironic. He was considered antiquated now, nothing but a living reminder of the old monarchy. Eccentric, and yes, somewhat theatrical and animated at times, and of outdated high ideals. Some of the youngest members of the cabinet suggested that he was certifiable. Yet, even sitting alone in his private library, Dedlin liked to believe that he carried about him an air of dignity, honor, and etiquette.

At one time, long ago, Dedlin Dane had been High Wyzard to the King. He had been young, powerful, and influential, his journeys far reaching, his wisdom vast, his magick deep and creative, his advice renowned and wellregarded. Indeed, at a time, his singular actions had shaped the foundations for civilization in central Galgariah as it currently existed.

Now, he was all but forgotten, tucked away into a dark corner of the castle like so much unneeded furniture. His mind often wandered to those glorious days, when Tungulin was little more than a few towers with one lone wall to keep the wolferines of the forest at bay, when the wilds were unknown and mostly uncharted, and the dealings of the evil Gharnians were not even whispered anymore.

He almost nodded off to sleep with those thoughts floating around his head like familiar ghosts, when something stirred in his old heart, causing him to suddenly sober. He looked up and glanced about his small room, as if expecting to find someone standing there in the shadows before him. He found this sensation most peculiar. But, instead, everything was perfectly sound, as it should be.

"It must be indigestion," he said aloud, forcing a burp. With a wheezing cough and a shake of his shaggy head, he managed to continue his repose.

Then he felt it again. It was as if there had been some psychic voice arise from the silence of his room, a harbinger of welcome news. Dedlin straightened up to listen better, his head cocked first one way, and then the other. He looked curiously about his study, focusing hard.

He realized then what it was. It was that *sense*... That special wyzardly *skill* he used to have, when somehow he just *knew* something...

"He's here," he said with a degree of excitement and awe. The cat looked up from the mat for a moment, and then it resumed his nap, purring loudly. Dedlin smiled warmly. "I have lived to see the day. He has arrived at last"

He placed a wide red bookmark between the pages to hold his place and placed the old manuscript in its exact place in the dusty bookshelf to his left. He turned his antique chair to stretch his old, cold legs. "My gracious me, the time has actually come," he said, cackling for a second, "And just in time for Council, too."

Walking up the stairs was painful; Dedlin's joints ached. He leaned heavily on his old, twisted walking stick, relying on it much more now than he used to. The chambers were empty and dark even from the landing. He hadn't realized how late it had gotten. An orchestra, somewhere far down the main hall, was playing a solemn symphony, but it was too far away to discern the melody.

Outside, the spherical lanterns along the garden path were still glowing hazily beyond the amber and crimson stained glass curtains that extended from the intricately painted ceilings to the polished wooden floors. The air grew cool in the music chambers on early summer evenings, so special attention was placed on protecting the rare and valuable instruments. It had been Dedlin's personal job to see to it, now that the matters of men and politics were in some younger wyzard's hands. "They'll have to get someone else to take care of all this now," he wheezed. "A new custodian, as it were..."

He ran his fingers across a harp as he passed it by; the random notes floated melodiously out into the darkness. The chambers were ghostly at night; the hazy light barely piercing the translucent curtains cast pillars of colored light up the carved walls beside the huge wooden doors. The adjacent hall, full of ancient treasures: borgonhorns, stringed golondolas, eloquent silver flutes from ancient Nordia that no one could master anymore, rare Eaophian tree drums and wind chimes, miniature takamines, and much more, was like a museum of the bizarre. "I will miss this old place," he muttered. "Yes, I will."

He hobbled on, his mind on the Secret Council, but more importantly, the uncertain future ahead. Many things needed to be revealed, and very quickly. But who would listen to an outdated, crippled, senile old wyzard? He allowed himself a cynical laugh. "I've got a few tricks left," he said to himself. "They oughtn't try to bury me just yet."

A young gythot secretary had just been walking by, carrying a stack of papers toward the choral hall. He nodded patronizingly to the old wyzard, who always seemed to be talking to himself.

Dedlin slipped through the thick wooden doors, over five times his height, and disappeared into the night beyond.

14

The twin suns began lowering in the southwest between two rugged peaks of the great Subring Mountain line, casting the long shadows of the giant toudra trees halfway up the gray bricked castle walls. The northeastern skies were deep violet, shading gradually across the heavens to pink and gold where the tall, billowy clouds chased the suns toward the horizon. Several silvery stars had presented themselves, frozen cold upon the deep velvet ceiling beyond the mountains, twinkling clearly.

One of the tallest towers in Tungulin was Westwatch. Lake Tobias and Qan Methalard, the same two guards who had so narrowly escaped death at the hands of Habad and Tursdah in Daerooge a couple of weeks before, had been assigned the evening rounds at Westwatch. They had just finished a light dinner, and were enjoying a good smoke as they watched the sights of the bustling city far below them, when, after a few minutes of pensive silence that had followed a dead end conversation concerning the weather, Qan asked his friend, "You think we'll ever get off this rock, my friend?"

Lake shrugged, absentmindedly. "Someday, probably. Maybe."

"I want to be an explorer, Lake, sometime before I die. I want to travel, to see the four corners of the kingdom. It's what I've always wanted to do, ever since I was a wee boy. I'm beginning to think it's never going to happen."

"Sure it will."

"Please. Don't patronize me," Qan said. "What about you? Don't you want to see the desert? The plains? The ocean? Other cities beyond the Rock?"

"Me? No. I'm fine right here in the mountains," Lake replied. "I like castle life. I'd like to visit a few places, sure, but I know where my home is." He took a deep puff on his pipe. "Besides, I'm getting too old to be running off out there somewhere now. It's time for me to settle down for good, I think. Get married. Have children. The wilds are no place for a man with a family."

Qan considered Lake's words. "I suppose," he replied. The wind, as always, was gusty. It blew their hair about and howled in the conical towers above their heads. "Oh, I almost forgot to tell you. I was down at Level Three near the king's hospital this afternoon, and guess what I heard? A doctor was talking about the prince of Bursia, Gaebryl Dindiane, being here. He's being treated for injuries from a fight or something."

"Oh? Well. There you go, then, Qan. You know his kind. Vagabond, really. Comes and goes as he pleases, willy nilly."

"See? That's what I'm talking about. What a lifestyle, being a ranger. He goes all over the place. His whole life is one great big adventure."

"Gaebryl trained for years to survive in the wilds, Qan. We didn't. It's that simple. I don't know why you just can't accept your place and be happy. It's not that bad, being a castleranger. I mean, the pay's not bad. It's a good, respectable life."

"I just think there's more to life than being a castleranger, that's all. Like, I don't know, being a scyropirate for awhile. Training as a masterpilot. I even thought about going to Irisia and competing in the Week of Eleven Trials. I'm not bad with a sword. With a little exercise, I think I'd have a chance of winning."

"We're nearing our thirties, my friend, and I don't know if you've looked in the mirror lately, but your midsection isn't getting any smaller. When is the last time you even trained?"

"You're a barrel of optimism, Lake," Qan replied, and they both took deep puffs again, blowing out their smoke in unison. Qan continued. "Anyway, Prince Gaebryl was injured fighting some monster they say, a famous assassin."

"Yeah? He must be a good fighter. I suppose I would like to see him in real life, see what he looks like. You think he's really as cold blooded as everyone says?"

"He trained here for years, sometimes in the same arenas that I did," Qan said. "Of course, I never met him because I was in public classes. Gaebryl trained personally with the king's wyzards and soldiers..."

Lake smiled. "Such is fate, Qan. Those who are born into royalty..." He paused, squinting out into the dim twilight. "Look!" he shouted, pointing out at the horizon. "Look at that! Do you see it? There! It's on fire!"

For a few fleeting seconds, Lake and Qan watched a burning skycraft with an orange flaming trail behind it come racing frantically through a low place in the nearest foothills. It went spiraling down into the Gaalothian Forest, not too far from the dark neighboring castlecity Bondoon, leaving behind it a thick, black, trail of smoke.

"By the gods," Lake said. "Could anyone have survived that?" Qan asked.

"I'm sure the gogmoors will get there before we do," Lake said. "Hand me the comm, and keep an eye out while I call this in."

Bondoon, a smaller adjacent castlecity that shared the valley with castlecity Tungulin, rose from the wispy fog like a withered, many fingered hand, rotten and decrepit. A fierce warlock called Gaorwyn had ruled the brutal gogmoors there for nearly a hundred years. Tungulin officials always kept a close watch on Bondoon, but did not interfere with them, respecting their simple laws and fluctuating boundaries. Before Gaorwyn's rule, the gogmoors had been much worse, a constant nuisance, looting, and occasionally attacking outlying Tungulin farms. Scattered confrontations with the gogmoors were still commonplace, but, over the decades, Gaorwyn had brought some semblance of order to the brutish race. Although they instituted no immediate threat to Tungulin or her inhabitants, away from the protection of walls, there was no telling what the gogmoors were capable of.

All castlerangers had been on alert recently, and they had been told to monitor any unusual or suspicious activity, and to immediately report the findings up the chain of command. Just as Lake through a priority pass into the comm to contact Commander Binder's staff at Defense Command, two more dark ships came cruising through the mountain pass, great silver, black, and red warships, each, themselves, the size of a small city.

"By the gods!" Lake repeated, but this time, much more emphatically.

15

There was a knock on the door. The boy, awakening from

a late nap, sat up and propped himself up in a nest of soft pillows, wondering about the time. He cleared his throat. "Come in," he said.

Gaebryl smiled as he entered, gently closing the door behind him. "Hello, there. It's been six days; I thought I'd visit you, if it's alright," he said.

"Yes, of course. Please come in."

The boy looked well. He was clean, well fed (finally), and dressed in a loose fitting cotton shirt and britches common to the youth of Tungulin. His leg was bandaged with clean, professional dressings. His eyes looked bright, his skin a healthy honey color.

"How are you?" the prince asked.

"Better. You?"

"Oh... I've seen better days," he admitted, pointing to the bandages on his head, elbows, and leg. "But, then again, I've seen worse. The physicians here, they're masters."

"Yes."

"My leg is still a mess. My head feels better, but, um, my back...I'm not used to being saddled for so long."

If the boy understood the joke, he did not show it. "I was just having a nap," he replied. "And I fear I've slept too long."

"Well," Gaebryl said, limping across the small room to a bedside chair. "Tonight is the New Year celebration. I was just out in the public park this evening, looking at the sights, enjoying a beautiful sunset, and trying to get this bum leg of mine to cooperate a little. It was very nice out. Should be a perfect night for a celebration."

"I'm sorry I missed it. I'm sure all the nice young ladies you talked to helped to make you feel better."

"I, uh..." he mumbled, then laughed. "You were watching?"

"I could see you from my window. Quite the ladies man, I'm led to believe..."

"Well, it's been awhile since I've had the company of a lady, if you know what I mean."

"Um. Yes. I'm afraid I do."

Gaebryl felt oddly scrutinized. "Anyway, I was thinking while I was out there. I wanted to ask you to do something with me tomorrow night, if you're not too busy. As I probably told you, King Vantoo is an old friend and ally of the family. He has summoned me to Secret Council, which was originally scheduled three days from now, but has been moved up to tomorrow after dinner. I thought that, maybe, you'd like to come along with me. Get out of this cramped room for a bit. Meet some of the local dignitaries."

The boy smiled and looked at him with eyes as sharp as arrows.

"It isn't as boring as it sounds. You might find it interesting," Gaebryl said. "It's quite an honor."

"Yes, we'll go to Council together," the boy replied. "I would be honored, sir."

"Always so formal," Gaebryl said, again displaying his unique smile, but only for a moment. When he looked up again, he felt as though the blood was leaving his face. He was troubled. "But that's not the only reason I wanted to see you."

"Yes?"

"I'm still... confused."

The boy nodded. "If you are referring to the event on the mountainside," he explained, "I can only suppose that your blaster fired a blank, or that Habad missed me altogether and hit the nearby rocks. I'm not sure. I am at a loss, just as you are."

"But I saw the whole thing... The impact..."

"I should be dead. That is what you mean to say."

"Y-yes."

"Yet, here I am, alive. I have no explanation for you. I've pondered this endlessly, and I'm as flummoxed as you are. I can only say that I remember nothing but an intense white flash, and then a moment of absolute darkness..."

Gaebryl sighed. "The mysteries continue to multiply and deepen, then," he replied. Habad, the only one who might know what happened for sure, had left no trail to follow. The old assassin had apparently disappeared into thin air, his mission, in retrospect, a failure.

The boy spun toward his nightstand and poured them both a glass of fresh cinnamon tea. "Well, here we are," he said. "Safe and sound, in the grandest castlecity in all Galgariah. I am immeasurably relieved and grateful. Thank you for getting me here safely, Gaebryl. I mean that. I could never have made it without you."

"You are welcome, sir," he answered, taking his glass. "And I hope you find what you seek here."

The boy sat back, making himself comfortable. He caught Gaebryl's curious glance and smiled in turn. After a deep sigh, he said, "Perhaps the time has finally come for a bit of explanation."

Gaebryl smiled.

"I cannot tell you all, not yet, but I can offer you a tidbit, I suppose, enough to hopefully satiate. Long overdue," he said, adjusting himself. He took a deep breath and squared himself, wondering where to begin as he cleared his throat. "Well, Gaebryl, essentially, I've come all the way to Tungulin just to find someone. A man. Probably very old now. A man who, I hope, still serves here. I've come to ask for his assistance and advice. He is called Dedlin Dane. He is a wyzard here, I've heard, if he is, in fact, still alive."

Gaebryl frowned. "I don't know him."

"Nor do I," the boy said. "Other than by story and reputation. And so, I do not know whether or not I can truly trust him since all that is known of him comes from sources long since discarded. I've heard he has old maps and knows the Old Stories better than anyone else in the kingdom. I was told, by many counselors and advisers, that he alone can help guide me on what I must do next. To help direct me to..." he chose his words carefully, "... a *place*. A secret place, reputedly lost now for eons. A place that I must now seek out with some urgency. And, hopefully, he can tell me what I must do once I arrive there."

Gaebryl was not a little intrigued with this story and vague riddles. He was, after all, an explorer by nature. What he wanted to know most of all about all of this is *why?*

"So, until I know for certain whether he, or King Vantoo, or anyone else here can be trusted, I must be very, very cautious. There are dangerous enemies about, as you have seen firsthand, and there are eyes and ears in every corner. At this juncture, I believe that there is only one individual I can now trust wholeheartedly. Because it has been proven. That individual is you. "

Gaebryl nodded. "Yes. You can."

"Therefore, I have a favor to ask."

"A favor?"

"Yes, a favor, if I may. I would like to entrust something to you. Something unique and precious. You have proven your valor to me, and so, on you alone I will depend. Hold onto this for me, and bear it safely until I ask for it again," he said, revealing a small stone key that now hung from a chain around his neck. "It is more precious than any amount of gold or jewels or magick power in this land. Habad and Tursdah are not the only ones who desire this trinket. There are far worse than they who would have it."

Gaebryl bore a puzzled, and yet an interested expression. "So, this is it. This is Habad's key."

"It is *the* key, but it is not Habad's by any means," the boy corrected. "It is holy and precious, Gaebryl."

Gaebryl stood, slightly reprimanded, playing along as if it were a game. "I am at your service, gladly, for as long as you require," he told him with a royal bow.

The boy held it up before them, dangling from a silver chain in the light coming through the open window. The key was slate gray, stone or metal Gaebryl could not tell, smooth, yet ornate, with tiny detailed thread thin markings on it that glistened like wet spider webs. It had an unusual, gothic shape. It did not appear as a key just so, but as a strange letter of some ancient alphabet. "It is very interesting."

"Hopefully, Dedlin will be able to explain its purpose," the boy said. He looked at him with fierce eyes. "Please guard it with your life."

Gaebryl nodded. "I already have," he said honestly.

"We both have." Another knock came from the door, and the boy acknowledged it. Lake Tobias, the castleranger captain, nervously stuck his head through. He looked at Gaebryl with eyes wide and unblinking. "Excuse me, Your Highness, but I was told you might be here. King Vantoo requests your presence in his meeting hall immediately. Secret Council has been called even earlier because of some new developments. It's an emergency."

"Very well," Gaebryl said, nodding. "Tell them I'm on my way. And let them know that I'll have a guest with me."

The nervous castle ranger bowed deeply and backed out of the door.

"New developments," the boy repeated. "I do not like the sound of it. I'll get dressed right away."

16

Outside, spontaneous fireworks were beginning to go off. Throughout the entire Kingdom Continent of Day, from one kingdom to the next, the good folks in castlecities, small towns, and remote villages alike were beginning to celebrate the arrival of the New Year, Y17, Dogmoon Toy II, 512 Age of Tears. Shortly after sunset, the king's royal fireworks show would begin for the good people of Tungulin. Since the city was known as the City of Science and Magick, and lay claim to the largest wyzard population in the kingdom, the royal fireworks show was to be unprecedented. The citizens of Tungulin and many foreign visitors looked forward to it with great anticipation.

Inside the royal reception hall, King Tital Vantoo sat at the head of his large, round meeting table, a cross section cut from a giant woodland toudra tree, staring at the latest arrivals with distant, unblinking eyes. His mind was not on fireworks and celebrations this night, but on urgent matters of his city. He was an intimidating presence, in stature, manner and demeanor. His robes were always green, tonight laced with thin strands of golden weave. His collar and sleeves were lined with fluffy white ocelot fur; on his head was an ornate crown of gold and jewels with green velvet interlays and sparkling green tassels. Gythots were born a light tan color and they darkened with age; old Tital Vantoo was nearly black. His white hair was like multiple braided strands of cotton, interwoven with black lace and gold beads. His two inch lower tusks, which rose from under his protruding pink lower lip and encompassed his broad, flaring nose, were capped with gold. His eyes were small, dark, and intense, flaring like flames from the cracked, black skin of his face. He looked grim and quick to anger, as did all elderly gythots, but Tital Vantoo was known as a compassionate, methodical, temperate king.

Gaebryl was ushered to his seat, directly across from the king; the boy stood complacently near the door behind him. The room was abuzz with quiet salutations, handshakes, and brief, shallow smiles. Dedlin Dane crept through the door without much notice and found his seat, a few chairs to the right of the king, where a small dish of koffik beans was set for him to munch. Benjyn Binder, the Defense Commander of Tungulin, was on the king's left. Also in attendance around the table were: Guy Huegart, second in command under Commander Binder; Gathargo, the current wyzard to the king; Drer Fregoode, the king's adviser, loremaster, ranger, and longtime friend, as well as Tungulin's chief historian; Sabre Jonhousan, captain in charge of the Tungulin police; the four castle governors; the mayor; the chief of castlerangers; the royal recorder; the king's personal secretary, and the city sentinel. All seven Royal Knights of the Guard were present. Behind the king sat the profound Inner Council, made up of eight: three exalted generals, who stared from their tall chairs, stern and grim, and five of the most renowned, celebrated, and wisest instructing wyzards in the kingdom, who watched the proceedings through old eyes buried deep in wrinkled faces. Around the perimeter sat the Outer Council, seventy seven other members, many soldiers and wyzards themselves. The two new castleranger captains, Lake and Qan, stood in the shadowy corner near the burgundy window curtains, at Binder's request.

Most had milled in with curious expressions and had seats as the meeting was called to order by the sentinel. All stood for the short prelude glorifying the king (who had just received kingship over the entire Galgarian quadrant less than a season ago), the castlecity Tungulin, and the great Kingdom Continent of Day.

King Vantoo took his seat first, leaned to the side and crossed his heavy legs. "Please, everyone, come in, have a seat," he said informally. His voice was gruff but precise. "I apologize for the lateness of the hour. I'd like to thank you all for coming on such short notice and succ a special evening. Much to discuss. We also have a welcome visitor, long overdue, His Majesty, Gaebryl Dindiane, the Prince of Bursia..."

"Thank you, Your Highness," Gaebryl replied, standing and bowing appropriately. "It is my pleasure to be here. Tungulin has always been my second home. And I would like to extend my congratulations on your new title and territory since I was unable to attend the coronation ceremony. I understand it was quickly ratified by the other kings."

"Give your father my best when you see him next," Vantoo said.

Gaebryl bowed again and had a seat.

"Hopefully, this meeting will be brief," Vantoo continued,

once again addressing the room. "I am expecting one crucial report, but outside of that, there should be no other interruptions. I have received some uncomfortable news this evening, a matter of some importance, hence the urgency, and I seek the wisdom and guidance of my Council, so let us begin. Listen closely," he said. "Commander Binder, you may have the floor."

Binder nodded his angular, clean shaven head and rose. He was a huge man, taller than the king, with broad, rounded shoulders and a massive square chest that stretched his military garb tight. His arms were large and brown from exposure to the suns, and his fingers were thick and stubby. He was scarred from many battles; in fact, it was rumored that he was largely reconstructed, surgically, in that many of his fractured bones had been reinforced and replaced with plasteel on the battlefield, sparking a controversial reputation for making him somewhat superhuman, physically. "Your Highness," he said to King Vantoo, bowing, then he turned to Prince Gaebryl, and did likewise. "Your Highness." Gaebryl acknowledged the Defense Commander with a polite nod.

"Ladies and gentlemen, members of the Council, honored guests, this is Lake Tobias and Qan Methalard," he began, acknowledging the two of them with a nod. "They are two of my castlerangers assigned to Westwatch this evening. Little more than an hour ago, two hours past inbound skycraft curfew, they sighted a small skycraft come in through Eyrie Pass, and go down in the forest near Bondoon. It was aflame. No comm link was ever made, and nothing from that direction had been scheduled for arrival at any port. Thermal tracing leads us to believe it came from the direction of Kalari and it must have passed Westhill City earlier without stopping. Shortly after the crash," he said, looking much more stern, "they then spotted two warships following it through the pass." His voice dropped an octave. "Worst of all. We have confirmed. They were Gharnian warships."

The room burst into an quiet uproar, and rightly so. The Gharnians were a militant race that lived thousands of miles away to the south, and had not been sighted in Galgariah for hundreds of years, not since they were defeated in the last Great Kingdom Continent War.

"Are we absolutely sure that they were Gharnian warships?" Jonhousan asked. "Not from Cissel or...or Oliader..?"

"Were they firing on the skycraft?" asked someone else.

"Please," the Commander continued, his thick eyebrows bristling. "I cannot answer everyone at once."

Slowly the room quieted. King Vantoo squinted hard, deep in thought. It was utterly brazen for Gharnian warships to enter territory that close to a major castlecity. It was nothing short of military aggression.

"As I said, it was confirmed. They were Gharnian make," Binder answered.

"The Gharnians have also been infiltrating towns and cities in the south," Drer Fregoode said. "And scoutcraft have been spotted near The City of Gold and Dindiane. Warships have been rumored seen in the wilds as far north as Gorn. It is suspected by many that they are preparing for maneuvers. Possibly on a major scale. Many men of all races are gathering to join them. It is a fact that the Gharnians are recruiting, and on the move again."

"Not fact. Just rumors," Jonhousan replied. "Rumors tossed about by gypsies and rogue scyropirates." Sabre Jonhousan was an elderly daksas, in Vantoo's police service for nearly thirty years. Like most of the daksas' race, Jonhousan was intellectual and confrontational, with a sharp mind for detail, facts, precise planning, and professional execution of his responsibilities. He was highly mathematical and concise, with the notorious ability to see beneath layers of lies and propaganda that most others might miss. Physically, he was short, even for a daksas, but he was stout and sturdier than most, with gray eyes set wide apart on his flat, frowning face. "We need to gather more intelligence before we overreact here, Your Highness."

"I do not believe that the Gharnians are planning an invasion or an attack on us here. Not at the time being," Binder continued, "but their presence in Gaaloth requires immediate attention and, perhaps, reprimand and sanctions. They have broken a seven hundred year old treaty that decrees that no warships are to encroach upon another territory's borders. Their presence is in direct violation of that treaty. It is my belief that the Gharnians pursued and disabled the aforementioned skycraft before it could reach our city, for whatever reason."

"We shouldn't underestimate the importance of protecting the integrity of this crash sight," Drer Fregoode said.

"Important how?" a governor asked.

"The skycraft was obviously trying to reach our city. Whoever was onboard was either escaping, or they were bringing a message, or news, here to us. They were fleeing two aggressive Gharnian warships. It is clear that they thought it was important enough for them to risk battle with warships with far superior weaponry," Drer replied. "And it was important enough to the Gharnians to shoot it down before it could get here, even if it meant exposing themselves to us right on our very doorstep."

"Or it could have been a fugitive," Jonhousan continued. "Or an escaped prisoner. We do not know for sure."

"What is the situation now?" Vantoo asked.

"According to screenscan and scouts, the warships have departed."

"Or are cloaked," Drer Fregoode added.

"And the skycraft?"

"It crashed four miles due east of Bondoon, near the river, seven miles from Westwatch," Binder answered.

"Bondoon's jurisdiction," the old king growled.

"Are you sure that it wasn't a craft bound for Bondoon?" he asked the two nervous castlerangers.

Lake and Qan shrugged, blank faced. They were too ill equipped and inexperienced to answer that logistic.

"It was too far away to tell for sure, Your Highness," Binder answered for them. "I agree that we should avoid contact with the gogmoors at all costs; we cannot afford another incident with Gaorwyn."

"On the other hand," Drer argued, "we can't afford to let them ramshackle the crash sight either, looting and destroying whatever was meant for us. Possibly killing whoever was on board."

"How much time before the gogmoors investigate?"

"They could be there even now," Binder advised.

"I see," Vantoo replied. "This Gharnian presence is dark news," he said. He turned to his secretary. "Prepare a response to the Gharnians, demanding an explanation. Include a copy of our treaty, highlighting the sections stipulating the encroachment upon neutral territories with armed warships, unprovoked. State our position firmly. Tell them they can expect retaliation if it occurs again. Find what trade we currently have with them that we might sanction. I believe we sell them quite an amount of foodstuffs and mercantile.

"I suppose we should send a team to investigate this crash sight, a small team of three to five. Should be experienced in evasive tactics, guerilla warfare, know the territory, and be familiar with the gogmoors. Binder, you take care of that."

"Your Highness."

"Report back to me with any news. And quickly," he stated, then he turned toward the Knights of the Guard. "As far as the warships go, let's send out scouts right away, as many as we can afford, in all directions. If there are Gharnian warships out there in the Subrings, I want to know where they are and what they are doing."

The knights nodded in response.

"Huegart, have your people send out coded messages to the other kings via message spheres. Tell them what has happened here and seek their advice," he said. "What else?" Vantoo asked the room in general. "What are your thoughts?"

"Your Highness, perhaps we should go on alert until we know something for sure, one way or another," Gathargo suggested. The generals nodded in agreement. "A quiet alert, so that we don't panic the general populace."

"Good," Vantoo replied. "Make it so. Generals, prepare our warships. I want all soldiers on standby. Chief, put all castlerangers on full alert as well, and have them fully involved in the internal security as well. Mayor, prepare a report for a city briefing."

She nodded. "Yes, Your Highness."

"Anything else? Commander Binder?"

"No, Your Highness."

"Very good. Keep me informed on all fronts. We'll meet again here first thing in the morning, an hour after sunrise breakfast."

King Vantoo stood to depart, but, instead, he paused and took a pensive breath. He walked toward the windows facing the south with long, confident strides. There, he paused once again, looking out into the night. His voice was not much more than a whisper. "Friends, I have been sleepless lately," he said to all those in the room. "I've had a loss of appetite. I've felt very strange. Helpless. And yet I feel as fit as I ever have been. I am restless, as if something very ominous is looming right before my eyes, making all else trivial and pale by comparison, and yet I cannot see what it is. Something important is happening, something grave, and we are not aware of it, although we very well need to be. It is close enough to touch, but, like vapor, it is intangible. I feel a movement out there, working its way inward, like the continent is shifting beneath our feet. There are great currents at work, of dark ambition, and of evil spirit, and I fear we will be swept away if we do not soon recognize and anticipate what it is that is coming for us. I fear dark days ahead, my friends. Dark days and hopeful moments. Keep your eyes and ears on alert. Hearts true. Swords at hand. Let us be prepared."

"Sire," the room spoke in unison.

"Thank you for coming. Thank you all. If there is nothing else, you may be excused until further notice."

The room began to rise.

"Sire, if I may," said a feeble voice from amongst the rising chatter. It was a bit croaky, but still clear and sharp.

Everyone turned to the elderly wyzard sitting slumped nearby, stirring now like an old faithful dog who had thus far, apparently, been asleep.

"If you'll permit me, there is one more thing," Dedlin Dane said.

Vantoo turned to him. "Yes, Dedlin?"

At the name 'Dedlin', Gaebryl and the boy made instant eye contact. This was *him*. The wyzard Dedlin Dane.

"It's, well, an announcement, no less," the old wyzard said, and then, under his breath, he said to himself, "This is going to be interesting." He laughed, just a little bit, as though he were both amused and delighted. Admittedly, the sound of his laughter sounded very odd under the serious circumstances. He pulled his chair back and slowly stood, obviously very stiff. "Yes, an announcement of some, dare I say, dramatic importance, Your Highness. An epiphany revealed, actually, if I may say so. Yes, yes, quite so. An epiphany, a legend, and a prophecy uncovered all at the same time. An announcement that directly relates to this meeting as well, I am sure. In fact, in some way, it is the very cause of it, and certainly the cause of this Gharnian encroachment."

"Do get on with it then," Binder moaned.

Dedlin slowly circled the table. "Firstly, important introductions are very much in order here tonight."

"Introductions?" murmured the king, looking about at all the familiar faces in his chamber. "Introductions to who?"

Dedlin then turned his back to his King, and to the Council, and faced the young boy who stood beyond in the shadows of the curtains just beyond Gaebryl's seat, silhouetted by the hazy evening light piercing through from beyond the large garden windows. His smile fell away as he threw his cloak back over his shoulder, and an expression of devout reverence replaced it. He bowed low, hand on the hilt of his sword. Then, as everyone gawked at him in bewilderment, Dedlin went to one knee before the young boy and addressed himself thus: "I bid you welcome, Your Highness. I am Dedlin Dane, Sire, wyzard deluxe, at your service and command. I have been awaiting your arrival with great anticipation for quite some time...."

For a moment there was an awkward silence, then there came an insulted uproar.

"What is this nonsense?" cried someone.

"Old fool," muttered another.

"He's fallen off one too many horses," replied yet another.

"Too much of that hazelnut liqueur."

Without any hesitation, the boy stepped confidently forward into the light, and all eyes fell upon him. His face shown bright, his eyes were like dual fires as he gazed upon them, one by one. He was grim for one so young, standing before such an impressive group of elders and peers. Despite his common clothes, his lordly stance and confident demeanor was very much like that of high royalty, ancient, wizened, and strong.

Tital Vantoo stepped forward, frowning. His jowls shook. "Dedlin," he said, trying hard to grasp what was being implied here and still contain his composure. The room quieted for him to speak. "There is no time for this now. We will do this later, privately in my chambers, if you want..."

Dedlin looked at his king. "Forgive me, Sire, but

respectfully, I must continue, for everything else now pales in comparison. What to do about the Gharnians, you ask? Neither you, nor I, nor anyone else here can make such important decisions, now," he said. "I cannot sit still any longer and be silent, while a dignitary of such magnitude stands aside, unrecognized, in your hall! In fact, Your Highness..."

"He's a traitor!" a general shouted.

"In fact, Your Highness," Dedlin continued, raising his voice louder, "No further discussions should be made concerning the Gharnians or what actions we should or shouldn't take, without *his* consent and approval..."

"Dedlin!" King Vantoo snapped. The room, full of tension, grew still again. "I'm not sure what has happened to you over the years, but because you have served me, my father and my grandfather so well, I am willing to grant some leniency toward your disrespectful behavior and allow it to pass as senile dementia. But right now, we have pressing matters to attend to. Please stand down."

Dedlin cocked his head. "I cannot," he replied. "For this boy's kingdom outranks your own."

Vantoo took another menacing step closer. "Does it, indeed? Who is he then?" he asked. "Who is this boy whom you call 'Sire' above me in my presence? In my own hall?"

Gaebryl sat on the very edge of his seat, squeezing the stone key tight in his fist. *Who indeed!?*

Dedlin was still smiling. He turned from King Vantoo and looked into the faces of his would be accusers, undaunted by their scowls, insults, and accusations. He looked no less than enlightened. "Members of the great Council, elders and authoritarians, King Vantoo, and all other presiding, may I introduce to you (before you panic and have me executed for high treason), the Ruler, Heir, and Namesake of this entire Kingdom Continent, His Majesty, King Day of Mead."

All eyes went to the boy. Vantoo looked at the wyzard for

a moment longer, and then his eyes locked with the boy's. They stared at each other as if in some contest of defiant wills. But the boy's will easily equaled King Vantoo's.

"This declaration is nothing less than preposterous," Jonhousa blurted.

1   The room instantly rose into another tumultuous uproar. Dedlin's proclamation was ludicrous and extremely inappropriate at such a dire time, they cried. Several stood, shouting and shaking their fists in the air. Some sat and sadly shook their heads.

Drer Fregoode wasn't one to pass judgment so quickly. He was one of those who stood, but for different reason. He stared at the boy keenly, considering and measuring, and within a few moments, he, too, joined Dedlin Dane, bowing toward the lad and taking one knee on the floor. "Your Highness," he said.

The boy nodded to the king's longtime friend and adviser.

"Drer Fregoode?" the king squawked. "You, too?"

"Ridiculous," Commander Binder snarled, not sharing in this revelation.

"There is no such place as Mead," Jonhousan replied, eyeing the boy with vicious contempt. "We're wasting time, King Vantoo!"

Gathargo, the head wyzard in the proceedings, also eyed the boy with sharp interest. "There is certainly an isle Mead," he said. "But these claims are nigh on impossible..."

Voices bantered in wild debate, rising in a chaotic cacophony. Gaebryl looked from one to the next as they blurted out their opinions, but always he returned gaze back to his recent traveling companion, the young man who had remained so secretive throughout their journey together and who now remained so patiently stoic throughout the raucous proceedings. The boy seemed eager to get on with things now, as well, rather than needlessly quip and banter.

"Quiet!" Vantoo suddenly cried out. "Enough of this! Silence, I tell you!"

Gaebryl glanced up at the paintings on the king's walls. There were many scenes from the Old Stories, simplified and romantic: the Great Flood, washing over all the lands; the first Day, with his arms spread to the skies, golden light beaming from his fingertips as he lit the suns in the sky during Creation; the Dragon Wars of Eaoph; the great sorcerer Oziah Aabx and the floating Stones of Power; the first coronation of Day as king during his voyage to the Island of Mead in the White Sea as a new mortal man; and, the birth of his first son, Mikael Day, complete with silver aura. Gaebryl had been taught the old religions in school, literally hundreds, perhaps thousands of stories and fables and tales and parables, and they were all about this boy's royal, sometimes godlike, ancestors, if he were truly who Dedlin Dane was claiming he was. King Day of Mead! Gaebryl had never fancied himself a believer, even though he felt as though all the Old Stories were probably *based* on reality. What generation of Day was he then? According to the stories, weren't they all supposedly immortal? Could that explain the impossible event on the mountainside with Habad..?

The boy stepped up onto a vacant chair to get a better view of his doubters. "Thank you, Dedlin Dane," he acknowledged with a respectful nod. The wyzard bowed once again. Then, the boy addressed himself to the rest of the room. "Indeed, I am who he says I am," he stated in a loud, clear voice. The room quieted to listen. "I am your king. I am Jamesyn Day of Mead, son of Mikael Day the Third, great-great-grandson of the first King Day, Ruler of the Kingdom Continent of Day. I come here to you, Tungulin, in peace. I come here, too, in dire need.

"Indeed, I come to you for your assistance and your prudent advice, great castlecity Tungulin. I come to you thus, begging if I must. Unfortunately, your presumptions concerning the Gharnians are correct, and I come bearing darker tidings than those shared here tonight. The Gharnians, formidable as they are, are not the worst of your oncoming foes."

"Are you going to allow this?" Jonhousan asked King Vantoo. "This is a ruse! We have the security and well being of the castle city and the entire Galgarian territory to think about now..." Several others concurred.

The boy paused his oration, gleaning with an impatient eye.

"Silence, I say," Vantoo responded, marching around the table, his eyes glancing from the floor to the boy, then back to the floor. "I know what is at stake here!" he snapped at his police captain, Sabre Jonhousan. "I must have a moment to think. I must think!"

The room fell into hushed whispers. The boy stood patiently on the chair, watching King Vantoo with a degree of respect and humility. Dedlin Dane remained more than ever pleased with himself. Drer Fregoode and Prince Gaebryl both looked somewhat pale. Binder seemed genuinely frustrated, as did most of the rest. Vantoo continued circling the table in thought, hands clasped behind his broad back, glancing toward his elder advisers for counsel and insight.

Gathargo and the wyzards of the Inner Council were quietly conferring amongst themselves, glancing again and again in wonder at the boy. They seemed rightly suspicious of him, yet they seemed to be nodding favorably. Everyone else began watching them, because their powers of intuition, observation and renowned wisdom were reputably infallible. They would know if this boy were a fake or not.

"Well?" Vantoo said in a voice that sounded both tired and angry. "What say you, wyzards? If there are those who can say whether this be a ruse, it is you."

Gathargo stepped forth. "Sire, there are some discrepancies with the known stories and prophecies..."

"I see..."

"But," the wyzard interrupted, continuing. "There is always room for human error when prophecies are derived from divine inspiration, written and rewritten throughout many generations. We, the high wyzards of the Inner Council, concur and believe unanimously," he said, "that he *is* a descendant to the Great Throne of Day, as he claims he is."

The room gasped in unison. Many stood, watching the proceedings in stark amazement and disbelief. This was nothing short of living history unfolding right before their eyes.

Vantoo stared at many of the faces in the room, first one, then the next. "Gaebryl?" he said, almost pleadingly, spinning toward him. "I must be sure on this before taking any course of action. You understand this. You traveled with this young man, for quite some time. No one here knows him better than you do. What have you to say in this matter? Is this boy who he claims to be?"

Gaebryl looked into the face and eyes of his young companion. *The demeanor. The infamous assassins. The key. The accent and strange clothes. The Gharnians. The event on the mountainside where he witnessed this boy somehow cheat certain death. The confirmation by the wise. What else could explain all this?* The boy's gaze was nothing short of piercing.

Gaebryl faced the room and spoke. "King Vantoo, this young man before you, before us all, *is* King Day of Mead. Of that I am absolutely certain."

The boy gave him a warm, affectionate smile.

"By the gods!" Vantoo replied. "Could the Old Stories be true, then?"

Just at that moment, two skycraft fighter pilots came dashing into the hall, the scouts that Binder had sent out to investigate the crash. This was the one interruption Vantoo had been expecting. Everyone turned to them as they stopped at Binder's side, breathing heavily. Seeming apprehensive for some reason, they knelt at Binder's side and began to speak to him in whispers.

"Speak aloud, Perce," Vantoo ordered sternly, recognizing one of them, a mahekian masterpilot of some reputation. The king was no longer in the mood for formalities. "What have you seen?

Speak!"

"Your Highness," Perce said. "We have just returned from the crash sight. The gogmoors have just begun investigating it themselves. They did not see us, though, of that, we are certain. We detected no less than two dozen small skycraft, fighters, on our screens. We also detected, fleetingly, as if being blocked, an occasional reading much larger nearby. A reading that could be interpreted as a mega hull warship, maybe two, but we could not pinpoint them. They must be cloaked, somewhere in the nearby mountains."

"Survivors?"

"Unable to confirm. We could not get close enough. We could only just see the hull of the crashed skycraft. But..."

"Yes, Masterpilot?" Vantoo said. "Speak up!"

"The markings on this craft, Sire. I've never seen a skycraft quite like it. It's sleek and unusual. Futuristic, if I may be permitted to say. I've never seen a ship like it. And the markings, well, they say it's from... Isle *Mead*."

"Mead!" Jamesyn Day responded fearfully. "They are trying to reach me!"

Gasps and more whispers filled the room. Certainly, the boy was who he said he was. He had to be. Even Binder, who was always cynical, seemed curiously persuadable now.

Gaebryl could scarcely breathe.

"I see," Vantoo replied. "Thank you, Perce, that will be all."

The pilots bowed and departed quickly from the chamber.

Vantoo turned to the boy and lowered his head. "This is very awkward. And I apologize most sincerely, Your Highness, but I did not know. I could not know. Especially with all that is going on."

"I understand, wise king. I came most unexpectedly, not the way I had intended at all. I never knew that I and my family had become a myth to you here on the mainland. Your misgivings are no fault of your own. Yet, here I stand before you, laid bare, now awaiting your official response."

"King Day," Vantoo said with all humility, bowing, "I, King Tital Vantoo of Tungulin, am at your service, as are all my subjects, possessions, and power. They are yours to command. Yea, I am troubled by your presence here. Pray, please tell us why you have come here at this troubled time."

The boy king Day continued to address the room. "I come by choice and by destiny," he decreed. "By absolute necessity. By duty. If you'll permit, I come to consult with your wyzard, Dedlin Dane, post haste, over matters and mysteries and nearly forgotten secrets hidden ages ago, when the deeds of war were passed down not by pen and scroll, but by fireside tales, from father to son to son. And to consult with you, as well, Your Highness. For I also need your wisdom and guidance."

Vantoo looked at the wyzard standing nearby, bent and frail looking. "Consider it done," he said. "Dedlin has already made his intentions known to everyone here tonight. I grant him my permission to serve you as he will. May he serve you well, in any capacity you deem necessary. I also have other wyzards, younger and stronger, should you desire. If you have come now to face the Gharnians in battle, I have legions of great warriors, trained for combat. My army is at your disposal. I believe we have the best army in the Kingdom of...well, *Day*, if you'll forgive me. And a fleet of the finest warships ever constructed."

Day nodded, gratefully acknowledging this generosity. "Soon it may be necessary to enlist the aid of these fine warriors, but, thankfully, not yet. I seek only quiet counsel with Dedlin, with Your Kingship, and with Prince Gaebryl, now, in more private chambers. I believe that you have handled the rest of your business here tonight more than effectively.

"I apologize for appearing to you so abruptly here today, members of this great Council," Day then said boldly to the rest of the Tungulinians. "And as I said, this was never my intended course of introduction. I had planned to make my presence known here differently, with a bit more pomp and ceremony, but what's done is done. Under the circumstances it could not be helped. Perhaps for the best, too. Please, forgive me now, but leave me to your king for rest of the evening."

The members of the Council, still in a mild state of shock, squirmed a bit, still staring wide eyed, hesitant to move, not sure if they had been properly dismissed or not. They looked to King Vantoo for guidance.

"Yes, thank you, everyone," Vantoo said, addressing his exasperated audience to their relief. "I'm sure you're as overwhelmed with all of this as I am. Obey your king tonight and go home. Please. Go and await your orders. I will brief you again in the morning. And, before you depart, a warning. Not a word about these events to anyone. Even mentioning it to your wives or husbands or friends or sisters or brothers will be immediate cause for dismissal from the Council and grounds for punishment. Consider yourself warned. Consider yourselves personally sequestered." He turned to signal his sentinel to close the Secret Council. "This meeting is hereby adjourned. Now, good night. Sleep if you can!"

Everyone reluctantly complied. They wanted to see more. They wanted to hear more. They mumbled their thoughts and concerns quietly to one another, gawking in awe at the young king as they stood and filed out. Sabre Jonhousan seemed particularly interested in the boy; he stared at him grimly, frowning as he departed. Gaebryl did not like the way he looked at his young friend.

Vantoo turned and addressed Benjyn Binder. "Go now, Commander. Be careful. I await your report," he said. "Especially now that we know the origin of this craft. This event may have an even greater significance than we first imagined."

"I will take Drer Fregoode with me, by your leave."

"Agreed. And one other."

"I will go," Gaebryl volunteered. "I know the land. I've

dealt with gogmoors."

"I cannot permit it," King Vantoo said. "You are both a guest and a diplomat here."

"You are not entirely healed," Day agreed. "You were badly injured. What good would you be to them, should things go awry? Do not be a hindrance to this search party, Gaebryl. Pray, come to counsel with King Vantoo and I, so that you may now learn all it is that you have desired to know.."

"Then I will go," Dedlin Dane said. "My personal skycraft is close by and ready for departure. And it wouldn't hurt to have someone along with a bit of majik, just in case..."

Binder straightened up, rigidly erect, obviously in protest.

"Agreed," Vantoo said. "You've taught me a lesson tonight, old man. I will think twice before ever doubting you again."

Dedlin nodded.

"Dedlin," Day said, coming toward him. "Perhaps you should not go. We have not yet spoken, and it is you that I have come here to find. I seek your valuable counsel. I need your expertise..."

The wyzard smiled. "Fear not, Your Highness, I already have everything in order for you," he said. "Trust me." Then he leaned over and whispered something into Day's ear. Just a few quick words. The boy's repose diminished and then he blushed from neck to forehead. They smiled knowingly at one another, then the wyzard spun on his heels. "We're off!" he said in high spirits, and exited the room, hot on Benjyn Binder and Drer Fregoode's trail. This left only Prince Gaebryl, a flustered King Vantoo, and the young King Day in the great Hall of the Council. The echoes of the retreating footsteps made the room feel ominous and hollow.

Gaebryl sat down next to young King Day and they smiled at each other. "So," Gaebryl said.

"So," said the boy.

"Shall I call you Jamesyn now? King Day?"

"Whatever you are comfortable with, Gaebryl. 'Day' is acceptable."

"Day," Gaebryl said, nodding pleasantly. "Dedlin seemed rather giddy for one so entangled in such a dark fate," he said. "What exactly did he whisper in your ear before he left? It definitely had an effect on you. I don't think I've ever seen you blush before."

"Nothing," Day said, blushing again instantaneously. He touched his fingers to his heart, smiling somewhat distantly, as if something both personal and painful had been revealed and eliminated all in one quick stroke. "Wyzards," he dismissed, pensively.

17

Gaebryl tried to recall what he could about the Old Stories, or the "original superstitions" as he used to call them privately to his friends, the ones concerning the founders and first rulers of the continent, but found that he retained very little from his school days. Just bits and pieces. He remembered only this: if the legend held true, then this boy was a direct descendant of one of the long lived first beings created after the Great Flood that destroyed nearly all life thousands and thousands of years ago, before written history. The first Day was, supposedly, the originator of the world as they now knew it, being chosen as righteous and fair by even greater gods, and given five great powers to use at His discretion, although what they were exactly had slipped Gaebryl's mind. There were Creation, and Time, he remembered, and Utter Destruction, but that was all he could muster from the cobwebs in his brain.

Gaebryl also recalled another being created after the flood by other gods, Gheelgahar, the Devil, who was granted the same five powers. There were wars and conflicts as both Day and Gheelgahar recreated the new emerging world as they had been instructed to do. In its most simplistic and idealistic explanation, the purists believed that Day created mostly good beings, animals, trees, and plants, while Gheelgahar spent His talents creating evil creatures and mutations of Day's good creatures, an effort to institute some kind of universal natural balance. It was a constant competition between them that went on off and on for centuries. Others believed that neither of them were truly good or evil. They were just two monumental powers locked in godlike combat.

Finally, after more than a millennium of struggle, Gheelgahar was eventually defeated once and for all. Unable to kill Gheelgahar outright, since Gheelgahar was created by a greater god than He, Day imprisoned him under the sea to the south of Gharne, which was thereafter called the Sea of Death, to await judgment, release, or rehabilitation from the original gods when they someday returned. If ever.

It was at that time that the desire to become human became too great (over love, Gaebryl seemed to remember), the first Day relinquished His five great powers into small stones, to be kept safely hidden should he ever need them again. He then became as an ageless immortal human, supposedly to live out eternity as a normal, powerless, yet spiritually fulfilled man, and he was named king of the continent. He married soon thereafter and had an offspring, a son. Then, shortly after, something went wrong, and immortal or not, he somehow died. Gaebryl's recollections of that part of the tale was unclear; there were a few things about all this in his memory that he couldn't quite remember correctly.

But, before his death, King Day built his great watchtower palace on the distant island of Mead in the ocean he had named the White Sea, and for countless generations his family dwelled there in peace, watching over the Kingdom Continent of Day omnipotently. Or something like that.

After Gheelgahar's demise, there were other wars as different breeds fought for dominance around the continent. The Gharnians continued fighting, and for another three hundred years, that lesser war continued, until the mysterious pacifistic mahekians arose from quiet obscurity to unite in war, which then tilted the table in the direction of all good men. The Gharnian's were finally defeated and banned from all lands but their own southern domain. This war, unlike the stories of Day's family history, was substantiated historically in numerous written accounts, and it was much more realistic and believable to historians and rational thinkers.

There had been another round of rumors from the religious fringe a few years back that had circulated around the kingdom that King Mikael Nicholias Day and his Queen (who would be this boy's father and mother) had both passed away from some strange sickness, as had all their predecessors before them. Gaebryl had just figured that this was part of the same ongoing fairy tale, kept alive by the pious fanatics who wanted to believe that the kingdom continent, indeed, was ruled by a just, all knowing, omnipresent king, somewhere too far away to substantiate or disprove.

Unfortunately, that was the extent of Gaebryl's limited knowledge. He walked quietly in tow behind the two kings, trying hard to remember more.

The king's personal chambers were dark. It only took a moment, however, for the pages to light up row upon row of candles around the perimeter of the circular meditation suite. Gaebryl tossed some new wood on the fire in the center hearth, and it blazed up like dried summer grass, golden and warm. As soon as Vantoo waved his hand, the pages scurried from the room. Outside the windows, the great fireworks continued going off over the river. The colors were vivid and breathtaking upon the smooth surface of the dark water.

Young King Day sat near the balcony and asked the other two to join him there. "Let us now relax for a brief respite while I finish my tale and make my requests of you ere I depart again."

"Depart? So soon? You've just arrived. Is it not possible to remain here for a time and recuperate after your long travels?" asked the old king, pouring some red wine into goblets. "I have many noble warriors who would take any dreadful chore from you."

Day shook his head. "It is not that simple. I fear this first quest will only be the beginning of a long and harrowing road that lies ahead of me. It is merely opening a door to what inevitably lies beyond."

"I can go in your stead," Gaebryl offered. "What can you do that I cannot? Give me your quest and remain here safe."

"Thank you, but that is impossible, Gaebryl. For I am the heir of the Kingdom of Day, not you. I am the Stonebearer. No other can be. Or, rather, I soon shall be, if we are successful. I am being pursued as much for what I *seek* as for who I *am*."

"The Stones," Gaebryl muttered, remembering the Old Stories. "You seek the Stones."

"Yes. But just one Stone for now. At least at first. Then, we'll see."

"A quest now begins to take shape."

"Yes, but it is actually more of a race than a quest, and not just with the Gharnians. It may be true that they are your foremost concern presently, but they are but foot henchmen to the One who has now returned in the south and will soon follow if he can. He who lost all, but now seeks to regain what He once deemed was his all along: our world. Now, here within this safe haven, I will tell you this. I will never be left alone and unsearched for, no matter where I hold up. Even in this mighty fortress. Because He and his agents are coming for me, and for the Stones I now seek. He knows that it is only I and my lineage who can reclaim the power from them. That is all He now fears. This reunion."

"You speak of Gheelgahar?" Tital Vantoo asked. At every mention of that dark name, the lights in the room seemed to mysteriously dim. The air seemed somehow thicker and smoky.

"The Dark One of Old has surely returned. The same my forefathers banned from the world so long ago to await judgment. Yes, it is He, the Ancient One, the Black Tyrant, who has risen from the Sea of Death and now resides in the walled fortresses of deepest Gharne once again, slowly recovering and regaining his focus and strength. Long has he waited. How long ago He came, creeping up from out of the depths of that murky sea, no one is for certain. But His return was foretold by many, and now the greatest seers have all agreed that this horrid prophecy has come to pass. Gheelgahar has indeed risen, and so His five great powers of darkness are emerging again with him. Sleepless and tireless, He is fashioning them and honing them to His will as we sit here tonight. He grows stronger every day, and He is ever angry and vengeful."

"Gheelgahar,' Gaebryl whispered.

"Seeing more and more signs of Him and his agents, my counselors concluded that time was of the essence and bade me depart hastily and clandestinely, before Mead could be sought out and destroyed. He has begun to send out assassins and legions of evil soldiers, infiltrating every castlecity on the continent, to both hunt me down and to seek out and destroy what it is that I now seek. Even now, armies and dark creatures search high and low for the Stones of Power. Perhaps Gaorwyn and the gogmoors are already under his command. Perhaps there are traitors within these very walls."

"This is the reason for the strange feelings and uneasy dreams I have been having. I feel in my heart it is so," Vantoo said.

"The key that I have entrusted to you, Gaebryl, is integral to releasing the first Stone, which awaits discovery, the scholars believe, somewhere in a secretive cave. This will initiate the mystical link between me and my inheritance. Or so the legends say. I will go with all haste to this place, and pray that there is some truth to these ancient stories. We must believe, because certainly the enemy does."

"This is a vast land, Your Highness. Where does this cave lie? Gorn, Eaoph, Galgariah?"

"That is where your wyzard, Dedlin Dane, comes into this story. It is said that he, alone, holds the knowledge to find this sacred place, and the ancient words that will release the magick and powers within..."

"If he can still remember them," Vantoo mused under his

breath, with some concern. "And from there?" he asked.

"To the next Stone, wherever that may be. It seems a task impossible, but hopefully not," Day replied sadly. "Now that my identity has been compromised, I must leave immediately, because the news will travel like wildfire. Tomorrow, if at all possible, or as soon as I may be prepared."

"Of course," Vantoo said politely. "I will do all I can do for you. But this is very sudden. I would realistically need a few days to prepare adequately for such a journey. I can perhaps prepare ten legions by morning."

"No. No army," Day stated adamantly. "Use them to protect this city."

"I'll contact the kings of all the great territories. We shall unite. There is none who could withstand the strength of many kings. Together, we can surprise them at their borders. We can attack preemptively."

"Once the enemy detected a movement of that size, they would know that we know. Do not start this war prematurely, before the first Stone has been found. To muster now would thwart all our plans," Day advised. "Do have your armies prepared to fight right here when they are called upon, Vantoo. While we prepare, we must appear unprepared. That is our only advantage. The appearance of ignorance and complacency."

"I understand," Vantoo replied. "Wise counsel. Yet, you're not planning on traveling the continent alone?"

"Only a handful will accompany me on this journey. Five or six. No more than ten. Secrecy will be our ally."

Vantoo nodded. "As you wish."

"Before the end, the prophecies have predicted unprecedented forces shall arise, both against us and to our aid, from places we know and places we have never heard of, from all around the world. We shall put off that horrible day for as long as we're able."

Gaebryl saw dispair in the boy's face. There were so many things he wanted to ask him. So many things he wanted to know. But all that would have to wait. "We will prevail," he simply said, in an attempt to comfort.

"When I left Mead, nearly three months ago," Day said, his eyes staring distantly into some other world, some other time, "there were fourteen others from the Palace alongside. We were so... so *proud* of this undertaking. We felt not only valiant, but essential. Invincible. Unfortunately, we were quickly put to the test and proven wrong. We were all novices, and no one was used to ranging the wilds. The way was not easy. At sea, a serpent haunted us for days. There were seamaids, as green as the algae that swirled beneath our boat, who stole onto the ship at night while we slept, and... their cruel deeds are too horrible to retell. The incredible distance and bizarre navigation kept us at sea for a month and a half."

"The others..." Gaebryl asked.

"All gone. Seven at sea, the remainder after we began our trek across the mainland. The last two were killed by Habad, trying to protect me to the end, just days before you and I met. A good crew. A great crew. Many of them were very close to me. Advisers. Seers. A longtime family doctor. Only three of them had ever done any traveling, and like myself, none of them had ever been to the mainland. But they volunteered. They knew how important it was and were willing to make that supreme sacrifice. Little did they know how they would meet their end. They were very courageous. All of them."

"I am sorry."

"They would be very happy seeing that I made it this far. There were many times when our situation looked grim, and all seemed lost. So, I will not reflect on them with sadness, but will try to remember their valor and be proud. They will not be forgotten."

King Vantoo cleared his throat. "The mahekians keep the stories of your family kindled, though most common folk do not believe them anymore. All searches for Mead have been fruitless.

It has become a fable land that only children and religious folk speak of."

Day glanced up at him. "Dedlin obviously believes."

"As does Drer Fregoode. I thought he was going to faint when you stepped out into the light," Gaebryl said. The three of them laughed. It was a merry sound, and welcome. The conversation turned for awhile to lighter subjects, and Gaebryl joined King Vantoo in another drink of wine. Day had a cup of cold mead instead. The king ordered up a tray of meats, cheeses, breads, and desserts, which they devoured as they spoke. Outside, the spectacular cacophony of fireworks continued to rain colorful bursts of fire across the skies; it sounded as though they were nearing the climax of the presentation.

The king's crickets in their blackwood cages chirped loudly for several seconds, marking the lateness of the hour. "Your chambers have been made ready, King Day. We all have a big day ahead of us tomorrow, and many plans to make before your departure. Please accept my offer of at least one night's peace."

He acknowledged King Vantoo with a tired nod. They rose to disband and head their separate ways. But before they had gotten too far, Day looked at the prince. "And as for you..."

"As for me," Gaebryl said, shrugging, "I'm sure you've been made aware that I am planning to be married soon. "

"That is the rumor circulating the kingdom," Day replied. "I believe you are betrothed to a certain princess in Cissel who is surely awaiting your anticipated arrival?"

King Tital Vantoo nodded. "Hmmm."

"Well," the prince went on, "Now, as inconvenient as it may be to all those involved, and in light of tonight's many revelations, it appears that I just may have to postpone that event and rearrange my priorities now," he said.

"Yes?"

"Yes."

"I have not made any request of you yet."

"There is no need to bother, "Gaebryl replied. "Because I will not be left behind, whether I am invited along or not. Even injured I will follow you across mountains, over seas, through deserts, even into the heart of darkest Gharne. I would be like an unrelenting shadow. I will see this done, whether you like it or not. Er, Your Highness.

"I'm sure that marriage ceremony will wait," King Vantoo said. "The princess may not, but I'm sure that your father, and hers, will understand. In the long run."

"Vantoo, I'll need a pilot and a good crew, a brave, loyal crew, and they must be, above all things, uncompromisingly trustworthy."

"I have a few in mind," the king said. "I will dispatch them immediately since I do not foresee any rest for me this night, and I will brief them myself personally. They will be ready to go when you are."

"The fireworks have ended, I believe," Gaebryl said.

"You have brought dark tidings, King Day, and, also, some inspirational revelations, both of which will need some time to sink in. In the meantime, sleep well tonight, if you can, both of you, for this may be the last night of peaceful sleep we will all have for a long, long time to come."

Five

THE TIGRE

18

Commander Binder was the first to reach the king's Royal Skycraft Depot. As protocol dictated, he quickly cleared their departure with Central Tower Control and officially registered the flight with the nearest timeclock office, all within the matter of minutes.

This was a dark business, this Gharnian affair, and he found the thought of King Day of Mead as hero sadly preposterous. Even if he was this illustrious make believe king, from Mead or anywhere else, what practical purpose could that serve? Did he command the allegiance of some great army? Had he brought some secret weapon that had not yet been spoken of? In Binder's educated opinion, these harrowing events called for nothing short of a massive military strategy, not just some symbolic display of ancient royal lineage, there to muster some religious or patriotic enthusiasm from the hopeless masses. His mind swirled with defensive precautions that needed to be initiated for Tungulin's safekeeping: strategic personnel changes, numerous security command delegations, immediate armament preparations. There were surplus warships hidden in secret underground mountain fortress facilities that could be actuated. Tungulin was certainly not prepared for an attack the size that multiple Gharnian warships could constitute in a surprise attack. How far had the Gharnians infiltrated? Were there already parasitic spies in the city? Assassins? Was King Vantoo safe? Binder was uncomfortable. Investigating this crashed skycraft near Bondoon seemed to pale in comparison to the importance of preparing Tungulin for a possible Gharnian incursion.

He guided Dedlin's compact skycraft, the streamlined six man fighter Stardeer, from its dock slot manually, unwilling to wait for the docking wench, and sent it on its descent toward the transport level via the skycraft conveyor. He paralleled the craft on foot for a few yards, and then he headed down the stone spiral staircase and through the grand archway leading to the private launch site on the ground floor. The main thoroughfare was still active outside through the tall, slender windows, but the depot itself was empty, except for the night cleaning crew in their tan and blue uniforms. It was there that Dedlin Dane, now dressed for night in the woods, joined him. "Good evening, Binder," the wyzard said.

"Dedlin," he replied.

"I see you've taken care of everything."

Binder gave him but the slightest glance. "Yes."

"It has been awhile since we've worked together, Binder. I would have hoped that you would have looked upon my participation more favorably. And yet, I detect resentment," he said.

"The king agreed to allow you to join this party. It is not my place to argue with the king, no matter what I think. And I harbor no resentment, I assure you. But I am uncomfortable, yes, and greatly concerned. Some young boy has just popped up and claimed kingship over the entire Kingdom Continent. And now policy is being made based on the intuitions and beliefs of a senile old wyzard who is generations beyond his prime. Forgive me, Dedlin, but I'm not comfortable with any of this."

"We are coming upon some great times in history, Binder, my friend, believe me in this, and we will both be a part of it. This is another great beginning, and it is as exciting as it is historical."

Binder rolled up his sleeves, exposing his bulging, brown arms. "Exciting? Hmmph. I'm a realist. A pragmatist. If any of these rumors are true, Tungulin needs strong leaders, here, acting now. Enabling our forces. We cannot rely on old men and their religious fables and old wives' tales. You may see this as an exciting time, but you're not in charge of the security of this castlecity. I am. You have the naïve advantage of some bygone romanticism; I do not. You were great once. I know that, more than most. But now, you are lethargic, Dedlin, old, and crippled from arthritis. You should enjoy your retirement, tending to your old books and all those musical instruments, leaving these more important matters to those younger, more capable and keen minded."

Dedlin smiled at him. He popped a koffik bean into his mouth and crunched it between his koffik stained teeth. "After all we've been through together, you're now my judge, Benjyn?"

"I'm just making an observation. I'm not judging, wyzard. I've seen you hobbling about in the gardens these past years, reading your old, flaky books and scrolls, feeding that blight of birds. I do know you well, so I am forthright and speak openly, as I would want others to do when I have grown too old to serve in my current capacity. It is not meant as an insult, but comes only from professional concern and responsibility, so forgive me if my words seem harsh. I can't banter words. Heed my advice, old friend. Do the proper thing. You retired long ago for good reason. Your glory days in the wilds and in the king's court are long gone. Please. Keep what's left of your dignity intact. Go on home."

"The reasons that I chose to retire were my own," he said. "I had other matters to contend with. Now, in retrospect, I know I was right in taking those paths, because they led me here, tonight. I'll admit that I do rely on this cane a little more than I used to, Ben, but the wyzard you fought dhoellums with in Yuolli Duol has a few fights left in him yet."

"That was a long time ago. I was not more than a boy. You were in your prime then, old man."

"Heed my words, Commander," the wyzard said, checking the ship's level gauges along the dash. "Some vintages better with age and so can the spirit. I am old, but, I assure you, sir, in my case, that is an asset. I may surprise you, yet."

"It will surprise me if you don't get lost or killed tonight."

Dedlin laughed. "Don't worry about me. It is not my fate to die this night."

Attendants hurried to clear miscellaneous cargo from the runway for them as they mounted the bobbing jet. "Seeing into the future was never your greatest gift," the Commander said. He always had to get the last word in.

Drer Fregoode joined them there, slinging a small pack under a starboard seat. Binder and Dedlin could see the sheath of a horngarian warsword among his baggage. He was dressed in woodland garb, splotches of dark shadowy greens and dark browns, and he wore sturdy black boots. Drer kept his head shaved smooth, but his beard and moustache grew together in one long braid down his chest. "I had to pick up a few things," he said, clambering over the rail. He covered his head with a hooded cap. "We ready?"

Binder made an odd sound: half grunt, half laugh.

"Binder was just delighting me with his undaunted faithlessness in a senile old wyzard, and an untested boyking," Dedlin said.

"Not to mention Gaebryl Dindiane, the playboy prince of Bursia," the Commander added, buckling himself in. "Quite an effective group for arranging battle strategies."

Drer Fregoode and Dedlin laughed quietly at Binder's cynicism.

At the helm, Dedlin checked the algaestone storage gauge as he edged Stardeer toward the mouth of the depot exit. The tank was full, and the fuel was fully expanded. "Hold on to your knickers," he told them, carefully edging past the airgate. With a single thrust of the accelerator bar, Dedlin's faithful skycraft launched from the opening like a hissing rocket, accelerating at a tremendous speed, into the sweltering night sky. He took her steadily skyward, in a high arch over the glowering Gaalothian Forest, veering slightly toward the east as they began to level off just below the low hanging clouds. Dedlin kept her at midspeed, watching the dense, dark forest race past below them. The warm wind made his thin hair and beard dance. Despite the business at hand, he found himself smiling. He felt good.

The last traces of the day's lingering light faded in the west. A trace of deep blue on distant scarlet clouds was etched across the western horizon like fuzzy writing on ancient pages. Mon, the green moon, seemed perched upon the crest of Hiden's Peak to the east, crowned with four silver stars. Due southeast thirty degrees was Duan, the smaller blue moon, riding high in the deep indigo sky. The air was so clear that the moons looked but an arm's length away.

"What do you think? I'm going to risk coming in from the direction of Bondoon," Dedlin told them. "So, if the Gharnians are nearby, watching, we might have a better chance going in undetected."

"Agreed." Drer Fregoode charged his blaster and attached it to his belt, and then began polishing his warsword. Like the wyzard, there was a light in his eye. Drer had served in the Tungulin army for over twenty years, working his way up through the ranks under his commander and old friend, Tital Vantoo, from a foot soldier to a brigade commander by the age of twenty seven. Once retired, he traveled and studied languages and lore, writing many controversial books on philosophy, history and prophecy. He was a self proclaimed jack of many trades. He had ranged the lands with gypsies, competed in numerous knight tournaments, served five years in a mahekian monastery, and he had sailed the seas off the shores of Bursia for two hard years, fighting a scourge of marauding pirates until they were no longer a threat to the ports of those friendly shores anymore. He had served prison sentences three times for various minor incursions, mostly for political reasons. He was a florist, a beekeeper, and a winemaker, but claimed to be a master of none. He had been married three times, and had three children, whom he never saw anymore. He was a spiritualist, but still, a true warrior at heart, even at the ripe age of sixty five, and could handle his weapons with the finesse and masterful dexterity of one half his age when need arose.

Now, King Vantoo usually just enjoyed Drer's company, as friend and advisor, whenever he could keep him for any length of time in Tungulin. Drer fancied himself a rambling musician and a minstrel and often sang for Vantoo (and other kings) whenever he had the mind, which was how he came to know Dedlin Dane, the Keeper of the Musical Museum in Tungulin. Drer and Dedlin had spent the better part of the last ten years together: reading, speculating, arguing, ranging, and gathering information from distant travelers, tidbits they deemed pertinent or mutually interesting. Together, they had exasperated many, many cases of fine wines between them pouring over their theories together. They disagreed on as many things as they agreed.

"I see lights through the trees, Dedlin, and many fires," Drer said, squinting. He sheathed his sword with a snap. "It looks as if the whole forest floor is ablaze, and the flames are spreading up to the treetops."

Binder searched the distant forest with a pair of nightscans. After a minute, he spoke. "Yes. It's burning up. Decimated."

"We'll see what we see when we get there," the wyzard said. "We might find more than you think. Just keep your eyes sharp." They rode on in silence for less than a minute.

Dedlin lowered Stardeer, passing beneath the tops of the trees.

"There she is," Binder said. "Right there, over the next hill. Get lower, wyzard. Just as I feared; the gogmoors are swarming all over it. There is one gogmoor commandship...and ten or twelve fighters, but...no warships. No Gharnians."

A puffy, gagging cloud of electrical smoke rose from the trees as they drew in closer. The crash site was just to the south of them, flares of dancing red and gold reflecting from under the dark tree branches, and a community of small, dim skycraft lights swirling in a deep black pool of shadow. Now Dedlin and Drer could see the blunt, boxlike gogmoor ships through the trees, swarming around the crashed skycraft like vermin on a carcass.

Dedlin lowered his craft deeper into the trees and edged forward through the middle terraces. "If whoever was aboard that ship survived the crash, I fear they may have been taken prisoner. If this ship is truly from Mead, we must be willing to risk a rescue. It is imperative to find out why they came here."

"Yes, but we can't afford an incident with the gogmoors, either," Binder stated quietly. "We're square in Gaorwyn's territory, breaching our contract with him in the same fashion that the Gharnians have breached theirs with us."

"We're not in a warship, though," Drer added, "We're merely investigating, and doing that peacefully and respectfully."

"We're still trespassing, and we're clearly armed, so I don't think Gaorwyn would agree with you, Fregoode. The gogmoors got here first, so by rights, whatever crashes here is their responsibility. King Vantoo can begin diplomatic negotiations with Gaorwyn in the morning. This is good, right here, Dedlin. No closer. We can't risk it."

"Mmmm. Unacceptable," Dedlin said. "We can't see anything from here and we're too far away to get there on foot."

"On foot?"

Dedlin slowly circled the hill, descending deeper within the trees, advancing steadily toward the lights. The castle Bondoon swooned tall and crooked in the very near south; pale blue lights glowed from countless windows. Uran, the rose colored moon, began to rise in the northeast. Dedlin was careful not to fly between a moon and the gogmoors.

"There are a lot of lights just ahead, in the valley just beyond this next ridge," Drer warned. "Be careful. Nearing ground zero."

Dedlin whipped Stardeer around in a tight circle and came to a halt. "You're right. We can't get any closer this way."

"Now you're making some sense," the Commander replied.

"Who's joining me?"

They could hear the noisy shouts of the gogmoor monsters in the valley below. "What? Dedlin, don't be foolish," Binder said. "Listen to me! King Vantoo put me in charge of this investigation because he trusts my judgment. We need to report what we've seen to him right away. The gogmoors have unequivocally taken this ship. Midnight sunrise is drawing close, and surely the wolferines will be here soon!"

"I'm counting on both. We could use those factors to our advantage," Dedlin said, anchoring his craft to the closest tree. "Drer, tell him I'm right."

"I'm sorry, Binder, but I agree with Dedlin. We wouldn't be reporting any more than the pilots did at Council if we return now."

"You can stay here with the ship, if you prefer," Dedlin said quietly, tossing a rope ladder over the starboard side into the darkness below. He hopped a leg over the rail. "Come or stay, Commander. It's your prerogative."

Drer followed the wyzard over the side without uttering a word.

"I'm going to regret this," Binder moaned. He stepped over the side after them, following the wyzard and the loremaster down into the dark Gaalothian forest. The rope swayed from their combined weight. The heavy laden branches were rough, poking at them as they blindly descended. "Anyone could paint 'Mead" on the hull of their ship. Doesn't mean it's authentic," he continued to mumble.

Oily smoke came up the hill to meet them, burning their eyes and lungs. Dedlin suppressed a cough. They met together when they had all reached the bottom, waist deep in prickly bulbushes. "Look for survivors hiding in the woods first," he whispered to them. "And footprints. Tracks of any kind. Then, prisoners, and anything else of interest in, on, and around the skycraft."

"Or what's left of it," Binder replied.

"Stagger formation. Binder, you should remain back fifty yards or so and watch our flank."

Binder nodded; he was the only one of the three not properly dressed for the woods. He allowed Dedlin and Drer to slip away ahead of him, and then he followed quietly behind.

Not too far away from them, from behind the gnarled trunk of a nearby tree, yellow slitted eyes squinted warily at the three Tungulinians as the two humans separated from the third larger one as they headed stealthily down the wooded hill toward the melee from where he had just come. A growl rumbled quietly in the cavernous feline chest. Soon, they all disappeared from sight into the smoky barrage below. As soon as the coast was clear, he crawled on all fours up the wooded hill, toward Dedlin's fightercraft Stardeer, which he had seen as it had descended down into the trees just minutes before. Off in the distance, through the thicket of woods on the nearest hilltop, the brilliant nightlights of Tungulin could be seen, shining like hopeful beacons.

19

Dedlin Dane and Drer Fregoode were as silent as the wisps of silver/white clouds that hung above the treetops over their heads like shredded curtains. They moved like shadows down the hill toward the chaos below them: crackling flames, clanking metal and guttural gogmoor gibberish, creeping dangerously near the site, quickly finding cover behind a fallen tree on a nearby rise, very near the vaporous exhaust of a smelly gogmoor fightercraft. The scene beyond was clumsy and frantic. The gogmoors were large, loud beasts, lumbering noisily about in their heavy armor and iron boots. Flame and smoke were pinning the oafsome beasts back against the forest, keeping them from physically examining the wreckage. Dedlin and Drer knew the beasts couldn't see well in the dark, but their senses of hearing and smell were finely acute. Courage they lacked, but in brute strength, they could easily handle three men apiece. Their piglike snouts protruded from under the light magnifying visors of their clunky iron helmets, exaggeratedly sniffing every breeze. Dedlin estimated that there were at least fifty of them. He could see their mottled faces and their round, pale, animallike eyes, glowing dull red in the firelight, through their open visors.

He instructed Drer to circle the crash site

counterclockwise, and meet him on the far side. Drer disappeared into the nearby shadows, while Dedlin circled in the opposite direction. Binder had been right about one thing, though, Dedlin conceded to himself; between the crash and the gogmoor ships, the area was completely trampled.

At that moment, from a distance, several miles away, riding on a chill wind that still shrieked through the last wintery crevasses of the Subring mountains, Commander Binder heard a sound that stopped him in his tracks. Their eerie howls were like no other hunters' cries. It was a pack of black forest wolferines, great Gaalothian wolferines of the ancients, nicknamed 'cattlewolves' by local farmers who had lost entire herds to them. They were wild, ferocious beasts, often as large as small horses, intelligent, innately cruel, and they were coming fast. They roamed and hunted the hills and bleak mountains of Gaaloth in territorial packs at night, often attacking local villages if cattle herds and other livestock were scarce. And they were known man eaters. Binder stiffened to listen. Yes, they were closing in fast, and with all of the ruckus going on down below, he was sure that Dedlin and Drer would not be able to hear them coming.

20

Dedlin had found a safe hiding place behind two lichen covered boulders with a dead tree log lying across them. He squatted there and waited for Drer. A couple of the stouter gogmoors neared the shadowy forest one by one, sniffing the night air for scents, then they retreated back just as quickly. Occasionally, one would venture a few steps into the shadows beyond the searchlights, but only for a few nervous moments, then they would march pompously back to rejoin the others, puffed up like peacocks.

Diligently, obeying orders, the gogmoor foot soldiers shoveled dirt onto the craft to douse the flames, slowly making some progress. They had not found anything yet; that was plain enough. They seemed very perplexed and impatient. Dedlin was concerned that there would be an unusually bright midnight sunrise soon, when, for nearly a quarter of an hour, the small sun that circled the larger one would quickly rise over the eastern horizon and then set again within minutes until the larger broke the horizon, creating a brief but bright, sunsrise. It was a rare occurrence, but unfortunately, tonight was one of those nights. The gogmoors were not nocturnal by nature. Midnight sunsrise would give them just enough light to see the craft plainly, (and, also, anything else that might be hiding back within the nearest forest trees). Obviously now, they were waiting for that light, and for the retardant flames to die down a bit more, before stepping up their investigation any further. In fact, the fire was almost under control, good enough to read the name "Tigre" on the hull of the small, charred fighter sky craft. Perce, Vantoo's masterpilot, had been right; the craft was unlike anything the wyzard had ever seen. It was silver and white, sleek and trim, almost liquid looking. It shimmered in the fires. The passenger cabin was nearly untouched by flame or collision, which was encouraging. As the smoke began to clear with the slight wind that had just risen, Dedlin noted that the pilot's seat was empty. Could the pilot have ejected?

He watched as a group of curious gogmoors gathered together on the opposite side of the clearing, raising their rubbery snouts and sniffing along a particular path that led into the forest, repeating one word a lot, the gogmoor word for "thordian." Dedlin realized that that was the direction from which he had just come, the direction where Binder awaited them, and where Stardeer was anchored. Was it possible that the pilot or any other survivors had gone off that way and that they had somehow missed them in the darkness?

A twig snapped to Dedlin's right, from the direction Drer should be approaching. Dedlin hoped that he had learned something; Drer was an experienced woodsman and master of many dialects, fortunately fluent in the gogmoor tongue. Dedlin took in a breath to whisper, but then he paused—

Over the wind came a chilling sound, barely discernible at first, then, like wails of sheer evil, the shrill howls of the cattlewolves echoed eerily throughout the valley hollow. Gogmoor movement immediately ceased. They stood absolutely still, listening fearfully. For the first time, they went absolutely silent.

The night birds could now be heard, and summer crickets, and the wind in the trees, but nothing else. Still, they waited, as still as statues. Then, again, the terrible calls came to them again, the hunting cries of the black wolferines of Gaaloth, faintly riding the night wind above their heads, high among the swaying treetops.

The fearful gogmoors grew suddenly restless, anxious to finish their work and be gone from the woods as soon as possible. A few snapped at one another. It was a well known fact that cattlewolves loved gogmoor meat. One of the older gogmoor captains began barking orders, angrily pointing toward the smoldering Tigre. The others, grumbling but heeding his commands, tried advancing upon the ship as close as they could without getting singed. One of the bravest ones stepped into the galley of the ship for a few moments, then he jumped back off, proudly holding a charred lantern as a prize, coughing and rubbing his burning eyes. Dedlin quickly discerned that the gogmoors' main objective was not obtaining information from the Tigre, but just looting the ship, for weapons or valuables. Although, he was quite sure, the nearby Gharnians, wherever they were hidden, had other, more calculating, motives in mind.

The howls grew louder. It sounded like it was a large pack. Dedlin shivered at the sound; he had faced the wolferines and their destructive marauding on many occasions. He didn't relish the thought of confronting that carnivorous horde this night, not without sufficient preparation. He thankfully had brought his cane.

The gogmoors began mounting their skycrafts, despite their orders. The frustrated leader snapped at the deserters, one after another, pointing stubbornly at the Tigre and pushing them back in that direction. Finally, another large gogmoor, tired of being bullied on such a frustrating, fruitless night, turned and clubbed the elder in the head with his shovel, knocking him out cold. A few of the others gathered to help pick him up and dump him into his skycraft, chuckling between themselves. Gogmoors had difficulty with authority, and the positions of command rotated between them often because of fighting and rebellion amongst the ranks. The new general allowed whoever wanted to leave, to leave.

Dedlin heard Drer creep up beside him, although he was trampling much clumsier than he should have, dried leaves crackling loudly underfoot. Without glancing up at him, Dedlin whispered, "Shhh."

"Huh?" Dedlin heard from high above, deep and guttural.

He looked suddenly up from the corner of his eye, realizing before he even saw what was there that it was not his friend Drer Fregoode at all. It was a another huge gogmoor warrior, a fierce looking captain. Dedlin could now smell him as well, unwashed and urine foul.

The ugly warrior moved swiftly in Dedlin's direction with two, quick heavy steps, growling and brandishing his weapons. He had heard Dedlin's "Shhh", but fortunately, he could not see the old man crouching in the ferns at his feet. Dedlin peered up at the animal from between the fronds and saw his elongated nose dangling between his sharp lower tusks, sniffing hungrily for a scent. "I smell man," the gogmoor growled in his own dialect.

On the beast's leg was a twisted dagger, on his right hip, a hunting knife. A double edged sword hung beside an old charger pistol on his left hip, and on a leather strap that hung across his broad, hairy shoulders, was clipped an old, antiquated Galgarian blastrifle. He held a battle axe in one hand and a spiked club in the other. He was just about ready for anything. His armor was thick and heavy, imitating the form of muscles beneath it, adorned with brutal battle scars and corroded with rust. He wore an iron helmet and had a shield across his left forearm. He was, all in all, a fierce adversary should it come to a fight, a fine example of a gogmoor gladiator, with his long, stringy black hair and short, scraggly beard.

Without so much as inhaling, Dedlin tightened his grip on his twisted walking stick. He knew he could handle this one gogmoor, but where was Drer Fregoode? The moment this beast hit the ground, a dozen more would swarm into the forest after them. Drer could be caught off guard.

The gogmoor captain breathed hot and heavy, squatting lower, as if he were finally catching a scent. Yes, the beast smelled a man, and it knew that he was close by. A growl rumbled in his huge porcine chest.

Dedlin knew he needed the element of surprise to get out of this situation alive; he could not risk waiting until he was discovered. Very cautiously, he pointed his cane up toward the beast's hairy head. He whispered a few words so quietly that he could barely hear them himself, activating the deep but long dormant mystical power he once held at his command. He felt the unusual tingling sensation as the power began surging back into the connection between his clenched fist and the walking stick. He was ready. Just as he was about to spring to his feet and strike, Dedlin saw Drer Fregoode rise up directly behind the gogmoor soldier with his warsword raised high above his head.

"Garak!" called the gogmoor general near the Tigre, one of the last ones still on the ground. Drer withdrew, slinking back down into the leafy shadows. The great beast Garak, standing above Dedlin with legs spread wide, turned to acknowledge his comrade. The first one snapped orders, commanding an immediate retreat. Garak argued, pointing into the brush with jerky motions, but the general was adamant. Either Garak joined them, or he would be left behind for the wolferine cattlewolves.

Captain Garak took a few more sniffs in Dedlin's direction, then he stepped noisily past him, pushing his way through the small trees with his hands as easily as parting beaded curtains, back into the clearing with his ugly comrades. In his anger and frustration, he swung his club at a small tree, splintering it in half, cursing in his own tongue.

Dedlin relaxed, heart pounding. He was soaked to the skin by the damp ground and leaves; the cool air brought a wicked chill to his achy old bones. He tightened his cloak around his shoulders, fighting a shiver, glancing at the dying flames around the Tigre. The last of the gogmoor fighters were departing one by one into the safety of the sky. "Did you overhear anything?"

"They'll be back at midnight sunrise, when the wolferines find cover from the light," Drer whispered, squatting next to the wyzard. "The Tigre was already vacant when they arrived. Whoever was aboard had already escaped, fleeing into the forest in the direction that we came. They didn't find anything of value. And despite their fear of the Gharnians, they're more afraid of the wolferines right now."

"So they mentioned the Gharnians, then? As I suspected, they are in collusion," Dedlin said. "We don't have much time, either, Drer. I'm afraid of the wolferines, myself."

"As am I," Drer agreed.

They crept to the very edge of the clearing, still hidden behind a wall of thick leaves, as the last gogmoor, none other than Captain Garak, mounted his humming skycraft. The beast mumbled a bit, looking over his shoulder in their approximate direction with a suspicious eye. Then, with a heavy creak and a hiss of steam, his fighter rose and disappeared over the trees.

Without a word to one another, Dedlin and Drer dashed toward the smoking hull. The ship was tilted over onto its starboard side. Stretching the neck of his shirt up to cover his nose and mouth, Dedlin climbed into the blackened cabin and raced to the passenger and storage areas first, ripping into anything he could find. The smoke was still intolerable inside, and the heat was intense.

Drer checked the exterior of the Tigre, finding exactly what he had expected: holes and other damage from missile explosions. The Tigre had definitely been shot from the sky. He chipped some of the charred residue into a bag in his pack for further examination. Stepping back, he read the enshrined word, the name of the sleek silver craft, etched in a beautiful golden script near the bow, "Tigre", and in smaller gold print, yet just as elegant, the words, "White Palace," and, just below that, back in gold, "Mead."

Dedlin fought his way to the small lower deck, trying to suppress his need to breathe. The flames inside were smoldering out, but it was still as hot as an oven. He spotted a batch of maps, letters, and charts, flames licking at the corners, threatening to burn them up like dry tinder. He hastily smothered the flames with his sleeve, then stuffed the papers into his cloak. Eyes burning and tearing, he turned for the door, feeling suddenly faint.

Then they both heard it. From high on the nearest hill came a thunderous crashing, down toward the Tigre. Dedlin could hear the commotion from inside the Tigre, and as he sprang out onto the deck, wreathed in white smoke and with his cape tail aflame, he raised his sturdy cane at arm's length, chanting an incantation, awaiting the impending attack. Drer was already standing firm, hat off and feet spread wide, battleaxe at the ready, his blaster pointed toward the oncoming invaders.

Just as the frantic intruder burst through the foliage into the clearing, Dedlin bid Drer to hold fire. It was Commander Binder.

"The wolferines of Gaaloth are just over this hill," he cried abruptly. "They're circling and will be coming down this ravine in a matter of minutes. We must run now. And hard! Follow me!"

Dedlin leaped stiffly off of the Tigre, rolling upon the ground, then came up onto his feet. The three of them dashed back into the dark woods together, back up the steep hill from which they had come. The scrub was dense and unforgiving, barring their every step. Binder led the way, mowing down shrubs and small trees that stood in his way with his large feet and massive forearms. The other two followed close behind.

"Hurry on, Binder!" Drer cried. "They come!"

In the near distance, a sudden explosion lit up the sky. The three paused for a second, startled at the blast, then continued their harried run. It had sounded like a battleship missile. Then, another explosion shook the earth beneath their feet, and the flash of it lit the tops of the trees like bolts of bright lightning. Then another. Within a few seconds, a full fledged battle of some kind was raging in the south.

"What is going on?" Binder cried. "Are we at war?"

It was then that they heard the wolferines below them. The beasts had found the wreck and had started up the hill after them. Binder kept his steady pace, plowing through, clearing a trail as best he could for his friends. Drer was right behind him. Dedlin, however, had begun to slow and was falling behind; he hadn't remembered how steep and rocky it had been going down! He was covered with a cold sweat. His lungs were still full of smoke, so he struggled for every crucial breath. His tired heart pounded loudly in his ears.

"Hurry!" Binder cried. "They are nearly on us!"

Dedlin wanted to keep pace, but his body was unable. He watched the distance between him and his friends grow wider. A few seconds later and he couldn't see them at all. He heard Drer calling something, but his words were distant and dull in his ears. Each step he took became a mile to him, an almost impossible feat. Suddenly, his legs cramped and went numb. He heard the wolferines growling behind him as the explosions continued to increase above the nearby treetops. All this, teaming with a sudden, complete exhaustion, caused a fog of confusion to roll over the wyzard. He stopped on shaky legs and turned around, unable to take another step, and saw the team of wolferines throughout the woods, coming at him fast from every direction, their red eyes ablaze in the night. "Here I am, cursed beasts!"

21

"Dedlin! Where are you?" Drer cried. "Binder, he's not there! We have to go back!" He scanned the woods behind him, but there was no sign of the wyzard, only the snarling sounds of the wolferines advancing from the ravine below them. Their snarls and growls sounded as though they could have almost been made by human throats. Before him, Binder had gone on ahead and was now gone, too. "Binder! Can you hear me? Don't leave us! We have to wait for Dedlin!"

There was no answer. Drer turned to dash back down the hill after his aged friend.

Then, he heard the voice of the Commander, high atop the wooded hill. He was shouting. "The skycraft!" he cried out to them. His voice was tinny and frantic.

"Dedlin! Drer! Stardeer is not here! The skycraft is gone!"

Six

ON THE
WAY WHERE ?
22

The gagging smells in the lower dungeons were as vile as those who were imprisoned there. Unredeemable men and women of all races lived out the rest of their miserable sentences seven floors below the ground, caged behind a series of no less than eleven locked gates and seven armed guard stations, wallowing in the filth and enmity they had created. Grim voices echoed eerily through the mazelike corridors. There was distant coughing and an occasional wail of anguish or insanity. Slimy water dripped from the ceiling and walls of slippery, mossy bedrock. This was the realm of Tungulin's most notorious caged criminals: the perverse, the wicked, and the deadly. There were rats aplenty and foul disease, despite the guards' best efforts to keep some semblance of cleanliness and order.

King Tital Vantoo, flanked by his personal Knights of the Guard, held a kerchief over his nose as he passed the general population quarters toward a specially designed holding room. Gathargo the wyzard accompanied him, as did Huegart, there in Commander Binder's absence. Vantoo entered the room like a storm about ready to burst, facing five shackled men standing against the wall: two humans, two glaaki, and one tyberlian. Although, just a day ago, they had been dressed in the finest clothes of the Tungulin aristocracy, and were free to roam the streets, this morning, their clothes were torn to rags, and two of them were noticeably injured, one of the glaaki badly. Yet, King Vantoo had no pity for them. He eyed each of them with bitter contempt. "The punishment for an assassination attempt," he said sharply, "is death. Death by beheading."

He paced the room from one side to the other, glaring

angrily at the collaborators, all of them Gornian born. "The punishment for treason is the same. You are all guilty on both counts, and your executions will be carried out within the hour. Do you have anything to say in your defense?"

One man sobbed. Two stared vacantly. The remaining duo blazed back at him with eyes fearful, yet defiant.

"No," the single tyberlian replied for them. "Would it make any difference if we did?"

"No," Vantoo answered. "Just a formality to ask." He squeezed his hand over the wound in his side; he could feel the ooze of blood beneath the bandage. Had he reacted one second slower to their attack, the blast would have certainly killed him. His wrists were bruised from the wire they had used to bind him with, and his head sore from the blow that had been intended to render him unconscious. He had proven a greater adversary than they had expected. He edged closer to the would-be assassins, close enough to smell their sweat. He sneered in the face of one of them in particular, the badly wounded glaaki shooter, whose firing hand had been severed in the fray.

"Cowards," he hissed at them. "You disgust me. The lot of you. We bring you in from your country and treat you as our own, and provide you with opportunity to thrive here and lead happy, peaceful lives as free Galgarian men, and still you serve the Gharnians. What reward could they have offered you to tempt you to try something so foolish? What could corrupt you? Lies? Offers of riches? Lands? Life here is good for good people. You are free men in Tungulin, blessed with liberty and opportunity. Life under the Gharnians would be nothing short of slavery and animal servitude."

The one closest to Vantoo spoke. "You are naïve, local king," he said. "Things are going to change soon, continentwide. It is inevitable. We did not choose, condone or condemn it, but we have been forced to try to make the most of it. The Gharnian Dominion is inevitable, and it will be better to side with them than rise up against them. Most feel that it will be better to hope for any kind of opportunity from the victors than forgotten promises from the defeated."

"Know this," said the tyberlian. "It is written that a great leader will arise in the last Age of Tears 512, a great redeemer, a savior, a god, and that sorrowful age draws to a close even now. He is come. The pendulum has reached its apex and now begins to swing in the other direction. The Kingdom of Day wanes and will soon become the Empire of Lord Gheelgahar the Great and His Perfect Dominion. All signs point to it. The prophecies direct it.

"He will bring order to this barbaric world. Order, discipline and stability to these unruly, wild lands. We will have progress and civilization from sea to crashing sea. Roads and bridges. Safe transportation for all. Equal share of the riches and prosperity for all. The masses believe this. They want this. Recruits are volunteering for military service all across the continent, Vantoo. Like us, you will either be a party to this evolution, or you shall perish from it, and, in time, be forgotten to your children's children's children.."

"You are gullible fools," Huegart replied. "You are the ones who shall perish and be forgotten, long before you ever see that wretched day."

"Sire, I do not ask for forgiveness, because I know I deserve none," the tyberlian continued, trembling. His eyes looked lost. He then lowered his voice so that only King Vantoo could hear him. "The Gharnian resolve is strong, my lord, as strong as battle steel. They are persuasive in both strategy and voice..."

"Enough to turn you traitor? Where is your honor, man? Does that not stand for something?"

"They entice, your majesty, and they seduce with their offers of power, of privilege and prestige. But that is not all. They have dark magick behind them. Powerful dark magick. It enables and fulfills. It emboldens their persuasive tongue. It dominates the direction of reasonable debate and the interpretation of speech."

The prisoner most badly injured, the glaaki who had formerly been a chef in the King's service for over a decade, found the will and strength to speak. "And they have allies of which this world has not witnessed in eons. I've seen them in my dreams. Coming. Fearful titans that they can call upon at their whim and discretion. To do their bidding. Great ancient demons of the dark. Of which there is no defense. Demons."

The tiberlian smiled, a bit of insanity crossing over his face. "This is true."

Tital Vantoo looked down his nose at the defiant, condemned spy. He pulled back his lips, snarling at his enemy in the traditional gythot manner. Then he turned to Huegart and said as he departed the chamber, "They have lost themselves to madness. Execute them and bury them deep. Tell no one of their fate. They are hereby forgotten. Begin with the injured."

Huegart nodded.

"Gheelgahar returns!" the tyberlian called. "He has set loose the realm of morgoth! The morgothyon comes for you all!"

Vantoo left through the security door with Gathargo and his knights close by his side. Outside, the elder Inner Council wyzards awaited them, following in tow behind them as they passed.

"In my very own bedchamber," he snarled contemptuously. "Traitors and assassins in my very own bedroom, Gathargo. One of them my personal valet of three years! How I wish Binder were here. Please tell me good news. Any word on the search party yet?"

"None, sire," Gathargo answered, escorting Vantoo by the elbow. "Yet, the battle has subsided. We suspect that the Gharnian warships continue to linger cloaked and hidden somewhere in the nearby mountains, but they have left the gogmoor injured to the ravenous wolferines."

"The filthy animals," the king growled. "Not even the simpleminded gogmoors deserve such a fate. We must hasten King Day's departure immediately, with or without the wyzard. It is not safe for him here anymore. Assemble the crew I've selected. We will send Dedlin after them, once he returns. Any word from Jonhousan?"

"He is still missing, and cannot be found, Your Highness," Gathargo answered. "No one has seen him since the emergency Secret Council last evening."

"That concerns me greatly. He did not seem right last night. I fear ill tidings."

"Things are certainly in disarray this morning," the wyzard said. "But at least you are alive."

Vantoo nodded. "For the time being," he said. "Send word via sphere to Cissel, Dindiane, Oliader, Poed, and the City of Gold. Tell them what has transpired here today."

"It has already gone out by message sphere to those cities and more."

"Very good."

"And Sire..."

"Yes, Gathargo?"

"The gogmoor have begun attacking villagers near the southern wall in retaliation for last night. There are many townsfolk dead and injured. Gaorwyn is blaming us for the decimation of his soldiers. The local guard is holding them back, but we need to send military reinforcements to drive them back out."

Vantoo nodded. "Do it immediately," he ordered. "Send two guerilla squads, and a medical rescue unit. Bring in as many townsfolk as we are able. Get them behind our walls. Set up temporary shelters for all who need them. Make room for everyone."

Gathargo signaled to his associates to fulfill Vantoo's commands with a nod of his head. "It is still an hour before true sunrise, yet this is already a dark day for Tungulin," he said.

Vantoo mounted the next flight of steps like an athlete half his age. "It is a dark day for the entire kingdom, Gathargo."

"Sire, what of..." the old wyzard paused, as if he did not want to say the word aloud. "What of the morgothyon the prisoner spoke of?"

Vantoo's heart grew cold. He stopped at the top of the stairs and turned to his most able wyzard, grim and noticeably shaken by that name. He took a brief repose and a deep breath before exhaling. "Say nothing of it again, to anyone. We shall face that horror if and when it arrives, and not a minute sooner."

23

The morning suns came up over the mountains in the east as though they were prepared to do battle. It was hot and bright almost immediately, and not a cloud dared show itself for fear it would evaporate instantly into mist.

"We'd best be getting back," Gaebryl said to Day, shielding the morning light from his eyes with the palm of his hand. They had been strolling along the paths of the public gardens for awhile to get a breath of fresh air, dressed in common townsfolk attire to keep from attracting attention, but now stepped down the narrow stone stairway that led to the busy market thoroughfare, stretched out along the myriad of streets, far below them in multileveled tiers. He had a sturdy brace on his injured leg, which caused him to limp and occasionally stagger, but his recovery was well underway. Every step showed signs of progress. "I sense the need for haste this morning. There is bad vibration in the air."

Day's spirits had been down from the moment he had risen from a sleepless night's repose. His eyes were affixed on the ground before his heavy feet, his hands deep in his pockets. "I shouldn't have let him go," he said quietly. He had repeated those sentiments repeatedly all morning. "I had him right here, and I let him go before we ever had a chance to converse. I knew better, Gaebryl."

At the base of the market stairs, they mingled in with the flow of the crowd, heading back toward the palace of King Vantoo. Gaebryl carefully led the way through the populous streets, deflecting overly aggressive solicitors trying to ply their wares at every step and turn. He was alert and cautious, watching everyone that passed them with a sharp eye, even though it was probably safer for them there in the public streets than in the king's royal court that day. No one would expect them out mingling among the commoners.

Pasted freshly to stone obelisks along the outskirts of the landscaped promenade were royal proclamations from King Vantoo's office announcing the reinstatement of the volunteer Royal Knights of Galgariah. Young men continued to gather around the posts, reading the information with interest and a bit of trepidation. A mild electricity was abuzz in the conversation in the streets and pubs.

Gaebryl and Day passed across the rim of the outer wall of the fourth ground level garden, a terrace that overlooked many square miles of tilled farm acreage, and passed into the bustling livestock market. The rich, fertile odor of the domestic beasts rose from the pens and stables: various breeds of cattle, sheep, deer, goats, oxen, ponies and domestic unicorn, asses, rrama, multen and pasture buffalo. Closer at hand were the smaller domestic breeds being bought, sold, and traded: chicken, geese, dove, turkey, rabbit, ground pig, several varieties of duck, and colorful ghurro hens from Haas. Nearby, a brazen pig roasted over a hot pit; the delicious aroma of beer and cooking meat was a welcome reprieve from the pungent dung of the barnyard.

"Do you think he's dead?"

"Who? Dedlin? Dedlin's not dead," Gaebryl said. "He's fashionably late, as wyzards are prone to be. He'll be back. If not this morning, then this afternoon. Nightfall, at the latest. He's probably busy doing, you know, wyzardly things. Who knows with those guys? There's no need to worry, though, I'm telling you. Dedlin Dane strikes me as one who can take care of himself. He no doubt has the nine lives of a cat."

"Unless eight have been spent already," the boy said, turning to face the new suns. The silver morning light brightened his unblemished, youthful face. There were no wrinkles yet around his watery, slate blue/grey eyes, no worry lines that long years have a tendency to draw out. But Gaebryl saw a burden there, nonetheless, back beyond those eyes, a weight of great responsibility beginning to now take its toll. "I would hate to have come this far and sacrifice this much to have this quest now dead in the water."

Gaebryl paused momentarily to observe an anxious crowd gathering ahead of them. "If I've learned anything, there is always more than one solution to every problem. If Dedlin knows where this Stone is, chances are so will others. Perhaps he has spoken to others about it. Have hope. The day is young and full of promise."

Castlefolk were busy clustering together along the northern walls on all levels, watching something that was going on beyond the castle reach. Whatever it was, it was clearly distressing. The mixed murmurs sounded troubled. Fortunately, Day was preoccupied and did not notice the commotion.

"Let's get back to the Depot," Gaebryl said, guiding him by the shoulder away from it. They passed back inside the market gate, and up toward the fifth level, toward the Skycraft Depot. "There's an old overused saying that I still find true more often than not. Things must be worse before they can get better."

24

The tenth ground level was amass with panicked Tungulinians. From his balcony suite, high within the royal tower terrace, King Vantoo watched them swarming below him. He was as provoked and angered as they were, even more so, for out beyond the wheat and cornfields of Tungulin, less than a hundred feet above the Gaalothian Forest, were two glistening, brazen, black Gharnian warships, poised like two great massive birds of prey, hovering on a warm, hazy updraft, missile chutes wide open and heated for firing. One of them, as the silver Gharnian script on the bow revealed, was aptly named the Mount of Steel, and the other, in fiery red script, the Godstrike V. The claws on Vantoo's four fingered hands scraped the rail as he gripped it. He had, only minutes before their appearance, sent out the third search party of the morning after Dedlin, Binder, and Drer Fregoode. Things were certainly speeding up since the Council the night before, and he found himself caught up in this unexpected whirling dervish of a storm quite unprepared. It seemed like, with each passing minute, there were new dark developments to contend with. Yet, remarkably, despite his injuries and lack of sleep, Vantoo's mind was acute and sharp, his body invigorated. His heart swelled with determination. The heat of battle was obviously upon him.

From above and on both sides, a regatta of seven silver/white Tungulinian warships advanced slowly in the direction of the enemy warships, descending to strategically position themselves directly between the Gharnians and the castlecity, halting above the golden crested wheat fields protectively before their great king. They were sleek, polished, streamlined warcraft, large and ferocious in appearance. The cheers from the Tungulinians perched upon the walls rose to such a tumult that it caused goose bumps to ride up King Vantoo's arms and neck. It was out of his hands now, this confrontation. Whatever was to be, would be. It was up to the battle seasoned warship admirals now to answer this Gharnian threat as only they knew best.

Despite counsel by his advisers who bade him remain somewhere safely hidden, Vantoo had decided instead to face his enemy forthright. His Inner Council warriors and wyzards surrounded him protectively.

From one of Vantoo's foremost Tungulinian warships, a small delivery pod was ejected and jettisoned toward the Gharnian ships. It held the heads of the five would be assassins of the king. A larger spherical pod was released from the foremost enemy ship to intercept it.

"Your Highness," a voice said from behind him. Vantoo turned to find Huegart bowing. "Good news, sire. Commander Binder has returned from the forest. He is on his way here now."

"Excellent. Excellent. And Drer? Dedlin?"

"Drer Fregoode has returned as well, but there is no news yet of the wyzard Dedlin Dane. He did not return with them. Just the two."

"I see," he said, deeply concerned. Through a pair of scanners, he watched as the Godstrike V intercepted the funeral pod with a crane beneath its hull and pull it on board. "Find Prince Gaebryl and King Day at once. Assemble everyone at the Depot immediately. Ready or not, it is time for them to depart."

Huegart bowed. "Yes, Sire. At once," he said, and made his way from the suite.

A low frequency, reverberating horn blast emitted from the Mount of Steel, the sound so loud that it shook the castlecity walls like an earthquake, rattling windows, mortar, and loose stones to crumble, causing dust to rise, and deafening all who were there listening. Afterward, an eternity seemed to pass as anticipation swelled. Then, through the scanners, King Vantoo detected a small skysled detach from a breech in the base of the forward hull. There were three men onboard the sled. No flag was flown, so the intention of this parley could only be guessed. They flew incredibly fast and low, brushing the tips of the long grasses of the outlying fields, heading fearlessly toward Vantoo's Tungulinian warships. Two of the men, by their dress, were Gharnian soldiers, large and battleready. The third one, however, standing on the bow, was smaller in stature, presenting himself, no doubt, as the Gharnian mouthpiece for this morning's standoff.

The skysled first approached the foremost Tungulin commandship, slowed, and wheeled to a halt less than a hundred yards from the bow. Vantoo was unable to discern much from that distance.

Then, two Tungulin fightercraft launched from one of his warships and advanced to meet the Gharnian party, midway. Cautiously, with their weapons drawn and at the ready, the three aircraft drew together midfield to confer. The conference between them was surprisingly short.

The three Gharnians voluntarily surrendered their weapons, and their small craft was securely attached between two larger Tungulinian fightercraft with sturdy plasteel lines. Together, they eased forward toward Vantoo's balcony suite for a parley.

As they approached, King Vantoo was both surprised and distraught to find that the lone figure standing with the Gharnians was none other than Sabre Jonhousan, the man who had been in charge of the Tungulin police for the past decade. Inconceivably, Jonhousan was, in fact, another dubious traitor.

The skysled drew close enough to the tower so that words could be spoken between them, but still far enough away that Vantoo could be protected by firepower and the magick of his wyzards. The gythot king shook with rage. "Sabre Jonhousan! I do hope that you are a prisoner of the Gharnians and have not gone over to them of your own accord," he called.

"The five men you executed. Why send their heads to us?" the man called back, his voice sounding different now, in an accent that Vantoo had never heard him use before. "They were not ours. They are Gornian born."

"You have less than one minute's time to speak your mind, traitor. At that time, I will give the order for you and your two escorts to be dispatched, and your warships blown from the sky."

"First of all, Your Highness, I am no traitor. I am a lifelong Gharnian patriot. I am Gharnian born and bred," Jonhousan declared. "I've not worn a soldier's uniform in some time, but I still have some value to the Power in Gharne. I am nearly three hundred years old, Vantoo, blessed with long life by powers you dare not know. And in those three centuries, I've only spent the last thirty with you in Tungulin, gathering vital information for my homeland. Even before that, I traveled all over this kingdom doing various deeds for the cause, mostly testing the political climate, and gathering intelligence of interest. You've been invaluable to me, and I thank you.

"Secondly, do not be a fool. Do you not see that I've come forward to you unarmed? That is because I know that we have the upper hand here. Should you have us 'dispatched', the Mount of Steel and the Godstrike V will open fire on the populace of Tungulin gathered there upon the walls. No doubt your warships would then certainly shoot us down, but not before we had unloaded ten to twenty powerful missiles into your precious city, and the thousands of onlookers I see before me. Then, by tomorrow morning, a hundred more ships will be here.

We will destroy your city in one day. Tungulin will be little more than a great pile of smoky rubble in the hollow of this valley by this time tomorrow night. That is a certainty. But it does not need to happen. It is entirely up to you."

Vantoo felt his left eyelid twitching nervously.

"Do you want to end this standoff peacefully or do you want to die?" Jonhousan called loudly to the king. "No battle. No bloodshed. The terms are quite simple. We want the boy and the key. Then we will go. That's it. Just the boy and the key. You know that I know he is here."

A growl came from deep within the king's chest.

"Consider this carefully, King Vantoo. I know we are outnumbered. But the weapons onboard these two warships are unlike anything you have ever seen. We have not been idle since the last great war," Jonhousan forewarned. "We have advanced our technology beyond your wildest nightmares. Just give us the boy and the key now, and we will go peacefully. I beg you, for old times sake. Choose peace here today."

"Look around you now," the king cried out in response. "Look at the beautiful morning sky above you, and the grasses, and trees, and these great city walls. Look upon them well, for these are the last things you will ever lay your traitorous eyes upon, Sabre Jonhousan, or whatever your true name may be. Not only do I dismiss your threats, I mock your terms. I am King Tital Vantoo, a free man until death, ruler of the great city of Tungulin and the territory of Galgariah, and neither I, nor my people, fear you, your threats, or your dogs of war. Jonhousan, know that you have served your Master for the last time here today!"

"Don't be a fool, Vantoo!" Jonhousan bellowed back. "Do you believe me stupid enough to stand here before you unprepared? I am offering you and your citizens mercy! There are scores of weapons trained directly on you! If you do not fear the hundred ships surely here by tomorrow, then how about a thousand by the week's end? I assure you this is the truth! Call up the boy and live another day! Give your people another day!"

"Your parley is now up, and you have failed! Farewell!" Vantoo cried out, and then, almost as though, by some magick in his words, the two Gharnian warships began to quiver and dance spastically above the trees. Popping explosions could be heard coming from within them, and a great tearing, wrenching sound. Then blasts of fire belched through vents in their sides. The Mount of Steel began a slow spin, down toward the forest. It exploded, just above the treetops, raining fire and blue oil into the jungle below. Then the Godstrike V followed suit. The crowds along the walls cheered at the spectacle, and praised their brave king, repeatedly chanting his name.

Sabre Jonhousan, witnessing the destruction of the two Gharnian warships, stood there aghast and suddenly speechless.

"Behold, your mighty warships!" the king mocked.

"How is this possible?" Jonhousan cried, terror now in his quaking voice.

"It was not me or my wyzards!" Gathargo explained from behind the king, as perplexed and amazed as was King Vantoo. "But blessings be! I'd say they were both sabotaged somehow from within!"

Vantoo felt as if he had just witnessed some kind of a karmic miracle. "We are truly blessed by the gods this day," he murmured.

"Excuse me, Sire," someone said from behind him. Vantoo turned to find Commander Binder advancing through the room like an angry bull. He brought a large blastrifle up to his shoulder and quickly aimed. "I apologize for being tardy," he said, and fired three shots.

Jonhousan's body exploded into pieces, and the two Gharnians did likewise. They tumbled from the unbalanced sled, falling a hundred feet to the hard ground below.

"Apology accepted," Vantoo said, slapping him on the

shoulder. He turned toward his window. "Fire upon those ships!" he cried to his generals. "Destroy them! There will be no prisoners! We will show Gharne what they can henceforth expect!"

The word traveled fast. Within moments the Gharnian warships were bombarded by heavy missile fire, the likes of which had never been witnessed by anyone there before. A square mile of Gaalothian Forest was soon aflame, the smoke billowing toward the heavens like a pyre fit for the gods.

"Jonhousan was right, though," a frazzled Binder told his king. "There will be many more Gharnian warships to come. Many more."

25

Gaebryl and Day had heard the vast explosions. The news of what had just happened spread quickly through the castle city. Tungulinians were running for safety in every direction, telling and retelling the story of their brave king and how he fearlessly faced down and somehow defeated the two great Gharnian warships singlehandedly with brave words alone. Gaebryl guarded Day closely as they ran with the chaotic streams of panicked crowds through the streets.

Before entering the Depot where their group was gathering, Gaebryl suddenly pulled Day into a corner behind a stone arch doorway, giving them a good vantage point from which to study things a little bit first. "What say we have us a look for a second," he said.

There was a lot of added security at the entrances and exits, but the way things were falling apart, that offered them little comfort. The room was currently being cleared of all unnecessary personnel. A small crowd was gathering around the skycraft that had apparently been chosen for them, a sleek fightercraft obviously designed for its speed and maneuverability. The name Sunshaft Aurielus was written in a beautiful flowing script on the bow in fiery golden letters. "Should serve us nicely enough," the prince warrior replied. "Now, let's see who the king has decided will accompany us on this little journey of ours."

"Look! There is Drer Fregoode!" Day said. "They have returned from the forest! Do you see Dedlin?"

"No," Gaebryl said. "Not yet. But look over there. Stardeer, the wyzard's craft is docked. That's encouraging."

"A mahekian," Day said, spotting him making preparations near the pilot's seat. "I believe that is the same masterpilot that we met in the Council last evening, is it not?"

"Yes. Perce was his name. He's packing as if coming along."

A small, determined promenade marched fervently through the adjacent door of the Depot; the Knights of the Guard scattered toward the corners of the room to set up a perimeter.
"There's King Vantoo's entourage," Day said. "Binder is there with him, too. It looks as if they are arguing. Come, Gaebryl, let's join them. I must find Dedlin Dane..."

"Wait, wait," he said, holding Day back by the arm. "Look over in the shadows, near the far corner, behind the exhaust fan louvers."

Day squinted. "I don't see anything."

"Keep looking."

Day did as Gaebryl said. He watched the shadows without blinking. As his eyes adjusted, he discerned a figure lurking there, a large figure, draped and hooded. "Who do you think that is?"

"Not who, but what," Gaebryl replied. "It is no man. He is a thordian, I'm quite sure, and a large one at that. I'd like to make sure of his intentions before we go parading down there. I don't see any reason why he would be skulking back there in the shadows like that."

"As we are?" Day pointed out.

As King Vantoo neared the Sunshaft Aurielus, all his

subjects halted and bowed respectfully, but the king immediately insisted that they get on with their preparations. Gaebryl watched keenly as the thordian stepped carefully and reservedly from his hiding spot, uncovering the hood from his head. His mane was thick, hanging in long braids over his massive shoulders. His brows were taut as he glared about the chamber with his bright, golden eyes.

"Okay, come on, I think we're safe enough," Gaebryl said. "The thordian has come from the shadows and I saw King Vantoo acknowledge him. They are acquainted. Still, stay close by my side. I trust no one today."

Before the workers and crew had finished bowing to King Vantoo, they spotted Gaebryl and King Day coming up the back ramp almost simultaneously, and began bowing again to them as well.

"Thank you," King Vantoo announced abruptly, wisely drawing attention away from them. "Please continue with your work. We are in dire haste."

Everyone did as they were bid and went on about their business.

The old gythot king hurriedly made his way over to join Gaebryl and Day near the rear of their new craft. "Good, good. It's good to find you both here. We have pressing business. Listen. Gaebryl, because of events that have transpired this morning, I am insisting that you be returned henceforth to Bursia for your own safety, along with your young personal 'valet' here, aboard this craft, as soon as possible. At least that is the information that my staff has allowed to pass to the public, if you catch my meaning." He had nodded to King Day when he had referred to him as Gaebryl's "personal valet", and given a wink. This was an excellent ploy devised by Commander Binder just minutes before, to keep from attracting any more unnecessary attention to King Day's presence there. "Simultaneously, we're going to send out a good number of fightercrafts similar to this one, in all directions, to help confuse and lose anyone who might be waiting to follow you," he said in a soft voice. "Whatever is packed now goes, whatever isn't, stays. I have had my Inner

Council preparing this craft for your departure all morning. I think you will find it adequate. To remain here any longer would surely be folly."

"We heard the news," Gaebryl said. "Are you hurt badly?"

"I'll mend," Vantoo said. "But those I have trusted for years have turned out to be murderous traitors. And already this morning we have seen the aggression, and then the mysterious destruction, of two Gharnian warships at our very doorstep. How this happened, I am unsure, but there is no doubt that Tungulin will be to blame and we will surely suffer the repercussions."

"We have seen Drer Fregoode and Commander Binder, and there in the docking bay is Stardeer, but what word of Dedlin Dane, Vantoo?" Day asked fearfully. "Where is the wyzard?"

"Alas, I am sorry. We have no word of him yet, Your Majesty, although the tale of their incredible night will be presented to you shortly," Vantoo told them. "I will not patronize you. Dedlin has yet to return from the forest, and when last seen, things looked dire for him. But be heartened. I have had years of experience with many wyzards, Dedlin among them, and I can only give you this advice: Do not fear for him. Wyzards work in their own ways, and work best when things seem their bleakest. They are secretive, and notorious for entertaining their own schemes and schedules, to the aggravation of the rest of us. Expect him when you least expect him, or, then again, possibly never again."

Day shook his head. "Without him we are stumbling around in the dark."

"Maybe, hopefully, he will still come for you," Vantoo said. "Otherwise, you may have to seek another light. For you cannot stay here now, that is clear.

"Come," he said. "Let me introduce you to your crew, and a finer one has never been assembled. As for your primary pilot, I commend my very own masterpilot, Perce. This delightful craft, Sunshaft Aurielus, is his. May they both serve you as well as they have served me. Perce," he said, as the mahekian stepped down toward them, "This is Prince Gaebryl of Bursia, and his *valet*."

The mouthless, noseless, and earless mahekian bowed toward Gaebryl, leaning somewhat respectfully toward the young valet at his side. He was a proud looking, fierce mahekian warrior, tall, muscled, and pale. "It is my deepest honor to serve you," he said telepathically in a voice as smooth as cream. Gaebryl returned the gesture; Day nodded. Already, Day liked this Perce.

Vantoo continued around the craft. "Drer Fregoode, whom you have already met, will also accompany you. He is well traveled in the lands and in the ways of the wilds and he will be a great asset to your crew. He has been one of my greatest and most stalwart advisers," the king advised. "We served together in the military for many years. He is masterful with the old stories and has many friends abroad, from the greatest castles to the smallest village pubs. He will help you in many ways in Dedlin's stead, until which time the wyzard returns. They were close friends."

"And should you need a story or song around the campfire, I'm a decent loremaster and a minstrel of some reputation, as well," Drer told them, smiling as he bowed.

"And my reluctant servant Commander Benjyn Binder will also be your escort," King Vantoo said. Binder was busy tossing his few bundles into the lower hold. He nodded, but his bow was not as sincere. "At least until you grow tired of his sour demeanor and send him scurrying back here to me."

A few chuckles quickly passed at Binder's expense.

"Commander," Gaebryl acknowledged.

"Truly, Binder is the most trustworthy man I've ever known. Ignore his sometimes cross demeanor if you are able. He did not want to accompany your party, out of his loyalty to me and his beloved station here in Tungulin, but I have insisted, because I value his services so highly. He is smart and strong, with a keen ability to see things more objectively than most, especially when it comes to the safety and security of that which he has sworn to protect. He will bring a certain balance to your group you may not have otherwise. His body may be covered with the scars of battle and war, but his heart remains unblemished."

"We are honored to have his valuable services," Gaebryl said.

"And lastly, a latecomer. This is Otthagorus, a thordian knight of some renown and distant reputation," King Vantoo said, nodding toward the thordian that Gaebryl had seen lurking before in the shadows. "I bid you to welcome him warmly and to accept his valuable services graciously. Heed his instincts and you won't go wrong. He will be of great aid, should you encounter any unexpected adversaries of the Gharnian nature."

The cloaked figure stepped respectfully forward, but still Gaebryl poised protectively by Day's side, nearly between them. Commander Binder, too, straightened up, and scowled at the thordian with knotted brows. Otthagorus's yellow slit eyes glowed like amber fires within the thick wool of his catlike face. He strode forward with prowess, strength and feline grace, evident in his every movement. Cautious eyes were upon him, since he was the only stranger amongst the group.

The thordian averted his eyes from Gaebryl, and bowed deeply before the two of them.

"It is a pleasure to meet you, Sir Otthagorus," Gaebryl responded carefully. "If King Vantoo trusts you, then so shall we."

"You are as wise as the stories say you are," said the thordian in a deep, resonating voice, as he straightened. "Please, you may address me simply as Ott."

"Well, for the record, I don't approve of his presence at all," Commander Binder growled, stepping forward toward them. He gleamed threateningly at the thordian. "He should be gagged and bound until we..."

"Binder!" King Vantoo snapped. "This is not the time!"

Commander Binder clenched his jaws tight. He glanced at the king, glared vehemently toward the thordian Otthagorus again for a few tense seconds, then went back to the matter at hand: packing away his belongings. "My apologies," he mumbled. "Obviously it is no matter what I think..."

"See?" Vantoo told them. "He'll be fine. Stress and a lack of sleep. Binder has had a bad history with thordians, which I'm sure you'll hear about soon enough," Vantoo said, hurrying them along. "Please, board your ship. I have much to do now myself, and your destiny awaits you."

Perce fired up the turbines on Sunshaft Aurielus. It was a clean, powerful sound. Several other skycrafts, sizes similar to Perce's Sunshaft, were departing at intervals at the mouth of the Depot, heading off in many different directions as decoys, according to the king's plan. Day watched another decoy crew mounting a nearby ship for departure, including another blonde boy his same age and stature.

The small accompanying crew of five climbed on board the Sunshaft and found their seats and positions, all but young King Day, who dallied reluctantly near the lowered stair ramp, scanning around the room for any last hope of spotting Dedlin Dane scurrying in, frantic, tattered, and late.

"Please," Vantoo pleaded. "Keep your eyes on your goal now. Remember, there is always more than one solution to every problem, and Dedlin's absence may very well be a blessing in disguise down the road. We will do all that we can do here, while we await your good news. In the meantime, continue steadily and swiftly on, never tiring, and utilize every available resource at your disposal. Keep your face in the wind, and a shadow far below you."

Gaebryl reached over to guide Day aboard. "We really should go."

"No one here knows in what direction you now proceed, my friends, not even I. I suggest you keep the details of your mission a secret from even your crew. The less that they know about it, the better. I will keep your departure here a secret for as long as I possibly can."

"Thank you, Tital," Gaebryl said, fondly gripping the old king's arm. Vantoo's face grimaced. It was then that the bloodstains seeping through his royal robes could be seen between his clenched fingers. "Get to your doctors soon," Gaebryl told him.

"Be careful, my son," the gythot king said softly, and squeezed Gaebryl close with one arm. "A blessing you are to your father."

"Take care of yourself, old man. Get some sleep."

Vantoo smiled painfully. "Soon. And you take care of this boy."

"I will. I promise."

"I await good news. Now, fly like the wind! And pray, don't look back until you have reached your destiny. Go!"

Within a few minutes, the silvery towers of Tungulin had receded into the distant morning mists, Westwatch tower gleaming proudly above them all. Perce, the mahekian masterpilot, was at the helm, guiding his craft straight and true. Binder and Drer, not having slept through the previous night's escapades in the forest, went below to rest, so no story or explanation of Dedlin's deeds or demise was yet given to the curious few. That left only Day, Gaebryl, and the mysterious thordian, Ott, who sat glaring suspiciously at everyone from his perch on the rear deck, awake and on guard. A half hour later, leaning against Gaebryl's shoulder, Day, too, fell asleep in the warm glow of the morning suns.

Holding loosely to the thick rail, wind in his hair, Gaebryl watched the tops of the trees racing past below them. He wondered if it were possible that the old wyzard could still be alive down there somehow, somewhere. The boy king was right, though; without Dedlin's guidance, what good was any of this other than to temporarily elude the Gharnians a few days longer? They were sailing absolutely blind, without any destination or direction whatsoever.

26

Day awoke from his nap just as Sunshaft approached the edge of the Great Rock Gaaloth. Behind them, the rugged, lavender Subring Mountains faded toward the curved horizon; before them yawned new blue skies. To the south and east, large black thunderclouds rolled menacingly toward them, as if trying to cut them off before they reached the edge of the great cliffs. The storm rumbled and growled and sent bolts of jagged lightning down into the cowering jungles far below.

Gaebryl was up at the helm, speaking with Perce while on watch. Aloof as ever, Ott the thordian had gone below to rest. Day sat alone, spinning in his chair, round and round, watching the colorful heavens along the horizon. Once again, he thought, he was heading out into the great unknown. Until recently, he had spent his waking days pampered and spoiled by chambermaids, nurses, and handservants in the palace of Mead. He was schooled by the greatest teachers every afternoon, and at night he cavorted with his multitudes of friends in and around his palace, and out in the rolling fields beneath the cold summer stars. But not anymore. That life was gone forever. Even the memories of it seemed distant and as faded as a waking dream. A crooked bolt of lightning tore the southern sky in half. The air shook and vibrated with the thunder that followed.

Day knew in his heart that Gaebryl and Tital Vantoo were right. With or without Dedlin Dane, they had to go on. There had to be some other alternative. Some other viable source of information. Some other way to locate this cave. The Kingdom Continent was a massive, barbaric land, and Day had no clue of where to even begin looking. Still, there was a certain sense of relief now, escaping the tumultuous uprising in Tungulin unscathed. The ride he was now on, with this fine new crew, was somewhat refreshing to him under the circumstances, despite their lack of direction. It was good to be off again.

He smiled when he thought of Dedlin Dane whispering in his ear just before he had left. How had he known? Day had thought that his secret was safe and secure, but apparently not... Had the other wyzards known as well? Maybe that's why they hesitated so when debating and revealing his identity to Vantoo and the Council. He could only wonder. As far as he knew, with no wyzard on board, his secret remained that now. *His* personal secret. As his feelings for Gaebryl had grown, Day wondered if he should share this secret with him, too. Or if he should still wait.

"Not yet," he whispered to himself, smiling.

Sunshaft Aurielus shot out over the last mountain cliff of Gaaloth, leaving the Subrings, the forests and steaming jungles, and the land of Tungulin and Tital Vantoo, far behind. The sheer mountain wall dropped straight down for nearly five thousand feet, to the strange lands over which they now flew, the wilds of Galgariah. As Sunshaft began her long descent, Day watched the monstrous plateau fall farther and farther behind, the details becoming less and less clear as the distance between them increased. Such a massive rock!

He remembered seeing the Great Rock Gaaloth for the first time, while fleeing in Habad's nasty ship. It had come out of the sky like a great wall, stretching from the earth to the heavens above the sky. From a distance it had looked like a dark cloud approaching... How glad he had been to have found it, and yet, how terrified he had been that he was not going to be able to reach the top before the skycraft ran out of fuel. He had been so sick from the knife wound, too... Delirious and hallucinating...

Now, behind him, the racing storm reached the edge of the Rock. Turbulent storm clouds fell over the side in an incredible display of whirlwinds and frantic netted lightning, an extremely awesome display of nature's strength and beauty.

He peered over the handrail. Far below their ship, between the clouds, a river wound like a green ribbon between the solemn brown hills. The air grew chilly, and the atmosphere thin. Day's stomach growled. The return of his appetite was a good sign.

27

Later that evening, Binder and Drer stirred and began moving about just as everyone else had finished eating and were preparing to get a good night's rest themselves. Drer took the first night watch and was lingering portside, searching the horizons in every direction with a pair of scanners. Binder took control of Sunshaft Aurielus from Perce, so that the mahekian could get some well deserved rest. Drer and Gaebryl spoke quietly together in the hold, discussing their options, and Ott was below, still asleep, purring.

Day had made small talk with the crew throughout the day, but conversations were short and purposeful. He found that sitting in the spinning hammock armchair suited him, and so, just at sunset, he was relaxing there when Perce came below deck and squatted nearby to reorganize his small pack of supplies. Day stared at the strange looking man curiously. He wore a gray hooded robe that was tied about the waist by a white braided cord. A crystal heatsaber, his only weapon, hung from a clip on his belt. Though he looked young, his hair, like most mahekians, was characteristically white, trimmed short and neat upon his oval shaped head. Like all mahekians, he wore a thin pair of dark eyeglasses, like a band across his face, protecting his deeply recessed, light sensitive eyes. His pale white skin glistened, as if covered by a crystalline rubber.

"Good evening, Your Highness," Perce said, working diligently with nimble fingers. Instead of fingernails, the mahekian had retractable claws, resembling those of an eagle's talons. "Are you traveling well this evening?"

Day nodded. "I saw you in the king's chambers the night of the Secret Council," he said.

"Yes," Perce answered. "I saw you there as well. We had a busy night that night."

Day was astounded how clear the voice seemed, since Perce had no mouth. "We have no mahekians in my palace back home in Mead," he said. "That I was aware of. They are rumored to live in secret places there, but all I have seen of your race are pictures. I am intrigued now that I have met you and seen your kind, here on the mainland."

"Ah," Perce said. "Curiosity has surfaced. Well, we are, by

nature, a peaceful and reclusive people, Your Majesty, content to live quiet lives away from the rest of the world whenever possible. Mead must be a very peaceful island, then, if my brethren are that well secluded."

"It is," he answered. "Or at least it was when I left."

"Let us hope it remains so," the masterpilot replied, and from the tone Day received, the mahekian was internally smiling. "So, what have you learned of my people then, Sire, if you have not had the benefit of associating with us?"

"Much, but whether it is true or not it is up to you to say. I was always curious about your people in my studies. I learned that you are a noble elder race, origins unknown. Ancient and, as you said, solitary. Kind to a fault, but can be ruthless and deadly if need arises. Humble, thoughtful, and generous by nature. Fierce in battle, and loyal to the end. Artistic. Prolific. Mahekians are the kingdom's collectors of knowledge."

"Librarians," Perce suggested.

"Yes. Librarians."

"You flatter me, Your Highness," the mahekian said. "Your insight and observations are very astute. I am most honored by your words."

"Well, in brevity, I suppose. However, I am sure that my limited knowledge does not scratch the surface of the depths of mahekian history and lore." Day nodded, smiling. "It is a comfort, though, knowing you are on board," he said. "But may I ask you a question?"

"Please."

"I'm puzzled. How is it that I can hear you speaking so clearly? Can you explain it to me further?"

Perce looked at him. "You have not been taught how mahekians communicate?"

"That it is through a sort of mental projection, instead of sound."

"Well, yes, in a simplified manner, that is it."

Day's brows tightened. "Then how is it that I can actually hear you?"

"I am... *projecting* to you."

Day considered this. "No, I can actually hear you, the same as I hear anyone when they speak to me."

"That is the effect, yes," Perce explained. "Whether sound comes as waves to your ears, or you are projected to mentally, these thoughts, these messages, are still translated in your brain the exact same way. However, a mahekian may choose with whom he speaks at will, or with whom he does not speak. He may choose his own voice, or imitate another. The projection is as controllable as one's own imagination. And we hear each other by *feeling* those projections in our minds."

"And you can hear me..."

"We can 'hear' you telekinetically as you speak. All sounds have a distinct vibration. Each voice, each sound, has a different vibration that we mahekians, to a certain degree, can register, both in our minds, and with our skin. As you probably know, we breathe, hear, taste and smell through our skin. We can gauge the temperature, detect changes in pressure and altitude (which aids in weather prediction), sense movement in the air, light density, life direction, water direction, heat, electric fields, vibration, and more. It's very convenient and useful."

"Can you read my mind?"

"No," Perce said, as if he had answered this same question many times before. "Only audible sound."

"Can you change colors?"

"To a limited degree, usually from intense emotion rather

than intentional camouflage, though, if that is what you are asking. That skill seems to be passing from us through the ages because of neglected use. It must have been an important defense mechanism in the elder days."

Day smiled and shrugged. "Thank you for today's lesson, Masterpilot Perce. I found it very enlightening."

"You are welcome," the mahekian replied, bowing his head. "You are both an honorable, and an inquisitive, king, Jamesyn Day."

28

The next morning, breakfast was served in the waning dark, just hours before suns up, with just a hint of pink and fiery orange easing from the bleak edge of the otherwise cloudless eastern sky for them all to see by. Drer had been cooking, and a grand camp chef he was, too. He had two seasoned soft boiled turkey eggs for each of them, and had warmed a roasted ham on a spit over a small hickory cooking pit in the small kitchen area that opened on a retractable shelf to the outside of the skycraft. The aroma of the smoking ham teased both nostrils and bellies. There was warm bitterbread for everyone, with pats of melting butter and jars of honey set on the side. The tea was fresh and hot. Except for Perce, who always ate his meals in private, the rest of the company ate together on the rear deck, even though it was windy and cramped: it was the only area on the fightercraft large enough for them all to sit in one place.

As they were finishing up, they all gathered for a brief meeting. Drer Fregoode relieved Perce from the helm so that he could excuse himself to go below to eat his breakfast privately, as was the wont of his race. Drer swung Sunshaft Aurielus angling skyward, arching in an upward circle, and then accelerated, leveling off low in the sky, cutting hard just above the treetops.

The troop took a quick vote and unanimously elected Gaebryl temporary leader of the expedition in Dedlin's absence, with Drer as his adviser and first mate.

"Okay. Let's get officially acquainted," Gaebryl said to the small group. His first order of business was to tell them his place in the story so far, beginning with his discovery of the lost mahekian city of Sweria Taaluu, which enthralled the lot of them, particularly Drer Fregoode and Masterpilot Perce (who was listening intently from just below the galley door). He described it to them, and pointed out its location on a map, so that if he could not for some reason ever return there, at least others would know of its existence, and someday make time to report and explore it.

Then, he described, in detail, the circumstances surrounding the discovery of young King Day in the coils of the snake, his rescue, and of the vicious leg wound that

he had treated. He told the story of their difficulties and travels, and of the assassins, Habad and Tursdah, who most had heard of. He told of the battle on the cliff, and of their arrival in Tungulin, bringing them up to date.

Day then took his turn as well, going back even further, describing his ordeals before meeting Gaebryl in the jungles of the Gaalothian Forest. He described his last days in his palace in Mead, the final meetings where all agreed that it was time to depart for the mainland, the journey across the White Sea by ship, the loss of his crew, and the harrowing events with Habad and Tursdah, including his miraculous escape aboard their assassin's craft. The crew was fascinated with his story, hanging onto his every word. In fact, Drer had himself a goblet of wine to cheer the adventures. It was too early yet for any of the rest of them to indulge.

"And so, for now, in the most simplest terms, we are heading east, to Gorn," Gaebryl relayed to them. "I spoke throughout the night with Drer Fregoode, and after much consideration, we believe we've come up with what we both agree is a good initial plan of action, in Dedlin's absence.

"Drer, you can explain more, if you will."

Drer nodded to the crew. "Well, truthfully, we are going on what I would call an optimistic supposition. Unfortunately, that's all we really have at this point. Dedlin and I spoke often in the past few years and became very close. As friends do, we spoke of things both professional and personal. Months ago, Dedlin told me about a recurring dream that he kept having, a dream that both moved and haunted him. He believed it to be relevant in some way as of yet unknown, he said, and, using his own word, 'prophetic'. He told me that in this dream his ears had been drawn eastward, like to a calling of some desperation, or as from some ethereal voice, weak and uninterpretable, from far beyond our borders and all the way to distant Gorn. He spoke of this dream to me several times, but it never occurred to me until his recent disappearance and our current plight that that vision could be in some way relevant. I realize that it's not much, but knowing the precognitive visions of wyzards, I believe it's the best we have."

Binder scoffed quietly. "Dreams," he mumbled.

Day, however, felt a very slight relief hearing this news. At least it was something. A direction. He chose to believe.

"To Gorn. To do...what exactly..?" Commander Binder inquired.

"Firstly, to safely elude all eyes," Drer answered. "And to keep the king safe. For the time being, we'll leave it at that."

"And more secrets. Wonderful. Nothing like not being in the loop."

Near midday, they paused briefly at a rugged cliffside outpost for more food and supplies. Near the wayroad, they briefly spoke to a group of young men passing by who had already heard about the previous day's occurrences at Tungulin, inspiring them to volunteer and take up arms to join the fight there as soon as was possible. "We want to join the crew of a Tungulin warship. We heard that several brigades have left for battle already," said one eager lad, no more than eighteen years old. "We heard that several Tungulin warships have departed to the west and southwest to bring the battle to the rabble Gharnian infidels there. We want to do our part!"

The Sunshaft crew fearfully wished the eager young patriots much luck and honor before departing. If this was the harbinger of what was to come, it was surely premature and disheartening.

They spent the day onboard organizing their meager belongings and assigning basic chores, such as cleaning, piloting the ship, and night watch, all shifts done equally on a rotating basis. It was important for them to keep busy with some semblance of order and discipline, to keep them from thinking too much and getting antsy or frustrated. In the meantime, keeping to plan, they flew in a direct line toward the southeast, toward distant Gorn.

After dinner, as they crowded into the cabin to split a bottle or two of Drer's potent wine to lighten the spirits, the conversation turned to the events of two nights before, when Dedlin, Drer and Binder had gone off to investigate the Meadian skycraft Tigre, amongst the marauding gogmoors of Bondoon. Everyone was most interested to hear what had happened, and Drer and Binder were happy and eager to oblige.

First and foremost, before even getting started, Binder defensively reiterated that, beforehand, not only had he made his point to anyone listening that Dedlin should not have gone along in the first place, but that he had told both Dedlin and Drer themselves while aboard Stardeer, in the most adamant terms, that the whole investigating in the forest at night on foot thing was an extremely bad idea.

And Drer concurred. "Yes, he was quite clear on that. Now, in retrospect, it appears that the Commander's stodgy, overbearing advice may have been wise."

"Stodgy? Over..?"

"Now, can we get on with it," Drer said, and he presented the story to them all in full detail. Drer was a natural, masterful storyteller. It was a craft he had perfected over many years traveling the kingdom as a wayward minstrel, and so everyone hung onto each and every word. When it came to the part where the three were racing up the hill to escape the cattlewolves, Binder took over:

"Suddenly, we heard a lot of missile fire above our heads, which momentarily disoriented us. We then realized that the Gharnians had returned, and that they were destroying the gogmoor fighters as they rose from investigating the Tigre. Their burning ships crashed down through the trees, falling to the ground all around us. We were perplexed at first, but then we understood. The Gharnians wanted to ensure that they destroyed anything and everything that the gogmoor soldiers might have found there."

"And *everyone*," Drer added. "They could not risk any messages from Mead reaching Tungulin, or any potential evidence from the wreck reaching Gaorwyn in Bondoon. They had to be sure that nothing from the Tigre was left intact, so they destroyed every last gogmoor, then blamed the attack on Tungulin. Why shouldn't Gaorwyn believe them? The Gharnians have been supplying Bondoon with weapons, ammunition, and supplies for years, while Tungulin only offers them trade sanctions and territorial legal skirmishes. They've made an alliance, Gharne and Bondoon, and Gaorwyn wrongly trusts them. Once the gogmoors were cleared from the sky, the Gharnians dropped a firebomb on the Tigre, destroying it beyond any hope of recognition. Ruthless, efficient, and thorough."

"And by all accounts, they succeeded," Binder droned. "We'll never know who or what was aboard the Tigre now."

"I am sure that Dedlin had found something before we left," Drer said. "He was clenching some maps and documents that he had managed to seize from the flames in the lower hold of the ship. His very cape was on fire from the feat! I'm sure he could have shed some light on that mystery."

"I, for one, will not believe that Dedlin Dane ended up in a wolferine's belly," Gaebryl said.

"Nor I," said Drer. "I know him too well. He's far too wily for that. And stubborn."

"How did you two escape the wolferines, if Dedlin didn't?" Day asked them.

"We found Stardeer just moments before the wolferines reached us," Binder said. "Drer climbed up first and I followed. A wolferine tried for a bite of me, but got a heel in his mouth instead. I'm sure he lost a few teeth. Then the beasts gnawed off the bottom rungs of the ladder before we could get it away from them. One held on for nearly an hour, growling and twisting in the air, as we waited nearby for Dedlin's return. Hateful beast."

"We searched for the wyzard for the rest of the night, while, at the same time, eluding the Gharnian searchlights," Drer said. "We never found a trace of him."

With that solemn thought, the conversation ended. Dinner dishes were done and evening's chores were finished. That night seemed particularly lonely. A bit of rain passed after midnight, but not much more than a sprinkling.

There was not much to do as the following day wore on, or the next. The crew took turns at the helm, always steering in a southeasterly course. They began discussing possible options, once they reached Tuus. They thought about trying other wyzards in that territory, possibly in Oliader or bustling Irisia, on the possible location of secretive caves. They agreed to attempt to reach King Vantoo by message sphere the first chance they got, to see how the city was faring since their departure, or to see if there were any word on the wyzard.

Ott remained acceptably cordial enough when addressed, yet rather unsociable and distant at all other times. He did not mingle with the crew, but always eyed them with some degree of disdain and scrutiny when he was not staring pensively off the back of the ship at the distant horizon. Concern about his demeanor was often a quiet topic of conversation among the rest of the crew. Day, however, generally defended the thordian. He seemed to feel oddly comfortable around him, as he would a bodyguard, and in fact, in some strange way, felt as if he had seen Ott somewhere before, although that could not have been possible.

Two more days passed without any change, even in the weather, which remained mild. The trees in the forests below them were mostly the broad leafed deciduous variety. The streams were green and heavy from recent rains; the few fields, crisscrossed with animal trails, were speckled with yellow flowers. There were rising buttes of stout rock along the eastern horizon, sheer walls of smoky granite, similar to the Gaaloth Rock, yet smaller in stature and girth, diminishing off into the northeast and southeastern mists.

The trees below began to thin, and in some places they cleared altogether, revealing wide expanses of knotty hills covered with the lushest green grasses Day could ever remember seeing. Perce took Sunshaft Aurielus down toward the earth, closer to the fragrant meadows, guiding the craft masterfully between the sparse thick bodied oaks that grew in random clusters in the folds of the lumpy hills.

Gaebryl spoke a few words to Perce, and the mahekian nodded in agreement. Sunshaft began slowing as Perce drew back on the acceleration bar. The skycraft glided to a smooth stop just off the crest of a grassy knob, hovering about three feet from the surface. A sparkling stream gurgled down near the base of the odd, knotted hill, forced to twist and drop over the irregular stones in a series of falls and clear pools.

"Why are we stopping?" Binder asked, coming up from the lower deck.

"Water," Gaebryl answered. They had traveled nonstop for several days. "We're nearly out."

Drer looked around the area suspiciously, as if something there was making him uncomfortable, though he could not quite place it. He hopped over the side into the tall grass, which rose up over his knees, and surveyed the area around him. From the port side of Sunshaft Aurielus, he opened a panel and began unrolling a vacuum siphon hose, rolling it over his arm and shoulder in loops, keeping a ready eye on their surroundings. Perce clambered over the side to assist him.

"You want to get out and stretch your legs a bit?" Gaebryl asked Day. "It might be a long time before we stop again."

Across the hillside on the opposite side of the creek, Day could see remnants of an old, crooked road, lined with weatherworn stone markers that ran somewhat east to west. It was all but covered with the lush grasses and peat, probably unused for years. He looked at the windswept reeds swaying all about, beneath Sunshaft Aurielus.

"No," he answered. There was something unwholesome about the knotted hills that he did not like, as if they harbored snakes and spiders. "I'll wait here."

"See you shortly, then."

Gaebryl, Perce and Drer headed down the hill to the stream, pulling the siphon hose along with them. Binder stood near the vacuum motor and awaited their signal.

Otthagorus was lying prone on the back bench, watching the dark trees behind them while grooming himself: licking the fur on his forearms with his rough, sandpaper tongue, and combing his long white whiskers with his clawed, pawlike hands. Day looked closely at the thordian, studying his striking face: soft, cream colored fur, surrounded by golden brown, with a distinguishable white stripe up the middle of his face. The fur of his entire mane was wreathed with black tips. He had fierce yellow eyes, and large white canines that showed only when he spoke, all in all a magnificent beast. His face seemed particularly tense since they had stopped, though. His ears occasionally pricked up, as if he sensed something beyond the trees, out in the brush.

Yet, look as he might, Day did not see or hear anything out there, but he was curious, just the same. He drew in, closer to Ott, joining the thordian near the aft of the ship.

The thordian bowed his head respectfully as the young king drew close.

"You keep staring off the stern of the ship as though there is something back there following us. I assure you, we took all precautions."

"You can never be too cautious, Your Highness."

"I'm wondering, Otthagorus. You look strangely familiar to me. Have we met somewhere before? Is that even possible?" he asked. He leaned out over the rail, looking into the same dark trees. "My homeland has many thordians, so I could be mistaken."

Ott shifted in his seat, adjusting the strap which pinned his arrowjet rifle to his back. "No, we have never before met, Your Highness," he answered, with the odd accent thordians had when pronouncing human words. "Still, I have always served the good Kingdom of Day, as I will continue to do, to the best of my abilities."

Day continued to study him curiously. "You choose to remain distant from the rest of the crew. Why is that? You may notice, the others grow suspicious of you."

Ott spoke slowly, choosing his words with precision, as he always did. "I have found that sometimes it is good to be suspicious of one another sometimes." His long lashes batted at a gray moth that fluttered near his face. "Especially during these days. I am cautious, that is all. I am a stranger to this land. It takes time and experience for a thordian to grant trust and friendship to strangers. I beg your patience, Your Highness."

Gaebryl called from the hollow; the hose was in place in the stream. Binder kicked on the vacuum motor, and the craft began taking on water in her two lower holding tanks. Binder checked to make sure the filters were properly activated and functioning correctly.

"I understand that," Day said. "I do. I've had to do the same thing myself. I traveled with Gaebryl for many days before I even spoke a word to him."

Ott smiled; Day saw a mouthful of sharp canines.

"But soon it will be time for you to tell your own story as well. We are all curious about you, and why King Vantoo placed you in this fellowship."

"My story will be told very soon, Your Highness. That I promise."

Binder came up from the lower deck and saw them speaking together. "Well, since you seem to have nothing to do once again, Mr. Ott, would you care to take a break from sunning and get out and stretch your legs for a bit? All four of them? Perhaps have a drink of water from the stream? Have a bath?" he asked. "We could set you up a hammock in the shade. Or you can just stay here and relax and groom yourself while everyone else does all the work as usual."

"Forgive Binder and his sarcasm," Day said, frowning at the commander. "He's still cross for having to leave Tungulin, and he has the manners of a bear, besides. He should learn to be more civil, especially when the one he is addressing is already active in conversation with someone else."

"My apologies," Binder said, nodding to King Day. "I mean no disrespect, Your Majesty. It's just frustrating to watch this one, reclined back here on his furry backside, watching every sunrise and sunset, day after day, doing little more than scowl at the rest of us while we're doing his work. I mean, none of us here know him. We don't know where he's from or why he is here. I just don't trust him. I've never liked thordians, and with good reason, and this one is giving me no reason to start."

"I do not serve you," Ott told Binder blandly. "Therefore, I do not need to answer to you."

Before Binder could reply, Day stepped in, speaking sharply. "It would serve you both well to attempt to get along together while aboard this ship. It is far too small for you to try to choose corners to hide from one another. We may be together for awhile, and you may very well end up depending upon one another for your very lives soon. If you have an issue, either of you, I insist you work it out diplomatically, as gentlemen warriors. This crew must work together as a team while we travel together. We are all on the same side here."

"I'm not so sure of that," the Commander said.

"I, for one, shall try," Ott growled, eyes on the angry commander.

"Binder, so what do you suggest, then? Should our guest, who King Vantoo himself requested join us, be ejected from our ship and be off on his own here?"

"No. Of course not. I also apologize," Binder said. "I have a lot on my mind."

"We all do, Commander," Day said. "But what say we trust king Vantoo for now? I suspect that our new friend here has purposes we have yet to discover. If he chooses to save his words and strength for the time being, it could be for good reason. I, for one, understand the importance of keeping secrets."

Ott slowly rose, eyes squinting toward the trees beyond the rise of the hill behind them, neck craned and fur bristling on his broad neck. Both Day and Commander Binder followed his gaze. "And, at this opportune moment, in my own defense, I would like to point out that I have not been as idle as I've been accused of being, nor have I been able to enjoy a single sunset since the morning we left. This is probably a good time to inform you both that we are being followed, as I suspected, and have been for days, although no one else has seemed to notice it, somehow, or care."

Day looked back to the trees, where Ott had been staring earlier. "Followed? What do you mean? By whom?"

"By them," the thordian answered, discreetly directing his glance to a spot, low within the trees. "You can see them plainly now. Look closely. Right there, where the bit of sky is showing through the opening above that clump of thickets. They are being careless. You can see them clearly now."

Binder joined him at the rail.

"I...I don't see anything," Day said, squinting.

"Just below the middle terraces, about thirty feet back into the trees," Ott replied. "A ship."

"I see them," Binder hissed. "Scouts. Probably Gharnian. Damn! They've followed us. I don't know how, but they've followed us."

"Don't be too conspicuous."

"They're using a small shadowcraft," Binder said. "It's a cloaked scoutship, used for spying, maybe holding three soldiers. Wait, there is another. A one man skysled gliding alongside the first."

"I thought I briefly spotted the smaller craft three nights ago," Ott told them. "The larger one appeared only early this morning."

"You should have told us the moment you saw them," Binder snapped.

"I was the only one not assigned to watch for some reason," Ott replied casually. "But I have anyway, since it is obvious that I have the best eye for this. I didn't report it right away because I had to be sure. Also, I wanted to test the abilities and, perhaps, loyalty of this crew."

"Loyalty of this crew?" Binder snapped.

"There are Gharnian spies in the highest offices kingdomwide," Ott replied. "How can I be sure there are none aboard this ship? You are all as strange to me as I am to you."

Binder frowned at Ott. "You're a fool."

The thordian continued. "There were many Gharnian scoutships tailing the other decoy skycrafts when we first left Tungulin. These two are the only ones I've seen since then. They are clever, and careful until now, and are armed adequately enough, but they know that we outgun them. They are merely scouts, information gatherers. They are monitoring Tungulin traffic. Learning trade routes. Potential escape routes and defense strategies."

"Or they could be looking specifically for us," Day added.

"They're certainly taking every precaution," Binder said. "And they more than likely know that we know about them now. If they've seen us, they've seen you, Your Majesty, and there could be some suspicion at the very least. Hopefully, they still believe you're not you, and that the real King day is still in Tungulin taking refuge. Because, if not, as soon as they know that you are here, every Gharnian ship in Galgariah will be after us."

"We need to inform the others," Day said. "We need to get out of here. Can we outrun them?"

"We could sabotage them," Binder said, heading for the helm. He didn't want to raise alarm by shouting to Gaebryl and the others. "Chances are we could destroy them both, right here, before they made any contact with their superiors."

"Gharnians have an excellent communications system," Ott advised, still remaining as calm as before. "We would have to be swift. Perhaps split up and ambush them from behind as well."

Binder shifted the ship control out of idle, and the Sunshaft Aurielus began to slide down the rim of the hill toward the stream as smoothly as melting butter off a biscuit.

Suddenly, the skycraft jerked and stopped, spinning a bit, but she would not budge another inch.

"What's wrong?" Day asked, looking around. "Are we snagged? On a stump or something?"

Binder raised the throttle, but Sunshaft Aurielus would not respond to it. In fact, the craft began surging back up the hill in the opposite direction, as if being gently pulled. "Impossible. The bottom of this craft is smooth. There is nothing extending below to get stuck on anything..."

"I saw no log to get stuck on..."

Ott and Day peered over the rail on opposite sides of the ship. "I didn't like the look of this place as soon as I saw it," Day replied. "It looked like snakes to me."

Sunshaft veered slightly to the right and to the left, as if something from below was firmly tugging at it. Binder, looking over his shoulder at the spies in the dark trees, increased the throttle. "We're certainly either stuck on something, or we're having a major skycraft malfunction," he said. The whirring turbines began to rattle as the frequency rose, the exhaust pipes emitting a fine black smoke that began to cover the grass behind them with a dusty pale ash. "Either way, not good."

"Not so hard! Whatever has us, if it lets loose, we're going to shoot into the clouds as if from a cannon," Day said, holding tightly to the vibrating rail.

Ott volunteered to have a look below. He opened the starboard gate and hung his hairy head over the side. He glanced right and left. Suddenly, he scrambled back, falling to the deck, rolling frantically backwards. From the open gate, a long, green tentacle rose up, wrapping tightly around the perimeter rail where Ott had just lay prone, and it pulled down hard enough to bend the plasteel bar.

"What is that?" Day cried.

Binder seized a fire axe from the cabin wall. "It's a creeper!" he said, as if this were the worst luck of all. "The biggest one I've ever seen." He raised the heavy axe above his head and brought it down hard on the smooth tentacle. The thick rail bent from the blow, the wood beneath splintered, but the rubbery skin of the creeper did not sever. It was pinched enough, though, that it released its hold and disappeared back over the side.

"It's gone," Ott exclaimed.

"Oh, no it's not," Binder replied. "They're relentless."

Two more tentacles rose up, gripping the rail on the port side. "There's more of them!" Day cried.

"It's but one creature," Binder said, pounding on the splotchy green and brown arms like a crazed machine, but with little or no effect. Two more tentacles had seized the rails. "One hundred and eleven arms," he said between strikes. "Sometimes more."

Ott unwrapped one of the tentacles by hand; it retreated,

then it arose a few feet away to tighten around the rail again. "It feels no pain?"

"Pain? It's a plant!" Binder answered, grabbing a woodsaw from the nearby tool chest. "A carnivorous plant. It lives in muddy holes under the ground, preying on whatever passes by. If we can't free this ship in the next few seconds, this insipid creeper is going to pull it down into the ground and attempt to eat it."

Gaebryl, still hobbling on his bad leg, came up over the hill with the others just then, winding up the siphon hose around his shoulder and arm. When he saw what was happening, he dropped the hose and quickly unsheathed his blaster. He fired a few rounds, but the huge creeper went unfazed. Two stumps waved ineffectively in the air, leaking oozy sap. "Get out!" he called to them "We've lost it!"

"We can't lose the ship!" Day cried.

"We can't beat this thing," Gaebryl reiterated. "I've seen these things devour dhoellums! It's already damaged the ship beyond repair. It's already into the open water tanks!"

"We can't lose the ship!" Binder then repeated, sawing heartily at a rubbery tentacle that had seized a mooring hook. "Look!" he said, pointing into the trees.

"We've been discovered!"

Drer Fregoode and Perce had reached Gaebryl's side and they all spotted the Gharnian scoutships at the same time.

The three of them circled Sunshaft Aurielus, firing again and again at the creeper with their blasters. Many arms were severed, hewn and cut. Many more arms replaced them, faster than they could be destroyed. They slid from muddy holes everywhere, securing themselves to Perce's floundering skycraft with hungry determination, pulling it steadily downward.

Binder had left the craft at full throttle; it bolted again, stretching the rubbery coils that secured it. The earth below seemed to rise from the force, but the ancient creeper held on tight.

Ott had been throwing as much of their food and equipment overboard as he was able. Perce and Drer hurried to retrieve it before the creeper could.

"Jump!" Gaebryl called to them. "And be careful where you land!"

Day did not hesitate for a second. He leaped hard from the failing craft and rolled into the grasses as yet another tentacle rose up beside him. Perce came to his aid and pulled him to safety.

Ott sprang nimbly from the sinking ship, landing squarely on all fours, and then he leaped away in two mighty bounds.

Binder was still onboard, tossing guns and packs over the side.

"Forget about the guns, Commander," Gaebryl called to him. "We've got all that we can carry as it is. Save yourself!"

Binder nearly fell from the tilting deck, just as a groping feeler brushed past his leg. It seized a loose blaster and pulled it over the side and down into a muddy hole. Beneath the ground they could hear a rapid succession of shots before the gun fell silent. Binder leaped off and rolled away, toward the others.

The once beautiful Sunshaft Aurielus began giving way, splitting and folding in half down the middle. The mighty creature pulled the skycraft's rattling air exhausts into the soft ground. The turbines, unable to take the pressure, ruptured at the seams, sending up a cloud of black smoke and ash. Having no thrust left, Sunshaft Aurielus yielded finally to the creeper, a great beast to a conquering predator. It began sinking into the earth like a dying ship at sea.

"The brainless thing thinks it has a huge meal," Drer replied. "Once it sinks its teeth into it, it's going to get a big surprise."

"By tomorrow, it'll reject the ship, and up will come a crushed chunk of useless wood and plasteel to the surface," Binder said.

The crew gathered their belongings and sorted through them, minimizing their packs. Perce watched his ship sink lower and lower into the earth, enwrapped with seemingly countless green tendrils. He was saddened by the loss of his ship, but true to his nature, he commented that they were just fortunate not to have lost a member of the crew to the thing. "Farewell, my Sunshaft Aurielus," he concluded thoughtfully.

"What now?" Ott asked. "Does anyone know where we are or where we can find another ship?"

"I know a place," Drer said. "Small town. But it's quite a walk. I think it's due east of here still, so that serves our purpose well enough. I'm just not sure if there are any skycraft there large enough to bear the lot of us."

"Where is that?" Gaebryl inquired. "Longray Bluffs?"

Drer nodded.

Gaebryl sighed. He had no better idea. "We're a long way from anywhere," he commented.

Ironically, out of all of them, Day seemed to be in the best of spirits. "Firstly, I suggest we get off these bumpy, knobby, snaky hills and onto that little road over there. It runs due east, as best as I can tell."

"At least we have an anxious escort," Drer said, referring to the Gharnian scouts, still hidden back among the dark foliage. "Even if we could take both of their crafts from them by force, we couldn't all fit aboard them."

"We should still destroy them," Ott replied. "No good can come from this now. We're sitting ducks out here."

Binder picked up two heavy packs and several guns. "I knew things would get bad, but not like this, and not this soon.

What are we now? Five days out? Six?"

Day waved at a small gray moth that fluttered playfully about his face. "Come on, then, gentlemen," he said. "Things could be worse."

Seven

AEROGREEN

29

As though the heavens reacted on cue, the skies soon filled with heavy gray clouds as the afternoon came on, and just as evening arrived, the air cooled, the wind rose, and it began to rain. Disheartened and uncomfortable, the troop of six marched on without conversation, hoping to put as many miles behind them as possible before bedding down for the night. Gaebryl was in the lead, pressing them to a brisk pace, even with his stiff leg. Then came Day and Perce, then Otthagorus, Drer Fregoode, and finally, following up at the end of the column, Commander Benjyn Binder. The drizzle was constant, and at times it came down in bitter, soaking torrents.

The crumbling road wound over gray featureless hills and through shadow darkened valleys, but it remained true toward the eastern mists. Day turned his face from the sharp sting of the rain, using the back of Gaebryl's pack as a visual focal point. It was a tiresome march, on and on, cold and dreary. The rain made a constant ambient drone on the rocks, grass, and leaves all around them, spattering in deepening puddles, tapping relentlessly on their packs and soaking everything that they carried. New streams arose, flowing down freshly eroded gullies on the hillsides and across their path, swathing them in ankle deep mires of deep, sucking mud that tugged at their weary feet. The shapes and silhouettes of the hills and trees were dreamlike in the twilight mists, gray and ghostly.

Over their shoulders, the two Gharnian scoutships cruised silently behind, as if secured to towlines, low above the treetops, unconcerned that their presence was now known. Nothing could be seen beyond their dark windows, but one thing was for certain: the Gharnians were warmer and drier than the marching troop.

The suns never showed, so night came quickly. Just as Day began stumbling over roots and stones in the dark, Gaebryl suggested that they find a place to make camp. They closed in together under a cluster of trees, up against a short stone wall, but it was neither dry nor warm there. For nearly an hour, they constructed a lean-to of limbs and pine branches to help shield out the wind and rain, roofing it with large, flat poplar leaves, layered one over the other like flimsy tiles, and fresh pine boughs on top of that for insulation. Drer got a roaring fire going near the wall, and they ate a wet dinner, but nothing they did could warm or cheer them.

Gaebryl and Drer blamed themselves for the mishap with the creeper, and Binder, perhaps in the worst spirits of all, felt inclined to blame them both.

The wind whirled over and around them throughout the long night, sometimes able to reach into their tiny space and pass through their wet garments like cold, ghostly hands. Although all were exhausted, most could not sleep, so the posting of a rotating guard was done, but was never necessary.

Day spent the night sitting up, shivering, pressed between Drer Fregoode and Prince Gaebryl for body warmth. His waterproof cloak could only do so much; the persistent rain still found ample access through the flimsy roof of leaves, dripping down into his collar, sleeves and boot tops.

He found that if he closed his eyes and pictured his homeland Mead, with its daisy dappled meadows and fountains and crystal palaces, for brief moments he could dismiss the ugly weather, and occasionally ignore the jagged little rock that pressed against his spine, no matter which way he spun. However, these moments were few and far too brief. Whenever he opened his eyes and peered out into the gloom, the dark shapes of the Gharnian scoutships were always vaguely discernible in the distant trees to the south, small red lights blinking like the blinking eyes of cattlewolves.

Eventually somewhat of a dawn did break, and at once they were up and moving to get circulation back into their chilled, stiff limbs. They ate breakfast on the move, only a handful of dried fruit, dried meat, and wet bread for each of them, except for the carnivorous thordian Ott, who had only the strips of meat, and he ate them ravenously. The bothersome rain came and went all day. Sometimes the clouds separated to display a vivid blue sky beyond, fringed in rainbow colors where the sunlight grazed past, but then, like dark curtains, the walls of rain and clouds closed it all out again. The trail was swampy, and thick with muck. Dark mud clung heavily to their boots and pant legs. There was a lot of quiet mumbling and cursing. Day often thought of Dedlin, and wished that he were there, guiding them. He believed that things would have turned out very differently had the wyzard been there with them the day before on the creeper's hill.

They stopped frequently to rest. Feet were sore, wet and blistered. Skin was chapped and irritated from the friction of wet clothes. Everything in the packs was soaked through, and this made them heavy and burdensome to carry. Ott's fur was tangled, lumpy and flattened, but oddly enough, he didn't seem to mind. Outside of Perce, Ott was, perhaps, the one member of the troop who complained the least about the rain.

Before the suns set that next night, outdoorsman Drer optimistically predicted the coming of a dry night and morning ahead of them, and the others concurred. The signs were clear: 'Red in the morning, travelers take warning. Red at night, travelers delight'. Usually that old saying held true. The nurturing rains had more than done their job there, cleaning the air, feeding the trees, and refreshing the earth, and now the custodial rainclouds had moved on elsewhere to continue their work. Spirits began to rise. The troop found a clearing among a circle of ancient pines and before dark they warmed themselves against a raging fire that could be seen for miles. No wood was spared. The wet logs steamed, hissed, popped and whistled before eventually drying out and catching ablaze. Then they burned through the firewood's cycle, from full on red/golden glory to piles of blackened ash and smoldering coals, hotter than any oven, perfect for the stew of pork, onions, wild tubers and pine nuts Drer was busily preparing for them.

Clothes and blankets were hung to dry in the tree branches and small A-frames made of sticks they had set up near the roaring blaze. The food was soggy, but the tea, and the wine, were perfect. The crew took time to pull burrs from stockings, mend cuts and scratches, and check each other over for woodticks and leeches. The feeling of warmth was a welcome reprieve, and a reason for occasional laughter and song. Drer brought out a mandolin and serenaded them until they began to nod off. After a full belly and a draught of wine, Day could not hold his eyes open a minute longer. His clothes and sleeping blanket were warm and wonderfully dry, laid upon a thick bed of moss and dry pine boughs, only yards away from the glow of throbbing orange coals. Above the treetops, a thousand diamondlike stars twisted and twinkled, as if there on display exclusively for the weary campers.

Day dreamed of Dedlin Dane. The wyzard, oddly enough, was made out of smoke in this dream, a dark, swirling mass of thick, gray smoke. Day could smell him, too, (although it wasn't until the next morning that he would realize that it was probably the smell of a spark that had burned a small hole in his pillow that had inspired that illusion). Dedlin was in a small, dark room that was filled from floor to ceiling with books. He was searching for something, frustrated and anxious. He pulled the books from the shelves with both hands, but they turned to ash before hitting the floor with an explosion of dust. Day was looking in, as if from a thick glass window, and he cried out to him, but no sound came from his mouth. He tried and tried, but was unable to reach the old man. The Dedlin of smoke was encased within a thick glass sphere, upon an old cluttered table, within a dark, forgotten room, within a dark, forgotten castle, thousands of miles away and hundreds of years ago.

30

Three more days passed in a similar manner, the troop marching diligently during the day, and resting as best they could (much more comfortably, thanks to the kindlier weather) through the cool nights. They had left the knotted grassy knolls of the creeper land far behind them. There were clusters of woods before them now as the hills steadily rose and fell, and they passed many lakes and ponds full of cattails and lillipads, swollen full from the recent rains. The choruses of what must have been millions of hidden tree frogs was often overbearing. Fording fattened streams was a common, but necessary, nuisance for the traveling party, keeping them soggy from the knees down.

When Day awoke the next morning, Gaebryl was sitting close to the fire with a curious smile upon his face. Drer and Ott had already finished packing and were busily cleaning up their camp. They seemed ready to depart. The suns were warm, and the skies were clear and bright. The morning air was brisk and refreshing to the palate, and small gray moths fluttered in the nearby trees. Day was instantly famished.

"Good morning," Gaebryl said, bringing Day his breakfast. "Hope you slept well."

"Like a proverbial log," he answered, brushing leaves from his hair with his fingertips. "The best since we lost the ship."

"Good. Ready for another day of it?"

Day pulled his blanket aside and reached for his boots, feeling inside each of them to see if they had dried sufficiently next to the fire. "I do believe I can go on," he said with a small degree of humor and forced enthusiasm. "It would be nice to have a carriage about now, though, drawn by sturdy horses, if you could arrange it. Or at least have my breakfast served to me in a warm, dry parlor somewhere away from these moths..."

Just then, Binder and Perce came jogging into view from the distant trees on the far rise. They crossed the hollow and came jogging up the hill through a narrow fissure between the rocks, looking tired and apprehensive. The rest of the troop paused, as if awaiting news from them.

"We lost him," Binder replied between labored breaths when he had drawn near. "About four miles to the south."

"Lost...who?" Day asked. Apparently, he had missed something that morning as he slept.

"The uusyrapi was just too swift," Binder continued. "We didn't have a chance in hell of following them on foot..."

"But the good news is that it drew the smaller Gharnian

sledship away, maybe for good," Perce added. "But to what purpose we don't know. Their motives remain unclear. I do not believe they were friendly to one another."

"What? What have I missed?" Day stammered. "Apparently quite a lot."

"You are a deep sleeper when you do sleep, that is for certain," Gaebryl answered.

"I'm awake now."

Gaebryl found a seat next to him, tightening his bootlaces. "Just a bit of harmless excitement is all. Last night, while most everyone was asleep, we had a visitor of sorts," he said. "I was still on watch. It was as pitch as tar. Perce and I were stoking the fire a final time for the night when we heard a strange noise coming from the other side of this very hill, from around that stand of beech trees on that exposed ridge right up there," he said, pointing. "It was a shrill animal cry...of distress. Like some large predatory raptor. The smaller Gharnian scoutship immediately turned aside to investigate. We thought it best to wake Binder to stand guard while we went to see what it was as well. We followed the tree line over the shoulder of the hilltop, staying near or under the overhanging thickets wherever we could.

"In the pale light we did indeed discover a large bird up there, a fullgrown uusyrapi, saddled and bridled, but at the time riderless, and it appeared to be embattled with something that we were at first unable to discern in the darkness. The bird was quite evidently struggling and fighting with some dire foe by the desperate cries it was making, crashing through the underbrush and stirring up clouds of dead leaves and dirt. We crept in on hands and knees as near as we were able. Its right leg was stuck, or trapped, in something, judging by the way it was hopping about in circles, like it was caught in a hunter's trap. It flapped its featherless wings ferociously, and pecked vehemently at whatever it was that held it.

"We slid in a bit closer on our bellies, and as our eyes finally adjusted to the night's blackness, we could finally see the flightless bird's adversary. Coiled and twisting at its feet was a huge, black and white striped syngoleus dragon. Its jaws were clamped tight upon the great bird's foot, and it was attempting to pull it back into its cave to devour."

"A what?" Day asked.

"A syngoleus," Gaebryl repeated. "It's a large, multi-horned snake. A rare legless dragon of some ancient origin. A constrictor. Ambush predator. The uusyrapi and syngoleus were engaged in mortal combat. Quite the spectacle to behold."

"I wish to have seen it!" Day declared.

"It was over before we knew it," Gaebryl said. "As we squatted there in the brush, a man suddenly emerged from the brush on the opposite side of the vale, the uusyrapi rider himself, silver warsword unsheathed and flashing. He was a large, strange-looking man, dressed in violet and gold stripes, with a strange helmet and armor. He struck at the syngoleus with incredible speed and dexterity, and within moments, the dragon was dead.

"Binder joined us there, and advised us that the second Gharnian scoutship had also gone missing. Fearing for our safety, he had come looking for us.

"We watched the rider check his steed over, soothing it in his strange tongue, and then he mounted it, looking continuously over his shoulder into the trees above his head. It was then that we saw our two Gharnian scoutships hovering silently there above him. The rider goaded his steed, and, in a flash, they fled down the slope in the opposite direction, into the shadows and were instantly gone."

"Curious! Who was he, I wonder?" Day asked.

"What kind of a man was he? What was he doing out here? Does it in any way involve us or our mission, do you think?"

"It all remains a mystery. He was an odd looking fellow for sure, with strange helmet fixtures and tubes connected to cylindrical packs on his shoulder harness."

"We tried to follow him," Binder added. "But he left us in his dust, and the trail grew cold. A mature uusyrapi can cross territory impossible by men on foot, and, at speed, they can often outrace a horse."

Drer curiously added: "It was strange that the Gharnians would take such an interest in this lone uusyrapi rider. They forsook us to pursue him."

"When we saw the larger of the two scoutships circle back toward our camp, we turned aside and headed back," Perce said.

"I have never even heard of a uusyrapi," Day said, flabbergasted. "Or a syngoleus dragon," Day said. "They sound terrifying."

"There are many strange and fantastical creatures throughout this kingdom, that is for sure. Both these creatures are infamous."

"I once witnessed a flock of wild uusyrapi destroy an entire mining village," Drer Fregoode went on to say. "And not all in one night. I was but a young man still, in my first year of flight school, and we were camped in a cave on a hillside near Fhughal, near the river Mease. Down below us was a strip mining village, mostly gythot, but a fair number of tyberlians made their home there as well. The uusyrapi flock came charging in one night unexpectedly, like a stampede. It's said that traditionally they're scavengers by nature, carrion eaters, but these birds were not scavenging anything. They were vicious hunters and killers. They went for the easy targets, too: children, small women, livestock, and pets. For three nights in a row this went on, always around twilight. The miners made a stand the best that they could. No one stayed the fourth night."

"And I once saw a syngoleus swallow a man whole," Gaebryl interjected. "In the syngoleus' defense, this particular man deserved his fate."

"I'd rather face a nest of syngoleus's," Ott said, waving at two small gray moths that fluttered around his face, "than one of these pesky moths. Infernal insects! They tortured me all night, fluttering in and out of my nose and my ears while I tried to sleep!"

"If we're on the road that I believe we are," Drer forewarned, shoveling dirt onto the dead campfire, "I can tell you we'll be seeing a lot more of them before we see less of them."

31

Gaebryl's limp had worsened as the long march continued, but he said nothing about it. Distant thunder from the north kept them moving at a brisk pace, tired and apprehensive.

The trail widened as it crossed a broad, flat, featureless meadow. All the tall, straight pines disappeared behind them, and ahead, in their stead, loomed large, twisted ordes pines. These unusual evergreens bore very long, dark needles, a corky, umber colored bark, and pulpy cones. They were covered with hanging lichens and parasitic tree eels that dangled like decorative ornaments from the twisting branches. Beyond the trees, dark jagged rocks jutted up like watchful giants, boulders bordering the corners of the nearby hills.

As they drew closer and entered the trees, a large population of shaggy gray squirrels took turns dashing in and out of the large community nests they had made from the long, thin ordes needles and thick, olive green moss. With eager curiosity they watched the troop pass by underneath them. They chattered with short barks and whipped their fluffy white tails threateningly.

Ott said something in passing about squirrel meat, but the crew hurried on without stopping.

The ground beneath the trees was covered with debris from the trees, but the trail, for the most part, was clear and dry. Still, they often found themselves dodging muddy water holes. As Drer had predicted, the moths became more abundant as the day wore on. They danced hither and thither in the trees, and in the tangles of the underbrush along the trail sides. They fluttered gaily in the air all around them, the males chasing the females in an aggressive courtship ritual.

"How much further until Longray Bluffs?" Day asked as the trail took a hard turn, heading up a steep embankment. "This road has been heading uphill since we began today, and I need a rest. My legs are burning! And these moths are more than I can bear."

"Four more days," Drer said. "Three if we rise a few hours before dawn each morning and press a bit harder before we camp each night. Longray Bluffs is a small town, not much more than a busy crossroads of sorts really, run by a rich old tyrant and his sons. I don't know how much luck we'll have when we get there. I haven't seen the old coot in thirty years, and he wasn't known as the friendliest host in Galgariah, even then."

"We can negotiate with him, I'm sure," Binder mumbled. "I think we could be a fairly persuasive team if we set our minds to it."

A soft thunder rumbled continuously in the distance.

Ott shook himself like a dog shaking off water. Moths flew from his fur like a cloud of gray dust. He roared in anger. "Pestilence!" he growled. "They're nesting in my fur!"

"Yes. These moths are called aerodares," Drer told them. "Gray aerodares."

"Aerodares?" Gaebryl siad. "I fear I know what fate soon awaits us, if the aerodares here are like the aerodares of my own country."

Drer acknowledged him with a respective nod. "I'm afraid they are. As I suspected, this road does indeed lead through Aerogreen, their breeding ground. I'm not exactly sure if they are in season, but I have a feeling we're going to time it just about right."

"Then we'd best travel through Aerogreen by day if we can," Gaebryl said. "If they're nocturnal, like the red aerodares in Bursia, they should be a bit more docile and complacent in the sunslight."

"More docile? Moths? How dangerous could they be?" Day asked. "They're just moths."

"I've always strived to avoid Aerogreen when hunting around in this land," Gaebryl answered.

"There's a story of an entire brigade that was wiped out in that cursed valley."

"By moths?" Ott growled.

"Aerogreen can be a very dangerous place," Drer continued. "The moths have an effect on those who cross their sacred valley. They can be completely overpowering. And sometimes even devastating. They somehow can collectively alter one's mind in both fascinating and horrible ways that I cannot wholly describe. I, myself, have been through this valley once, though it was a long time ago, during midwinter when their numbers were small, and, still, it was not an enjoyable experience. But yet, even still to this day, I deeply crave that magickal hypnosis again. Once you've crossed Aerogreen, you will never be the same again. You will always want to go back there, submerge yourself again in the pain and pleasure that it offers. You will be haunted by that desire of comfort and welcome doom your entire life thereafter. It is like knowing the inevitable peace of death, without any more fear of it."

"I don't care for the sound of that at all," Day responded.

"Can't we find another way?" Binder suggested. "Let's go around to the north."

"On foot, it would add more than a week to our schedule, maybe two, and that is if you have cliffclingers carrying you, which we don't. You can see the cliff walls from here," Drer told them, pointing. The gray walls were sheer and featureless. "And there are no supply stores along that route. Barren, at best. To the south, the ordes pines are so dense and tangled that no road has ever been cleared through them, blanketing the hills and valleys for hundreds of miles in all directions, and beyond those pines is yet another wall of rock that nearly equals the cliffs of the Great Rock Gaaloth. And, again, slim pickings as far as hunting for food. No, unfortunately, for us, without skycraft, the road through Aerogreen is the only road forward."

"We should be safe enough if we stay on the path and hold ourselves together," Gaebryl said. "It is navigatible. After all, this road was made by men and it does pass straight through the valley of the moths."

Drer agreed. "Most mishaps are caused by travelers who advance into the swarm foolheartedly. Since we know what to expect somewhat, we should be able to pass safely and quickly if we keep our heads. Now, listen closely, here's what I know of the place:

"Aerogreen is a vast, bowl shaped valley with a long and sordid history," he began. "Our road crosses it, west to east. There is a deep green stream that enters the vale from out of the root walls of the impenetrable ordes pine forests to the north, the Aerogreen River Run. It churns though the cliff drain of the valley, through twisting rapids and waterfalls, intersecting our road over a wide, shallow ford, crossable by foot. Then the River Run continues its way downstream from there and eventually exits Aerogreen over a great waterfall some distance directly south, over an immeasurable cliff.

"Now, be prepared. The water of Aerogreen is icy cold, and filled with the aquatic aerodare eggs and caterpillar larvae, although the moths were so thick during my first journey through that I could barely see the stream at all. The aerodares breed along the banks, billions of them, so thick that it is nearly a solid mass. When the eggs hatch, the caterpillars eat their way up the banks toward the ordes pines, where they cocoon. There they hatch as aerodares and the cycle continues.

"When we reach the stream, we'll be blind, but at least you'll know that we are halfway through the Aerogreen valley. Keep your head. Holdfast to your concentration, don't get distracted, and we should be able to make it to the other side in less than an hour from the time we head down into it."

"What is going to happen to us down there?" Day asked.

"I can't entirely remember what effect the moths had on me when I passed through Aerogreen. I only know that I was in danger of losing my way, and my mind. And I was willing to gratefully accept that happening."

Ott growled. "We have worse problems than moths right now," he said. "Look behind us, gentlemen. They have returned. With reinforcements."

Above the pines, in plain sight, were not just two, but three Gharnian scoutships, and one good sized fighter, and they were making no attempt to hide themselves anymore. They flew at a walking pace, like abominable kites.

Day sucked in his breath as yet another Gharnain fightership edged over the treetops. "There are four of them now!"

"I think they may be on to us," Binder said. "We can't defend ourselves against that fightercraft from the ground like this."

"We have no choice but to continue forward," Gaebryl answered. "Let's move quickly."

"I think we could take them," Ott said. "Anyone with me?"

"Keep your weapons at hand," Gaebryl continued. "If they do attack, we should separate and meet again together on this side of the Aerogreen valley, or, if that fails, move on forward and rendezvous at Longray Bluffs." Gaebryl glanced at the hovering ships. "Day, come, stay close by my side."

"I hear thunder again," Day said, batting at the moths in front of his face. "But the skies are cloudless, and the thunder does not end. It sounds as though we're marching directly into it."

"That's not thunder," Drer said. "Those are moth wings."

32

The muddy, weedy dirt road they had been following

eventually turned to smooth stone beneath their feet. At one time, long ago, it had been an active thoroughfare between two flourishing towns, long since extinct. A million wagon wheels had farmed two smooth wheel ruts in the stone, but what cities and civilizations they had been, no one could now remember. There were no major cities within hundreds of miles of them in any direction now. Countless rains had continued the work, keeping the stone road as smooth as spotted sienna silk.

The troop continued to climb as the road weaved up the sloping mountainside. Directly before them, the road divided. An ivy covered marker of faded brown stone stood in the center of the divide, etched with an ancient script of tyberlian letters, indiscernible to all. One route went off to their right on a long, gradual, curving slope to the top. The other, to their left, zigzagged much more steeply up stones and broken steps, directly up the hillside, joining the longer, easier way at the crest. The aerodares had grown so thick around them that the hillside and the scrubby trees were now gray and alive with movement.

Gaebryl chose the steeper of the two paths, and all agreed. The stairs were weatherbeaten, old and crumbling. Each step they took unintentionally crushed moths underfoot. The thunder from the beating wings of the aerodares in the valley over the next rise was not unlike the thunder of a waterfall, mixed with the sound of a massive wind. The roar was *alive.*

"The smell!" Day cried out, coughing. "It's unbearable!"

The stairs had eroded away at one point, so Gaebryl paused to boost Day up onto the next large stone. The young king stood and turned, looking back over the long valley from which they had come. Shielding his eyes, he could see the path they had taken, winding for miles back through the trees and far beyond, into the warm, hazy distance. The Gharnians were now nowhere in sight, which made all of them nervous. All six members of the troop were weary from the road and distracted by the moths, making them ever more vulnerable to a surprise attack.

As Day helped to pull Gaebryl up beside him, for one quick second, he thought he saw movement on the hilltop above them, just two small shadows beyond the veil of dead bushes and swirling moths, dashing quickly across the upper corner rim of the nearby rise. He squinted; the blazing sunslight was shining directly into his eyes, but he saw nothing else. Whatever it was, was gone like a puff of smoke.

"Did you see something?" Gaebryl asked.

"I'm not sure," Day said. "Shadows. I think."

"Something has to cast a shadow," the prince advised. "They do not exist on their own."

One by one the troop climbed to the top level shelf at the head of the staircase and paused to have a drink of water to clear their throats and to catch their breaths. Never had their packs seemed more burdensome. Years and years worth of accumulated dead and dying moths had accrued, piling a foot deep beneath their feet, like a dry, dusty, ashy gray snow. Drer took the lead, advising them to ready their ropes so that they could secure themselves to one another at the top before plunging through.

"Aerogreen is right over this ridge," he called out from the summit. The rumble of tiny wings was incredibly loud. "You can see the far side from here..."

"That'll be thirty dillins, please," said an odd little voice from behind a dead tree. It was as sharp and clear as a bell.

Day was the closest to the strange voice. He spun around and stepped quickly backwards, almost stumbling. Gaebryl's hand went swiftly to his sword.

From behind the gnarly tree, two little people stepped spryly out, a little old man and a little old woman who matched, palms outstretched, shy eyes blinking as rapidly as the moths' wings around them. They were dressed in colorful, tattered clothing from head to foot: apricot, cream and mint green. Both were balding, nearly toothless, and covered with gray aerodares.

"That'll be thirty dillins," repeated the little old man. "Apiece."

Day smiled at them, supposing that the odd little couple were the ones who had cast the shadows he had seen just moments before, while climbing up the hill.

"Thirty dillins?" Gaebryl replied, drawing closer to them. "For what?"

"No closer!" they piped, signaling him as they stepped nervously back. They both leaned, humped over, to the left. "Thirty dillins...to pass," they said together, now smiling their wide, toothless smiles.

"Don't sneeze or you'll frighten the bookends away," Binder replied.

"Why should we pay to pass here?" Gaebryl asked. "You don't own this valley. The moths do."

The two elflike characters giggled and hugged each other. "Must pay to pass, great warrior man," insisted the little blushing lady. "Caretakers."

"Thirty each, times six of you, that's...two hundred dillins even!"

"I think your math is off," Binder replied.

"I'm sorry, but we have no dillins with us today, little friends." He stepped toward them and at once they were gone, somehow blending instantly into the moths and trees and bushes all around them.

"No, no!" came a little scolding voice behind them. The troop spun to find the couple standing on a tree stump on the opposite side of the small clearing. "No closer!" the little man said, shaking an angry finger. He stomped his foot. "Thirty dillins apiece to cross. And fifty for each of your airboats!"

The troop followed the woodelf's gaze to the trees behind them. There hovered the Gharnian skycrafts. They had returned and were drawing in close.

"No dillins," Gaebryl reiterated. "You folk have no need for man's money. You only hoard it and never spend it. And, besides, those aren't our 'airboats'; they're unwanted tagalongs. You'll have to speak to them if you want gold or silver." He pressed past them, toward the rumbling mass. "Let's go. Let's get this over with!"

"Wait!" cried the elf. "Twenty dillins!" The others filed past them. Drer was laughing.

"Go bother someone else," Ott growled at them as he went by. "We're busy today, little man."

Day reached into his pocket and found one shiny gold dillin, and he flipped it toward them with his thumb. It landed on the ground near their shoeless feet.

They jumped on it, laughing and singing. "Thank you!" they said. "Thank you!"

Day turned and ran, quickly joining the rest of the troop at the crest of the hill. What opened up there before them was beyond the grasp of reality or belief. The valley of Aerogreen lay open at their feet, an ocean of hypnotic movement in a million shades of gray. It was an awesome, incredible theater of nature, more immense and powerful than Day, or any of the rest of the troop, had previously envisioned. Day felt suddenly minute in comparison to it.

"I have never seen anything like this before," Perce said.

"Nor I," said Ott. "It is a sea of life."

"When I passed through here before," Drer told them, "it was not a quarter of this size. I fear we have arrived at the height of their breeding season. It will be very difficult to pass. I fear we will have much trouble once we're inside..."

Just ten or fifteen yards ahead of them, the road at their feet disappeared completely down into the massive swarm, and then, on the far side, directly across from them, barely discernable, it resurfaced again, rising from the swirling gray sea in between. However, the distance to the other side was deceiving. It could have been a quarter of a mile across; it could have been four. The perspective continued to shift before their squinted eyes, creating an optical illusion. One thing was for certain: beckoning green hills, dotted with golden summer flowers awaited them on that distant shore.

To the north, on their left, a forest of netted, impenetrable ordes closed in upon the cylindrical, bowl shaped valley; the rocks and cliffs beyond stood steep and jagged. To the south, a blue sky beckoned; it was there that the River Run flowed out of the heart of Aerogreen and left that land, falling over a sheer cliff of unfathomable depths in the shadowy, sunless lands far, far below.

"Get your ropes!" Gaebryl shouted. A moth flew into his mouth and he spit it out. "Secure ourselves in a straight line, one after the other. If one is lost, then we're all lost. Hold tight!"

"Cover your mouths with kerchiefs, if you have them," Drer advised. "It will help you breath. You're going to feel as if you're being smothered."

Day found himself oddly enthralled with the rippling, swirling, surfaceless waves dancing before his eyes. He began to experience a form of mild hypnosis that a flowing brook or the coals of a campfire could likewise inspire in him. Was this what Drer had warned them about? Because it wasn't bad. It wasn't that bad at all. It was nice. He barely noticed the moths crawling about on his hands and face anymore.

"There are two things to remember as we cross," Drer cried to the others. "First, the moths have a natural pull to the right, toward the cliffs. Remember Gaebryl's story about the doomed army? Such was their demise. Avoid that pull; the moths will lead you over the edge of the cliff if they can. Overcompensate an inch to the left with every step, as if fighting a wind.

"Secondly, remember to concentrate on the task at hand, and avoid the overwhelming call of the moths. Hold onto the rope tight, because we will have no further communication once we enter their domain. Stay together. Breathe when you can.

Concentrate. Veer slightly to the left. The River Run was only knee deep when I crossed it, and perhaps twenty feet from shore to shore, but it will be deeper now, what with the recent rains, so take all appropriate precautions. Focus! Focus!"

"Day, come and stay close by me," Gaebryl said. "Tie this loop around your wrist and hold on at all costs." He stepped toward the thunderous living mass. The rope went taut and all followed. "See you on the other side!"

"Wait! Wait!" they heard from behind them as they were one by one enveloped by the swarm. "Wait, I say!"

Day turned quickly, squinting through the moths at the figure dashing up the rise toward them. He waved his hand at the moths before his eyes. "Who is that?" he cried, stalling. He was yanked along like a dead weight.

Perce disappeared into the moths, then Binder.

"Sire! The rope!" shouted Ott above the roar. He took King Day by the hand and forced the rope into it. "You must hold on, or be left behind, or worse! It's just the woodelves! Don't be deceived!"

"No, it's not the woodelves!" cried Day, although now no one could hear him anymore. "Stop! Go back! It's Dedlin!"

33

Down they descended into the living insect sea. Moths immediately filled all the space around them, delving deeply into their clothes and packs. Even if it were possible to open their eyes, which it was not, the sunlight could not have penetrated the deep, dark cloud of solid gray. Deeper and deeper they submerged, the pressure of the moths against their skin increasing as they descended.

"I have some good news for everyone," a voice suddenly said, as clear as day. It was Perce. "The moths do not seem to have an effect on me and I am able to communicate."

They were glad to hear his voice, a clear bell of sanity in a world without dimensions or conscious control.

"I can feel the slight pull to the right, as Drer foretold," he said. "I will remind you of his words. Do not compromise with them. Stay to the left, move slowly, one step at a time."

The ascent was not smooth. It was steep and rough. They felt their way forward blindly with their feet, stepping off shelves of slimy rock and often stumbling together. There was no way to tell if they were still on the road anymore at that point, or if they had headed off the bank toward some perilous hidden chasm. The moths underfoot, alive and dead, were as soft as cotton, as fine as dust, and several feet deep. It was slow going and awkward.

The smell was of sweet rot and decay.

Then, the moths began to call to them. It was almost like a song, the soft thrum of millions and millions of moth wings that surrounded and penetrated. The troop of six were now totally immersed in a resonating, somber rumble, as if slowly and methodically becoming a part of it. As their bodies became one with the frequencies that spanned all audible ranges and beyond, they assimilated. Almost immediately, the effects of the strange valley began to work on them, each one responding differently to the exotic, erotic song.

Gaebryl's concentrated on one feat alone: stepping one foot over the other until he reached the far side. Then, in one flashing moment of weakness, he briefly listened. For one split second, he allowed himself to experience the sensations of the tiny wings fluttering all over his body, in his clothes, on his face, in his hair, and instantly he forgot everything, his mission, his name, the rest of the troop... It was as if they had never existed. He was immediately alone, and in slumbering bliss. There was a constant weight, a comforting pressure all over him. It was very peaceful and forever. He suddenly realized, to his delight and astonishment, that he was not even awake, but asleep at home in his bedchambers in some other place, fast asleep and dreaming soundly, the weight upon him nothing but his own soft down blankets on the bed surrounding him. It was a sleep so divine that it felt like love, and he chose never to wake again.

"Onward!" Perce said to them all. The troop was wavering, struggling in different directions. The ground began to rise underfoot and he wondered if they had headed back in a circle. "To the left! Stay focused!"

Drer Fregoode had long ago forgotten what the effects his first experience in Aerogreen had had on him all those years ago, but now it returned as if that journey had only occurred the day before. The moths were so ticklish! The tiny, featherlike creatures were everywhere: on his neck, in his shirt, in his shoes and between his toes. It was sheer torture! It was so much more intense than his first trip through Aerogreen. There were so many more of them! He squeezed the loop of rope tight with his right hand, attempting to fight off the aerodares with his left, but to no avail. He laughed out loud, and squirmed, and then he laughed louder, and within seconds his laughter was muffled as if he were trying to laugh with a mouthful of bread.

Day wanted to tell them all to go back, but he had forgotten why. The moths were singing to him. The beating of their wings were some kind of soothing orchestral instrument and he was adrift on the music they made. It was not unlike the soft melody of harps or the gentle coursing of water on glass. He was flying between the world of wake and sleep, desiring only to lie down and listen for a few minutes. Couldn't they hear the lullaby? It was so dark and lovely.

"What is happening to you all?" Perce cried to them. He jerked at the rope. "Stay together! Don't veer off or we're all doomed!"

Ott roared, cursed, and then he fell silent. He occasionally slashed at the swarm with claws outstretched, feeling the resistance as if he were in water. He could not fight this foe by any means that he knew, which frustrated him to the point of madness.

Binder found himself leading them onward from the center of the rope, with the rest of them dangling like weights on either end of it. He could not exactly tell where he was heading, but he continued to march, foot over foot, deaf, dumb, and blind. It was dark now, with nothing but gray: gray light through his eyelids, gray sound, gray taste. And the smell, the taste, was so musty. The dust of chalk. The flavor of ashy dust. He was walking through gray stone, pulling the weight of the world behind him. Or, was he part of that stone, he wondered? That was certainly it. He was, himself, part of the stone that surrounded him, and it was pointless to walk. Why attempt it? Could rocks walk? Why should they? Rocks were made to rest, firmly and solidly. Rocks were unmovable.

"Take one more step!" Perce cried. "One more! And another!"

Binder's existence in that great gray stone was of no consequence. His life existence was now trivial in the grand scheme of the universe. Rocks did not move on their own. They held things down. They weighted the earth under their feet so that it would not float away into space. They sat for eons and just slowly eroded. He had to stop now, because he realized he was not alive, and in fact, he had never existed at all. He was a great rock, important, strong and heavy.

Gaebryl stumbled back into the lead, stepping suddenly knee deep into the stream of Aerogreen. It was icy cold and swift, instantly sobering him. It jarred his senses back to life for a moment, and he fought to retain them. The moths around him were at their thickest, nearly a solid mass, and it was choking the air out of him.

"Keep on!" he heard Perce cry, and the voice inspired him to do so. He pulled hard at the rope, encouraging his fellow travelers onward, into the stream of Aerogreen. Halfway there.

"Remember, concentrate!" the mahekian cried. "Ignore the urge! Ignore! Ignore! Remember the far shore!"

Binder splashed into the stream, followed by Ott. It revived them both, just enough.

"I am beginning to feel strange now," Perce said. "I feel so helpless, like a little child, but I do feel so happy."

Ott roared. He was infuriated with this loss of control.

"I am happy! I'm a child again!" Perce sang deliriously. He pulled against the rope as though he wanted to run off and play. "Come with me!" He tried to free his hand from the tight loop he had secured around his wrist.

They stumbled through the water, and instantly it grew deeper. It was remarkably cold and biting, ice water from the mountain snows, and it was running swiftly. They suddenly realized their peril as it rose up higher on them with every step that they took.

"Hold on!" Perce called. "The bottom is slick. The aerodare larvae are as slick as snails!"

Day was up to his hips, and he was having trouble keeping his footing. "Gaebryl! I'm slipping!"

He stumbled and slid over and over again, grasping desperately onto Ott's belt for support. His pack came loose and drifted away with the torrents. The thordian was growling with every struggling breath he was able to take.

Binder was the first to fall and go under. He held onto the rope with one hand while grappling at larvae covered boulders under the surface with the other.

"Binder fell in!" Perce cried. "Help him up! Commander Binder is under the water!"

"Hold onto Day!" Gaebryl cried out, pulling his hand free from the knotted loop, but he could say nothing further. He traversed down the rope, hand over hand, past Perce, and seized Binder's wrist beneath the water, pulling on him with all his might. The rapids pushed hard against him, but he was somehow able to keep his footing. Binder found a foothold and stood, momentarily crying out before his mouth was filled with moths.

"Come on!" Perce cried. "Let's cross it! We're halfway there! We can make it! Don't stop now, don't give up, we're halfway across!"

With all his strength and concentration, Gaebryl moved

back down the rope to find Day, grasping onto each of his comrades for support along the way. Even if he had to carry the boy to the far shore on his shoulders, his only thought now was to get young King Day up and out of that hellish nightmare as soon as was possible. The rest of the troop would just have to fend for themselves now.

They were all moving again, step by step, making good progress across the stream of Aerogreen, when suddenly, Binder slipped and fell in again, coming free of the rope, and drug Ott off along with him. Then they heard Day cry out, "Gaebryl!" and he, too, was gone beneath the raging waters with them.

"Something's wrong," Perce said, holding on to a limp rope.

"They've fallen in!" "Go on!" Gaebryl cried out to Drer and Perce, and then he dove blindly and without thought into the swift, icy water, allowing the current to pull him along with it. He stretched out his arms and legs, feeling for the sides or the bottom. His hands slid through the squirming aquatic caterpillar larvae like oil on mud. He scraped his shoulder against a sharp rock, unable to cry out.

The current was carrying him faster and faster. He swam with it, stretching his hands out in front of him, hoping to seize the boy, or anyone floating along ahead of him. If only he could catch hold of Day, and pull him to the side! He could not rise for a breath, no matter how badly he needed one, nor open his eyes underwater; it was too dark and murky to see.

He tried one last time to swim ahead, but the current tossed him from side to side. His head hit a rock, sending flashes of sparkling white spots before his clenched eyes. He was sucked mercilessly along, unable to control his movement, desperately needing to take a breath. He reached for the side, for the bottom, for anything, but there was nothing there. He could not tell which direction was up, down, left or right anymore. He realized he was floating downstream backwards now. Any second he half expected vertigo to hit, as he shot out over the waterfalls and off into the oblivion of death. The thunder was coming, just ahead. It thrummed in his aching ears. He screamed under the water, and tensed all of his muscles in preparation for the launch.

His hand touched something in the water, and he seized it as fast as a snake striking its prey. It was shirt cloth. He pulled and clenched onto an arm. He could tell. It was young King Day.

Suddenly, Gaebryl himself was caught by someone, seizing him by his hair and collar, yanking him to a stop. He felt the water pull hard against him as he swung around and crashed to a halt into the rocks at the side of the stream. Another hand seized him by his wrist. His face rose above the surface and he sucked in as much air as he could between his clenched teeth, spitting out the omnipresent moths, clinging precariously to a greasy, slimy rock, with Day, choking, at his bosom. Someone still held him by his hair, and they yanked him up and out of the stream with struggling effort, pulling the boy up along with him. Another hand, a strong one, seized his belt and lifted him up and out of the river. Gaebryl thought that it was Binder, but he could not be sure. He tried to speak, but he could not; in fact he felt as though he were smothering to death. The boy encircled his arms around Gaebryl's waist. They were on solid ground again at least, but on which shore he was unsure. He was so weak that he nearly faltered to his knees several times. He felt a loop go around his wrist, and it jerked him forward.

Exhausted, confused, and in shock, Gaebryl came to his feet and began to follow whoever it was who had saved him. At that point, he didn't care who it was. He just wanted out of that hell.

Once again, the moths began calling to him. "Shut up!" he cried to them. He tried to ignore them, but even his anger and fear of disgrace did not aid him while passing through the great domain of the gray aerodares. Down there, in their valley, the insects ruled, not him, nor any man. In another few seconds, he was hypnotized again, dreamily and blissfully sleepwalking again under the powerful spell of the horrible moths of Aerogreen, without a single care left in the world. Fortunately for him this time, his wrists were securely tied, and someone else was now in control.

Eight

THE WYZARD'S STORY

34

"There will be time for questions and lengthy explanations and all the 'thank you's' and other nonsense that needs to be said soon enough," Dedlin Dane snapped irritably, shaking moths from his hat. He was wet, angry, and anxious to get moving now that everyone was out of danger and accounted for. He glared across the fold at the Gharnian scouts hovering in the trees and he frowned. "First of all, we've got to get rid of *them.*"

"We lost most our packs," Day said, feeling somewhat like a drowned rat. Gaebryl handed him a towel to dry himself with.

"You've lost more than your packs, I'd say. Since I saw you last, you lost a perfectly fine fightercraft to a creeper that's been living in the same hill for a hundred and fifty years, wasted at least three days walking in the wrong blessed direction, and nearly drowned in the rising floodwaters of Aerogreen. You now have four Gharnian ships escorting you across the country, with more on the way, no doubt, *and* you lost your packs. That probably doesn't cover it. You didn't happen to offend any woodelfs along the way, did you? Never mind. I don't want to know."

The troop looked sickly at one another.

"I hope not," Dedlin said. "Anyway, fear not. I brought ample food and some extra clothes, although I wouldn't hope that everything is going to fit that well." He leaned over to Gaebryl, and with a concerned and inquisitive eye, he whispered, "And how is the... *you know...*"

Feeling suddenly flushed, Gaebryl felt for the chain around his neck. Thank goodness, the key was still on it. "F-fine, Dedlin," he said. What a disaster *that* could have been. "We're fine."

"Well, good. All's not lost then, despite everyone's best efforts. Stardeer is just ahead of us here, among the rocks. I expect no one's against air travel this evening, then?"

"No," they mumbled.

"Good. Get onboard then. I've brought along two more crew members who are new to the Wilds, Lake Tobias and Qan Methalard, whom you might remember as the same two Tungulin castlerangers who first sighted the distressed Meadian skycraft Tigre last week. They have recently joined the voluntary Knights of Galgariah, and since they were in attendance at the Secret Council and heard much of what was going on, I agreed with their request to come along with us. We could use an extra pair of hands or two. They will be acting as your pages on this journey, but don't be too hard on them. They're nervous enough about all this as it is. I'll trust you all to bring them up to speed. "We'll need to travel through the night now to make up for lost time. I suspect that we've been discovered and that bigger warships will soon be on the way. Things are going to start getting very dangerous before long, so let's start preparing for it. It's time to start *thinking* for a change."

"It's good to see you, too, old man," Drer Fregoode ventured to say. He pulled a moth from his ear. "What took you so long, anyway?"

Dedlin snorted at the question, and continued marching crossly up the hill. "Let's go find that magickal cave."

35

Within the hour, Stardeer was sailing swiftly through the summer evening sky with Dedlin at the helm of his own skycraft, leaving the valley of Aerogreen far behind. King Day had changed into loose, dry clothes and had joined the wyzard at the helm. Drer, Perce and Ott were below, trying to get an early sleep so that they could take the long night shift later. Binder was cleaning up and Gaebryl was introducing himself to Lake and Qan near the starboard rail. The two castlerangers stared at the Bursian prince warrior with eyes as wide as coins, engaging him in nervous conversation as best they could.

Day studied the old man briefly. The wyzard looked a decade younger than he had back in Tungulin to him. There was color in his sallow cheeks, and some suns on his skin. His hair and beard were now braided, pulled back and tied, much more practical for skycraft flight. His dark eyes were sharp and bright beneath the shadow of his bushy gray eyebrows. "You don't know how glad I am to see you," Day said to the wyzard. "I feared that you were dead."

"I do have some idea how glad you are," Dedlin replied with a wry smile. "I am sorry, but I was tied up with other matters. You'll hear about my recent escapades soon enough. In the meanwhile, how is our little secret? Is it still safe?"

Day shook his head. "Yes."

"That's amazing," Dedlin replied quietly. "Not even Gaebryl suspects?"

"I don't think so," Day said. "I suppose I could tell him."

"No need to rush. You will when you are ready. It has served your purposes well enough so far."

A moment of comfortable silence passed between them.

"Did the wyzards at the Council know? I was very nervous."

"Oh, yes, they knew. That was the reason they hesitated before confirming your identity. I had to explain things to them later, to better help them understand. They found the entire premise delightful."

"I'm glad."

"But it does brings up other questions," Dedlin said. "Shhh, we have company. We'll talk about this later..."

Gaebryl walked across the deck and joined them. "Good evening," he said. "All together again."

"As it should be," the wyzard replied with a wink. "Dedlin, I...I just wanted to say that I feel responsible for the mishaps we've encountered over the last few days. I was in charge in your stead and I failed on several counts. I hope that your faith in me hasn't wavered irreparably."

"Oh, don't be so hard on yourself." He leisurely banked Stardeer around a cluster of oak trees, then leveled off again, maintaining the ship less than twenty feet above the scrubby terrain. "To be honest, things might have turned out much worse had those 'mishaps' not occurred," he said. "In fact, they turned out to be blessings in disguise. By being delayed by the creeper, there is a good chance that you escaped capture... The day after the creeper took Perce's skycraft, a fleet of Gharnian warships was reported to be crossing your intended flight path. That old wretched creeper just might have saved your lives, and this mission."

"By the gods..."

"When I heard the report, I flew like a gale wind. I was very encouraged when I found the crumpled hull of Sunshaft (and none of your gnawed bones) strewn around the creeper's den. I shouted with joy," the wyzard said. "I was a bit too rough on everyone earlier this evening. I was just cross and wet and tired and fearful at Aerogreen. You *were* heading in the right approximate direction for those three days on foot. Generally."

Day glanced over his shoulder at the four specks on the horizon following behind as though tethered to the back of the ship.

"Don't worry about them," the wyzard said, with devilish light in his eye. "I have a plan."

"I'm anxious to hear," Gaebryl said.

"Tonight," was all he would say. "Tonight we will lose them. In the meantime, I've made a nice dark brew of roasted koffik beans in the pantry that should just about be ready. Please have some and share it with the rest of the crew. But don't drink too much! It will make you as jittery as a dragonfly."

36

Lake and Qan had been given the charge as lookouts that evening, and stood as sentinels on the front and back of Dedlin's skycraft. The remaining six were below, getting much needed, and well deserved, rest. Dedlin alone remained at the helm, keeping Stardeer at full speed through the twilight and into the coming night, steering a straight arrow course toward the southeast for many ongoing hours. But try as he might to outrun them, his ship was no equal to the Gharnians' sleek crafts. A very mild midnight sunsrise came and went, and now the moonless night was as pitch as coal. It was nearly time for a shift change at the helm, but before he relieved himself from duty, Dedlin began to make preparations to lose the Gharnians once and for all before he, himself, retired for the night, as he had promised.

Three of the Gharnian scoutships were smaller than Dedlin's Stardeer, but one fighter was thrice its size. All four of them loomed much closer now that night was upon them, most likely keeping Dedlin's ship under surveillance with high powered nightscans. Sometimes Dedlin spotted red beacon lights on their bellies, and occasionally a spotlight would come on, aimed in one direction or another, but most of the time the Gharnian ships flew without lights, in sheer and utter darkness.

Dedlin strapped himself into the helmsman's chair and took a deep breath. It was time. "Lake, Qan, hold on to something," he forewarned them. "It's going to be a wild one."

They hurriedly did as he suggested. And no sooner had they snapped the safety latches on their seat harnesses, they heard him mutter to himself, "I feel as though I'm forgetting something. Hmm... Anyway, here goes..."

He shut off all the lights.

Without slowing, he jerked the steering bar hard to the right, spinning Stardeer directly around in a circle, now facing the oncoming Gharnians ships, firing no less than ten missiles in rapid succession straight at them. At the same time, he flipped a switch that caused Stardeer's levitation vents to open. It released the inert gases that kept her afloat, and she fell like a rock, backwards, into the thick forest trees. From throughout the craft Dedlin heard frenzied voices. He realized then that he had forgotten to forewarn the rest of the crew to strap themselves in! "I knew I forgot something!"

The missiles had missed the Gharnians, but that was of no concern to the wyzard. They hit trees in the forest all around them, lighting the night with bright orange fireballs. "That should blind them for awhile, nightscans or no," he said to himself.

He quickly flipped the switch again, closing off the gas vents, and the powerful turbines quickly filled them again. He leveled Stardeer off, still crashing backwards through the treetops, pushing the accelerator bar forward with all his might. The ship slowed and slid to a complete stop with a hissing, swooshing roar of air, just as several Gharnian missiles flew past overhead, exploding in the trees behind him. Everyone and everything onboard tumbled and rolled to the back of the ship, and once again, frantic voices cried out below.

"Sorry!" he said.

A few seconds later, with Stardeer descending slowly down under the dense cover of the trees back they way they had come, like a cautious fish sinking slowly out of sight in a dark, deep lake, the Gharnians flew swiftly past him overhead, all searchlights ablaze, firing wildly into the distance beyond.

Immediately, the wyzard turned ninety degrees to the north and began creeping along at a ridiculously slow snail's pace, descending lower and lower into the ancient forest boughs in complete blindness. He lit his console with a faint blue luminescent glow that was undetectable from more than even a few feet away.

By now, everyone was scrambling up onto the deck,

clinging onto whatever they could for dear life.

Perce raced to the helm. "Did we crash?" he cried. "Dedlin! Is everyone okay?"

"Are we hit?" Binder called.

"Shhh," the wyzard simply told them. "Good night, good friends," he said quietly, heading below for a long needed rest. "Someone take over, if you please. Stardeer is now yours. We are free of the Gharnian fleas. Go north until dawn, east until breakfast, then south until lunch. See you then, if not sooner."

The crew watched him retire below, then they looked around, puzzled and still completely stunned. Where in the world were they? It was pitch black. The foliage that brushed past them was thick and wet, the air was cool and the insects were loud. Stardeer squeezed past a thick and ungiving tree trunk and then some heavy limbs, causing the ship to scrape and tilt just to wedge through. Strange noises surrounded them: birds, bugs, unnamable tree creatures who did not like being disturbed at all. They were immersed, somewhere, deep within some primordial jungle, and there was an unexplainable creepy feeling all around them.

"That wyzard is out of his ever loving mind," Binder mumbled. "Where in the hell are we?"

Qan had not yet opened his eyes or released the rail; his arms were locked solidly around it. There was a small branch protruding from his hat. He was whispering a prayer that he remembered recanting as a child.

"I don't know," Day said, "But I'm going below to try to go back to sleep, if I can. I doubt I'll be able to close my eyes anytime soon after that jolt."

Suddenly, blinding spotlights pierced the trees from above, grazing past them on the right. The crew instinctively took cover. The searchlights, trickling down through the leaves in roving circles as the Gharnians frantically scanned, caused strange shadows to dance all around the forest depths.

"They're searching for us," Gaebryl whispered, smiling out the side of his mouth. "The old coot escaped from them after all."

"He said he would," King Day replied, smiling.

They knew that the smaller Gharnian scoutships would have no trouble following Stardeer beneath the woodland terraces, if they knew where to look, but the dark fightership above them was much too large to enter the trees. It slowly moved off in the direction of another spotlight that had just come on somewhere to the south, where a golden blaze, ignited from the missile fire, had begun to spread along a short line of dead pine trees.

"Good night," Day whispered as he crept below after the wyzard.

"Night," the rest quietly replied. They were still rattled and in a mild, and somehow jubilant, state of shock.

"Ingenious," Binder said beneath his breath. He watched the Gharnian searchlights fade off into the distance. "But don't tell him I said so."

Drer Fregoode smiled to himself. "Yes, he certainly can be."

37

Dedlin came back up on deck a few hours before dawn, rubbing his puffy eyes. He had been dreaming again, the same uneasy dream that kept haunting him night after night as of late: he was fleeing from something that was trailing him, something fell and evil, as dark as midnight shadow and as cruel as death, but he could not see what it was, for it kept no earthly shape. It was always coming behind him, always on the move, sniffing, hunting, searching hungrily. It was smart, horrible, and existed nearly in the ethereal. It acted without remorse, and Dedlin feared that he held no power over this thing. This recurring nightmare had frightened him from his sleep on several occasions, as it had this night. He began thinking that it wasn't a nightmare at all, but, instead, a premonition, a vision of something that was soon to come. He vowed not to speak of it to anyone yet, not until he had to. There was no need to frighten them any further. But he knew, *something evil was on its way,* and this crew would inevitably have to face it.

He took a deep breath to help calm his nerves. He figured he could use some herb smoke. Outside, it was serenely quiet, except for some strange nocturnal waterfowl that cried eerily from some dark river beneath the trees to the west. Perce was at the helm; Ott was standing statuesquely close by on watch, his keen feline eyes gleaming gold in the dark. Stardeer had gotten stuck once or twice through the night as she coasted diligently along, but Perce had just backed her up and found another way through. At this juncture, it was smooth sailing through the middle terraces, and they were enjoying a relatively good speed. The wyzard glanced up at the sky through the levels of gloomy leaves, yawning as he stretched.   "Ready to get on out of here?" he said, reaching for the onboard light switch.

Ott seized the wyzard's hand, startling him. Perce directed the wyzard's attention to the southern skies. There, past the dark silhouettes of the trees, was a large, black space in the heavens where the stars did not shine through. Dedlin realized then that it was a Gharnian warship, a large mega hull warship, a hundred times larger than Stardeer, hovering silently above the forest with its lights off, watching and waiting, and hoping that the crew of Stardeer would do something careless to reveal her position. The large ships had arrived, and even the tiniest glimmer of light could be detected from above.

Dedlin whispered: "Like I said earlier, I'll see you gentlemen in the morning, and I'll try to leave my overconfidence with my humility, under my pillow from now on, where it belongs."

38

A gold and crimson sunrise foretold of more rain to come later that morning. A stoic Commander Binder had relieved Perce, taking control of the helm of Stardeer shortly after they had risen from the sweltering jungle canopies. The ship was still covered with debris from the forest: leaves, sticks, seeds, insects, a tree snake, and a strange little brown animal resembling a lemur or a sloth, which they caught and released without incident. The crew busied themselves by tidying things up on the ship. Binder flew low, once again at full throttle, heading directly south, following a ridge of hills that rose like the lumpy spine of some great animal. Drer had risen early and was working on breakfast for everyone. Lake and Qan were setting plates and spoons, filling mugs, washing countertops. Despite the cramped quarters, the crew was in good spirits, because, thanks to Dedlin's ingenious scheme, they had successfully eluded the Gharnian scoutships once and for all.

     The trees were thinning out below them, now clumped together in sparse patches between the rolling hills and mossy tundra. The grass of the oncoming plains was a resplendent green, dotted with wildflowers in the vivid colors of summer: bright gold, ivory, white, black, yellow, orange, and lavender. The ship would soon pass the rough outskirts bordering the far west reaches of Galgariah and enter the vast rolling treeless plains of Tuus. Day came to an aromatic table of fried ham and fresh baked bread. He was the last to eat, but had two portions of eggs, ham, and toast, and topped off his meal with a glass of cold rrama's milk, a welcome treat. He cleaned his own utensils and whisked the crumbs off of the small square box that he had used as a seat. The box, he noticed after a closer inspection, was strange in its design. It was apparently carved out of some kind of hardwood, but it was as lightweight as a feather. It looked very old, and its surface was covered with handcarvings of the moons, and of trees, and large, elegant waterfowl. There was a rippling ocean with a score of large, flat bottomed boats, sails full of wind. The box appeared to have no seams, nor nails, or screws holding it together, as if it had been carved from a solid block of wood, although, by its weight, it appeared to be hollow inside. As Day continued to turn it, images changed, disappeared and then reappeared upon its surface, as if telling a story. "What is this?" he asked, intrigued.

     "Oh, careful with that, Your Highness," Dedlin replied, coming up from the lower deck with an old crumpled map in his hands. "It's a box made by the wyzard Jaas in Kengingtal Fway.

You may examine it, and be amazed, but do be careful. It can be dangerous. Jaas was a box maker, you see, but not just any boxes. He was the master of designing and constructing *passage* boxes, such as the one you are holding. They are strange items, with magick that I, myself, have never fully understood. I brought it along, because you never know. It may come in handy."

"Passage boxes," Day repeated. He found a button latch and pressed it. A seam formed and the lid popped open. Inside, it was empty.

"It's so light I thought it must have been filled with algaestone gas."

"No," Dedlin said. "Alas, the trees from which this wood was crafted no longer exist on this continent, or any other, I fear. Barone trees they were called, and they were rare, even in the elder days, growing along the coasts of Kengingtal Fway in ancient Nordia. The trees began dying there, out of loneliness some used to claim, despite the efforts of the mahekian caregivers who tried to preserve their kind. Jaas took the wood from the trees, just before they passed, to construct the most wondrous items from them. See, the wood of a young, thriving barone tree, or from one already dead, held no power; but the wood taken from one, just *before* its passing, could be used for all sorts of wyzards' manipulations. It is lightweight and strong, unlike any other, as you can most probably see."

"This box is magick, then?"

"True magick is only achieved by the complete understanding of physical laws of nature, so that ways may be found to bend or break them without interrupting the natural flow of everything else. This passage box by Jaas is a perfect example of that theory."

"It looks perfectly normal to me."

"It is perfectly normal," the wyzard explained. "All magick is normal. Magick is nothing but precise scientific formulas that alter existing laws of nature: gravity, thought, energy, motion, sight, light, sound, fire, animals, and so on and so forth. There are nature's functions happening all around us, at all times. Wyzards learn how to cause these laws to malfunction and/or alter, while controlling them, through exact calculation, experimentation, manipulation and faith. Magick can be very simple," he said, opening his hand, palm up, with a ball of fire appearing to float and roll just above it, "or it can be very complicated." The ball of fire exploded, startling everyone who was watching. The sparks turned into tiny blue butterflies, flying away in all directions. "I began learning levitation, or the undoing of gravity, when I was about, oh, half your age. That was my favorite. Then I worked my way up from there."

Day spun the box. "You said to be careful," he said. "Why, Dedlin? What does it do?"

"Several things. Most importantly, it teaches. Start by putting your hand in the box."

Curiously, Day did as Dedlin suggested. He did not know what to expect, so he did this slowly.

"Further," Dedlin encouraged.

Day did as he said, further and further. "There's no bottom!" he finally sputtered. He put his entire arm inside, all the way up to his shoulder, and, although, on the outside, the passage box was only threevquarters of the length of his arm, Day's fingertips could not find the bottom or the sides of it. "How far does it go?" he asked.

"No further than the opposite end of the box," Dedlin answered, smiling.

"So," Day said, searching for a logical explanation, "actually, my arm shrinks when it goes inside the box?"

"See for yourself," the wyzard encouraged. "See for yourself."

Day peered into Dedlin's box and shook his head in fascinated wonder. "My whole arm is right there, as normal as can be, but it is nowhere near the bottom of the box. The space inside the passage box is different from the space out here."

"That is correct, Your Highness," Dedlin said, looking pleased. "Good. You figured it out. There is nearly a square mile in this particular box. Works wonders for storage, sometimes."

Commander Binder had been watching and listening to this instruction, but he shook his head in disbelief. "A square mile," he mumbled. "That's ridiculous."

Day held it up to him. "Try it yourself, Commander."

Binder took the passage box. "There's not a square mile inside this box," he said, holding the open side of it up to his face. "That's just preposterous." He reached his massive arm inside of it to tap the box bottom with his fingers, but he could not do it, experiencing the same remarkable phenomenon that Day had. He stretched his entire arm inside, up to his shoulder, and looking in, the bottom was still far, far away.

"Don't fall in, Binder!" Dedlin warned. "It's a long way to the bottom."

Binder sat the box down beside him, with the opening facing upwards, toward the sky. "You're hypnotizing us, or using some other sort of wyzard's trick," he groaned. "A square mile, indeed. Silliest thing I've ever heard!"

"Watch this," Day said. He dropped an apple into the top of the box and watched it falling inside. Everyone crowded around to watch. The apple dropped farther and farther away until they could hardly see it. Then, Day grasped the box and flipped it over, holding it out before him. A few seconds later, the apple fell out and hit the deck at their feet, splattering in all directions as if it had been thrown off of a cliff. Everyone cheered, except Commander Binder, of course.

39

After pouring over the maps and charts, mumbling and measuring, Dedlin called a meeting. "Okay! Time for explanations and answers. Time for revelations and some honesty for a change," he said, marching through them. "Time for planning and intelligent preparation." He pulled a wooden pipe from a small cabinet. "Most importantly of all, time for a good smoke of Tungulin's best pipeweed. It's been far too long since I've had a decent smoke, and my head could use some clouding this morning. Let's see if I can get this lit with all this confounded wind."

Dedlin found a spot next to Masterpilot Perce at the front helm, and the rest of the crew gathered around them on the four curved stairs that rose from the lower deck up along both sides of the helm. Lake and Qan stood quietly behind the rest, watching the horizons for unfriendlys. Off the port bow, the sky turned a deep grayish purple. Heavy, threatening clouds billowed and a new wind blew from that direction. Distant thunder rumbled and bolts of stark lightning lit the earth and sky beneath. It was going to be the kind of storm one strove to avoid.

A trail of smoke left the wyzard's mouth and dissipated in the wind; his expression showed that he savored it. "So, Gaebryl," he began, coming back into focus. "How is your leg, then, son?"

"Fine."

Dedlin's eyes sharpened. "The truth, prince."

"Better," he said. "I wouldn't win a foot race if I had to, but it's getting better. The countryside hike was not good for it."

"And how are you, Your Highness?" he asked the young king, who stood next to Masterpilot Perce.

"Good," he said. "Great, now that you decided to become involved."

"Well, I have much to tell you. Qan, be a good lad and pour an old man a vessel of ale," Dedlin requested. "We're making good time now, and it is time that everyone knew the truth about our mission: where we are going, what it is we seek, and who our enemy is. And if you'll allow, it will be storytime. I'll take the time to tell you about the night I was nearly devoured by cattlewolves, and who it was who flew to Tungulin in the Tigre that fateful night. Let me explain how I was captured by the Gharnians, and then how I destroyed the two Gharnian warships Godstrike V and Mount of Steel, right on Tungulin's doorstep, and how I barely escaped with my life. And permit me, if you will, to tell you why I changed King Tital Vantoo into a miniature green aardvark and threw him into the royal fountain!"

40

Dedlin would not say another word until he had drunk not one, but two flasks of ale, and held another full flask tight in his fist. Then did he talk!

"Everything I said was true except for the Tital Vantoo episode. I did not change him into an aardvark, whatever an aardvark might be. He was doing well enough when I saw him last, although there were dark deeds astir. But I'm getting ahead of myself. I'll back up to the events on the night we investigated the wreck of the Tigre... I was nearly eaten alive by the black wolferines of hell!"

"Yes, Dedlin, tell us about the wolferines," Day said. "How did you get away from them?"

"Not as easily as you might think," the wyzard said. "Once the cattlewolves of Gaaloth have your scent, or even worse, have you in their sights, there is usually no chance of escape from them. And yet, I managed to do just that. The black devils were closing in on me fast, and I was too weak to go on. Binder and Drer had gone on ahead, which was exactly as I had planned. The wolferines slowed when they found me, giving my dear friends a better opportunity to escape. I, however, was forced to stand and do battle.

"There was enough dry timber around to suit my needs. So, uttering a carefully chosen word, I encircled myself within a ring of protective blue fire. This startled the wolferines momentarily, for they do not love fire of any color, giving me just enough time to mount the lower branches of a sturdy pine tree. From this exercise I was so exhausted that I feared that I might faint and fall from my perch and right into their snapping, drooling jaws. I was able to taunt them from there, angering them even more, allowing Drer and Commander Binder a few precious seconds more.

"One unusually large wolferine jumped the fiery blue ring and came at me. I called to the beast in the ancient tongue that it feared before it could seize my leg, and it went temporarily mad, rolling in the sticky blue flames, and it quickly returned the way it came, madly attacking his brethren. Thus, I was able to climb one step higher.

"Another wolferine broke through and lunged, seized my cape, ripping it from around my neck, nearly yanking me down from the tree. I tried to set him ablaze, but my aim was off, and I missed. Another tree lit up instead, with flames of gold.

"I was too weary to perform any more magick, so all I could do was climb higher with the last of my quickly waning strength. Somehow, I clung to my cane. High enough now for a brief respite, all but two wolferines gave up on me and passed on by, up the trail after our good Drer Fregoode and Commander Benjyn Binder, a pack of nearly fifty of those foul dread beasts, if my count was right. I clung to the tree trunk like an infant to his mother, and recited my blessings. The two wolferines circled hungrily below me, snarling and gnashing their teeth, their red eyes glowing as hellish fiery coals. It was literally a nightmare come to life.

"I continued to slowly climb whenever I could, hoping to somehow signal Stardeer from the top of the tree. Although the thin limbs swayed dangerously with my weight, I was able to get my head up above the treetops and take a good look around. I could not locate Stardeer, but I did see many other disturbing things. Two great Gharnian warships, the aforementioned Mount of Steel and the Godstrike V, were methodically destroying each one of the gogmoor ships with missile blasts as they rose from the forest, as easily as knocking flies from a window with a swatter. The warships were flying low, riding the tops of the trees to avoid being spotted by the towers of Tungulin or Bondoon. One of them, the Godstrike V, came right for me. I thought it would knock me from my perch if I didn't descend immediately, but I took my chances and waited there, hoping to learn something new or perhaps do some kind of damage before my inevitable demise.

"Fortunately, I was able to seize a horizontal fin as the huge craft turned past me. It was as easy as stepping off of a step and onto a conveyor. I held on tight because the ship raked through the treetops, shearing off limbs and sharp needles. I had no way of getting inside the ship from there. Or off of it. I had to hold on for dear life, knuckles red with blood, and just ride it out for as long as I could, all the while praying for a miracle. I was dragged up against the trees many times, and many times I nearly fell to my death. My greatest fear was that the warship would take off into the heavens at speed, and, unable to maintain my precarious hold, I would then fall from on high and plummet to my death.

"Miraculously, that did not happen. The destruction of the gogmoor warriors continued on until none were left alive, at which point, the two great ships headed back toward Bondoon. The Gharnians were going there to lie to Gaorwyn, to say that it had been King Vantoo's Tungulin warships that had destroyed his gogmoors. As soon as we began our descent into Gaorwyn's courtyard in the heart of the castlecity, I was spotted by the gogmoor soldiers in their watchtowers, clinging to that fin. They surrounded me in great numbers as we landed, and apprehended me without a fight and cast me to the ground without mercy, vowing to skin me alive and take me before the great warlock Gaorwyn to slowly die at his feet. Then, the Gharnians came forward to claim me, and I was taken into their custody instead. There, I was beaten in the courtyard, but I feigned deaf mute. The Gharnian general in charge, Shandhark was his name, had his soldiers take me inside his ship for further interrogation. He told me that he had some very particular tools and techniques that would make me tell him everything he wanted to know, and I believed him. I was convincingly terrified and naïve, quaking and cowering before the lot of them, although I had already been scheming up a delicious plot of my own.

"I had never before been inside a Gharnian warship (and I hope that I never will again). They are not what I imagined them to be at all. They are very clean, pristinely so, and dark. The Gharnians favor black and red, but much inside was polished silver. Everything is organized and precise: the controls, the décor, the soldier's quarters, the layout and design of the pathways and catwalks, and the prison. This proved to be their detriment and their ultimate downfall, for the layout of the ship was so predictable that I felt as though I knew my way around almost immediately.

"To my dismay, they stripped me nude, took the charts and maps I had recovered from the Tigre, and then they snapped my cane in two. I do not believe that they knew I was a wyzard, because they took very few precautions. I was thrown headlong into a holding cell. Thankfully, I had removed the crystal from the head of my cane beforehand, and had hidden it by sleight of hand while they searched me. That crystal was just enough to soften the tumblers in the lock of my cell so that I could force the heavy door open after all had departed.

"I moved fast, not knowing how much time I had before they discovered my escape. I wasn't sure from moment to moment what was going to happen. I climbed, crawled, and jumped. I slithered where I could, and still naked, ran across a brightly lit tarmac. Eventually, I found where the engineers kept their uniforms, although the one I chose, the smallest that there was, was still too large for me. I then moved throughout the ship for awhile disguised as one of them, hiding from soldiers when I needed to, investigating the components, and always searching for a door or an escape route. There was enough ammunition on board to blow the warship sky high, so I wired a detonator and hid it near the turbines where it wouldn't be found. I set a small box of explosives near the expander motor. As soon as the turbines went, I knew a chain of reactions would ensue, and the ship would soon follow.

"I then rigged a second detonator and hid it in the bottom of a satchel. I used the ship's comm to call the other ship to have someone come pick it up. I told them that it was some highly classified paperwork from the wrecked Tigre that had been found on a deceased gogmoor, and that General Shandhark had suggested that they have a look at it as well. This intrigued them and they were fooled. They said they were sending a troop of gogmoors to escort me from my ship to their ship, and that they would rendezvous with me in the other's loading foyer in ten minutes. This barely gave me enough time to find the exit ramp before my anxious escorts arrived.

"The gogmoors were suspicious of me right from the outset, sniffing at me with their keen noses. After all, I was the smallest Gharnian they had ever seen and my clothes were comically oversized. I handed the sealed satchel with the detonator to the foremost gogmoor and ordered them to follow me. "Keep an eye out!" I barked at them in their own tongue (using a Gharnian accent as best I could). That's some mean feat when you're as nervous as I was! "Hurry on, now! No dawdling! Keep up! There's a good lad!" and such. We were marching down the ramp and across the bustling courtyard, beneath the very noses of the preoccupied Gharnians, just as the alarms went off everywhere. My escape had been discovered!"

He paused for a moment, extending his empty flask toward Drer to have it refilled. "Another, kind sir. This oration has me parched!"

"How is it that you were able to use the Gharnian comm to signal the other ship?" Binder asked. "Surely the comms are coded, and the military dialogue is not known to any other than the Gharnians..."

"Excellent question, young Commander," Dedlin said. "I took a great risk, jeopardizing my own safety, to attempt this, but I felt as though I had nothing to lose. Fortunately, in my recent studies, (even during the very night of our Secret Council in Tungulin), I had been analyzing a stolen daksas manuscript containing Gharnian field tactics and communications, although it was still very antiquated. I memorized the very basics: how to use the equipment, how to signal, transmit, and receive messages, how to mimic an officer, you know, just enough to get by. My intentions, at that time, were to learn as much as I could about their field codes and comm dialogue, in case we intercepted random transmissions at our stations in Tungulin. I had no idea that I would ever put that knowledge to such practical use! And so soon!"

"Amazing!" Day replied.

"The wyzard's luck is the most amazing," Binder was

inclined to agree. "Please continue, sir."

"'You smell of humans', the lead gogmoor said to me as we crossed the loading dock toward the other ship. There was utter chaos everywhere, what with the destruction of so many of their fightercraft. 'You are the smallest Gharnian I have ever seen,' he said in his guttural tongue. 'Why do you wear a blaster helmet to cover your face, when there is no blaster fire here in the city?' His suspicions were getting the better of him, and I feared that I would not be able to get much further before they discovered me. I was so exhausted!

"Too many questions!" I snapped at him. "Mind your duties! I have much to discuss with very important people!" and so on and so forth.

"Once onboard the Mount of Steel, I took the detonator back from them, and left the confused gogmoor soldiers behind at the service door. I do believe that it was at that moment that I was the closest to getting caught. When I left that boorish gogmoor brute standing there with his finger in his ear, he knew that I was no Gharnian soldier.

"Behind me, the real Gharnians began boarding the ship in waves to prepare for departure from Bondoon. I slid into the shadows and crept down a ventilation shaft to find the engine room of that great ship.

"After sabotaging the Mount of Steel in the same way that I had sabotaged the Godstrike V, I tried to go quickly back the way I had come, but I could not. The only way out was past an inspection station that had filled with a garrison of rowdy Gharnian soldiers coming back onboard, alert and snappy, and they would not be as easily fooled as the dimwitted gogmoors had been. I was then trapped inside. And I knew that I did not have much time before the explosions began. I had no choice then but to hide and wait, and to look for some other opportunity to escape. I found a service stairwell leading to the lowest decks, and crept into the belly of the warship to explore."

At this time, Dedlin stopped his oration again momentarily to savor a drink of ale and a puff on his pipe. "Talking makes me thirsty," he reiterated. "Another refill if you would, my dear friend."

The suns went behind a deep cloud, covering them in summer shadow. To the northeast, great monolithic stones stood starkly from the horizon like crooked spires and towers. The sunslight upon them glowed a brazen summer gold. The crewmembers had been enraptured by Dedlin's every word, and were waiting anxiously for him to continue on. He was about to do just that, but something out on the horizon beyond the next chunk of hills caught his attention.

He squinted. "So, then, I waited there... Hold on one moment," he said, eyes widening. He rose to his toes, peering out at the horizon. "What is that? Is that what I think it is?"

To the south of them, there were tiny wisps of white clouds rising from the trees on one hillside. Not a misty wet cloud, like dew or fog, but a dry fluffy cloud, comprised of millions of fuzzy white specks.

"It is! My story can wait a moment, for we have a rare opportunity here, I believe."

"W-what is it?" Qan asked nervously.

"Drop the fishnets," Drer suggested. "We'll pull some on board and have us a treat while Dedlin finishes his fine oration."

"What is it?" Qan repeated.

"Candytrees," Drer answered.

"Must be a grove down in these woods," Gaebryl answered. "I see a few clouds floating up in the wind."

"The seedpods open and release the seedflux every year around this time. They float skyward in the wind and travel miles before falling. Very tasty, too."

"Head right for it, Perce, my friend," the wyzard said. "What an unexpected treat."

"My pleasure," the mahekian said, pulling the guidestick slightly to the right.

"The fuzz is tangy and sweet. It melts right on your tongue," Drer told them. "And at the heart there's a tasty little brown nut..."

Drer had joined Perce at the helm. "Here's what I was looking for," he replied, pressing a button. Just before Stardeer plunged through the fluffy cloud, two oval fishnets protruded from the hull beneath Stardeer. For a few seconds, the crew was enveloped by the swarm, but, in a flash, they emerged from the seed cloud again, the fishnets, filled with hundreds of fist sized balls of candytree cotton retracted quickly back into the holding tanks of the hull automatically.

"Whoo hoo!" they called.

Dedlin laughed long and hard. It was a merry sound.

"I'll go get our treats!" Drer Fregoode piped, dashing eagerly down into the hold. "Go ahead, Dedlin! Don't wait for me!"

"Very well, Fregoode," the wyzard replied. "But you're not tricking anyone! We know you want the best candy for yourself! Just don't eat too much of it or you'll get sick!"

"Another round of ales," Lake Tobias said, bringing up a jug to pour.

"Where was I? Oh, yes! In the belly of the beast!" Dedlin said, finally continuing. "I waited long in the lowest level of the ship, down where the Gharnians store their food supplies," he said. "It was cold and dark. My body was aching and I had suffered some minor injuries that night, so I probably needed a spot of rest before going on, anyway. However, at my ripening old age, sleep can sometimes be a powerful enemy as well. Before I knew it, I was hard asleep.

"When I awoke, the ship was moving. My heart leaped, because I knew it was going to blow and I wasn't sure how long I had been asleep there. There were no windows at that level, so I had no idea where we had flown to, and for how long. I only knew that I had to get off that ship immediately before I perished there.

"Just then, the door opened, and an old, pudgy glaaki cook came down the stairs. He hit a switch and the lights came on. I was instantly discovered. He asked me who I was and what I was doing, so I told him, and I told him what I had done. I had a blaster pointed at him, so he was a very attentive listener. I told him that if he didn't help me get off that ship right away that we were both going to die there. He made me promise that I would take him with me if he showed me a way out, and I agreed to save the poor sod. He was barely more than a slave anyway, and claimed that he would be forever grateful if I could free him from the Gharnians' brutal control. How could I resist such a request?

"Simply enough, there was a garbage chute in the next room and it opened by the pull of a lever. We found, by peering through, that the ship was just then standing nearly still above a forest, and that it was now daylight outside. I wondered why the bombs had not yet gone off, and prayed that they had not somehow been discovered. The trees below us were very close, but still, too far to jump to. We tried hard to come up with some kind of plan, but there were no sleds, ropes or cables.

"Just then, an explosion went off that knocked us to the floor. I could hear the gases blowing from the turbines; it was so loud that I thought my ears would burst. Then there were more explosions from above, and the warship turned up onto its side. Everything began sliding across the floor. The cook and I were nearly buried alive by overturned trays of frozen meats and fish. Then I heard the other ship explode and I knew at once that the detonators had done their job. I think I yelped with successful joy. Those great warships are virtually indestructible by an outside attack, but, thankfully, I had discovered that they are certainly susceptible to sabotage from within.

"The cook and I crawled back to the garbage chute, watching the trees draw closer as the ship fell, spinning toward them. Our only hope was to jump at precisely the right moment to catch the branches and hold on with all our might. If we waited too long, we knew that the great ship could fall right on top of us and crush us.

"We took our chances and leaped, tumbling down and out of the chute, reaching for the nearest pine tree. Both of us hit a tree and desperately seized the sharp branches. Our combined weight pulled the treetop over so much that we heard wood splintering.

"The warship came spinning down toward us, pressing against the tops of the trees. The very same fin that I had clung to on the other ship the night before hit me on the head as it passed. I was dazed, but somehow I hung on. The Mount of Steel veered off and crashed a hundred yards away in a swirling dervish of gases and flame, and beyond that, the Godstrike V suffered a similar fate. The pair of ships were destroyed.

"After a time, the cook and I managed to climb down and we headed back to Tungulin with the aid of an overgrown hog and a saddle, but that story is long and embarrassing, and has no real bearing on the outcome of this particular tale. When I reached the king's chambers that afternoon, you had already left, and I was glad. Things were not safe for King Day in Tungulin anymore. Traitors, spies and Gharnian sympathizers were being rousted by the dozens.

"I told Vantoo my story, and he told me his. He had seen the warships go down, and told me of his encounter with the traitor Sabre Jonhousan. I was disheartened from his words, and weary from the night's tiresome exploits. I longed to leave immediately while your trail was still warm, but Vantoo ordered me to rest while he made preparations for my departure. So, with bottle in hand, I retired to my quarters beneath the music chambers and slept the night through."

"My, what adventures you had!" Gaebryl said. "I'll have a flagon of ale myself, to cheer this wyzard among wyzards."

"As will I!" consented Drer Fregoode. "And some more candy!"

"I'll have some of that," Day said, seizing a handful of white fluff from Drer's bowl.

"Let me pour," Commander Binder said. "I insist!

If nothing else, wyzard, you can still tell a marvelous story!"

"And yet! It does not end there!" Dedlin told them. "The most ironic may yet still be to come!"

"What about the charts and maps you recovered from the Tigre?" Day wanted to know. "What news of Mead? Were there any messages for me?"

"There were none. I read what I could while I had them, and learned much about the pilot of the doomed craft, but, alas, the Gharnians took from me all the scraps I had, save this crystal, which I have now remounted on a new and improved walking stick," Dedlin answered, displaying his fine new instrument. "However, that loss pales in comparison to what has been gained, the next tidbit of wonderful news that I present to you now. You see, *one* substantial thing *was* saved from the wreck of the Tigre. The pilot, himself! He not only survived the crash, but he spoke with King Vantoo in great lengths the very night before your departure. In fact, they became very close, and King Vantoo insisted that the pilot of the Tigre should join this very expeditionary party. Which he did, gladly!"

"I am he," Otthagorus admitted. "The Tigre was my craft."

"Ott!" Binder piped, nearly spilling his drink.

The thordian came forward to give his part of the tale. "I flew solo from the great fortresses of Isle Mead, not with a message for King Day, as you all once suspected, but with information for King Vantoo: lists of spies who had infiltrated Mead, Tungulin, Poed, Cissel, and Dindiane. The maps and charts I left behind (and that Dedlin found) were little more than utilitarian and would have served little purpose. I was attempting to reach Tungulin before King Day did, to give Commander Binder lists of spies and assassins that I had long since memorized before my overseas departure. That is how we were able to thwart the assassination attempt on King Vantoo's life! I had arrived with that information only just in time!

"It was a harrowing flight from the onset. Once I had arrived on the mainland, the Gharnian sentries were at once on my trail. They tracked me for a week, but gave full chase as I neared Tungulin. The Mount of Steel and the Godstrike V appeared as I crossed the last few miles of Gaaloth. Once they surmised my destination, they signaled me to stop, and tried to force me to the ground. When I would not, they opened fire upon me. I survived the crash mostly unscathed, and went forward from there on foot to Tungulin at full haste, to make my case. I had been deprived of sleep for many days, and I was hungry and weary. Forgive me for my clandestine manner and standoffish demeanor, but I hope you now understand. I could not let that information fall into the wrong hands. I have long been a stalwart patriot in the service of the family of Day my entire life, and could not accept failure."

"A fellow Meadian," Day said, delighted. "We have much to discuss."

"Yes, Your Highness," Ott said, winking. "I have served as one of your Secret Guards in Mead since I was a cub. My order works in secrecy, as you know, and am adept in keeping my own secrets as well. Your Highness thought that he might have recognized me before, and perhaps he had, for I, with my brethren, have been close by your side in one way or another for many events for many years, holding that oath and position by vow of honor and the threat of death. Until I could be certain every person on this craft could be trusted, I thought it best to shield my identity.

"I insisted that King Vantoo order this departure immediately. With the list of spies in hand, Vantoo's own safety was at great further risk. His plate was full with the assassination attempt, the gogmoor invasion, Jonhousan's deceit, and until Dedlin Dane perchance returned, there was nothing else he could do for you there."

Gaebryl and Day shared a glance. What a remarkable revelation!

Dedlin continued his part of the story. "My turn!", he started. "After I awoke the next morning, I was so relieved to hear about Ott's involvement and presence on this quest, and that Drer and Binder had also joined in, and that Perce, the king's very own masterpilot was along as well, manning the helm, that I went back to my room and slept the rest of the day and night through. The gogmoors were attacking on several fronts, but Huite had matters well in hand. I needed to reload, recover, and to think.

"There were some things to do in Tungulin before I left. I found the freed cook a job for one thing, and I hope he enjoys his newfound citizenship. He made me a wonderful grilled fish dinner and chocolate soufflé before I left! Also, there was much ado surrounding the news of the death of the assassin Tursdah the Brute. There appeared to have been several rewards for his insidious hide, from all around the kingdom, so I let the authorities know that Prince Gaebryl Dindiane had insisted that his share of the reward money go to the farmer Feren Den and his good family..."

"Why not?" Gaebryl replied with a smile. "He pulled me up from a long fall."

The wyzard continued. "Vantoo had received information that a Gharnian air fleet was crossing Galgariah, right in your flight path, and he bid me haste my own departure to intercept you before you crossed paths with them. I persuaded Lake and Qan to join me, and I left hours before dawn that next day.

"I searched far and wide, questioning townsfolk and travelers I passed. When I found Perce's Sunshaft I feared the worst, but hoped for the best. I knew you'd have to follow the old east road on foot, so I came hard and fast after you. I found one of your camps, and the coals beneath the earth were still warm. There were rumors of Gharnian scoutships in the area, so I was fearful.

"By the time I reached Aerogreen, you were toying with the woodelfs. I tried to make my presence known then, except that I spotted the Gharnian soldiers disembarking from their ship in numbers. I couldn't risk exposing myself to them just yet."

"I saw you," Day added. "I tried to stop..."

"It was good you dove into Aerogreen right then and

there! They were heavily armed and coming to capture you to take you hostage before you could disappear into that valley. Aerogreen is a true marvel of the world," Dedlin said. "But I wasn't sure what effect it would have on you all. I used to play in the moths as a boy, mostly on the outskirts, and later, as a young wyzard's apprentice, I would cross Aerogreen with other novice wyzards, just to entertain myself. I am nearly immune to their influence now, and I know a spell or two to make them disperse temporarily (although smoke works wonders, too; they loathe it). Therefore, I am very much at ease in Aerogreen.

"I hid Stardeer on the opposite side and found my way into the swarm on foot, praying that I was not too late. I ran down a different path than the one you used to cross the valley, a shortcut that I knew thast would get me further downstream, ahead of you. I knew that, with the storms of the last few days, Aerogreen's waters would be flood swollen, and that you would never make it across without some kind of trouble. When I reached the last bridge, I heard splashing coming my way. I went to the bank just in time to pull Commander Binder and Sir Otthagorus to safety at the side. A moment later, King Day and Prince Gaebryl came floating by, and they, too, were rescued there."

"There's a bridge in Aerogreen?" Drer asked.

"There are four. As I said, I found our doomed swimmers as they passed the last one, right at the head of the Falls of the Sky," Dedlin said. "Just inches before they went over the side."

Shivers rode up Gaebryl's spine. He quivered.

"As soon as I was sure that no one else was floating past, I located Drer and Perce, wandering foolishly about. I believe you know the rest of the story."

They each took turns thanking the wyzard, and drinking to his health and prosperity. Dedlin drank one more flask himself, looking at the suns, sailing high in the cobalt sky. "The morning has turned into afternoon and this drink is going to my head. I'm ready for a spot of lunch, if no one else is," he said. "Then we'll get down to the important matters closer at hand."

With Lake and Qan's assistance, Drer Fregoode brought out trays laden with cheese, bread and butter, leftover ham and eggs from that morning's breakfast, fried mushrooms and two fat ghurro hens that had been marinating in a tart lemon garlic sauce overnight, served with wild rice and onions. There was no time for baking potatoes, but there were fresh fruits for whoever wanted them: apples, strawberries, brownberries, and miniature coreless pears. The candytree seeds made a wonderful dessert. Everyone was full, even Otthagorus, whose belly, it seemed had no bottom to it sometimes when there was meat.

The great monolithic stones had passed into the distance, and now there were rolling fields and gently sloping hills on all sides of them. An occasional singular tree appeared now and again with wide, outspread branches, usually one every two or three miles or so. It was a lonely land, but wholesome and welcoming.

They ate and drank together, marveling at both Dedlin's and Ott's remarkable stories over and over again. They were asked to repeat parts of it, or explain things further, which the wyzard and the thordian were both more than willing to oblige. Dedlin was apparently delighted at his own exploits, too, praising his luck often. Ott found his place as a guest of honor among the crew there that evening, and experienced more backslapping than he cared for. He was a humble servant, and seemed a bit uncomfortable with the newfound respect, praise, and admiration he was being shown.

When the plates were empty and the flasks not more than half full, Dedlin placed his eyeglasses on the hook of his elongated nose, appearing crosseyed as he lit up his pipe once more. "And now, down to it, my good friends. What only a few here know in full, we will now share with the rest," he said. "Gather 'round and hear me well so that you may decide your path, for there is still time to turn aside, if you should choose to. The way ahead will not be easy, and is fraught with perils unknown, greater than any you have experienced thus far. I will give our enemy His name, and reveal what it is that young King Day now seeks. You will understand why he has sought our help and assistance. Then, choose to remain, or to be on your way at our next stopping. No ill thoughts will befall you from those who choose to go on, should you decide to stand down, for no greater task has ever been asked of good men. Do we all understand?"

All nodded to him. He cleared his throat and began.

"This is it, then," he said. "In essence, gentlemen. We are in, with no simpler word for it, a race," the wyzard told them. "An absolute crucial race that affects the fate of all who live on the Kingdom Continent. Presently, we are ahead of the enemy at this early stage, but not by much. We will soon pass from Galgariah into Tuus, and from there to Commander Binder's own homeland, Gorn. Somewhere in a desolate region of Gorn our destiny awaits us. That is our final destination, if we can make it. I say *somewhere* in Gorn, because currently, the exact finish line of this race, in its final detail, is still a bit unknown. It is a very secretive, sacred place, a cave in a mystical wood, surrounded by old magick and cribs of forever blooming jasmine nightflowers, but its precise location is known to no living being now, including myself. Unless the great sorcerer Oziah Aabx, who I've not seen or heard from in years, still knows. I have found no maps or books that describe the location of this sacred cave, if any ever existed. I only have a vague idea, and that is the best we can hope for. But, once we get close enough, things will run by themselves if my theories are correct.

"In the meantime, our adversaries in this race pursue us in increasing numbers. Gharnians and assassins, and some creatures more foul than I now wish to tell you. You'll know too soon. They will stop at nothing. They will follow or apprehend us if they must, because they, too, do not know where this finish line is. Fortunately for us, they believe that we do know, and that may ensure a degree of temporary reprieve. They cannot kill us. Yet. Because they need us to show them the way.

"They seek this sacred place tirelessly now, pressing all their thought and might to find it. Why do they do this? They are led to do so by an enemy we must now speak of. An enemy of old who has returned to this land. An enemy dark and powerful, whose ancient powers are returning to Him after eons of neglect and complacency. It is He who now drives our adversaries like a cruel whip. If you have never heard the name of Gheelgahar before, then hear it now, for Gheelgahar has returned to the fortresses of Gharne and is the might, the inspiration, and the force behind the ambitious Gharnian army, and many other dark, foul creatures now traveling abroad. We are reliving the tales of old, my friends. We are swept up in them now. Whether you believe the tales of old or not is unimportant, because, obviously, Gheelgahar and the Gharnians do. Otherwise they would not be putting all of their efforts into keeping this one small boy from reaching the destination of his ancestors before they do. He wants what we want from that sacred cave. A magickal Stone. Gaebryl, the key, if you will."

Gaebryl reached into his shirt and revealed the stone key.

"Many of you have heard of the legendary Stones of Power. The ancient stories tell of how the original Lord of this Kingdom Continent, the first Day of Mead, released one or more of His great powers into the safekeeping of these mystical Stones and hid them throughout this vast kingdom when he decided to choose human mortality. This key, and a few sacred words that I have yet to reveal, unlocks one of these Stones, about the size of an apricot I'm led to understand, from its hold within this extraordinary Gornian cave.

"There are some, on both sides of this conflict, who believe that by rejoining King Day to this Stone, that one or more of the five great powers in the universe: creation, love, life, time, or utter destruction, will become his to command. Gheelgahar fears no army, but He fears the same fate that sent Him into exile in the beginning of our age. He fears that Day will reach this Stone first, and will acquire a power equal to or greater than His own, and He cannot allow this to happen. Again. He will try to stop us by all means at His command. His will follow us to this cave to destroy the Stone, or to try to take it for His own, and then He will kill the young king and all who aided him. Then, His rise will go henceforth unchecked."

There was a moment of contemplative silence.

"Questions?"

"What do we do after we reach this cave and acquire this Stone?" Drer asked. "What then?"

"Only the future knows," Dedlin answered. "I personally believe that there are four other Stones besides this one, one for each of the great powers. When we obtain the first one, we will reassess our mission then. I am hoping an answer will present itself, for better or worse, as it often does. Right now, we have a race to win, and a prize to seize."

Day then spoke up. "I knew of this sorcerer Oziah Aabx that Dedlin speaks of. I knew him well. He was the greatest counselor to my father in Mead, and his years with my family went further back than anyone alive could guess, nearly to the beginning of the age, many said.

"As you know, my family's reign had enjoyed many generations of peace and prosperity, the kingdom over. Then, some years before I was born, my father began growing concerned about what he sensed as a 'shifting' in the kingdom tides, and was often in counsel with his staff and the great sorceror discussing these intuitions and adjacent matters. As a symbolic gift to me on my seventh birthday, Oziah Aabx entrusted my parents with this key, and told them that he may someday return, if need be, to recover it. But for the time being, he said the key was not safe in his possession while he traveled abroad. And off he went to a place called Benminer's Village. After the passing of my parents, Oziah's visits became less and less frequent, and then one day stopped altogether. He was not heard from since.

"We watched as subversive events unfolded across the continent, with no word or sign from him, and still we yearned for his return. Over two harrowing years, without his guidance and wisdom, my counselors and I began many meetings concerning the quest for the Stone. We could not decide if we were acting too late, or if I was leaving Mead prematurely. We desperately needed the counsel of Oziah Aabx the Great, but there was none to be had.

"Spies began to appear, and the rumors of assassins. Our scouts reported seeing Gharnians leaving their southern gates in multitudes and building walls and fortresses along the seas to the west and the mountain rims in the south. Good men were being seduced with false promises and lies and were marching southward to join the armies there. One evening, during

Midsummer's Eve Festival, word reached us that they were making preparations to come across the seas to Mead. They had begun their search for me in earnest, and for the family's Stones of Power.

"I can tell you that my father was right. The tides have certainly turned and we are set on a irrevocable course. There is no more stalling. I am moving forward, with anyone who will come along, or by myself.

"This is our only chance, and it is terrifying. Gheelgahar is a primal god and an all powerful enemy. I am not. I'm just me. I must retake the Stone of my forefathers and all the power and responsibility that it bears if we are to stand up to this oncoming onslaught. Otherwise, we can fight and toil, and crumble and die. Our way of life as we know it will cease to exist.

"And I believe that what Dedlin says is right. I have never said this before, never told a living soul, but I believe what he said about things moving on their own course... I can honestly say that I feel the Stone drawing closer. I can hear it in the ghost of my soul. With each passing day, its signal becomes stronger. It knows that I am coming for it. It awaits our reunion. It calls me."

"And until that reunion, no Gharnian shall ever lay a hand upon you," Otthagorus said grimly. "To that cause I pledge my life."

"As do I," Gaebryl said. "No Gharnian or any other fell man or beast."

"I pledge the same," Drer Fregoode said.

"As do I," said Commander Binder, then Perce.

Dedlin puffed. "Lake? Qan? You are both part of this crew now. What say you?"

They looked at one another, then back to the wyzard. "We're in," they said.

"Then we are one," Dedlin decreed. "And we are making

history together."

"To the Stone of Power!" Drer cheered, holding his flagon aloft. "And to the Stonebearer, King Day of Mead!"

They toasted.

"To the wyzard!" Gaebryl said. "May his stories never cease to amaze!"

"And to the illustrious crew of Stardeer, with whom the Stonebearer gladly entrusts his life," Day gratefully acknowledged. "We shall not fail!"

"I, for one, am enlightened, delighted and impressed with each of you," Perce said. "And now the story is told in full. It is good to know you all, and even better that no secrets may build any walls between us anymore on this most noble and gallant journey!"

Day looked up to see Dedlin's kind eyes watching him.

Otthagorus, too, knew his secret and had said nothing of it so far. The thordian nodded knowingly at him, and winked supportively.

Perhaps the time had come for him to shed his skin, he thought, at this time of honesty and forthright declarations. No more secrets. The thought of that sounded liberating. "I have one last thing I would like to say," he began, a rosy flush rising from his neck to his cheeks.

Dedlin nodded supportively.

"For the sake of complete honesty. Especially since everyone is opening up so..."

The crew looked toward him, but it was directly to Gaebryl that Day intended to direct his message.

"I...I am not..."

"Excuse me!" Qan suddenly blurted out witlessly,

uncomfortable about interrupting, but unable to keep silent. "But, um, there's something out there that I think someone ought to see! Please! Hurry!"

Nine

TUUS

41

"Masterpilot Perce!" Dedlin cried, turning quickly toward the locked cases where he kept his larger rail mounted weapons. "Take this ship down lower! There is a lot of movement off the starboard bow!" He unlocked two brass latches with the flick of his thumbs, opened the case, and heaved out a large blastrifle. "Let's hold up here until we can see what is going on out there!"

Perce quickly obeyed Dedlin's command. Stardeer was close enough to the ground to send ripples across the tall grass like a boat on water. Perce drew Stardeer abruptly around to a halt. The fightercraft rocked gently backward and forward, turbines hissing.

"There it is," Qan said, pointing. "Do you see it?"

A two legged figure could be seen racing over the grassy knobs about a mile away from them, sometimes disappearing from view in shallow valleys, then reappearing again on each rise. It turned from a near parallel course with Stardeer, heading directly into the path of an oncoming plains storm.

"That's suicide," Drer exclaimed.

Gaebryl brought a pair of scans to his eyes and flipped the night lenses to the side. The next time the figure came into view on a rise, Gaebryl focused. "As I thought," he said. "It's that same uusyrapi rider we saw the other night."

"He's not going to beat the storm going that way," Drer said.

"He's not trying to beat the storm, Drer Fregoode," Dedlin said, securing the blastrifle to a mounted revolving hinge near the helm. "He's escaping *into* it. Perce, be a good fellow and back us up into the shadows of that bluff. The rocks might hide us better there. What I wouldn't give for a cloaking shield right about now."

"Dedlin's right," Ott said. "There are three Gharnian scoutships closing in on the rider from all sides. For whatever reason, they're in pursuit. They're firing upon the rider, and he's returning fire."

Gaebryl found them in the scans. "Could be the same ones that were tailing us... But I don't see any fighters." He searched the peripheral horizons for other Gharnian ships.

"Have they seen us?" Binder asked, bringing a pair of scans to his eyes.

"I don't know. I don't think so."

"I hope not. There's not a decent place to hide for miles," the Commander said. "We're sitting ducks out here."

Dedlin squinted. "Plenty of places to hide," he said. "If we need to."

They watched the ships bank and close in on the uusyrapi rider as he faded over the last misty hill into torrential distant rain. It appeared as if the Gharnians were firing upon the rider in a succession of exploding volleys, just as they passed the line of the horizon, but they could not be certain; it might have been the lightning, instead. A few seconds later and they were all gone from sight. "We can relax," Binder reported. "I think they missed us."

"Wrong," Gaebryl blurted from the other side of the deck. "Look behind us! There are more of them, and they're heading this way!"

"We've been spotted," Ott responded. "Arm yourselves!"

"Get us out of here, Masterpilot Perce," Dedlin said, fastening the mount on a second blastgun. "Everyone! Prepare to move! Prepare to fight!"

Perce pressed the accelerator bar to full throttle. The noise of the turbines rose to a high pitch as Stardeer's nose rose skyward. The ship leaped like a rocket from the vale, accelerating into the sky at an incredible rate.

42

"How many?" Dedlin asked, coming to the aft rail.

"I count nine," Gaebryl answered.

"Nine," Binder confirmed, seizing a blastrifle. "Mostly fighters. This could be part of that fleet we had missed earlier."

"I didn't lose them last night to be found by them again today!" Dedlin snapped.

"That's not the worst of it," Ott said suddenly. "Look to the east!"

"Warship at nine o'clock!" Binder cried.

From the east it came, a flying city fortress of silver, black, and red, arcing in a calculated sweep of the sky to try to cut them off. It was incredibly malevolent looking.

"We can't fight that!" Binder cried.

"Faster!" Dedlin shouted above the wind. "Follow the uusyrapi! Head directly into that storm!"

Three of the nine ships separated from the rest and advanced toward Stardeer. Two others veered off toward the uusyrapi rider. Perce scanned the oncoming storm, keeping Stardeer just feet above the ground. The wall of rain from the purple storm clouds directly before them resembled a ferocious, live, pulsating entity of some sort, a solid, wavering mass. Nets of lightning ripped through the sky. Thunder reverberated through air, through earth, ship, and bone. Tuus' homicidal storms, like this one, often rolled across the flatlands for miles and miles, building into nightmarishly destructive maelstroms that were reputed to be able to rip flesh from bone.

A cool front passed over them, whipping at Stardeer's flimsy interior dewtarp; the temperature dropped nearly twenty degrees almost instantly. The wind lashed from one direction then another as alternating cool and warm fronts taunted the delicate atmosphere. A few miles south, they saw twin twisters raging destruction in the fields, as if dancing with one another.

"Visitor approaching port side!" Ott cried out above the wind.

One of the Gharnian fighterships drew within thirty yards of them. Suddenly, it fired a warning missile, startling the crew. It exploded two shiplengths ahead of Stardeer, causing dirt and shrubbery to rain down upon their heads.

"Get the young king below!" Dedlin called. "Binder, you're in charge!"

The commander quickly assessed the situation and took decisive control. "Drer, get King Day below and take care of him there. Lake and Qan, below! Otthagorus and Gaebryl, defend this ship with me, and fire to destroy. Dedlin, you are free to use your own means, but I suggest you remain close to Perce at the helm in case we have mishaps there. Try and get us out of this!"

The uusyrapi rider had been engulfed by the storm and could not be seen now, followed by the scoutships and two fightercrafts. There were now two fighters coming up on the left of Stardeer, and three on the right, with the great warship closing in aggressively from behind.

Another missile exploded in front of Stardeer. This one was close enough to send a shockwave throughout the frame of the ship. The nose bounced a bit from the impact, but Perce was able to level her off and maintain his course and speed. One of the fighters closed in in front of them, slowing to block their way. Perce steered masterfully around it without pause.

"They're going to try to drive us to the ground before we can reach the cover of the storm," Dedlin said. "They may try and clip us."

"But we have an advantage," Gaebryl said, aiming one of the mounted blastguns. "Their orders are to bring us in *alive*." He fired the huge gun. The side of the nearest Gharnian vessel exploded into a cloud of fire and spirals of smoke. The heat from the explosion washed past them. Tiny shrapnel noisily littered the Stardeer's flank like nails against a steel drum. The fightership arced to the side and crashed, rolling and bouncing in a ball of fire until it laid to rest, upside down in the windswept flowers and reeds below.

Binder fired. Again, a hit, and another Gharnian ship was disabled, and fell off and behind.

"Banking to port!" Perce warned. Two ships were squeezing in, directly ahead of them.

"Hold on!" Dedlin called to those below. Stardeer rose and arced gracefully to the portside, rising up and over the Gharnians. They passed swiftly beneath, and then, immediately, they banked in opposite directions to circle back.

Perce took Stardeer up at a dangerously steep incline, keeping her at full throttle, then shifted, heading back toward the mountainous and tumultuous purple/black storm clouds. Raindrops the size of olives began spotting the deck with loud, hammering splats. Perce, who had just closed the back wall of the helmsman's cabin with his free hand, quickly fastened the hardcover rainshield roof over the pilot's chair. A burst of marble sized hail drummed on them, and then it stopped.

The warship was now below them and to their left, less than fifty yards away. A strange hollow "tube" sound could be heard, and Binder cried out, "Get down!" Everyone dropped to the deck, even Perce, holding onto the guidestick above him with one hand. "Cover your ears!" the Commander warned.

A red cylindrical canister reached its arc height a few feet away from the helm at midship, and it exploded in the air with a heavy thrum. It was a pressure stunner. Dedlin, who was the closest to the blast, fell to the ground, unconscious.

"Masterpilot Perce!" Gaebryl cried out, unable to hear his own voice because of the ringing in his ears. "Dedlin is down! How are you?"

Binder fired another shot at the closest fightership, missing. But, Ott connected, instantly vaporizing the closest Gharnian fightercraft into a rainbow of fiery colors. He had hit the fuel tank.

"They are as mad as hornets now," Binder said. "They could blow us out of the sky with ease if they wanted to. We've got to get out of here!"

"What?" Ott cried. "Did you call for me?" His hearing was also temporarily impaired.

"Perce!" Gaebryl cried again. It was an incredible effort just to speak; the pressure stunner had knocked his breath from him, and he was struggling to get it back. "Report!"

"I need help," the mahekian answered finally, his telepathic voice hazy and faint. "Take the helm, someone. I need help."

"I've got it," Gaebryl shouted, running low across the deck. "Dedlin! Can you hear me? Are you all right? Dedlin, answer me!"

A missile flew by them, dangerously close.

"They're trying to clip us now," Binder called. "They'd rather take their chances and hit us rather than to lose us completely in the storm."

The sky ahead was as dark as night. Long, crooked bolts of lightning ripped through the sky, burrowing into a distant hill. The dark hills turned white with each vivid electrical display. The smell of burnt sulfur filled the air. The first wave of hard rain poured down on Stardeer in drenching gushes like added weight, saturating everything instantly.

"Get below," Gaebryl ordered Perce. "Take the wyzard, if you can. I've got Stardeer. Here comes the storm! Hold on!"

Rain blew in so hard that all visibility was instantly gone. Hail pounded in ferocious spurts like meteors, denting the plasteel hull and tearing holes in the thick canvas tarps. Binder and Ott joined Gaebryl at the helm, both soaked to the bone, but with the fire of battle flaring boldly in their eyes. They looked out through the wide rear window; the sunslit, frosted green hills of Tuus were soon obscured and then lost from view behind them. Gaebryl kept a dangerously fast pace, flying blindly just a few feet above the whipping grasses, but eventually he was forced to slow down to compensate for his lack of vision and the increasing turbulence. The wind was incredibly loud. It wailed and shrieked and roared, tossing them first in one direction, then another. The rain fell hard enough to press the ship almost to the ground.

"I can hardly breathe!" Ott exclaimed. "Are we underwater?"

A Gharnian ship cruised slowly past, just a few feet above them. Binder stretched his arm up and touched the rear dorsal fin as it crept blindly past. Fortunately, their scanners would be as useless in this storm as they were aboard Stardeer. Gaebryl turned his ship directly south and crept away at the same snail's pace they had used the night before in the jungle forests.

"The warship won't come in after us," Binder supposed. "They'll circle the storm and wait for us on the other side, with reinforcements."

Perce had not yet gone below. He sat with his head in his hands near Gaebryl's feet. Dedlin, on the ground beside him, began to stir, shaking his head as though clearing stifling webs from his mind. He looked around, empty eyed. A leak in the roof poured a trail of rainwater on his head and face, but he didn't seem to notice or mind. Part of the roof suddenly blew back from the wind, dousing all of them anew with cold rainwater. Ott and Binder seized it and began reattaching it more securely.

"I think we're safe for the time being," Gaebryl said. "The Gharnians are as lost in this storm as we are. Everyone okay? Advise me on any injuries."

Drer poked his head up from below. "I've turned on the internal cabin pump. We've got a lot of water coming in. We're flooded down here."

"I'll be all right," Perce advised, nodding. "I just need a few minutes."

Suddenly the wind scooped under the ship like a giant hand, pushing Stardeer nearly onto her side. Gaebryl fought to keep her steady and right side up. "By the gods!" he swore.

"Let's hope this storm doesn't prove worse than the Gharnians," Dedlin said, grunting with every movement. He tried to stand, but he was unable. He lay back, resting beneath the console. "What was it? A pressure stunner? It feels as though my insides have been knocked out of me. And, oh, my aching head!"

The ship moaned and whistled in the wind.

Drer came up onto the deck, squeezing in with the rest. "Everyone's fine below," he reported. "We're battened down pretty good. King Day is secured in his favorite hammock chair. Let me help secure this area and get the weapons out of this rain before they're ruined. We don't want them malfunctioning when we need them next. Where are the Gharnians? Can you see them? Can you see anything in this?"

"Not a thing," Gaebryl answered, checking over the helmsman console. Water was dripping in all around them. "This overhang is hardly adequate for rain blowing in at this angle. It's pouring through the gaps around the edges." He rolled the tarp handle tighter, taking up all the slack he could.

"Turn on the lights," Dedlin said. "We don't want to accidentally hit anything or run aground. The Gharnians won't see us unless they run into us now, anyway."

Gaebryl turned to the wyzard and grimaced, but he

complied.

The torrential rain continued.

43

Two days passed without reprieve from the rain.
Sometimes it was a mild downpour, and other times it was
impossible to do anything but hunker down and wait for it to
subside. They had kept on course in any case, despite the efforts
of an angry wind, and had covered many, many miles without any
sight of the Gharnian fleet. In fact, there was not much to see in
Tuus on the best and brightest of days, no trees, no hills to speak
of, and very little wildlife; only slow, flat, sloping fields of grasses
and reeds, mostly mired in swampy mires and new lakes that
came and went with the rains.

Ott had provided a fine dinner by hunting for a few hours
that second evening. He had simply crept over the rail of the ship
and disappeared into the mists and rain, and then, hardly any time
later, returned with a wild pig and two medium sized wild plains
turkeys. He had also come across a goodly number of wild red
yams and a batch of late blooming mayapples for everyone else
(he was a strict carnivore himself), which Drer Fregoode
combined with butter, sugar, cinnamon, and pears into a delicious
baked pie. Dinner was served below a few hours after sunset, with
some mirth provided by Drer's fine voice and musical abilities.

On the third day traversing Tuus, the skies had nearly
cleared except for spotty patches of rain clouds that could still
attack quite suddenly at times. But as evening came, it was certain
that they were about to enter another major storm system, visible
at every corner, perhaps the worse system they had encountered
thus far. They assessed their options, and saw no other choice but
to stay on course and manage as best they could. Luck had served
them well enough thus far, they thought. They secured everything
down and watersealed the spots that had previously opened and
leaked. They ate a fastidious dinner of leftovers and prepared for
the worst as the next substantial rain began to fall.

Most of the crew were below deck, warm and dry. Ott was

at the helm, braving the elements, and Commander Binder was at his side, surveying the frightening skies ahead through scans. A twister dove from the spinning clouds like a jabbing finger, a few miles to the west, cut into the earth, then dissipated back up into nothingness within a matter of seconds.

"This looks bad," the thordian said, holding white knuckled to the guidebar. Despite his steady steer, the ship was being heaved as much sideways by the relentless wind as it was moving forward. "Very bad. Curse this flat land."

Binder didn't disagree. "I've never seen so much rain," he replied. "This country soaks it up like a sponge. By my estimates, Tuus should be ten feet underwater by now."

Otthagorus nodded. "I suspect vast underground caverns and rivers that wash the rainwater away, off to the sea. Perhaps a great subterranean ocean lies beneath this land."

The heavy skies opened up on top of them and they passed through another leaden curtain of water that blew in nearly horizontal from their port side. Despite the sound of the rain pounding on their ship and the raging wind in their ears, the two of them could partially hear a song starting below. Drer had pulled out his mandolin once again, and had begun to entertain the rest of the crew. It had a miraculous effect on weary hearts and minds whenever he did that. It even made the two of them smile, as drenched and as cold as they were.

"Otthagorus, I'm not much for apologies, but I'll admit that I was wrong about you." Commander Binder said, in a rare moment of sincerity and openness. "I'm sorry for the way I treated you before."

Ott looked at the man sidelong. "Eh. That's not necessary, Commander. We're professional soldiers."

Binder shrugged. "I didn't behave professionally. I let a personal bias cloud me. A long-time prejudice. And it was wrong of me."

Ott nodded, gratefully. "Apology accepted, my friend."

"I was taken prisoner as a child," Binder reluctantly explained. "Forced to work the algaestone mines for several years," he explained.

Ott stared out the front window. It was nearly impossible to see anything at all. A strong gust of wind pushed the ship sideways with a bump, then let it go. "Your captors were thordians?"

"We lived in a small, rustic, coastal town a hundred miles south of Poed, near an inlet of a beautiful little lagoon in Gorn, my family and me. A wayside for pirates and travelers selling their wares to the north and south of us. We had an inn there, and a livery stable, run by my parents and my uncle. Thordians and humans did not get along in those parts. They hadn't for decades. Skirmishes were common, as was kidnapping and slavery, on both sides. Thordian mercenaries killed my parents one winter night and took me to the caves in the southern swamps. I was but twelve years old. My village was burned to the ground, and I was enslaved. I survived there for nearly two years before a truce was negotiated and they finally released me."

"Dedlin and Drer have told me of your past. I am sorry. I have found that there are good and bad in every race, mine included. No one can be held accountable for the actions of a few others who tarnish their own reputations, otherwise we would all be held in contempt. I do not condone, nor am I responsible, for the actions of any other living creature, thordian or otherwise. Only for myself, Commander. As are you."

"Yes, I understand that," he said. "But sometimes it's a matter of the fears in your heart suppressing the rationale in your mind. When your nightmares are filled with images burned deep from events of your childhood, it is hard to let go of the hate and mistrust that they created subconsciously. That may be no excuse," he replied, shouting above the wail of the weather. "but it is the truth. However, what I mean to say is, I will try."

A battering ram of wind littered the portside hull of the ship with a barrage of uprooted reeds and grasses in several prolonged, pounding blasts, some bursting through the tarp like shrapnel. They stung the skin like pins and needles. The Stardeer tipped far up onto it's side with a metallic groan, caught atop a wave of gale force wind, sliding and spinning counterclockwise, until Ott could finally right it and regain control once again. The ship was being pressed hard to the west. Ott gripped the guidestick and accelerator bar with steel fists, gritting his teeth. "Perhaps our new friendship will go a long way toward the therapy you require," he said, clearly straining. The wind increased even more. The ship shook and rattled. "And I am not trying to be rude, but I'm sorry, I am unable to give you the undivided attention you deserve right now. I may be losing control here. I think I'm losing the ship."

"What is it? What is wrong? Should I relieve you?" Binder asked.

Part of the roof above the helmsman's chair ripped off, twisting on a flimsy attachment pin in the frame like a battered flag. Ott tried to seize it, but it tore off and was instantly gone, spinning off into the misty deluge. "Damn!" he cried. "Hold on!"

Three times the battering ram returned to punch and pummel the skycraft. Stardeer was knocked sideways by terrible bursts of wind, spinning like flicked coin on a table. Ott's footing slipped, and he released his grip. The wind caught the ship, pulling it up into the sky, then released it. It rolled completely up and over, nearly onto its back. The ship's plasteel frame groaned under the pressure. Binder tumbled, sliding across the deck; Ott nearly fell from the ship out the side door. Whatever was not strapped down on deck was now lost.

"Damnation!" Binder cried, rolling onto his head. "Ott, grab the guidestick before we flip over!"

A wide, hot bolt of lightning pierced the sky and buried itself into the earth less than twenty yards from the ship, and thunder pounded down upon them like a massive drum. There was an instant smell of char, and a taste of copper on their tongues. Static electricity wreaked havok on both the crew and the instruments of the Stardeer.

Then, for a moment, the wind gently released the ship. Sprawled across the roof of the helmsman's cabin, Ott leaned in and twisted the bent guidestick over, and Stardeer leveled off with a sad, beaten hiss. The ship bounced and bobbed as though on a spring, slowly spinning as the wind pushed it along to the northeast, like a paper boat loose in a rushing stream, up and then over a wide hill.

Dedlin's fuzzy head popped up from below. "Take her down!" he said. "Anchor my ship! This is ludicrous. We'll sit it out for awhile. This storm will kill us all! Everything is topsy turvy down here! We're rolling around like balls in a box! Down! Down!"

"I broke another string!" Drer cried from below.

They eased slowly into a pinch in a shallow hollow, where they hoped the majority of the wind might pass them by overhead, and secured the four corner anchors as best they could into the soggy earth. As Ott began shutting down the controls of the ship, ironically, the storm seemed to slacken, and then even pause altogether. Just the thrum of a constant falling vertical rain and distant thunder rolling around the hills in all directions, out beyond any hope of visibility. As Ott looked up and around, the skies turned a pale shade of green. The guidestick and accelerator bar went completely limp in his grasp. "It's...green," he said.

"That's weird," Binder said.

Down below, everything was in disarray. "Let's take stock of our supplies and get this mess cleaned up. My poor ship! She held together, but I'll wager she needs some tending to. Check for any significant damage," the wyzard instructed the crew. Outside, the sound of the roaring wind had swirled off and died away, barely more than a vacant carnival whistle. "From one extreme to the other in this forsaken land..."

"I don't like it," Gaebryl said. "It's too quiet out there. Like a tiger eyeing us from the bushes..."

The rain and wind then stopped completely. There was an eerie dead silence all around them. It was so quiet that they could hear solitary drops of water plopping from the cracks in the ceiling into puddles all around them. The air pressure around them then changed, too, as if they were now sitting in some type of great vacuum that made it difficult for them to breathe.

Day peered out the window. "Look," he said. "The skies are as green as clover."

"Not only that... What kind of sorcery is this?" Gaebryl said as he joined Day by the window, his voice barely above a whisper, as though he was seeing something that he just couldn't believe. He rubbed the condensation from the porthole with his sleeve. "Look outside, Dedlin. The rain is falling *upward.*"

Dedlin looked out one window, then quickly out another on the other side. His eyes confirmed Gaebryl's observation. Droplets of water were riding up the stems of the reeds and grasses, and they were falling upward into the sky. "Oh, no. It's... It's coming," he whispered.

From somewhere miles above them, a distant noise was fast approaching, like the amplified roar of a mighty, thunderous engine. As it fell down from the heavens toward them, it got exponentially louder and louder. The air pressure squeezed in their ears and Stardeer began rattling uncontrollably.

"Grab onto something!" Dedlin cried out, diving for an affixed table leg. "It's a twister!"

The tornado's first blast rendered all controls useless. Stardeer was ripped from the earth, her anchors flailing, useless. They were sucked up skywards, thrown across the hill, rolling, bouncing, and spinning. The ship spun like a top, pinning the crew against the walls. Panels burst, windows shattered, doors cracked and the ship's frame squealed in an effort to resist snapping and holding together. They were upside down, then right side up. The rainwater found every new way to get inside. Lightning flashed nearby them; electricity burnt the air. Gaebryl was screaming up at Ott and Binder, but the roar was too great for him to be heard. His mouth moved soundlessly.

Commander Binder had gripped onto the guidestick alongside Otthagorus, with welded fists. Both of them fought to regain some stability, but it was no use.

The interior lights flickered off and on in rapid succession. Stardeer was pointed nose up, rising and falling, then she began spinning like a turnwheel. They slammed one way then another. There were screams all throughout the skycraft. Day clenched his eyes tight, spinning uncontrollably in his chair, arms wrapped tightly about the taut ropes. Dedlin was lodged underneath a wedged cabinet on the ceiling, powerless.

Then, as quickly as it came, the tornado then let them go. It dissipated in a whoosh, and died, ending as abruptly as it had started. The fightercraft skidded and slid to a tilted stop, right side up, with a gentle thump, her nose brushing the ground. The rain returned in earnest. Somehow, thankfully, everyone was still alive and, miraculously, still onboard. The entire incident took less than twenty seconds start to finish.

The power returned. The lights flickered on. Stardeer's turbines kicked in and, with a groan, she righted herself. And in the aftermath, now only the rain could be heard, tapping nonchalantly upon the dented and damaged fightercraft hull.

"I'm going to be sick," Day moaned from his chair.

Lake, lying on the floor, had already vomited.

Ott fired up the turbines and Stardeer rose up a few more feet from the ground with some effort. Through the cracked front window, he and Binder watched a new funnel cloud as it swirled away toward the west, riding the sky like a rodeo rider.

Still, it poured, the wind howled, and grass and bushes rained down on them from the sky. Ott steered Stardeer to another low spot between the hills and let her hover a few feet above a newly formed raging stream.

Then, he rested against the wall, exhausted. Gaebryl's head popped up from below. "Drer's hurt," he said. "A toolbox got him in the head and he's losing a lot of blood. Dedlin, Lake and Qan all suffered some minor injuries as well. How are you faring topside?"

The two nodded, but there was trail of blood dripping

down Ott's face. He, too, had a minor head wound.

"The worst of it is over," Dedlin replied below. A drip of water hung from his hooked nose. "At least for a minute. Anchor this ship again if you can. Let us all come below, where it's drier, and rest. Let us see to Drer Fregoode's injury. We must mend while we check this ship over. What an episode. What else could befall us in this place, I dare not chance to think. Oh, my poor Stardeer, you are a wreck!"

44

The storm raged for two more hours, and the temperature outside dropped dramatically. Night had fallen like a wet velvet blanket all around them. Inside Stardeer, however, for the most part, although still damp in spots, it was warm and cozy. The crew moved about the lower deck with only the pale light cast from the stove fire and the blue stone at the tip of Dedlin's walking cane. Occasionally, the windows were lit by flashes of lingering lightning.

Gaebryl, Binder, and Ott had spent a good bit of time outside in the rain, repairing damage to the hull and roof. A lot of provisions topside were gone, including one of the three small skyslcds. Pcrcc had stitched and bandaged both Ott and Drer's head wounds and had seen to the others' injuries as well. Shortly thereafter, he crept into one of the darkened lofts and slept; his sensitive skin had been severely shocked by both the Gharnian stunner and the static electricity emitted by the proximate lightning strikes, so he needed some rest. It would take a couple of days for him to recover completely. Until then it would be up to the others to divide the piloting responsibilities. Other than that, the crew was fine, although the interior of the ship was a disastrous wreck. Charts, maps, lamp oil, clothes, blankets, utensils, weapons, boxes, and small equipment were scattered around on the cots and shelves, and piled up in the corners. With Dedlin's occasional direction, Day helped Lake and Qan clean up. Gaebryl jumped in as well, circling and recircling the main galley and smaller side rooms with a mop.

There were a few substantial leaks to repair. One window

that had been boarded up was not watertight, and two broken lower windows were letting water in around their frames. There were a number of moist streaks showing between slats in the rear, above the food compartment, and the roof had several circles of pooling moisture, two of which dripped constantly. The drain in the center of the galley floor kept a puddle three feet in diameter and an inch deep. The bilge pump hummed continuously below.

Binder reported that the turbines appeared undamaged, and that, after a minor repair, the vacuum fuselage tank was as airtight and as stable as ever. The foremost windshield had a large crack in it and two other windows topside were completely shattered. Thankfully, none of the major flight mechanisms had been affected, although they were wet and steaming a lot.

Clothes were hung about the galley hall on makeshift clotheslines. Their bedding and most their food was wet. They saved what meats and cheeses they could. Most bottles were broken. Lake separated the good from the bad while Qan tried diligently to dry the shelves and storage areas.

"All in all," Gaebryl reported as he emerged from the dressing room in moderately dry attire, "we're in good shape, considering that we were inside a tornado. The rain has slackened. I suggest we move on."

"Not until after dinner," Drer replied from his bunk. "I can't travel another inch on an empty stomach. Besides, we need to eat this food before it goes bad."

"An evening of rest could not hurt," Dedlin advised. "We all need it. But the storms are ending and the skies are relatively clear at times, so I suggest a quiet night on our part, no singing or loud voices. We have been lucky insofar as the Gharnians go, so let's not get careless. We're in no shape to fight tonight. Surely they have circled these storms and now search the plains high and low for us. One tiny spark of light could be detected for miles out here. Let's eat and use this time to think, organize, and strategize."

A soggy dinner was made and consumed on what was left of their cracked cups and shared dishes. Spirits were as damp as their food and clothes, but appetites were eventually satisfied.

Except for a few meager scraps, the cupboards were now virtually empty. Dedlin's cache of koffik was one item of luxury that went unscathed; the small burlap bag of beans was safe and dry within an airtight oak box, secured fastidiously upon a narrow shelf. Drer kept everyone's mugs filled with the warm, invigorating brew.

Shortly after supper, Dedlin had his smoke, things were cleared from the center table, and a map was rolled out to begin plotting an alternative, more unpredictable course into Gorn. Dedlin called the crew to gather around. He placed one finger on their present location, and another at the western border of central Gorn. "It is my assumption that the Gharnians are amassing along the Gornian River now, and are waiting to ambush us there..."

Abruptly, Drer stood and cocked his head, as if he had heard a noise from above. "Did anyone hear that? I think there's someone outside at the door."

The gentle spattering of rain on the deck above and the whistle of wind were the only sounds they could hear.

"I didn't hear anything..." Gaebryl said.

Then, they all heard it. A knocking. Three gentle raps. From the outer galley door. No one from the crew was missing; all nine members were present and accounted for. Quietly, they readied their weapons, and together edged toward the short flight of stairs that led to the upper deck. It was as black as tar in the stairwell.

"Stay back, Your Highness," Ott urged, whispering to Day. "I fear the worst. The fur on my neck is bristling."

Dedlin led the way toward the door. "Behind me," he whispered to them. He eased his way up the three narrow steps and placed his hand on the door latch, cane ready in the other. "Let us have a see," he said, peering through the foggy circular window. "Hmm, interesting," he said, curiously. "Prepare yourselves." Then, with a twist of the handle and a jerk, he popped the door open and a flood of water poured in through the doorway, down the steps, and across the galley floor.

Lightning flashed beyond, silhouetting a huge figure of a man standing just outside in a sheer wall of icy blue rain.

"Do not move!" Commander Binder ordered, his blast rifle extending over the wyzard's right shoulder. "We have weapons drawn upon you."

There was no response for a moment. The figure staggered, and then, in a deep, rumbling voice, he spoke: "I do not wish to fight...I need...I need help," he simply said, and his request was followed by another bellow of ominous thunder.

Dedlin, still the closest to the door, addressed the man again. "Tell us who you are!" he said. "What is your name? And where are you from? Quickly, I say!"

A gust of wind brought another shower of chilly rain into the galley.

"Speak!" Dedlin commanded.

The man put one hand up, as if surrendering to them, the other hung listlessly at his side; blood ran from it in rivulets to the floor. His knees buckled and he almost fell, just catching himself against the door jam, where he remained leaning, chin against his chest. There was a metallic sound of rushing, rattling air, as if he was forced to breathe through a series of metal tubes. The lightning flashed again, outlining his massive form. He was immense!

"My name is Kadazaat," he answered. "I am from Gharne, although I am no longer a soldier. Not anymore. I mean you no harm. I am... I am hurt. Quite seriously. Perhaps mortally. There was nowhere else to turn, and I fear I am in shock and losing consciousness."

Day stepped forward. Gaebryl's hand shot out to stop him, but Day pushed it aside. "Come in," he said to the Gharnian. "Come in out of this weather and find the aid you need here, sir. Are you armed?"

A wheeze. An airy rattle. "I am, but I have no intention of

using them. You may unarm me. I will not resist."

Weapons, ready to fire at the slightest provocation, were held at bay. Dedlin stepped back, allowing the huge man passage inside the ship. Everyone took a step back, forming a circle around the stranger who was so large he had to bend down to pass within the doorframe. King Day braved another step toward him. Gaebryl stood close behind, his blaster aimed at the man's throat.

"One false move," Binder warned. "Do you understand?"

The shadow took form as the lights eased on. "Yes, I can see well in the dark," he replied in the same rumbling voice. "And... Couldn't if I wanted to. Which I don't."

The Gharnian was broad shouldered and tall, at least seven feet, if not more. His striped garb was torn and bloody, dripping with rain water into puddles on the floor at his feet. A bone protruded from his right forearm.

"You are the rider of the uusyrapi," Gaebryl said. "We have seen you before."

"Yes," Kadazaat answered. His odd facemask had air tubes that connected to a pack upon his back. It hid all his facial features except for one eye that was visible where part of his helmet had been blown off. "The bird is mine." He turned and looked at Gaebryl. "You must be the one that I saw among the trees near Aerogreen," he said.

"Where is your steed?"

"She is under your fightercraft, hiding from the storm. She, too, is badly injured and may not survive the night."

"I'll check outside," Ott said, stealing past the Gharnian, back up out through the door, closing it behind him.

"We saw your brethren pursuing you," Day said to him.

"Aye. I lost them in the storm."

"How could it be that they pursue you, and you are forced

to flee from your own kind?"

"That is a long saga..." Kadazaat answered. He looked down at Day and stared at him for a few moments, as if suddenly aware of his presence for the first time. It was a strange and uncomfortable moment of focus and recognition. The air suddenly grew tense again and weapons were readied once again. Kadazaat took a deep breath; the sound was like that of congested air swirling in a leaky barrel. "Are you He?" he asked, somewhat in awe. "Are you the One? The One they seek?"

Day stood fixed and confident, eyeing the Gharnian with caution.

"Who is it that you believe he is?" Dedlin questioned.

Kadazaat seemed shaken, as if encountering the most paradoxical irony in his entire life.

"Answer!" Dedlin commanded.

"Of all ironies and coincidences," he replied, and even mustered a sound that might have been an attempt at a sad chuckle. "The Heir of the All Powerful. Ancestor of the First. Descendant from the Family Immortal. The One my kindred seek," Kadazaat rumbled, then he mumbled almost unintelligibly as he began to fade: "The Stonebearer."

Suddenly his knees buckled and he fell headlong, crashing onto the floor with a thud, out cold.

"Don't kill him!" Day cried. "He may tell us more."

"Could be a trap," Binder said, straddling the Gharnian with his blaster pointed at his head.

"I believe he fainted," Drer Fregoode said.

"Suicide soldiers," Gaebryl reminded them. He crept in closer with a pair of handcuffs from the galley stockade. "We'd best take no chances. Secure him."

"He must be a traitor," Day said. "Or...or an escaped

prisoner."

"And a fugitive," Dedlin agreed, helping the prince with the shackles. "With a story to tell. But to what purpose? We should beware. Traitors and escaped prisoners are desperate and unstable at best, particularly fanatical soldiers. Who knows what types of brainwashing and tortures have befallen him. He could be confused. Or quite insane."

Lightning lit the skies outside. It was followed by a pounding hammerlike thunder that rattled the broken glass in the windows: boom, boom, boom, boom, BOOM.

Drer Fregoode approached the soldier to get a better look at him. "He is hurt badly," he said. "And remember, he's been out in this storm without any cover, and you know what the twister did to us, protected as we were by this ship. Before that, he's been at battle with the Gharnians, for whatever reason. I doubt, with the distance he's covered from Aerogreen, that he's slept for days."

Binder was removing Kadazaat's unique and varied weapons. There were many. "Most of the ammo has been spent," he remarked. "His breathing apparatus is damaged, too."

"I find it odd that we keep crossing paths with this fellow out here in the wilds," Dedlin ventured to say. "Nothing happens without a reason. Nothing is coincidence."

Ott came back inside, soaked to the skin. "Uusyrapi's below us, like he said, curled up beneath the turbines to keep warm. But she's badly injured. Wings are broken. She's lost an eye and she's burned very badly. One of her feet is mangled. She's going to die," he said.

"I'll see to her," Drer volunteered. "I have substances for pain. If she's as you say, she should be put out of her misery. Poor beast."

"Let's move our prisoner to a cot," Binder said. "Let's see to his injuries before we begin interrogating him."

"So much for resting, thinking, organizing, and

strategizing. Let's forego our respite. We should get on out of here before we have anymore unwanted visitors," Dedlin advised. "Make haste. Let's get out of these plains and cross that next border."

45

Kadazaat remained unconscious and with fever for four days, and then, for the next three, he faded in and out of consciousness without exchanging any coherent dialogue with them. Just moans and indiscernible mumbles. He was secured steadfast to a reinforced bunk with shackles and chains, but everyone did their best to see to his minimal comfort. Upon investigation, they found his multiple wounds much more complex and severe than they had first suspected. Injuries that would have killed any normal man. Somehow, either out of a lifetime of discipline and intense training, or by the strength of will alone, under the keen watchful care of Drer Fregoode and the crew of Stardeer, Kadazaat began pulling through, slowly forward, toward a long and painful recovery. His bones were set, his wounds were sutured, his burns were salved, and he was tended constantly to ward off infection.

Drer was usually at his bedside during the day, Gaebryl through the night, and Dedlin and Day always remained close by, waiting anxiously to talk with him. At all times either Commander Binder or Sir Otthagorus was on guard by the door, armed to the teeth and always ready, should the Gharnian somehow regain his strength and attempt anything devious or unexpected.

While nursing him back to health, they were never able to completely remove his mask or breathing apparatus while repairing it, for fear of smothering him; it was an integral part of his Gharnian physiology. He had hydraulic plasteel implants on and in his ribs, arms and legs, not unlike those that Binder had, and plates of biomechanical exoskeleton armor implanted in strategic places upon his body. There was a complex, oval, dome shaped glass box that they guessed regulated his heartbeat and blood flow, affixed surgically in his chest just below his skin, right above his heart, powered by what source they could not successfully determine. Drer had never seen anything like it, and was in awe of the medical technology. He admitted that it was far beyond the realm of his expertise. He still did the best he could.

On the morning of his eighth day aboard Stardeer, Kadazaat awoke for a few minutes, mumbling something about his wife and son, and then he slipped away again. Perce came in and asked if he could relieve Drer at Kadazaat's bedside. "You've been down here for over a week, my friend," the mahekian said. "Let me take your shift for you today."

"A mahekian caring for a Gharnian," Drer replied. "I would have never expected to see that in my lifetime. I'll be on deck getting some air if you need anything, my friend."

Drer went up to find a glorious day outside, stiff legs aching. The suns were blazing and the fields of Tuus were aflame with colors and life. The rains had inspired a myriad of wildflower growth and blossom, and the wildlife was taking full advantage of the fair weather. There were large white cranes feeding everywhere, leaping to flight as Stardeer whizzed quickly past, only to circle and land again after they felt it was safe. The songs of insects, birds, and multitudes of frogs filled the air. From above, they heard the screech of some great predatory eagle or hawk high overhead, on the hunt.

Drer found newcomers Lake and Qan near the rear of the ship, assisting one another as they futilely attempted to change Ott's head bandage. The thordian seemed to be napping by the sound of his cavernous purr. "A little tighter or it will slip off," Drer said. "Thordians have big heads."

"I heard that," Ott retorted sleepily, then snorted and resumed his repose.

"I'm having a bit of trouble," Qan admitted. "I've never bandaged a thordian's head before. It's so... furry.""

"I'm sure you're doing quite a few things that you've never done before, aren't you, Qan?"

"True," he said. "Very true."

"I was thinking about you two earlier, and what an experience all this must be for you. Your first excursion off Rock Gaaloth," Drer said, finishing the dressing up for them. "There you go," he said to Ott.

Ott inspected the work with his paws. Satisfied and rested, he stood and stretched, then left the three of them to chat while he went below to check on the prisoner.

"So, what do you think of all this?" Drer continued. "This adventure in the Wilds, I mean?"

Lake smiled. "We never had storms like these in Tungulin," he admitted.

Qan nodded. "It's amazing," he said. "Everything is so big and beautiful."

"And dangerous," Lake added.

"We're very grateful and honored to be along," Qan said. "And I hope we're not a hindrance. We want to do our part.'

"Don't be silly," Drer said. "You're good men. We're fortunate to have you along with us. You're an essential part of this team, so never think otherwise."

The two castle rangers nodded gratefully.

"It does take a little getting used to at first," Drer told them. "You never know what each day will bring, or what surprise may suddenly just pop up out of nowhere. Out here, you must often live by your wits, if you are to live at all, and without any of the comforts of home..."

Lake nodded. "Like food," he said. "I'm starved! Our shelves are as bare as a bone. Where are we going to find something to eat? I'm afraid we may become Ott's next meal if we don't find something soon."

"We'll eat again," Drer assured them. "I guarantee you that, my young friends. We'll find a meal somewhere. We might get hungry first, but, eventually, I guarantee you, we will eat again. Just tighten your belts a notch and don't think about it!"

46

Now, the rain was not more than a spritz of fine mist. There were wide blue stretches in the heavens, devoid of any rain clouds at all. Dedlin was at the helm of his battered but fully functioning Stardeer, heading due south along a steppe of small brown hills. The warm wind tousled his reddish white beard. "Hello!" he called out to the crew behind him. "Want to see something? Ask King Day to come up for a moment. There's a bit of Tuusian history just ahead of us."

Drer opened the rear trapdoor to the lower deck and called to the rest of the crew. Except for Binder, who remained at Kadazaat's bedside, all came topside to see what all the commotion was about. Dedlin told them to look straight ahead and report what they saw there.

Gaebryl and Drer recognized the shape instantly, and were delighted, but the rest of the crew were at a loss. "I don't see anything," Day replied.

"Nor I," Ott admitted. "That hill is strange, though. Is there something on that big black hill just ahead of us?"

"On the hill? I don't believe so, other than some scrub brush and a few small trees," the wyzard answered with a laugh.

"Interesting patterns though," Perce replied. "Almost like a network of trails crossing over it, or irrigation troughs. It looks manmade. I can definitely detect patterns now."

"I'll give you a clue;" Dedlin said. "That is no hill at all, my friends. Look closer."

"A rock?" Day asked. "A big round rock? I give up, Dedlin. What is it?"

Suddenly, the entire hill moved. It actually rose up from the ground, lunged forward ten or twelve yards, then it settled to the earth again, shaking the trees on top of it.

"The hill is moving! It's alive!" Day exclaimed.

"Indeed it is alive," Dedlin remarked, exceedingly pleased. "It is a great Tuusian prairie tortoise, a Tuus tortoise for short, if you will. One of the last, if not the very last. We'll be coming up upon her in a moment or two and we can all have a closer look. The beast is ancient. I have no idea how old, as old as the planet itself, I've been told."

"She's beautiful," Gaebryl replied.

"Beautiful?" Day refuted. "She's hideously ugly!"

"Her shell is so immense that we used to hold wyzard initiations and alumnus conventions upon her back when I was a younger wyzard. You can see a great pyre of ash right there at the summit! I suppose she's three hundred yards long if she's an inch, and two hundred yards wide. A small forest grows upon her shell, and, indeed, that forest is old itself, older than any forests in these lands. It's said an old hermit lives somewhere up there, but he's so shy that he's rarely seen."

As they drew in upon her, circling the monster's flank to the right, the huge, flattened hind limbs and tail became visibly evident, appearing almost as the rise of great brown hills before a mountain. Each scale was the size of a boulder. Her claws were as large as great tree trunks.

"So amazing!" Day replied.

They swept past in a long arc. The beast's old eyes were dull and fixed, paying them no mind. She opened her huge shovellike mouth to scoop up a hunk of earth from the ground, and then she shook the dirt loose through a massive baleen filter on her lower throat and jaw with great twists of her massive head, to easier feed on the scrubby vegetation alone.

"She's immense!" Perce decreed. "And look there! On the rise to the west! A nest!"

"Oh, my! Eggs!" Drer cried. "She's laid eggs, Dedlin!"

"Well, I'll be," the wyzard said, shaking his head. "She's probably been in gestation for centuries. I wonder how long before they hatch? Certainly not in our lifetime."

"When was the last sighting of a male tortoise?" Gaebryl asked.

"I've heard of none. But they do burrow and sleep for many, many years at a time. Any one of those distant hills could be a sleeping tortoise, overgrown with forest vegetation."

"Someday our party will reunite here for a victory celebration as was done in the days of old," Drer declared. "We will rejoice and build a great fire, and sing and dance, and get drunk and have merrymaking for a month, for all these harrowing days will be long past, and all but our most valiant of times will be forgotten."

"If any of you are still alive," said a hollow, rumbling, barely lucid voice from behind them. Kadazaat the Gharnian was there, on his unsteady feet, still heavily shackled, standing before Binder, who guarded him with two drawn blasters. "If any of *us* are still alive. I see that I am now your prisoner, although I have done you no wrong. Our countries are not presently at war. I ask to be unshackled and released immediately. Return me my weapons and set me on the ground. I'll be gone and trouble you no more."

Day stepped toward him. "No. Not yet," he answered. "Not before we have a chance to talk, Kadazaat of Gharne. You owe us that. Then we'll decide your fate. There is much at stake here. Setting you free creates a whole new set of problems for us."

Kadazaat bowed slightly at the waist. "As you wish," he said. " I will tell you all I know. I have no reason not to anymore."

"Alright, back in the hold," Binder instructed the prisoner, leading him by his shackles.

Lunch, if you could call it that, since it was the last of their food scraps, was served. The last of the ale accompanied bits of dried meats and cheeses, cold beans, some crushed nuts and raisins. There was still enough water to last for several days. The Gharnian chose not to eat, but accepted a flask of water gratefully. The suns were declining, and Perce found a shadowy vale to slide Stardeer into, out of sight, among the scrub and creeping shadows, so that they confer in earnest with their prisoner, uninterrupted. The crew crowded around Kadazaat the Gharnian in the galley, with Lake and Qan remaining above on watch.

"Are all in this land now also my enemies?" the Gharnian asked as the crew encircled about him. "In all lands on this earth? Am I cursed to be shunned on sight, and hunted and imprisoned for no other reason than my national origin and my past? I am homeless and without allies, north or south, east or west. I am ostracized. I am without a country to call my own, ever again. I flee with every waking breath. That is all I do now. Flee from all. Shall I abandon all hope of redemption? Will I ever know peace? Was I ever given a chance to be something other than what I was made, even after my betrayal?"

Dedlin began. "We shall see," he said. "You must have an interesting backstory, most of which I have deduced already or can guess, but for the sake of the rest of the crew I will ask you to submit it in full detail for their benefit. My concern is to what depth your knowledge of us delves."

"I know no more than any other of my kind."

"We'll see. You said a few interesting things in your delirium before you collapsed the night we found each other that I find quite curious, but we'll get to that later. First, tell us about yourself. What possible series of events led you to our particular cabin door?"

"Where to begin? My story is not a short one."

"We are here for the duration, sir, and you will appease our ears until we are satiated. From the beginning."

The large man paused in thought, took a breath through his

mask, and then he began. "Very well," he said thoughtfully. "I was born in Ash, Gharne, fifty seven years ago, under the House of Anghor, prince warrior Lord Fhargak. My revered father was a temple builder by trade. As is our custom, I left home at five years old to begin my training in Kaldash. I originally planned to return to the Fhargak princedom when I finished my first tour of duty, usually, for most, at age thirty five.

"I excelled in my training. I worked as a policeman, and trained as a gladiator in the arenas. I had my hundredth kill by the age of eighteen, a new arena record, which gave me cult celebrity status in Kaldash, and the military took notice. I was recruited into intelligence, and worked my way up the officer's rank by organizing and executing secret covert operations for the Gharnian Elite. Life was very hard. We were trained to torture and to tolerate and endure torture ourselves. We were taught the ideas and philosophies of the Elite and of the Perfect Dominion. And we were taught about the ideas and philosophies of the complacent, evil woodan..."

"Woodan?" Day interrupted.

"Us," Drer said.

"You," Kadazaat said, nodding to all there, "You are all woodan."

"Go ahead, please. Continue."

He cleared his throat and continued. "When I graduated top in my brigade, I anxiously awaited the arrival of my family at the ceremony, but to my dismay, there was no representation from the House of Anghor, or any explanation for their absence. I had wondered if I had dishonored them somehow...

"I rose to the rank of Major Admiral within the next seven years, and sent to a base near the border of Ash, not far from my homeland, for more intensive training. I served there as Commandant for twelve years, reaching the Fourteenth Level of Discipline, and Awarded the Badge of Master of Secrecy for the Gharnian Elite. I did not have one blemish on my perfect record.

"I advanced to General in the Gharnian Warship Fleet at age forty four. Some of the elders were apprehensive about one so young having such an impressive responsibility. I alone commanded a force of 35,000 Gharnian warriors, nearly a twentieth of our entire active force at that time.

"However, here's the twist. Despite my varied accomplishments, I was...incomplete. At times, I was... miserable. I submersed myself in my duties to keep from thinking about my long lost family. I did not speak to anyone about this, because, as all Gharnians know, that is a weakness of a woodan, not a true warrior. Still, it ate at me every day, like a cancer, and nothing I did could dispel it. It seems that I was cursed somehow by feelings that I could not control, and I feared that my commanders, and some of my subordinates, sensed it in me.

"I was instructed to delve into the ancient prophecies for my peace and redemption. To give my heart and soul to it. And I tried. For years I tried, but it never happened. I was not a True Believer, because it is not in me to believe.

"To help me forget my family, and to help me fight the temptation to go hunting for my past, I requested a new tour of duty that would take me far from Gharne. The request was granted, and we rode the eastern coast from Gharne to Eaoph.

"Four years ago, I met a girl there, in the mountains of Eaoph. We had raided a village there for recruits for our ship, and she was one taken. Her name was then Elith." He paused to take a drink of water. The breathing tubes went through his lower trachia, bypassing his throat, allowing him to drink through his mouth. "I was struck by Elith's fierce eyes and her defiance in the face of death. So I took her to my bed that night, and I changed her name to Mayar. Less than a year later, my son, Illar, was born to me.

"My brigade was ordered to invade some towns in southern Gorn, to search the mines and caves for a mystical Stone, and I would not allow my wife and son to follow because there was strong resistance there from renegade scyropirates, and we were committed to a suicide task. I sent them both to Gharne, escorted by seven of my most trusted soldiers. Mayar had grown attached to me because I loved her and was good to her, and she vowed that she and my son would wait for me there, in Ash, until I returned for them. Our parting was sorrowful.

"As is often the case, the suicide mission turned out to be easier than we at first anticipated. We acquired two small towns, taking what is in balance with the Perfect Dominion, and destroyed what was in conflict with its ideals. We did not, however, find any Stone in any mine or cave.

"A short time afterwards, a messenger came to me in the middle of the night. I had a new assignment from my commander, Executive General Saargon. I opened the letter and read that my highly successful and fruitful career had been finalized. I was to complete my tour of duty by fulfilling my life's essence in glory to the One in ritual, honorably, before my men, the very next morning. Self termination.

"This prestigious ritual generally follows a long career of distinguished successes in battle. Not at a time where most of the glory still lies ahead. I was confused. And I silently questioned its rationality in my mind. Was it because the love I felt for my family back in Ash, my wife and child, could be sensed and determined a weakness? A liability? To all those around me, I feigned great pride of the upcoming ceremony.

"Although I did intend to obey (I had lived my entire life and career obedient to every wish of the Elite), the more I dwelled upon it that night, the more this request was beyond my comprehension to bear. There had to be something wrong at the core of it all, although I would never have been permitted to inquire. I made arrangements to gather my brigade at dawn, laid out my uniform, and I had my coffin officially prepared, as is our custom.

"Then, in a move none could have suspected, a spontaneous rebellion inexorably came over me from within. I disobeyed my orders for the first time in an otherwise illustrious career. During the night, I fled. I was forced to kill three of my own men to successfully escape. For sleepless weeks I flew, in one stolen scoutship after another, without light by night, and hiding like a coward during the day, eluding my trackers by whatever means necessary. None had expected my desertion. More than that, no one expected me to return to my homeland, Gharne.

"I went first to my home in Anghor, to find my parents. The prince warrior Lord Fhargak had become a warship admiral, I was told, and long gone from Gharne. My mother was still there. I cornered her in the servants' showers. She was blind and did not believe me when I told her who I was.

"She finally talked, but only to be rid of me because she was frightened. She said that my poor father, a true Gharnian patriot, had died of natural causes seven or eight years ago. The Elite, for whatever reasons I cannot even begin to fathom, had told my parents that I had been killed during my first year in warship training, killed by my comrades for cowardice. And, as our custom decrees, my parents' property and possessions had been absconded for the good of the movement, and my parents recruited as servants, to begin working their way back up the social ladder once again, from the bottom. In essence, my father became a slave in his own home to one Admiral Daamsarak, and my mother became the concubine of the admiral and his entire staff. All of this, because of some grand lie created to discredit, dishonor, and remove me. And if there is one thing that I cannot tolerate as a man, a soldier, and a Gharnian, is hypocrisy.

"That night I killed all members of Admiral Daamsarak's family, and then, once again, I fled a wanted man.

"I sought out my wife and my son, but soon found out that they had never reached Gharne. I have been searching for them, and running as a traitor with a formidable bounty on my head, for the last two years. So far, I have only reached dead ends. I fear that both my wife and my son are now dead, and I am out of leads to follow. I spend all my waking hours on the run, my sleeping hours hidden. I am tired and I am desperate, and I'm afraid I am going quite mad.

"I have stolen a small gardoon of Gornian diamonds from a Gharnian freighter, which I am offering as a reward for any information that will lead me to my family. I will not rest until I find my wife and son, or confirm their deaths, because I gave them my word. Unless, that is, I am killed first, which seems more likely with every passing moment.

"If I find any of the seven I sent as escorts, and I know them all by name and description, I will question them one by one, and kill them all, for they have failed me. Yet, they, too, have vanished into thin air.

"If I do find my family, we will flee this continent and go far, far away from all this subversion, scheming, and war. I will build them a home and provide for their needs.

"If I find that they are dead, then, having nothing left to live for, I will do as my last orders said, and honor my country by taking my own life."

The room went quiet for a few moments.

"Your story is indeed a hopeless one," Dedlin replied. "And I would not have believed it even possible had I not seen your own brethren hunting you down with my very own eyes."

"Still, Gharnians are adept at creating tales of deceit if it suits their needs and plans..." Binder reminded. "Lies, schemes, deception, false trust."

"Then you do not know the Gharnian Elite, Commander Binder. Gharnians, true patriot Gharnians, never lie," Kadazaat reiterated obstinately. "It is a sign of weakness. Lying is a common trait of your people, the woodan, not us."

"You may have believed that once," Dedlin replied. "But no more. You were betrayed by your own people. They have lied. To you and about you. You are a fugitive because of a Gharnian lie against you."

"Yes," he admitted. "There was a conspiracy of lies set against me. Someone, somewhere, grew fearful of me, and decided to have me removed. Unfortunately, that also included everyone who knew me, as well.

"Despite that injustice, I still adhere to the noble discipline of truth myself, even now. Their betrayal cannot corrupt me. I will not break. Better to die as an honorable man speaking the truth, than to save oneself as a weak man by lying."

"Show us you can be truthful, as you say. What do you know of our plight, then?" Gaebryl asked. "You seemed familiar with us when you collapsed on the floor from your injuries. Be thorough. Tell us what you've heard."

"As much as the rest of my brethren, I suppose," he answered after a moment's thought. "But I have learned much since I have been here resting as well. I was not always asleep when my eyes were closed, Prince Gaebryl."

"Careful," Commander Binder warned.

"I, myself, was never given any particular instructions regarding the pursuit, apprehension, or extermination of the Stonebearer during my own career, but I do know many who have. And I expect that, as of late, there are many more with like orders. I was in many meetings where this was discussed. I do know of the magnitude of the search to locate you now," he said, directing his attention toward Day. "Outside of the massive military migration and subversive infiltration of the eastern quadrant three years ago, it's the grandest endeavor ever taken by the Gharnian military forces in my lifetime.

"Honestly? Your presence, your *existence* here both awes me, but also embitters me. It has made my simple task of searching for my family much more dangerous. There are fighterships and warships incoming, from every corner of the continent, right to this very spot, to this damnable obscure corner of the world, just because of you. And likely, I'll be caught and killed soon because of it. Until it is known that you have passed Tuus and are in Gorn, they will be pouring into these plains and I will be at risk."

"We're all at risk," the wyzard snapped. "Now, to it. When you arrived, and you saw our young King Day here, you said, and I quote, 'Are you He? Are you the One? The One they seek?' and then you went on by saying, 'Of all ironies and coincidences. The Heir of the All-Powerful. Ancestor of the First. Descendant from the Family Immortal. The One my kindred seek. The Stonebearer.' What say you, now, Kadazaat of Gharne? Elaborate!"

The Gharnian soldier was taken aback by how well the wyzard had retained his every word. "That is what they believe," he answered. "That the Old Stories are true."

"And you didn't?"

"Not until now."

"A nonbeliever. He's a mirror image of you, Commander," Dedlin replied to Benjyn Binder. "So then, who is in charge in Gharne now?"

Binder asked with a scowl. "We've heard rumors. If the Old Stories are coming true, who is it that you serve?"

Kadazaat looked at the Commander. "I do not serve Him. But, you know who it is."

"Gheelgahar is indeed risen from death?"

"I have never seen Him, but there are those who have," he answered. "I, myself, have never been a believer in the Old Stories or the Dark Arts, hence my inevitable downfall. Despite all the fertile training of my youth. The capacity of faith is just not within me, despite my willingness to *try* to believe."

"Confirm to us then what you know of our mission," Dedlin asked.

Kadazaat looked at young King Day. "We have been led to believe that you are the heir of the Kingdom of Day, hidden until recently on the Island of Mead, and that you now seek one of the Stones of Power. In Gorn. The Stone with the potential to destroy anything. Everything. The power to destroy all."

His words were ominous and deep to hear.

"You said that I was from the Family of the Immortals," Day said. "What exactly did you mean by that? My father and mother died when I was but two years old," he said angrily. "That doesn't make my family immortal, does it? They died from natural causes. As did my father's parents before him."

The Gharnian seemed to be struggling. He had reached a crossroad, not knowing which direction he should now take. Finally, they were getting to the heart of it. Yet, on this matter, he would no longer speak. Most suspected that what he had was, for the first time, holding back his tongue.

"I wonder," said the wyzard, still circling him. "Hypothetically speaking, of course. If you could, would you take King Day prisoner to regain status with your peers?"

"That thought has crossed my mind as a possibility a few times, although I imagine I would have to kill the lot of you first," Kadazaat answered coolly and straightforward. "Of course it did. Why wouldn't it? Perhaps I would have tried under different circumstances, if I had been captured before stripped of my title and command. And everything else.

"But, no, I would not now. I will never return to Gharne, ever again, for any reason. It is a tainted place for me now. I told you that I seek no conflict here, and I gave you my word. I needed help, and have received it.

"Make no mistake, my loyalty to my country runs deep, as I'm sure does yours. We are all loyal to the lands that bore us. This continent is still so barbaric. People battle each other, village to village. Many starve while many have so much to waste. Once the kingdom is united, and the Perfect Dominion has been initiated, all of that will end. There will peace through discipline. Order through reward and punishment. Advancement through competition and enterprise. The weak will fall away, as chafe, the strong will endure and procreate. All this through the progression toward perfection, which is the only goal of the Perfect Dominion."

"So, to hell then with diversity and individuality?" Dedlin asked. "This is the crux of it. This is where our philosophies differ. To hell with grace and mercy? To the freedom to choose one's own destiny, be it grand or folly? Survival of the strongest and the smartest? What you suggest is living in fear, as puppets. A mere step away from living the lives of dumb barnyard animals."

"That is better than living under the threat of annihilation, disease, and hunger. It is evolution."

"We have more than a difference of opinion," Drer Fregoode said. "We have a difference of belief. I choose to do whatever I want, despite what I am told to do. Often, this gets me into trouble, but at least I'm a free man, living in a free world."

"You mean living lawlessly. Recklessly. Selfishly, and foolishly," Kadazaat replied. "And without discipline or order. Fragile as a butterfly. Living with temptation, vices, depravity and sin."

"Eh," Drer replied in turn. "Everything in moderation."

"Enough political bantering," Day finally said. "This is pointless. Our common ground is that we are both fleeing the Gharnians now, Kadazaat, you for your reasons, and we for ours. We should come to an accord if this is to end amicably. If you are released, and we are caught, I will not turn you in to them, and I would expect the same courtesy from you. Not because we snatched you from the jaws of death and nursed you back to health, which we did. But because it's the right thing to do. You won't find us to be hypocrites or liars, here, either. We are true to our words."

"You speak for all here?"

"I do."

Kadazaat nodded to Day. "Then I agree to your proposal, should you release me. It will be as if we never met on these plains."

"I also pledge you this, Kadazaat of Gharne, as a further token of good will, because your story has moved me. If I am able, after I succeed in our current mission, I will do all I can within my power to help you find out about Mayar and Illar, your wife and your son. I swear it to you and all here who hear my words."

The Gharnian stared at the young king.

"Perhaps they are in hiding someplace safe, where you are not allowed and have no eyes. Perhaps they are imprisoned by our allies," Day said. "We have access to many places that you do not."

Again, Kadazaat stared contemplatively in Day's direction, in a new, but very deep thought. "The gardoon of diamonds that I offer for reward is well hidden, but, should you succeed, the reward is the same. I could retrieve them in less than a week..."

"I do not want your reward. I had even forgotten that you had mentioned it."

"You are very strange," he then said. "Whatever your motives are, I cannot discern or understand them."

"My intent is just to be kind. To care."

"To be kind?"

"To show you kindness for what atrocities you have endured. I don't expect you've experienced a lot of it. It can be a wonderful thing, kindness."

"I know what kindness *is*. I do not understand its purpose. I do not understand your *motive*. What is your reward? What is it you want in trade, should your search for my family be fruitful?"

"Doing kindness *is* my motive, and it is its own reward."

The Gharnian remained confused.

Day sighed. "Okay, look. It can be a very powerful tool for building allies."

Kadazaat slowly shook his head, beginning to understand this strange, new way of thought. "Ah. I'm not sure if that will work, but I am willing to chew on the thought... This *kindness*... It is a gift, then?"

"A gift without reason, or maybe against all reason," Day said. "A gift without recompense."

Kadazaat shook his head. "I will consider this paradoxical philosophy."

"Good," Day said.

"Good," Dedlin said in agreement.

"Now, may I go free, or do I remain your prisoner this day, forced to attempt my own escape?" the Gharnian asked. "It would not end well for anyone on board."

"You are a most extraordinary man," Drer wagered. "But you are not fully healed yet. Your uusyrapi is dead, so you will be traveling on foot from here, undisguised and in the open. We should at the least put you down somewhere where you may find cover and supplies."

Day looked to Dedlin and Gaebryl, then back to Kadazaat. "Give us until morning before you attempt anything foolhardy. You'll have my answer then."

The general nodded.

48

The debate concerning Kadazaat's fate dwindled long into the night. He was Gharnian by birth, a soldier by trade, and probably guilty of many heinous crimes kingdomwide, (or so Commander Binder kept pointing out), so turning him over to any local law authority might be prudent and invariably wise. That way, he could be questioned, and interrogated further, possibly by more ruthless means. Valuable information might be ascertained, and justice better served. And he would still remain relatively safe from his own countrymen.

But, then, on the other hand, the act of locating a strong enough facility to securely hold him could take the crew far out of their flight path, and hinder their mission by days, if not longer. Gaebryl pointed out that banishment from country and stripping him his rank was worse punishment than any prison sentence anyone could impose on General Kadazaat, especially with his own countrymen trying to assassinate him at every turn. He was branded. Disgraced for life. What could be worse than being pursued by bounty hunters who were once your comrades and peers? He argued that their current mission took precedence over Kadazaat's uncertain legal future. "Our own quest is paramount," he continued to repeat. "Not cleaning up Tuus, one Gharnian soldier at a time."

They pondered the repercussions of setting him free. What was the worst he would do? Detract more Gharnians? Further divide their forces? Binder, for one, did not want to take the chance of Kadazaat getting captured, tortured, and inevitably exposing what he had learned about them... That he had actually engaged the Stonebearer personally and his (very small) troop on the fields of Tuus. That he could give them an accurate description of the course, speed, and direction that they were heading. Day, for one, perhaps naively, believed that Kadazaat would not break under that duress. But Binder explained that no being could endure intense torture without breaking before the end. No one.

When they asked him what he personally suggested, Commander Binder told them that they would not like his answer... But that it was war, and taking care of that one loose end, permanently, was what was undeniably best for the mission and the crew. He volunteered to handle it himself.

"No. We did not nurse him back to health only to execute him once he's recovered," Day reprimanded. "I will not relinquish my morality, decency, or our civilized ideals. That would make us no better than the gogmoors of Bondoon."

They went to bed that night without having made any unanimous decision, but all agreed that they would submit to whatever King Day came to by morning.

Morning did come, and, even before breakfast, they brought their prisoner up onto the deck for his sentencing, bound in plasteel chains and leggings. It was a tense, solemn gathering. Kadazaat stood before them silently, facing King Day and Dedlin Dane without a flinch or sign of fear or emotion. Commander Binder, Sir Otthagorus, Prince Gaebryl, and Drer Fregoode stood in a semicircle behind the prisoner with weapons drawn and ready, in the chance that Kadazaat might take some sort of aggressive or retributive action.

"Let's just get to it. Our final discourse, one way or the other," Day said informally, without any type of prelude or ceremonious oration. "I have made my decision. But first, I have one last request of you, Kadazaat."

The huge man nodded respectfully.

"I toiled long into the night over our predicament here. You must agree, it is quite a quandary. We can't keep you onboard, always bound and guarded. We can't deviate from our quest to find you a proper prison. So. To execute you or to set you free. Our only two remaining options... Or so it seemed to us all last night."

There was a hesitant silence.

"But the instant I awoke this morning, an idea popped into my head. There is a third option. A choicc. For you."

"I have a choice?" he said. "I have already asked you to set me free. That is my choice."

"There is another."

"And that might be..?" Dedlin said from behind.

"Would you consider joining us on our quest, Kadazaat of Gharne, as part of our crew?"

Stuttering gasps.

Dedlin smiled. "This young king never ceases to amaze me," he replied quietly to Drer Fregoode.

The rest of the crew, Commander Benjyn Binder in

particular, did not share in this novel revelation.

Day went on. "It makes perfect sense, if you think about it. The premise is blatantly simple. You're already at war with your own people, and so it would be safer for you to travel with us than to travel alone in the wilds. We could help protect one other," he said. "There is no doubt that you could be invaluable to us. And, if you'll aid us in our quest, then we can better aid you on yours, to help you find your wife and child. Can you see the wisdom in this?"

"Intriguing. There could be mutual benefits to this union," he said after a second. "And some wisdom."

"And, so?"

"Alas, I cannot accept your offer."

"Why not?"

"Because I do not belong here. I could not successfully assimilate very well. I do not fit in with your tiny, hopeless band of lost and desperate militiamen, at a base level. I am a lifelong, hardened soldier at the core, conformed to the great military body of Gharne. With all my heart, I still believe in the pursuit of the Perfect Dominion. I still believe in the domination, control, care, and education of those who cannot fend for themselves, or advance on their own. Woodan domination. Those beliefs are marrow deep. I know I cannot...*will* not change.

"True, I am what you might call a lone wolferine now, with no need for the great pack that once embraced me, and has now shunned me. I will not seek out any new pack who might welcome me anew.

"I am obsessed with my own personal vendettas now, and committed to a noble revenge I must fulfill before all is done and I sleep below the surface of the earth, which is my obligatory right as a man and a Gharnian soldier. That being said, I will still always love my great country, its ideals, and its people. My revenge is directed at corrupt individuals. Not the lands we serve. I cannot bring myself to fight against Gharne. If I remained with you, in the long run, it is likely that I would one day turn on you. I would one day commandeer the ship, and make any survivors my own. For the glory of Gharne. It is best to choose one of the other two remaining options you originally stated, Your Majesty."

Day sighed, regretfully. "Very well, sir," he said. "Thank you for your honesty. Should you ever reconsider, the offer stands."

"Thank you, Your Highness."

"Commander Binder, please free him from his restraints," Day said. "You are hereby free to go, Kadazaat, as was your wont," he then said. "Return him his weapons."

Reluctantly and cautiously, Binder did as he was bid. The chains and handcuffs fell to the ground at the Gharnian's heavily booted feet. Kadazaat rubbed his wrists. He squared himself and looked around the deck at each member of the odd fellowship, and then he turned and looked gravely at young King Day once more, with deep and thoughtful eyes. "May we speak privately before I go? I have decided something, myself. I have a gift of my own to give. A gift you may someday use gratefully, although you may not find it kind at all. At least not at first."

"Definitely not!" the wyzard piped, the same sentiment echoes immediately be the rest of the crew.

Day held up his hand. "Yes, we may speak privately, but only if Dedlin and Gaebryl chaperone as my advisers."

Kadazaat agreed. "Of course."

"We'll meet back here on the deck as soon as you've finished your preparations for departure."

49

"Are you sure this is a good idea?" Gaebryl asked a few minutes later as escorted Day up on deck. The entire crew was coming topside. Half went to the bow, the other half to the stern, so that Day, Dedlin, and Gaebryl could meet quietly and privately with Kadazaat in the middle, on the landing near the helm console.

Kadazaat was dressed in his full regalia once again, armed to the teeth, and ready to depart. He walked up the galley stairs with a forceful swagger, yet his every movement was as nimble and precise as a butterfly ballet. He was like a great bull moving masterfully and effortlessly through a room of crstal glassware, without disturbing a single thing.

Unexpectedly, before a word was passed between them, the great general went to his knees at the feet of King Day, bowed his head, and raised his palms supine before him in submission and respect. "I, too, have made an extraordinary decision, Your Highness," he said. "I make an offering to you. Of great value. I believe you will find this gift will more than repay my indebtedness in full, although it will hurt your heart to hear it.

"I sense I may die out in these fields today, or, if not, perhaps tomorrow, cut down by missiles that I, in a way, made myself. Yet, before my life ends, I am owed a revenge for the wrong that has been done to me. Against those who I once pledged my entire life to, who I served unquestioningly for forty years. To those who have done nearly all to destroy me and all that I ever cared for, and still continue to do so. They hunt me down like an animal, like a wild, rabid dog. Me! Well, they have chosen the wrong man to betray. For, in the names of my unjustly dishonored father and mother of the House of Anghor, and in the memory of my precious and innocent wife and son, I will give you something far greater than my skills as a Gharnian soldier, accompanying you on your quest.

"I give you the truth of the Curse of Lord Gheelgahar, The Day Family Bane, *the* Curse that has plagued the Family of Day since the end of the First Battle and the end of the First Age. I give you the secret of this ancient Curse to do with what you are able. And so, *this* will be my revenge.

"What you have heard in the stories of old is true," he said. "You and your family *are* immortal. Or *should've* been..."

Day squinted at him. "I don't understand."

"...except but for one powerful curse. The Curse of Gheelgahar. An ancient curse known only to a few, the topmost ranks of the Gharnian Elite.

Day frowned. "C-curse?"

"This may be the best guarded secret in the oldest scrolls in the deepest caverns in the tallest towers of Gharne," decreed Kadazaat. "And it comes to you at no easy price. The price of my soul. For, from this moment forward, my betrayal is complete."

"Day's Bane," Drer whispered. His ears were sharp, and from where he stood, he could overhear them talking. He crept closer to hear better.

"My very own people took my family from me! There may be nothing I can do about that now. We will see. But perhaps, this one broken secret may bring you some peace with your own family someday, if you can find a way to break it."

Dedlin's face grew pale. He looked over at his friend and confidant Drer Fregoode, who had placed one hand over his mouth and another one over his heart. Pieces of a great and ancient puzzle were about to fall into place before them, right then and there. An unanswered question of old, now being revealed, all because of Day's kindness to an abused Gharnian traitor. They had both heard of this Curse, the most significant missing puzzle piece in the struggle against Gheelgahar's ancient evil. Since nothing of it had ever been chronicled, or detected, scholars believed the Curse of Gheelgahar had done its dark work long ago, whatever it had been, and was long ago used up, forgotten, and henceforth became completely harmless.

"This Curse has been a crucial, active component of Lord Gheelgahar's ultimate design to keep the kings of Mead from passing their powers and secrets from one generation to the next. Like Gheelgahar, the First King Day was immortal, living life forever in the prime of His life, say, around the age of twenty five or thirty. Unless, of course, He was killed, and even still, the Family Day are extremely hearty beings and quick healers, rarely able to be hurt or get sick. Immortals rarely to never become ill, and they simply never grow old. This trait, supposedly, passes from the parents in your family to their offspring. An enviable characteristic.

"Everyone knows the story: Day the First defeated Lord Gheelgahar the Great and sent Him to a cruel, living death in the bowels of the Black Sea, south of Gharne. But what the Gharnian Elite has kept in secret is that Gheelgahar's powers were not completely spent before He was swept downward into that black whirlpool abyss. In His infinite foresight and wisdom, with the aid of his Sorceror Lords and Black Mystics, He gathered the last vestiges of His sacred magick and placed a curse on your forefather, and all that would follow in His line, from that time so long ago, to this. And since that time, this Curse has been cared for, nurtured, and enforced by the Mystics and Sorceror Lords of Gheelgahar, from deep within the sacred bowels of Gharne.

"This curse is designed to wait benign for the right moment before it takes effect, (just as it now awaits inside you). Just as King Day the First became a mortal man, as told in most historical accounts, He relinquished his godlike powers into a number of prepared magickal Stones. It was only then, since he was then powerless, that the Curse could take its strategic effect. That Curse, specifically, was, and is, this:

"No offspring of the family line of Day the First will ever know their parents, for shortly after their first child is born to them, the parents will both contract what appears to be a fatal disease, and they will die, painfully and slowly. But die they inevitably do. Lord Gheelgahar's Curse is a contrived disease that afflicts any new parents with quick illness and death."

"I... I don't believe you," Day said, scowling.

"It is the truth, nonetheless. Just think about the facts. How old were you when your parents died?" Kadazaat asked. "How did they die? How about your father's parents before Him? And His before that? There is a definite pattern that can now be discerned. If you first recognize it is even there."

"I don't believe you..." Day repeated, but it was clear that his words were now faltering as this new information filled in and fit the gaping holes in the mysteries of his family's history.

Kadazaat continued. "How long did your ancestors live before they first conceived a child? Thousands of years, am I not right? Or did you think it was only stories? They were all immortal, *until conception occurred.*"

Gaebryl focused his thoughts. "So, you're saying that Day here will live forever in his prime, unless he decides to procreate and have a child?"

Kadazaat nodded. "That is exactly right. Or, unless he is killed. No one can live without a head or heart."

"All my ancestors did die the same way," Day acknowledged, pensively staring into space. "Everyone always said that they thought it was just some strange island disease. But it is true. It has to be true. The children were always so young each generation when the parents passed away. It was not just some coincidence? It's so horrible."

"This is part of the foundation of what is to become His triumphant return. Lord Gheelgahar's Curse is a genealogical disease, mixed with dark magick. One generation to the next, in your family alone."

"It was said that my father was over three hundred years old when he died, but looked as though he were in the prime of his years," Day said to Dedlin, looking to him for some insight or reassurance. "My grandfather was older than that, and his father even older. Isn't that right?"

"Originally, I believe that Gheelgahar cast this Curse out of last minute desperation, for the sole purpose of exacting some kind of retributive revenge in the end, before his descent into the Black Sea. His last chance. Fleeting. The Curse would have never even worked had King Day the First not relinquished His powers into the Stones. Foolishly, He did. Why shouldn't He? Gheelgahar was gone, and the great king was in love with a mortal woman.

"Yet, Gheelgahar prevailed in the end and His Curse worked. Just like in the tale of the tortoise and the hare, Gheelgahar did survive, and Day the First has been long gone, as have his generational heirs. In the long run, the ingenious Curse has proven to be of much greater consequence and value than Gheelgahar had ever imagined. Because of it, no secrets have passed from generation to generation, other than partial, written messages that no one can even find anymore. No father to son and/or daughter talks. Nor a mother's nurturing love. Nor the locations of the five Stones of Power. After a few generations, the strength of the original family has dramatically diminished. Lord Gheelgahar, assumed entrapped for eternity, took that opportunity to slowly rise and grow again, unhindered by his enemies of old, perfecting His original plans. He could once again rebuild His forces, without any resistance. And that is what happened, and is still happening, even now."

All were silent for nearly a minute while these shards of information found painful places to lodge in everyone's hearts and minds.

"Your gift has done little to encourage," Gaebryl said, looking pale. "I would that it could be unsaid."

"Gheelgahar is indeed clever and devious," Day mumbled. It was as if the wind had been knocked out of him. "I feel more defeated than ever."

"Then, we'll hear no more of it!" Binder cried, pointing his weapon at the Gharnian soldier. Otthagorus raised his as well. They had both overheard enough of the conversation, and could see the duress on their friends' faces, to come forward into the fray. "Storytime is over."

Kadazaat was unfazed by the show of aggression. "Most importantly of all," he said, defiantly concluding. "I shall leave you with this, for surely the wyzard knows its importance more than even I do: Because of Gheelgahar's great Curse, the prophesied Five can never come. After the first child is born, the parents soon thereafter die. Only one child at a time, aging alone, parentless, and ne'er a brother or sister to be born. Any mere army can deal with just one Stonebearer. Even if you succeed in this quest, what are the chances of finding the other four Stones now? The world is closing in upon you."

"Enough!" Commander Binder ordered, even angrier. "I'm

warning you."

Kadazaat complied. He looked at Commander Binder from the corner of his eye, undaunted. "The truth sometimes hurts," he said, almost as a dare.

Dedlin was mumbling to himself, the wheels in his mind churning, his mouth reflecting the rapid succession of sequences flashing through his mind. "The Five? The Five? That's part of *this*? That would explain the searches in Eaoph... Each generation, but they must have figured it out somehow. But wait! How could the...oh, yes, that makes sense, then. The Five Powers! But th- then, she can't die anyway, so there has to be more to it than that. All hidden..? But how... A guardian? A protector? That makes some bit of sense. Five? Could there be four more? Impossible. I would've heard something."

Gaebryl, like the rest of the crew, was utterly confused. "Who or what are the Five? The five Stones of Power?"

"No," the Gharnian answered. "Five Stone*bearers*."

"But there is only one," Drer said to the wyzard. "Or do you think it's possible..."

"I don't know! I don't know!"

"So this Curse worked then?" Day cried. "That's what you're saying? Gheelgahar has returned, and His Curse has worked for another generation?"

Kadazaat nodded. "The *final* generation."

"Why couldn't this fate have come to my father instead of me?"

"You cannot win," Kadazaat said resolutely. "You are too late. He has already won. But at least you now know how it was accomplished."

"One more pessimistic remark and my blaster will go off accidentally," Binder told the Gharnian.

Dedlin shook his head. "There's so much I need to find out. I don't know! I have to read! I have to read! And blast! All my books are at home."

Drer and Dedlin walked away together, talking in hushed whispers.

"We won't hear from them for the rest of the night," Perce remarked.

Day was more perplexed now than ever, but remained steady before the Gharnian general. "You have borne us great knowledge and mystery which will offer us food for thought for a long time to come, Kadazaat, and truly, I am troubled to my core. You have sacrificed much to do so I believe, and I thank you as well as curse your name for this new information," he said. "And although I am bereaved, I now consider our contract to one another fulfilled. I will hold to our bargain and help you search for your missing family as soon as I am able."

"We are even, Your Highness," he said. "You will undoubtedly have more important things to do than search for my family if you reach the first Stone."

"We will see," Day replied. "After meeting you, I have a different viewpoint on your kind than I once did. I am still indebted, for that one revelation alone. Therefore, I ask you once more before you depart, will you not accept my offer? Come with us. Join our crew."

"Again, I must decline. I have done all for you that I am able. I am impassioned to follow my own life's journey, even to its doom, if fate decrees. My presence here endangers you all in ways you could not foresee. I must away, and soon. It is best, from this point on, to agree that our paths never have crossed."

50

The following two days were dreary ones. Skies were overcast and gray and moods were touchy. Dedlin and Drer poured through their meager cache of books, occasionally running back and forth to show one another something. Day was brooding and distant, always mumbling about the Curse, or the parents he had never really known. He began talking incessantly to anyone who would listen: how he had always longed to know his mother and father, to touch them and be held by them as a child, and to speak to them now, adult to adult. To ask them about these awful responsibilities he had been left with, that they had so selfishly passed on to him to bear. Sure, he had been raised by loving counselors, but there was never that loving touch that only a parent could give. He found himself increasingly hating his dead parents for deserting him, and passing on to him this unbearable responsibility. It just wasn't fair.

Binder and Otthagorus both argued that they should never have let Kadazaat go free the way that they had, but after stating their case to everyone plainly, they never mentioned it again. However, on the other hand, Commander Benjyn Binder was very humbled by the recent events, and now found himself a new, true believer. In the Old Stories, the Stonebearer, the Curse of Gheelgahar, and everything else he had previously scoffed at. Especially the judgmental ineptitude of his aged mentor, Dedlin Dane. He could not apologize enough for his doubting behavior and ignorance back in Tungulin. But he tried, to the point of irritating redundancy.

Ott found a new perch on top of the helm cabin from where he could lay on his belly in the sun and survey the distant horizons without obstructions. Thus far, travel had been good, for all he saw was the waving grasses of the great fields of Tuus vanishing off into all distances like a speckled sea of yellow/green waves.

Stardeer had been damaged irreparably by the storm, but she was still aloft and sailing along at three quarters speed. Perce was well again, once again at the guidestick, instructing castleranger Qan Methalard on the finer points of skycraft navigation. He even let him hold the acceleration bar for minutes at a time. The evening was waning, but they were warm and dry, so traveling was comfortable, if not sometimes even pleasant. They began bedding down wherever there was room, a few of them on the upper deck, beneath the stars. The darkening western sky was lit up like a stage above a city made of fiery orange candles.

"I hope that Kadazaat fellow is okay," Qan said to Perce before he retired for the evening. "Even if he is an ex-Gharnian General, I felt sorry for him. He's a lot like us, if you think about it, even though he's a lot bigger, partly metal, and he's killed a lot of people."

51

"Let's see if we can round up some food down there somewhere, for goodness sakes. I'm starving!" Dedlin said, waking everyone shortly after dawn. Mornings are when he tended to be his loudest. "You don't want to see a wyzard when he's really hungry. Anyone up for a hunt?"

Otthagorus resolutely volunteered.

Now the land below them was rocky, with patches of tough knots of brown grass in the clefts and cracks, and an occasional wood of dry, twisted trees pinched tightly in the infrequent hollows that opened like wide toothy smiles. The gray and golden hills rolled off in all directions, rising higher in the far distance southward.

The landscape below was dotted with immense handcut square stones, arranged sometimes in long, straight lines for miles at a time, for whatever purpose, long ago forgotten. The fog in the hollows began burning off as the suns crept lazily up into the morning sky.

"Let's set this thing down so that we can walk around a little bit," Gaebryl suggested. "I'm tired of being all cramped up on this little rowboat! I need to stretch my legs, and stop knocking elbows!"

"Thank you!" agreed the grumpy, hungry thordian.

"How far from Gorn?" Binder asked, coming up from the galley. "I can smell my homeland in the air this morning!"

"Drer said that we were about four hours away, and that

was three hours ago," Qan answered, proudly steering Stardeer on his own.

"One more hour says our new pilot!" Binder replied. "I must visit friends in Poed as soon as I have the chance. It's been far too many years since I've been there." Stardeer hit an air pocket and bounced. "Whoa!" Binder said. "Careful, Qan, please, don't kill us on your first day at the helm."

Below, a herd of small antelope bounded away up the rocks, fleeing from the oncoming Stardeer. Ott eyed them hungrily. Ironically, after all the rain they had endured in the fields, the creek beds there were as dry as bone. No rain had fallen on that part of Tuus for a long, long time. Ever so often, a cloud of silver steam sprayed brightly from hot geysers, hidden down in cloven piles of shattered rock and brick hard, cracked mud. It looked as if, at one time, much of the land had been irrigated for some irrigation or agricultural purpose. Dry, cracked culverts crisscrossed at various intersections between the huge blocks of stone.

"Anyone else interested in some antelope for breakfast?" the thordian asked from high on his perch. He cocked his arrowjet rifle theatrically. "I volunteer to hunt for all of us, although I daresay I could eat a whole stag myself."

"That looks like an orchard over there," Dedlin said, pointing to the southeast. The horizon, from the east to the south, was covered with dark rows of planted trees, in long, straight lines, as far as the eye could see. "I venture that we could accessorize our antelope steaks with some delicious ripened fruit this fine morning, if we're lucky. Qan, my good man, head for that oasis. Let's see what we can find there."

Ten

IN THE ORCHARDS

52

"Mmm, Drer, you are absolutely right. These are good," Gaebryl said, his mouth full of sweet apple. "The best apples I've ever tasted."

"Delicious!" Dedlin piped, wiping his chin on his sleeve. "Wonderful! Scrumptious!" He bit into another one with a loud crunch. "Includes nature's cinnamon!"

Seven crew members relaxed on and about the front bow of Stardeer, feasting upon a bountiful supply of large, red, shiny apples available in all directions at an arm's reach. Out on the lawn, Ott had a medium sized antelope on a spit above a fresh blaze for himself and anyone else who might be interested. The aroma of the charred meat was exceptional. Day had sat alone in the hold below all morning, staring out a window into the orchard forest, thinking and brooding.

The patched up skycraft hovered low under the heavily laden branches of a massive apple tree, wedged in like a treehouse, well within the cover of the immense orchard. The tall rows of overburdened fruit trees continued for miles in every direction, covering the patterned fields and rolling hills like a giant patchwork quilt. Once in awhile, small brown eyes could be seen staring at them from the leafy boughs, or a raucous laugh would echo up throughout the orchard forest nearby. Dedlin told them that they had nothing to fear. The laughs belonged to the playful luper monkeys that lived in the forests along the Gornian River region. Lake threw an apple core at two of them to watch them scramble away, chattering.

"I've only eaten one apple," Qan said. "Yet, I feel

remarkably full, and satiated, as though I've eaten a full, hearty meal."

Lake agreed with his friend.

Gaebryl was rubbing the area around his knee. "For the first time the aching in my leg has subsided," he said. "In fact, I'm invigorated overall, myself, just as Qan is. This is miracle fruit!"

As usual, Perce partook his meal privately behind a folding partition a few feet away from the other crew members, as was his custom. Like all mahekians, he consumed food through a slit opening in his stomach. Eating was a personal, private matter for their race, to be undertaken alone (or, should one be wed, with their life partner). "They are a type of healing fruit," he said as he rejoined them. He pulled back the folds of his robe sleeves, extended his bare arms and flexed his talons. "I can feel my damaged skin healing even as I stand here before you. The warmth of the sunslight filtering through the boughs is equally rejuvenating."

"Otthagorus, would you care for one?" Binder said, sarcastically. "For medicinal purposes, if not for the pure deliciousness of the fruit?"

Ott growled, his lip curling up in disgust. "I'd just as soon eat dirt," the carnivore replied. "Candytree seeds. Bah. Apples. Bah!"

"It might help your head wound. Like medicine," Gaebryl said.

"It will heal just fine on its own, I'm quite sure."

Binder held up a particularly large apple. "You're not afraid to eat one, are you?" he said playfully. "I would like to test your courage. Eat one, thordian, if you dare. Here. Catch."

A growl deepened, rumbling like an amplified cat's purr in Ott's chest. "Test my courage," he said, snatching the apple from the air. He took a whiff of it and his face wrinkled up repulsively. "By the gods! How can you eat these foul things?"

"Go ahead," Dedlin Dane said. "Take your medicine. An apertif will be good for you. You will feed on antelope soon enough."

Ott stared at the fruit one last time, gathered his wits, and tossed the entire apple into his open maw. He chewed on it for a few seconds, groaning the entire time, and then he swallowed it, nearly whole. "I'm going to be sick!" he said, spitting the remnants onto the ground.

The crew laughed, and continued to eat their fill.

The lower deck door came slowly open and Day came out to join them topside, his face long and his shoulders drooping.

"Here," Gaebryl called to him. "Have an apple." He tossed him a large one.

Day had not looked up, and so the fruit caught him off guard, hitting him squarely in the chest. Day's hand went up, gripping the spot painfully.

"Oh!" Gaebryl said. "I'm sorry. I didn't mean to do that..."

"It's okay," Day said. "Really. I'm all right. I just wasn't watching. My mind was on other things."

Gaebryl came toward him. "Join us?"

"No," Day answered. He turned away from them and swung a leg over the rail. "I'm going for a walk. I'll be right back."

"I'll go with you," Gaebryl said. "It might not be safe."

"I want some time alone," he said, stepping from the ladderstairs onto the ground. Their eyes briefly met. "I won't be gone long. I won't go far," he said as he turned away from them.

"Let him go," Dedlin said softly, holding the prince back by his arm. "The king is fine. He just needs some space from us for a bit."

Day walked away, his head hung low. The crew watched as he disappeared among the drooping branches, following the row above which they hovered.

Gaebryl looked up at Dedlin, almost resentfully. "Do not patronize me any longer, wyzard" he said to him. "No more games. You don't mean *he*. You mean *she*, don't you? I'm not stupid, and I'm certainly not blind. Day is not a king, and never was. Day is a queen if she is anything at all."

The crew suddenly stopped eating, confused faces on display everywhere.

"What...what was that you just said?" Binder asked. "He's a..."

Dedlin looked grim, yet relieved. "The prince is correct," he told them. "Our good King Jamesyn Day is indeed... a female. A girl, masquerading as a boy. I knew it the moment I first laid eyes on her. And, the subject of which, we have privately spoken."

"Loose clothes, bindings and padded shoulders cannot cover what nature does to a girl at her age," Gaebryl said. "And her features are much too fair and demure. Her hair too fine and silky. I suspected early on, and have been certain for awhile, but still said nothing. I figured there must be a good reason. I knew that you shared some secret with her, Dedlin, and I always found her modesty a bit overcompensating."

"She took on this disguise when she left Mead for the mainland," Ott added. "I, too, have always known her true identity and kept it hidden."

"Of course, this brings up more questions than answers," Drer Fregoode replied, somewhat still in shock himself. Dedlin had shared this revelation with his longtime confidante Drer shortly after Kadazaat's departure from them. "We are working on some interesting theories even now."

"I... I am bewildered and amazed! Why such a deception?" Binder asked. "Why take on the guise of a boy?"

"I am sure that is has something to do with her mission," Dedlin said. "I, too, had been expecting Day to be a man, and you can imagine my surprise when I discovered otherwise in King Vantoo's great meeting hall. I'm sure she was advised by her counselors to come to us as a young *king*. Would we have believed a young girl making the claims she has? Would we have followed her into peril? Would *you* have?" He cast a sharp eye in Gaebryl's direction. The prince averted his gaze. "It was hard enough to get things done with her posing as the prophesied Meadian King. The old prophecies told of the return of King Day, not Queen Day. This paradox caused the Inner Council to hesitate and stutter before authenticating her identity at the emergency Secret Council, but still, she was ratified by them. And rightly so. She is still the heir of the Stone."

"Are we sure she is?" Binder asked. "Does this change anything?"

"Yes," the wyzard simply replied with a shrug. "And no."

Gaebryl dropped his head shamefully. Sadly, Dedlin was right. He might not have followed *Queen* Day off on this mission in the same capacity as he had *King* Day, or even believed her tale. He might have just left her, safe in Daerooge or in Tungulin, and been on his own merry way. He knew that he would have most likely scoffed at her preposterous claims of Meadian royalty... He had been brought up to believe that men were superior to women. And he had embraced that belief, perhaps as a defense mechanism for his own insecurities. Or fear of desertion. He had never truly ever trusted women since his own mother's death when he was but a wee lad. He knew that he was guilty of chauvinism, more than any other there, and felt ashamed.

"Many armies will follow a king into battle before they will a queen," Ott told them. "Maybe the Meadian counselors feared what the Gharnians would do to her if they captured her along the way. Death as a male soldier is better than serving a life term as a concubine to some Gharnian general and his staff and family."

"It could aid in her attempt to elude the Gharnians," Drer interjected. "They will be looking for a king. This disguise could work to her advantage..."

"After hearing Kadazaat's explanation of the Curse of Gheelgahar, there may even be other, more relevant reasons for not disclosing her gender than these. Reasons that I suspect she does not even know, although I do have a theory... A theory that I am not ready to disclose just yet," the wyzard said to them. "Of this matter now, I am only sure of two things. One, Jasmine Day, which is her true name, is obligated wholeheartedly to this quest. And two, Gaebryl Dindiane," he said, slowing down, "she is in love with you."

"She is..?"

"...in love with you," he repeated.

Gaebryl suspected that could be.

"Ah, that's why she suffers so," Lake mumbled quietly. They had all seen it. "She cannot express her feelings... It must be terrible for her."

The prince of Bursia stared blankly at the wyzard, then off in the direction that Jasmine Day had taken. Yes, she may be in love with him, couldn't she? Hadn't he known it all along? She was too young for him he was thinking; that was part of his justification for denial. She was no more than thirteen or fourteen, and he was twenty five.

However, he did have feelings for her, protective and brotherly, and this hypocrisy was breaking his heart. "We mustn't let her stray too far," he said, strong emotion moving through him. "It would be safer for her to stay close to the ship, even if she does need time alone, not wander around this orchard maze unsupervised. I am going after her. Someone come with me."

53

The sound of voices passed behind Jasmine Day before she realized it. She strolled along, weaving through the trees, kicking at tumblegrass while trying to empty her troubled mind of all her anxieties. There was just too much for her to cope with; too many problems and not enough answers. Too many neverending paths, just like the one she was following through the apple orchard. Did the orchard have as many secrets as she had?

She picked an apple, nibbling as she went. Her chest ached where it had been hit. Had anyone suspected? She hadn't hidden the pain very well; it wouldn't have hurt a boy like that. She had been so tender there lately, perhaps because she tried to keep herself constantly flattened with a tight, specially made corset that was getting too small for her. She longed to pull it off and throw it into the weeds; it made her so sore. She did not know how much longer she would be able to keep up the façade; people would soon want to know why the king had breasts and no whiskers on his face.

The trail at her feet turned to stone as she made her way through an old stone archway, mostly hidden among the trees. From far above came the sound of silly laughter, but Jasmine didn't heed it. Nor did she notice the old walkway she was following, or the short stone walls on both sides of her, leading her deeper and deeper into the old orchard forest. It wasn't until she began a descent down a flight of stone stairs that she paused to look at her surroundings.

"I was daydreaming," she said to herself.

A couple of old yellow ochre colored monkeys sitting on the wall near her laughed at her words.

The stairway led diagonally down a dark hillside, cutting through great, massive leveled steps that each great row of apple trees grew upon. The stairs divided, then the ones she took were joined by a different set coming from a different direction. The apple trees around this vale were much older and wilder than the previous apple trees she had seen. The bark on the boles was black and curled. The huge, reaching branches, excessively fruitful, bent to the ground in great upswept arches.

The two monkeys followed her, she on the steps, they on the wall. They continued hooting and laughing, sometimes making silly faces at one another. One continually hit the other one on the head with a small stick. Jasmine found their antics amusing.

Besides the aromatic cinnamon apples, Jasmine detected a faint hint of sweet honey nectar on the air. The golden blooms on the trees swarmed with large, black and yellow striped hummingbees. The cool wind rode down the hillside with her, gently coaxing her forward. Monkeys of different sizes began to line the stairway to gawk at her, mounting themselves like comical gargoyles along the walls. At the bottom of the hill, the trail swerved crookedly through the apple trees, no longer in nice, neat rows anymore. The monkeys, all colors, all shapes and sizes, were still coming toward her from out of the trees, more and more of them, perching on limbs and on every ancient column. Some even gathered enough courage to touch Jasmine with their fingertips as she walked past. They hooted and howled, seeming to cheer her on as she began another descent of stairs, hundreds of them, down into a massive, shadowy valley, filled from rim to rim with dark, ancient apple trees.

"Where does this lead?" she said, squinting into the shadows beyond. The monkeys howled excitedly. They knew, didn't they?

The steps crossed over an immense ravine by means of a narrow stone arcbridge, covered with ivy and decades of woodland debris, and shrouded with the largest apple trees Jasmine Day had ever seen. Some of the apples that hung from the drooping limbs were the size of cantaloupes. She passed beneath cracked stone archways every twenty or so steps, thirty three of them in all, until she came to the last one on the opposite end of the bridge. It was larger than the rest, connected to large wall that circled away from her on both sides. Stepping inside, she found that it marked the entrance to a gateway of a great ancient amphitheater in the very heart of the mysterious orchard forest depths.

She passed curiously inside and looked about.

The entire amphitheater appeared to have been carved from a single great hollow bowl of bedrock, some time, long, long ago. Far down in the center there was what appeared to be a circular stage, or an altar of some kind, or perhaps even a well, since there was no floor on it. It was a bit frightening to look upon. In the center of it was a black hole, a strange void where light could not penetrate or pass, where one would not want to look directly into for fear of losing one's self in its deep, ancient magick.

Then, radiating outwards from the well, Jasmine counted sixty six smooth, concentric, flat rings of stone rising upward and outward as great primitive seats for giants, covered with decades, if not centuries, of rotting debris dropped from the overhanging trees. The brownish gray rock of the amphitheater was so old and worn by the elements that it appeared seamless and natural, created by nature rather than chiseled by civilized hands.

What had once been a grand theater to some extinct civilization of eons past, now had returned to nature's wilds. And it was beautiful.

The trees surrounding the theater were huge. They arched high over the clearing, blocking out nearly all the sunslight with their dense, leafy foliage. All the seats were complete in shadow, even though it was coming on noon. There was only one opening in the dome of leaves and branches above her, directly in the center of the amphitheater ceiling, high above the black void of the well, and somehow nearly as perfectly circular in shape. A bright column of sunslight shone through that opening, lighting a nearly perfect circle on the stone ground, just inches away from the well's strange emptiness.

It was amazing to Jasmine that such a beautiful, exotic place could ever have been forgotten by man. It was awesome, incredulous, and beyond amazing.

She started slowly down the steps to investigate the curious pulsating well, when a ruckus erupted behind her. She turned to find two white whiskered luper monkeys, one gray, one red, dashing from the trees, down the steps of the amphitheater, directly past her. They did not stop until they reached the front row, only a few feet away from the throbbing well. Then, from the other side of the arena, several more apes dropped from low hanging limbs and squealed exuberantly as they dashed to find seats down in front.

"How strange," she said.

As the minutes passed, crowds of crazily laughing monkeys began to fill the stands, finding seats as near to the well as they could, wailing, and waving their long arms and nimble tails in anticipation.

Jasmine's heart began to pound. Something exciting was about to happen there, she knew it, although she couldn't imagine what. She pushed some rotten apples aside and took a seat. She wished that Gaebryl were there with her.

The monkeys kept coming, but they were hesitant to sit too close to her. Like Jasmine, they were both nervous and excited. They screamed and jumped, and sometimes ran in anxious circles, keeping their eyes on the column of light as it approached the rim of the well as the suns approached their zeniths. They began to go into a wild, frenzylike trance, bobbing their round heads and baring their long white fangs. Soon the amphitheater was absolutely full of heckling simians, and the din was deafening.

The suns were almost directly overhead. Jasmine watched wide eyed as the column of light began to descend over and into the blackness of the well. She could not bring herself to blink. She wasn't even sure if she were breathing or not. She knew certainly that she did not hear the monkeys anymore, and that she was unable, or unwilling, to move, or to remove her eyes from the upcoming spectacle before her.

All became dark, silent, and dreamlike around her. The trees had blackened in, filling the amphitheater with the same consuming emptiness that had been waiting in the well. The single column of light stood tall and straight before her, stone pure and crystal white, reflecting her thoughts, memories and dreams like an open mirror into her soul. Somehow, time did not exist anymore.

Images came. Like in a dream, they might have been there all along, but she hadn't seen them, until, all at once, hundreds of them began flashing before her vacant eyes. They were moments and segments of her life, undistinguishable, but somehow, crystal clear and as vivid as reality in present time: faces, emotions, duties, fear, all alive and full of color and sound. Conversations from the future and the past. Everything she saw held a vital message for her, if she could only decipher and remember them. Others, including her new friends, were there with her, too.

She saw Commander Binder there in the void, in a dark place, running for his life. He was underground, in a filthy cave. There were others running with him, all afraid, trying to get away from something, but Jasmine did not see herself there among them. Ott was there, she saw. There were echoes coming from behind them, many padded feet, some heavy booted feet, flapping, echoing, and racing in dogged pursuit. Down a long, dark tunnel. Which way? *Run harder and don't stop, no matter what*, she wanted to tell them. A dead-end! Then there was a crash and a flash of light, and it was all over.

Then she saw other people and other places. A red headed boy named Thistle. An old man of great power on a great horse commanding bolts of lightning to obey his will. A forest of connected trees and vines where the leaves came to life as men who spoke like the wind. Another old man, lying on the ground. It was Dedlin! He was motionless. Dead.

She saw Gaebryl, but he looked different. His hair was short and tinged with gray. Like a flash, it passed.

There was Binder again, in another dark place at another time, caught within a collapsing crevasse. Straining! Hold the jaws open! Too late; he was swallowed and was gone. Sadness!

There was Stardeer. Jasmine saw the crew there just as though she were there riding along with them. All of the crew but one was onboard. Lake Tobias, the Tungulinian castleranger, was not among them. He was gone. But wait! They weren't on Stardeer. They were walking across a dusty field between clumps of dark trees and mounds of dirt. It was night. There was danger all around them, no, below them! They began dropping into holes, one by one, and hideous things were in the muddy holes, waiting to devour their helpless prey...

Then she was upon a great flying beast among the clouds. Although this vision was vague and distant, she felt strong and resolute. Powerful. But she was not alone there; in fact, there were four others, each riding beside her on their own magnificent beasts. They were beginning their descent down into a place of incomparable evil. Who were these four who looked so familiar to her?

She realized then who they were, and her heart began to pound joyously. They were her brothers and sisters! Two of each. She was one of five! This was the Five that Kadazaat had spoken of! Five siblings, five Stones -- five great powers! Damn the Curse of Gheelgahar! Somehow, it had already been defeated! They lived!

She was exhilarated. She was not alone! She had two sisters and two brothers somewhere else in the world, each one connected to their own Power Stone, and someday they were destined to meet and take on this awesome and horrendous responsibility together.

Someday they would unite and move as one to face the evil. Gheelgahar thought His Curse would end all hopes for the Five who were prophesied to destroy Him once and for all. However, He never foresaw the chance of quintuplets!

Another epiphany! She knew that their names were Legend August, Amber Leigh, Destiny Blue and Chance Brook. Every fiber in her body flowed with rapture at this newfound knowledge. She knew them already! She knew them and she loved them!

The vision faded. She tried to hold on to it, for fear of forgetting it, but it blew away like smoke. "Wait!" she cried.

Now who was this woman? She was grim, but so beautiful, her hair long and golden. She was filled with sweetness and life, as open as a book, a princess perhaps, but a warrior as well, with many years of toil behind her. She was sitting on a bench near a stream, braiding blue ribbons into her hair. A man draws near on horseback, handsome and fierce, long, dark hair and beard, kissed with strands of gray, braided over his shoulders. He is older, but regal and content. He looks familiar to her. He dismounts and kneels beside the woman, taking her hand in his.

Jasmine can see that they are in love. Is it Gaebryl? A fire of jealousy wells up inside her heart. Who is the woman? Who is she? And why is she crying?

Next, she saw a shadow of a face, and her heart instantly chilled with fear. It was a man. A man with the ability to frighten her to the core of her soul. This was the clearest vision of all, as though it were a vision in the present time. She could see this hideous face as if she were standing right before him, and he thing that terrorized her most was that she believed that, at that very moment, he could also see her as well. Still, she did not flinch before his piercing gaze. As he began to fade, like all the visions did, she stood firm and resolute. She had seen his face before, and she knew that she would see it again someday in the real world. His fiery green/gray eyes were unforgettable.

Then she saw a hazy vision from the past. It was her mother. She was so beautiful, with ice blonde hair, alabaster skin and slate blue/gray eyes. Jasmine was filled with warmness and comfort. Her mother was waiting for her somewhere, and she seemed so content. Jasmine longed to be held by her, to melt into the warmness of her embrace, but she looked so pale and sick...

"I'll be back, soon," her mother said tenderly, eyes filled with tears. She turned her head to cough. For a moment, Jasmine saw the outline of another figure coming through the mists toward them, hoping it to be her beloved father, Mikael Nicholias Day. How the people of Mead had loved him. Jasmine had been told how good he was and how much he was missed. As the figure came into view before her, the scene faded serenely away.

More visions came. They flashed before her eyes and in her mind for what seemed like a luxurious eternity. She tried to see them all, individually, but she could not. They were layered one on top of the other and running without time. She could not even retain the ones she could translate, each one knocking the last one into nothingness. It was a delirious torture. There were eyes everywhere: large mysterious green eyes in a plain of white, a man with violet eyes hiding among the trees. Who or what they were, she had no idea. Colors, faces, great things and places to come. Healing, knowledge, beautiful songs, worlds beyond her universe. A man in a kitchen poking keys at a small, black box. A boy with a scraggly scoundrel of a mutt, watching his friend trying to fly. A pestilence of insects a mile wide, marching, devouring. A great machine, the size of many cities, rolling over mountains, unstoppable, across the landscape. An angel in white. It was all there before her eyes. It was all revealed.

Jasmine shook her head and rubbed her eyes as she reluctantly emerged from this waking dream. She rubbed her eyes. She was chilled and wet. It had obviously been drizzling for awhile, and it was nearly dark.

A luper monkey was within inches of her face, watching her eye to eye as she awoke from the trance. Jasmine flinched when he came into focus before her, frightening him. He scrambled away, screaming angrily over his shoulder. Here and there throughout the dark amphitheater, several apes still sat, motionless and wide eyed, jaws slack, staring blankly at where the void had been, their limbs and tails limp. Now, nothing showed in the well. The light was gone, the sky was filled with wet clouds, and the visions had faded as fast as they had come. They seemed so distant and dreamlike to her now, so very, very distant. She was having much trouble remembering anything about them at all.

"It's almost dark!" she cried, drowsily. She rose to her wobbly legs and ran back up the wet stone seats toward the entrance from which she had entered the amphitheater earlier that day. "They're probably so worried," she said. "I've got to get back!"

She ran back up through the arches, back over the slippery arcbridge, and up the countless stairs in the fading twilight, trying hard not to stumble, and hoping to find the rest of the crew before nightfall was fully upon her. The monkeys that still remained watched her with pensive, half lidded eyes, not making a sound now. Only their heads turned to watch her as she raced past them.

"I've got two brothers and two sisters!" she cried, but her voice fell dead among the wet trees. Or did she? She was now suddenly unsure about all that, because it was all just a dream, wasn't it? Nothing more than wispy wishes of her hopeful, yet downhearted, subconscious, inspired by nothing but the mere words of others. Piece by fragmented piece, the strange visions she had witnessed dissipated into the ghostly orchard mists with every step she took, until they were, for the most part, completely forgotten.

54

It was nightfall, and Gaebryl and Drer Fregoode had not yet returned from their latest expedition. They had searched for Jasmine Day ever since she had departed, and there was still no sign of her whereabouts, no clues, no tracks. It was nigh on inconceivable, and all were frightfully concerned. She seemed to have virtually disappeared into thin air.

Dedlin, Otthagorus and Binder had all gone off in different directions throughout the afternoon and evening, and had returned without finding a single clue to her whereabouts. There were many master trackers among them, and all were stumped. They gathered beneath the dark umbrella canopy of a particularly stout apple tree and waited anxiously for some news. No one had yet suggested kidnap or capture, but that was surely foremost on everyone's worried minds. The suns had set and, just minutes before, Ott had spotted a Gharnian warship cruising above the orchard to the distant northwest, bathing the shadowy apple trees in floodlight.

Dedlin had been surveying the landscape from the top of the tree, but was quickly on his way back down. "Here they come," he said softly. "They've found her, bless them. Let's get going. We can be in Gorn before sunset tomorrow night, if we get a move on right now."

"Thank the gods," several of them said, very relieved.

They hurried out from under their cover and met Gaebryl, Drer, and Jasmine Day at Stardeer with many salutations of joy and relief.

"Your Highness," Otthagorus said, bowing. "We were worried."

"I'm sorry," she told them all. "I was delayed. I think I fell asleep and had the most unusual dreams..."

"We've spotted a warship close by, so we must be careful," Dedlin told her. "They are scouring the orchard."

Jasmine nodded to him. Everyone was looking at her and trying unsuccessfully to hide their smiles.

"Your Highness," Drer Fregoode said, bowing.

"Your Highness," replied Lake and Qan almost simultaneously.

"All right, let's not make a big fuss about all this," she said. "I am not Jamesyn Day. I am not a king. I am Jasmine Day, and I'm not at all sure that I am actually a queen, either, so please, dispense with all the 'Your Highness' stuff, at least for the time being. You all know the truth now, and I'm glad that my secret is finally out. However, it changes nothing. I am still the heir to the Stone. The mission remains the same."

"Of course," Dedlin exclaimed. "We are all the more dedicated. But we were dreadfully worried about you. Pray, come tell us where you've been and what you saw."

As they boarded Stardeer, Jasmine began to tell them what she had seen in the amphitheater, and her tale raised some eyebrows: the monkeys, the swirling void, and the visions. When it came to what she saw exactly in those visions, she found that she had forgotten almost everything except for the colors and beautiful sounds that she had heard. She did not even recall the visions of her friends in strange and dangerous situations, much less the knowledge of her newfound siblings. This mental blackout frustrated her. She kept repeating, "I know there is more. Something else...important."

"You found one of the lost sinkhole mirrors," Dedlin said with some admiration and awe. "There were four of them. One of them was found a few years ago in northern Galgariah, but its magick had faded. It was naught but a hole in the ground now, and trees had begun to grow from it. Many a ranger has searched unsuccessfully for the other three. They are sacred and mysterious, reflective mirrors of psychic transcendental space, memory, and time. No one has been able to locate them since the time of the Great Flood."

"I saw so many things," she said. "But I can't remember any of it now."

"You may remember your visions in pieces, when you need it and least expect it," he said to her. "You may have glimpses of them in your dreams, or right as you are waking in the morning. They are lost in the world between sleep and wake, but they will always remain there for you. Try to recount as much as you can, when you can. My advice is to write it down whenever you do, whatever you can remember. It could help you."

"I will. I will try, Dedlin."

"We searched the orchard for miles in every direction for you," Gaebryl said, somewhat cross from concern. "How did you elude us?"

Jasmine frowned. "I didn't go that far," she said. "I only followed this one nearby row. The path turned to stone less than a hundred yards away. The amphitheater was directly ahead, less than a mile from here."

Gaebryl and Drer looked questioningly at one another. "We searched every square inch of every row for many miles in every direction," the prince said. "We never found any stone path, or walls, or ravines, or any bridge. Certainly no ampithater."

Drer confirmed Gaebryl's story. "Only rows of apple trees over gently rolling hills. This land is basically flat and featureless."

"My," she simply said.

"Cherish your experience," Dedlin told her. "You will gain much by having had it."

They kept travel at a slow pace along the rows, low enough in the trees to remain hidden, but exposed enough to get a decent glance around them. As night came, they cruised smoothly without the benefit of lights, following a southerly course in the orchards that seemed to stretch out forever before them. Occasionally, they would pass above little cabins where farmers lived. Thin trails of gray smoke rose from the chimneys. Quiet voices from inside. The windows glowed with firelight, warm and inviting.

Ott paced around the deck nervously. He often spotted Gharnian searchlights off in the distance, and would advise Perce on a better course away from them. Two times they were forced to descend to the ground to wait until nearby danger passed, arming themselves in case of unwanted discovery. "I've never seen so many warships," he told them. "There won't be any sleep for us in this orchard tonight."

"We can't go any further and we cannot linger here," Dedlin said. "I fear that to land here would be folly, but to flee would be worse."

"I feel the same," Jasmine said. She turned to the wyzard, and with a shiver, she whispered to him: "Dedlin, I feel that something else nearby is hunting us."

"Yes. It is. I've known of it for some time. But do not speak of it!" he rebuked, looking sidelong out into the orchard mists. "Do not give it a reason to sense us here. It feeds on fear..."

"There are two Gharnian warships directly ahead of us," Ott said from his perch. "We cannot go further south tonight. Unless, maybe, we can circle them, but I don't see how."

"We cannot go back," Drer said. "There are scoutships behind us, as thick as a swarm of summer mosquitoes. We are trapped here. Perhaps we should hide somewhere close by and find shelter until the morning."

"What makes you think it won't be worse tomorrow?" Binder asked.

"Could it get any worse?" Drer said. "We're surrounded!"

"Perhaps, if we can elude them here for the night, the Gharnians will think they've searched this area thoroughly enough, and then they'll move on," Perce said. "There are many cabins below. Some of the farmers are mahekian, my brethren. I could solicit them for aid."

"There is a thick blanket of fog rolling in below," Gaebryl said. "It could help make a good cover."

"Against the Gharnians," Dedlin agreed. "But the fog might not cover us from other things. There are entities more at home in dark, foggy night than we."

Suddenly, a Gharnian fightercraft sailed past above them, less than twenty yards away, at full speed. The crew of Stardeer instantly spun toward it, planting their feet hard in battle stance, weapons drawn. Fortunately, the fightership had not spotted them. It was on some other errand, running urgently from warship to warship.

"This is ludicrous," Binder said. "If we go on, we might as well surrender to them here and now."

"Look over there," Ott said to them, pointing into the mists. "What about that?"

"What?" they asked. None of the rest of them could see anything in the dark. Gaebryl peered through nightscans, but they were no use in the fog.

"We just passed an empty cabin," he said. "It looks long deserted, but intact. The front door is hanging half off the hinges. It is down in a hollow, and shrouded with mist. We could spend the night there, undetected; I am sure of it."

"I'd love to spend a night on the ground," Gaebryl told them. "If we find a safe place to hide we could get a good, restful night's sleep. This ship is so drafty now."

They all seemed to be trying to convince Dedlin to go to the ground, but by his expression, he was not yet convinced. Usually outspoken about every aspect of everything, Dedlin, for once, stood silent and pensive, staring grimly into the night mists. "I don't like choosing the lesser of two evils tonight," he finally said, face grave. "And you may take those words literally. I am all at once unsettled."

"Let's just investigate Ott's cabin," Gaebryl suggested. "Then we'll decide."

Grimacing, Dedlin nodded to them. "I'm outnumbered."

"Dedlin –" Jasmine said, touching the wyzard's arm apprehensively. She was unsettled as well. "It's close," she whispered.

"Perce, take the ship to the ground," Gaebryl said. "We'll hide her and seek nearby shelter tonight."

"Landing gear is already down," Perce replied.

"We'll be fine," the wyzard said comfortably to Jasmine, though he looked unconvinced.

Stardeer appeared to be surfing on a cloud as they rode down into the cool mists that lingered heavily a few feet from the ground. They eased beneath the arched limbs of an apple tree, hugging the branches on all sides, and the fog covered them over. An owl hooted close by, and a cooter loon let out its lonely, eerie cry some miles away, answered by another one from even further, across some still, dark lake. The clouds above were heavy and they were getting heavier by the second. It smelled like more rain.

They unpacked blankets and packs. Drer and Perce volunteered to stay behind to camouflage the sky craft, and would join the rest of them later. Gaebryl led the way across the weedy ground between the trees, ducking under low hanging limbs. Jasmine Day remained close by his side. The diurnal luper monkeys slept in the forks of the limbs. Some hung from the boughs by their tails, undisturbed by the passing crew of Stardeer.

They found themselves following an old, soggy dirt road, covered with piles of rotten, half eaten apples. An old wagon wheel rested against a post on the side of the road, covered with vines. The crew kept northward, walking silently through the encompassing mists.

"There it is, just ahead," Ott finally said. He pointed through the fog. "It looks to be a one room structure, buried in apple ivy, like everything else around here. I see a front door; I suppose it has a back. Windows on all four sides. A porch out front, and a chimney. An empty stable in the rear. Hitching posts and a horse trough. What do you think?"

Binder squinted. "I'd think you were making it all up," he said. "I can't see my hand in front of my face."

"Nothing but trees on all sides," the thordian continued. "There's a small well out back."

"I see it," Gaebryl said. "Just a silhouette, but I see it."

They left the road and crossed a few rows of trees, coming in towards the cabin from the side.

"It should be nigh on invisible from above," Gaebryl said. "There are countless similar inhabited and more uninhabited cabins for miles in every direction. The chances of the Gharnians searching for us house to house tonight is very slim, if any at all. What do you say, Dedlin?"

The wyzard did not answer.

"We should investigate the interior first," Ott said. "Just to make sure."

"After you," Gaebryl said to him.

"What do you want here?!" cried a startled, frantic voice from inside the cabin. The crew dashed for cover in all directions, rolling into the weeds, and falling to their bellies, weapons drawn. They half expected hostile gunfire to erupt from within. "Don't come any closer, if you know what is good for you!"

Gaebryl had taken Jasmine to the ground next to him, covering her with a protective arm.

Dedlin was right beside them. "What is this tomfoolery?" the wyzard said. "What kind of a voice is that?"

"It does sound odd," Jasmine agreed.

"I'm going to circle around to the back to see what I can find," the prince said. "Keep an eye on her."

Gaebryl rolled away and disappeared into the fog and trees. Dedlin saw Otthagorus heading around in the opposite direction with his arrowjet rifle at the ready. The wyzard came up onto his knees and peered at the dark house. He called out, "Who is there?"

"Who are you, old man?" asked the angry, tinny voice that nearly squawked more than spoke. "You are trespassing here. Go away! Now! Leave this place if you know what is good for you!"

Drer Fregoode and Perce came slithering up from behind. "You're making a lot of noise," the mahekian warned. "We heard you from back at the Stardeer."

"I don't know what to make of this," Dedlin said to them. "It seems the cabin is occupied after all."

"By whom?" Drer asked. "Or by what? The windows are wide open and the front door is hanging ajar."

"I'm not sure," the wyzard said. "Although I know we have no reason to fear. The voice that comes from within is very unusual. It is not from the throat of any race of being that I'm familiar with. It is a voice bewitched."

Jasmine stood. "We need a place to stay the night, sir," she called out. "May we speak to you there? We are traveling through here, and we would like to share this cabin with you tonight, if we might. We have some food we can share with you. We will gladly pay you..."

"Go away!" the voice shouted. "Go away! All of you! Old man! Young girl! Mahekian! I saw the other two sneaking around back! I have...that is to say, *we* have no room for you here, see.

No visitors here tonight! Too many ships in the sky. Go away!"

"What should we do?" Drer asked. "We can't force our way. It wouldn't be right. We can sleep in Stardeer."

"Not just yet, friends," Dedlin said. "Something is not entirely right here. I don't believe this person, or whatever it is, has any more right here than we do. If the Voice is not the owner of this domicile, we are just as entitled to seek shelter here as it is."

Just then, Gaebryl stepped out from the cock eyed front door, onto the porch, followed by Ott. "Ahoy, there," he called to them. "We came in the back! It's empty! No one is in here, I assure you!"

"Empty?" Binder called out from the trees to the right. "That's impossible. No one came out. We could see all sides!"

"Well, come see for yourself, then. I came through the backdoor, and there is no one inside. This place is long ago abandoned. It will serve our purposes well enough tonight. Come!"

"How very strange," remarked Dedlin Dane, throwing his cloak back over his shoulder. "Lake! Qan! Come on then, boys. Let us make ourselves at home in this empty, talking house. Build a fire! Make some biscuits! I believe that it is starting to rain."

55

The fire in the hearth blazed with golden fervor. It cast dancing shadows throughout the small, wooden cabin. It was as vacant as Gaebryl had said, except for a bit of simple furniture, a few copper utensils and a storeload of apple wine. The aroma of the boiling soup was inviting: Ott had caught a goose and a goodsized rabbit within an hour, and was willing to share them both for soup stock. They had scrounged up some wild carrots, potatoes, tubers, onions, and various other herbs and spices thrown in to boot. Of course, there were enough apples to go around for everyone. If lucky, perhaps a Drer pie.

"How I'd go for some fresh baked bread and a dollop of melting butter!" Gaebryl told them, pulling a cork from a wine jug. "But biscuits will do. Who was silly enough to leave all this wine behind? These jugs are dusty!"

After fixing the hinges on the front door, Drer Fregoode had gone back to retrieve some additional items from Stardeer. He said that he had foreseen a rare night of mirth ahead, and brought enough mugs for all, and an assortment of musical instruments he'd been able to lug along. After all were settled in, he began to entertain them. He played his mandolin and sang a few songs that seemed to chase the shadows away. Lake and Qan acted as wine stewards, making sure that each and every mug remained full at all times.

The rain poured nonstop outside, tapping the roof like nails on tin sheets. Crickets, warm and dry within the foundations of the cabin, sang along with the minstrel, seemingly competing for dominance.

Finally shedding his skin (thanks to many mugs of wine), Dedlin relaxed and enjoyed the activities. "Let me try one," he said, taking the mandolin from his friend. "Accompany me, my good minstrel, if you can. I dedicate this little piece of verse to this fine crew. Bear with me, it has been awhile." With those words of warning, the wyzard began to sing in a fine baritone voice:

"Though the heat of day is flaming, The storm o'er the plain rolls to the sea, Though pursuit rages on behind us, Our quest is to keep this country free, It may mean we sleep in danger, But our quest is to keep our country free.

"Hey ho! The fear subsides at daybreak, As we watch the skies for foes above, When the Dark One sends out his dominion, Our hearts reach out for those we love, They wait at home 'til we rejoin them, But our hearts remain with those we love.

"Yea, the future is uncertain , Tomorrow is another day, Tonight we'll sing and tell our stories, Our songs will keep awful things at bay, And if my mug of wine drains empty, Fill it, fill it right away!"

They all laughed and applauded. Dedlin bowed deeply. Lightning flashed outside, and then soft thunder rolled past them shortly thereafter.

"Yes, Lake, my man, fill our mugs once again," Drer requested. "But that will be the last for me. My head is spinning and my eyelids are heavy."

At Jasmine's bidding, each one, in his turn, told a story about his homeland, beginning with the wyzard. But before Dedlin had finished, Jasmine had fallen asleep, leaning up against Gaebryl's shoulder. He laid her down near the fire, rolling a mat up beneath her head, and covering her with a blanket. All eyes looked upon her warmly.

Lake, more than most, was not used to the effects of the apple wine and had imbibed admittedly more than his share. He sat, dozing noisily in the corner. However, he would often wake up and cheer something or someone for no apparent reason. "Oh, such a great night!" he blurted out. "I shall remember this night forever!" Then, he began to doze off again, mumbling drunkenly, "Or as long as I live, whichever comes first. Where's the pisser?"

"I doubt you'll remember this night tomorrow morning, my friend," Dedlin said, rolling his own sleeping mat out upon the wooden floor. "Perhaps this was a good idea after all," he said. "Drer, please play something for us. Play something nice and peaceful, if you will. Something very, very old. From the elder days of my youth."

Drer obliged him.

Ott was curled up near the corner of the hearth, grooming his bronze fur with his tongue. "That's nice," he said, and tossed the last piece of dry firewood upon the dying embers.

"I feel like a young wyzard again," Dedlin said softly, lighting up his pipe. "This is where I belong. Not in some basement. Out here."

Gaebryl nodded. He belonged there, too. Out in the Wilds, actively involved in some purposeful crusade. Would he ever be able to put it all aside and remain content in one place? He wondered. Someday, maybe. But not this night.

He looked at Jasmine's face. Her eyes moved beneath her closed lids, as though peacefully dreaming. Her breath was deep and calm.

How she had changed since the first time they had met. Or at least his perception of her. It was remarkable. Gaebryl could scarcely believe that it was the same person he had met in the Gaalothian jungles so long ago, wrapped tight in the coils of a hungry snake. Each new day brought a new revelation, and he knew, deep down, that the last and greatest revelation of her was yet to be discovered.

He moved a lock of her hair aside to see her better. Her eyes were moving even more restlessly than they had been before. And it seemed as though her breathing had intensified. What could she be dreaming about?

"I'm going for firewood," Perce, who was first on guard, said. As he stepped through the creaking front door, gentle lightning flickered, illuminating the somber blue orchard beyond. "It's awfully quiet out there," he said as the door closed behind him.

Drer switched from mandolin to the softness of a wooden flute. Very softly, the notes poured from the instrument like warm honey, down and across the floor, against every wall, filling the corners like cotton, easing the weary crew into an enchanted state of rest.

Ott purred. Binder was snoring. The rain fell and the crickets sang accompaniment.

Almost all were asleep. Even Dedlin's eyes were half lidded above the dim red coal of his smoking pipe. Drer set his flute aside and drifted off to sleep himself, humming the last few notes of his sleepy lullaby.

56

Dedlin suddenly rose. His eyes lit like fiery coals as he looked this way and that. He was as rigid as steel.

Jasmine woke out of her dream with a start. Her eyes showed pure terror. "Dedlin," she whispered. "It's here. W-what is it? I feel—"

"Silence!" he whispered as loud as he was able. With a quick movement, outstretching his right palm, the fire and the candles about the room instantly extinguished without a thread of smoke.

One by one the crew awoke, but remained instinctively frozen as a seeping cold that they could feel to the marrow of their bones infiltrated the cracks in the cabin walls. Powerless against it, they shivered, motionless, and powerless.

"Something is upon us," Dedlin ventured to utter. His hands shook. "Do not move, breathe or make a sound if you can help it. Close your eyes and do not look up at the windows if you value your sanity. We are caught, and only by a miracle of providence may we be saved from the presence that draws nigh. May the gods have mercy--"

Just then, at Dedlin's last words, they heard a shuffle against the outside cabin wall in the back. It brushed by the corner, causing the cabin to splinter and lean. Dust fell from the rafters. Then, a shadow entity blackened the dim violet light beyond the sole eastern window.

Dedlin began chanting words so quietly that no one could hear them. Never before had they seen him so pale and grave. He was skeletal.

"Dedlin," Gaebryl whispered.

The wyzard put a finger to his lips, eyes pleading.

"Perce is out there."

An eye gazed in through the glass. Gaebryl ventured a glance at it, then turned from it and cowered. Then, it spoke to itself. "Anyone here?" they heard it say. Fear tore through the cabin interior like an icy winter wind, unexplainably terrifying the crew to immobile numbness. They clenched their cold, sweaty fists, and gnashed their teeth tightly as a feeling of intense evil swept over, around and through them, chilling their hearts to ice.

Gaebryl had never felt anything like this before, nothing even comparable. He could not even find the strength to reach for his blaster. With his arms tight around Jasmine Day, he clenched his own biceps with both hands so as to not unintentionally crush her, daring not to swallow for fear the sound might betray him. He even fretted for the sound of his pounding heart.

The creature was sniffing at the frail window. "Do I smell cat? Ahhh, thordian," it said. Its voice was so deep the earth shook at the sound of it. "A lion man."

Ott was curled into a ball, tail wrapped around him protectively, shivering, claws outstretched but frozen, each talon pierced through the wooden floor, his fur standing up on end.

Drer Fregoode felt tears rolling down his cheeks. Forcing himself to look up, he saw that even Dedlin Dane had tears of fear welling up in his eyes.

The thing's breath covered the window with steam. Its yellow eyes were aglow with the fires of hell, two circular rings of flame amid an infinite ocean of pitch black. Mucus streamed from pits in its face, dripping down the window ledge as thick as melting tar.

The window shattered as it pressed its head against it. The crew screamed, unable to conceal their insurmountable fear any longer. Its head, resembling a huge black dog's, came through the opening, up to the shoulders, twice the size of the largest living cattlewolf. The aura of terror it exuded was like that of a solid, living entity, filling the entire room en masse.

"It spoke again, sending rippling chills through the cabin like waves of an icy wind. "Day," it called in a menacing, whispery tone. "Where are you heading, little girl?"

Jasmine trembled, clinging tightly to Gaebryl Dindiane. "Master wants the Stone," it said, slowly and distinctly, although the voice was both ethereal and surreal, as from a different dimensional plane. "It seems that only *you* can find it. So I follow. We will follow. Little wyzard man cannot stop me, though he tries so hard with his conjuring and his protective spells. He cries in fear, like the weakest of you."

"Stop!" Lake screamed. He began writhing furiously on the floor, screaming and mouthing nonsense. His fear had gotten the best of him, and he went completely mad. Suddenly, he flung himself against a wall, and he fell to the floor, unconscious.

The dog thing continued. "You don't even know *what* you are," the beast said. "And you will never know. Because your life will be ended long before that day ever comes."

"No, you won't," Jasmine's tiny voice answered, a sudden beacon, weak yet discernible in the swell of a ferocious, raging hurricane. Exercising all her mortal effort, she wrenched her way from Gaebryl's seizing arms, and stood before it, knees almost faltering, facing the hell beast face to face. Its breath was cold and foul upon her face. She shook and her voice cracked as she spoke. "I will destroy you and your Master," she decreed with admirable valor.

"You dare--"

"Be gone!" she cried. The dog cursed in the name of Gheelgahar, and was at once gone. No one spoke for nearly a full minute, as the terror left the cottage like water swirling down a drain. There was a fluttering in the rafters, and the crickets in the cracks of the floor began chirping once again. Lake began mumbling again; Drer attended to him.

Binder was the first to break the silence. "Pray, tell," he said, voice quaking. "Dedlin, what in the fear of the gods of Gharne was that?"

"I was so utterly powerless," Ott said feebly. "I am so ashamed."

"I have never witnessed anything like that before," Gaebryl sputtered, wiping his face with his cloak. "It came upon us so suddenly, without warning."

"As any great predator does," Drer added.

Dedlin stealthily crept to the broken window from where the thing had invaded their resting place. The horrible stench, like animal dung and dead, rotten flesh, was so strong that the wyzard had to cover his face and turn away from it. "Shapeshifting morgoth," he said, naming it. "A nightmare of evil, come to physical life. One of many servants of Gheelgahar. You can see what we are up against."

"I'll never sleep on the ground again," Ott said.

"We're not safe anywhere anymore, now," the wyzard explained. "Not on earth, in air, or on water. Morgoth can take any shape, any form."

"Jasmine stood up to it," Gaebryl said. "She alone among us faced it. And it backed away from her. It obeyed her. It... *It fears her.*"

"Where is it now?" Binder asked.

"Waiting," Dedlin answered, looking out the window at the rain spattering in the puddles. "Waiting for us."

Suddenly, the front door swung open. Perce entered, carrying an armload of wet firewood, but he came to an abrupt halt when he found the barrels of three blastguns facing him. "I take it you don't want a brighter fire?" he exclaimed.

"Didn't you see it?" Binder said.

"See what?" Perce said, dropping the wood near the wall. "What? What happened? You all look like you've seen the dead come to life."

Again, there came a fluttering sound from the rafters above them. Then, from up in the ceiling beams, a familiar voice said sharply to them: "I told you not to come in here! But in you came anyway, uninvited, and big trouble came with you. Thank you very much!"

Dedlin pointed his cane toward the ceiling, its tip emitting a soft, glowing light. Perched on a crossbeam was a large, excited crow.

"Yes, now you see me!" it squawked. "Do you mind?"

"Who or what are you, raven?" Dedlin asked the bird. "Answer quickly. I'm in no mood for bantering with a bird!"

"You act as though you've never seen a talking bird before," it said proudly, strutting back and forth across the beam. "I'm Venni. I'm a crow from the old crow families of the annulara of Eaoph, sent here as a scout. According to my observations here tonight, there are obviously dark tidings indeed in Tuus, as we have long feared."

"Not Tuus alone. There are dark tidings across this wide continent," Dedlin said, eyeing the strange, enchanted bird. "I can see you are a crow, and wise, if birds can be so. But have you always been a crow, or are you something else, bewitched by some magick spell?"

"Come, come," snapped the bird irritably. With a flutter of its blue/black wings, Venni swooped down among them, alighting squarely on the table in the center of the room. "Did you not hear anything I said?" he squawked at Dedlin. He marched back and forth on the table, like a pigeon toed soldier. "There is no bewitching! I am a crow, as my father was a crow, as was his father before him, as far back as the earliest of days. I have always been a crow! How about you, sir? Have you always been a rude, meddling, pretentious old wyzard?"

Eleven

FLIGHT INTO GORN

57

The exhausted jailer entered the dark suite, back bent so that his hairy knuckles drug the ground. Chains hung from his belt, clanking as he waddled forward. He squinted into the darkness. "S-status report on the traitor, sir..."

A mechanical hiss. "Go ahead. Is he dead?"

"No," answered the mutant gythot recruit, breathing heavily. He went to all fours in the floor near the foot of the bed, head bowed obediently, and crawled forward. His knuckles were bloody; one bone showed through the skin. "Worked on him all day. Not dead. Not yet. He is drugged to stay alive. And sutured. The doctors give him blood and fluids even now."

The commander did not respond immediately, not even a movement of hand or eye. A minute later, his head gently nodded. "Good."

"M-more pain, General Jakarad?" the recruit muttered nervously. "Still, he suffers greatly even now."

The dark figure standing in the shadows paused to straighten his broad shoulders and square his jaw. "Let him rest tonight and suffer more as he is," he answered, ripping his collar open. The moon through the skylight cast a sullen blue line around his angular silhouette. "You may rest, too."

"Aye."

"When he dies, send his carcass to his mother in Fhargak. Do you understand?"

"Aye, General."

"Recruit?"

"Yes, sir?"

The General drew a pensive breath. "What do the others say about this soldier?"

"The others?"

General Jakarad turned toward him with an impatient glance.

"They call him a traitor, a blasphemer, a coward. They say he was strong once, but grew weak, and that he went insane."

"Insane?" he asked. Yes, you could call love insane.

"Yes," the gythot answered, stealing a look up from his place on the floor with one yellow eye. "He's very strong, sir. And resilient."

Yes, that he was. "He was my brother," the General said.

"Y-yes, sir..."

"Not by blood, of course..."

"No, sir."

The General stood in thought for a few more moments while the jailer uncomfortably waited to be dismissed. "Yes, well," he finally said. "Most importantly, recruit. Again. Did he ever speak of the Curse? Did he admit to revealing any part of it to the Stonebearer?"

The slave shook his lowered head. "No, sir. I could never detect any acknowledgement or awareness of any kind of curse, General. We interrogated brutally, with hallucinogens, until he lost consciousness this last time, and was unable to be revived."

"He never admitted even knowing about it? Are you sure,

recruit? He was one of the Elite. He knew of the Gheelgahar's Curse, of that I am sure. I only need to know if he betrayed it to our enemy."

"No sir. Nothing. No subtle indications at all."

"Nothing about the family of Nicholias Day and their inability to ever live past having children? The disease that ends their immortality? Did he speak of that?"

"N-no, sir. Nothing like that whatsoever," the jailer answered, somewhat confused.

"I see." General Jakarad turned back to the trees racing past outside the small porthole window of his private quarters. "That concerns me greatly. I fear that out of guilt and pride he is now denying any knowledge of ever knowing it, with his last vestiges of consciousness and mental control, to keep us from finding out the truth about what he has done. He is willing to endure torture and carry that one betrayal to the grave to keep us from knowing. Admirable. And tragic."

"Yes sir."

"Mmm. Has he asked for mercy? For death?"

The torturer shook his head. "No," he said.

"But..."

"Speak."

The slave cleared his throat. "In his klerim based delirium, he does keep asking for someone over and over, some Ozi-Arr Abbex, if I'm understanding him correctly. It's hard to make out any words with the damage we've done to his jaw. He has no tongue or teeth..."

The great Gharnian General looked at him flatly, emotionlessly. That name was not unknown to him. Oziah Aabx, the mythological sorcerer, savior of the first dynasty. But, Oziah Aabx did not truly exist... Just a woodan legend, nothing else. As most did while dying, the broken prisoner was hallucinating in the last phases of his life, seeking redemption, salvation, peace, mercy. Seeking the gods. And, even in the stories, Oziah Aabx was no god. "That's all, recruit. You may retire for the evening."

"Aye."

"Tell Captain Dhar to keep one fighter brigade hidden along the southeastern perimeter of this orchard tonight and send the rest on to the Gornian River, as we had previously discussed. I'm going to do some work here tonight and I don't want to be disturbed for a few hours. Let him know."

The recruit bowed obediently and left. General Jakarad watched the lead torturer hobble away, down the polished silver corridor. Gythots made such good slaves once broken, he thought. Of course, this one would have to be eliminated after Kadazaat passed on, because he knew of Gheelgahar's Curse, and Kadazaat's treachery notwithstanding, the Curse still had to remain a secret of the Gharnian Elite alone.

The General finished undressing and lay naked upon his hard bunk, fingers interlocked behind his plasteelcplated skull. This was such a sad irony. He had known General Kadazaat from the time he was a Minor Admiral and he had served with him for many years in Ash, while they both trained through several levels of the Gharnian Elite. Kadazaat had been an exemplary, dedicated soldier, whom Jakarad had admired and emulated. But Kadazaat had never been a Believer, and it eventually drove in a wedge. He had fallen in love. Fool. That was clear now. Even after taking that temptation away, Kadazaat's heart would not return to his career. All the training and military expertise in the world could not fill a longing soul... A Gharnian's heart should only seek the Religion. The One. SciGeneral Moon Jakarad, himself, was a true Believer, and it made him complete. Fulfilled. Righteous. Reflecting on his many experiences in the field with Prince Kadazaat, he was both saddened and angered. What a waste of life; what a waste of time and military resources.

He went to his study to write some notes in his journal before retiring:

*It is late. Sunborne the 27th, Meriday, 432.12C.
SciGeneral Moon Jakarad of the Caasar III, closing record of the
day. Update: the traitor Kadazaat has revealed much on this day,
yet his testimony reveals a troubling paradox for me.*

*It is true. The prophecy is realized, exactly as the Great
One revealed to the Elite. Under extreme duress, General
Kadazaat confirmed the existence and arrival of a very young
Meadian King Jamesyn Day, by his own personal contact in the
fields of Tuus, no less. He spent some time with young King Day
on his small skycraft Stardeer, while recuperating injuries. He
spoke to him, and they exchanged information. My fear is that it is
possible that the traitor committed the ultimate blasphemy by
revealing to the enemy the familial Curse of Gheelgahar, which
the Elite has kept in confidence for so many generations. This has
not been confirmed or denied, but we are still attempting to
assimilate relevant information while the prisoner yet lives.
Kadazaat's silence on the matter gives me cause to believe the
damage is now done and he intends to carry that treacherous
secret to his grave. This will be his great revenge for the wrongs
he believes we have done him.*

*However, the good news of the day is that Kadazaat
confirmed the boy king's pursuit of the Great Stone, somewhere
near our present location on the western border of central Gorn,
and we are currently in close pursuit. King Day is much younger
than we expected, perhaps no more than fifteen or sixteen years
old. He is traveling with a small group of soldiers and rangers,
including the prince warrior of Bursia, Gaebryl Dindiane, and
Commander Benjyn Binder of castlecity Tungulin of Galgariah,
suggesting the involvement of King Tital Vantoo, among others.
This crew has proven themselves resilient, resourceful as prey,
and amazingly elusive.*

*We have trailed them this far, hit or miss, and now that we
have lost them again, I am very concerned.*

General Jakarad scowled, hissing through his crooked
front teeth, frustrated. His mission seemed simple enough in
theory: locate the Stone of Power, and bring it back to Gharne.
The Elder Gharnian Elite had agreed that capturing King Day was
the key to fulfilling this mission, to guide them to it, willing or

unwilling. They had set all their roaming forces on this singular premise, so, as of yet, at least thy hav been following him toward it. But, the only catch to this plan was that the young king, himself, could not be allowed to reach this powerful instrument first, which could prove disastrous...

Yes, Jakarad's mission was simple in theory, but it was proving more difficult than he had ever imagined. In fact, now, he felt that he was on the brink of failure.

I now declare an executive mandate on a field decision, as described in Tabula 77, chapter 4.9, verses 83 through 91, concerning mission alteration from apprehension to termination under extreme prejudice, and seek Elite approval as soon as possible. Consideration point: the enemy draws nearer to the Stone with every passing hour and we have been unable to keep them in our sights. Their skycraft entered a large orchard grove at point 44B 887, less than one day ago. From the few clues we have been able to obtain, we have missed them here. Again. It is virtually impossible for them to have eluded our massive forces in this sector, but they somehow have, and we are rapidly running out of time and options. I believe that we have but days left before it is too late. They may reach the Great Stone of Power before we do, and escape with it. This is unacceptable. They cannot be allowed to slip through our fingers yet again.

Therefore, apprehension is no longer an option. It is time for more effective measures. I will be addressing our warship commanders at dawn with new instructions: We will take down this Stardeer and her crew upon the next sighting, by any means necessary, and scavenge what we may from the rubble, hopefully, a survivor. Best case scenario: King Day himself.

The traitor Kadazaat may have nothing left to offer us; he is now on the final brink of death and awaits us to release his life, which he will not be getting any time soon. I am retiring for the evening, for I expect a glorious day of hunting on the morn. Please respond with due speed via message sphere. For Gharne! End log; General Moon Jakarad, Commander of the Caasar III."

He sent his message, placed his journal aside, and pressed a bedside comm button.

"Sir?" came a voice.

"Send in a boy. I'm not to be disturbed until dawn."

"Aye, sir."

58

Stardeer was a hundred miles away from the orchards by that next morning, the crew having decided to leave shortly after the encounter with the fell beast at the cabin. They were haunted and exhausted by that encounter, unable to free themselves from the harrowing chill and heavy shadow it had left upon them. They hoped that the faster they flew, the better they would feel. They were trying to quickly put in some distance and escape from the weight of it, but that did not happen. The unrelenting dread and fear still clung to them like airy wisps of night.

They could not agree among themselves what form the beast had appeared to them, and argued about what they had heard and seen that past night, but most recalled that it was much like a great dog or wolferine. Dedlin explained that the morgoth was a shapeshifter, a demon from an elder age, appearing different to anyone that came across its path, and that it could, by will, take any form it chose. All they could agree upon was that it knew them and their purpose, and that it recognized Jasmine Day as a female, and as heir to one of the Stones. There were no more masquerades. The enemy now knew her true identity, and it wouldn't be long before Gheelgahar knew of the ruse, if He didn't somehow already. If the morgoth knew their location, so would the Gharnians now.

"No offense intended," Commander Binder said to Dedlin Dane, "but we may need a bigger and better skycraft for fierce warfare than your pleasurecraft Stardeer..."

The sky above was clear and the air was warming by the minute. Qan was at the controls once more with Perce close by his side. They kept a direct course southeast, zigzagging below the bristle treetops. The scraggly trees were scattered sparsely around the bases of the dry hills like brown, thorny crowns on bald pates.

The terrain below was rough and rocky, still dotted at intervals with an occasional barren, vagrant apple tree. Qan had become quite a decent pilot over the last few days; Perce had complimented his skills, suggesting that he was a natural born flyer. "Your forefathers must've been birds," he had commented.

Gaebryl, Drer, and Ott kept a vigilant watch for enemies on all fronts. They remained anxious and uneasy, circling the perimeter of the ship throughout the morning hours with scans. Dedlin and Drer were often off by themselves, deep in conversation; much had happened that required their sound expertise and interpretation.

Lake had not been idle; he had shown an interest in how the large mounted blasters worked, so Binder took time to show him operation and maintenance techniques between his watches. He showed him where the ammunition was stored and how it was loaded, and he gave him a brief lesson on the firing of the powerful guns. "Believe me, it's got a kick to it," he warned. Unfortunately, only two of the blasters were now functioning properly; the third one had suffered irreparable damage at the hands of the twister in Tuus.

Jasmine came up on deck for the first time that morning. All eyes turned to her, and more than one jaw dropped. She was certainly not the same girl they had watched retire the night before. The change in her was striking. Absolute and phenomenal, both inside and out. A strange and miraculous transformation had occurred overnight, like that of a homely caterpillar emerging as a beautiful butterfly in the rays of the morning suns. It was as if a curtain had been lifted from around her, revealing someone completely new, grim, and regal. She looked beautiful. Her clean, wispy hair was pulled back from her face and tied up with a white ribbon, revealing narrow shoulders and a long, statuesque neckline. The suns made her new eyes sparkle like jewels of sapphire blue. She had left her restraining corset and shoulderpads below, and she had cinched her thin waist with a fine belt. There was no denying her blossoming womanhood anymore. In fact, she was undeniably lovely. Looking at her, her demeanor and her regal air, caused some of the gloom that had lingered from the previous night's horror to immediately dissipate.

But that was not the only change they noted. She seemed to have suddenly matured and hardened, as if having stepped into a new, truer role, accepting another, more appropriate, identity. One by one she addressed the crew, asking for news and updates. She was curt and aloof when addressing them as she circled the craft, inspecting it and the men as they performed their various duties. There was no doubt that the encounter with the great dog had changed her, and marked her in a rather dark, serious way. She, alone, had had the innate courage and strength to stand before the Thing and confront it. Some of whatever force of will she had summoned the night before remained ingrained within her from that point forward, and the crew could feel it while in her presence. She was stronger, more resolved, as if her heart had hardened and her blood had chilled.

Dedlin made a brief attempt to be cordial, but Jasmine dismissed him. She was all business this morning. "We must get through this day," she told him curtly. "Continue your preparations."

The crew remained on edge throughout the afternoon. The provisions were low, so a meager lunch and dinner came and went under Drer Fregoode's apt supervision: fried apples and walnuts, candytree seeds, and some thin barley soup with hard bread for dipping.

Eventually, Dedlin grew more concerned for Jasmine as the evening wore on and her brooding continued. He watched her from beneath a furrowed brow, trying to discern her needs, but there are some subjects of which wyzards have little knowledge or understanding, and one of them is the science of women's emotions. If there even was a knowledge or understanding of the science of women's needs and emotions, he thought, which he doubted. The only sure predictions about them was that they were intuitive and unpredictable.

When Gaebryl, who was speaking quietly with Perce and Ott, happened to glance in his direction, the wyzard motioned toward her with a nod of his head, as if saying, 'Go talk to her, fool'.

Gaebryl nodded. He excused himself from his friends and

crossed the deck to join her at the front rail. She looked so grave and distant to him, detached and emotionless, like a sad statue of a bygone age. She did not notice him approaching at first. She peered toward the southeast as if staring into a dim, unknown future, the wind hard in her face. "Oh," she said as he drew close. "Hello."

"You seem preoccupied," he said to her.

Jasmine teased with a smile, but it was quickly extinguished. "Yes," she said. "I guess I am focused."

"You look very nice today."

She looked at him fleetingly, then back out at the horizon, making him wonder whether his compliment had been appropriate. "Thank you," she replied. A few moments passed, then Jasmine took the initiative and broke the awkward silence. "I've never heard of talking birds before," she said. "That was a strange and unexpected turn."

"They must be very rare," he said. "Intelligence must not be regulated by brain size."

She glanced from the corner of her eye. "Depends upon which human you're comparing them to..."

He smiled and shrugged, nodding in agreement.

Below them, a gypsy caravan was entrenched in a deep gully, cinched tight between three craggy hills, set up there to prey upon the slack morals of the nearby town to the west. There was a battle pit erected in the center of the camp, between the weather beaten brown tents, and two local fighters were visible, engaged in hand to hand combat. There was a decent crowd pressing in around the brutal event, placing wagers, cheering and booing in succession, and scarcely an eye was raised as Stardeer passed by silently overhead.

"You know," Gaebryl said, now choosing his words with care, "I can still remember hearing the news of your father's death when I was just a boy."

Jasmine looked firmly up at him.

"I wasn't much more than ten or twelve, I guess, training in the battle pits outside Dindiane, much like that one right down there," he replied. "My favorite mahekian warmaster, Jesse (I called him Jesse Boy), told me about it. Jesse was very smart, and funny, as far as mahekians go. The youngest warmaster in our Kingdom, so we got along famously. He often had news about things going on in the wide world beyond the Bursian territory. He was proud of his people and all their responsibilities. He considered the mahekians the stewards and protectors of the entire Kingdom Continent. He was deeply proud of that. He boasted to me about a secretive network that his brotherhood maintained. He said that, because of their telepathic abilities, they could pass information faster and more efficiently than comms or message spheres, anywhere throughout the kingdom, from coast to coast, north, south, east, and west. He said that his people were the blood in the veins of this land. I learned to believe him, because he always knew things even before my father did. But, sometimes, I didn't know whether I believed all of his tall tales, especially the strange stories coming out of the west.

"I remember him telling me once that mahekians had been secretively traveling from Isle Mead to the mainland for centuries. I found that both entertaining and amusing at the time. That's how the stories of your family would spread, he said, from the mahekian traders along the West Coast. By the time the news reached us, our people couldn't tell truth from rumor. I suppose that's why people stopped believing."

"Including you."

"That's not true," he said. "I didn't stop believing. I never believed in the first place. I just enjoyed Jesse's stories."

She put her hand on his for a moment, then withdrew. "And now?"

"Do you need to ask?"

She nodded with a melancholy eye. "Oddly enough, I never saw mahekians at home growing up. They are virtually invisible there."

"Watchers," Gaebryl said subtly. "They are like the Watchers. The Watchers of the North."

"Watchers of the North? Who are they?"

"A society of woodsmen. Very secretive, and very dangerous," he said. "But noble men. Good men. I've supped with them, and shared camp with them on occasion, but they don't talk much. They're very thoughtful and mysterious. I've always believed that they could be a formidable force should need arise."

"They are like the mahekians in many ways then," she nearly mumbled.

"Dedlin probably knows a lot more about the Watchers than I do. I'm sure Drer does."

Jasmine sighed. "I was just a baby when my parents died. Barely two years old, I was told, but now I wonder about the accuracy of anything I was taught about my life. My childhood is shrouded in protective lies. I'm beginning to see the sense in it now, though. Secrets and lies were crafted to protect me. And hopefully end the damned Curse, though that remains to be seen.

"I can't even remember them now, my parents, other than in dreams, and I can only wonder at the accuracy of those memories now," she said. She stood silent for a few moments as emotion welled up inside of her. "All of this... It's so hard bearing this burden alone without them. Gods, I long to hear their voices. I cannot recall the sound of my mother's voice, Gaebryl. I might not have known them, but still, I miss them terribly. I miss their love. You know what this means, Gaebryl, this Curse of Kadazaat's? I will never be able to share my love with my children, either. I will never even know my children. Just like all my forebears, my grandparents and my own parents, if I ever fall in love and have a child of my own, I will succumb, shrivel, and die, and I will never know them. I will never be able to sing to them. To teach them. To discipline or cherish them. And they will never remember my love, either." A tear broke loose and rolled down her cheek. "Knowing what I do now, I cannot do that to an innocent child. Never. It is just too cruel..."

"Jasmine..."

She turned to him. "I must face this reality. I can never have a baby of my own, Gaebryl."

He gently wiped her tears with his thumb. "Shhh," he said to soothe her. "Don't cry. Listen. We can break this damned Curse...'"

"What a horror..." she repeated. "It's not fair..."

"Shhh. Listen to me. We will find a way to break Gheelgahar's Curse," he said. "If it was made, it can be unmade just the same. I've already been speaking with Dedlin Dane and Drer Fregoode about this, and they agree. It was a blessing to have come across Kadazaat the Gharnian out there in the fields of Tuus, Jasmine. It was a blessing that he did not die, and a miracle that your kind words loosened his tongue. We know about this Curse now, which is an insight your forebears never had. You will not suffer the same fate as your parents did, and theirs before them, this I promise you. We will find a way to break this horrible black magick Curse. I will find a way. There is strong magick out there in this world, bad and good. I know. I have seen it all, firsthand."

"But at what price?" she said, eyes welling anew. "Magick costs, and not just in money, gold and jewels. The sacrifice is often the price of a soul..."

"Let me worry about that," he assured her. "You will raise your children, and your grandchildren, and even your great-great-great-great grandchildren. This, I swear to you, on my life and my kingdom."

A trembling smile crossed her wet face and new tears sprung forth upon her cheeks. He could always make her smile.

"I could never live with myself with that horrible Curse upon you," he said, gently stroking her hair. "You have become so very dear to me."

Jasmine stepped toward him, encircling her arms around his neck. "You always make me feel like everything will work out, even when I can't see it," she said. "Thank you so much, Gaebryl." She pressed her body tightly to him and held on for a good while, and it felt so good to her, just holding him there like that. He was big, strong, and warm. "Thank you for being here with me through all of this. For everything you've done. I don't know what I would have done without you."

"Just be patient about having those children," he bemused. "We still have time."

She laughed through her tears once again. "Yes. Yes, we do. Thank you, Gaebryl."

59

"Can we get any lower?" Dedlin said, scans at his eyes. "There's another warship about a mile to the south, heading north/northwest. We need to get below their field of vision!"

"Follow that cliff line," Perce advised, nodding toward a shallow limestone outcropping, and Qan obeyed. They were still at full speed, less than ten feet above the ground. The real danger of flying thusly was the possibility of crashing into a sudden tree or rock face. Qan often sheared through thin, leafless branches and withered saplings in order to keep their current speed and altitude. The branches were brittle and nearly exploded from the impact, littering the deck with dry kindling and splinters.

"There are Gharnian ships on every horizon," Ott snarled. "We're in a tightening snare, Dedlin. It's a miracle that we've not been spotted. We have to do something."

"Decide fast," Drer Fregoode said. "Gornian River just ahead."

"Stop here then! Find a place to dock," Dedlin said, eyeing the greenish blue strip of water appearing between the heels of the sienna hills directly in their path. "It is just too dangerous to cross the river openly during the day until we've had a chance to reconnoiter. They'll be monitoring this river for a hundred miles in all directions."

The crew nervously looked for any possible refuge that could hide a fightership.

"There," Gaebryl said, pointing. "Look there. That oak tree. It's big enough, and the foliage is thick. Find a way to wedge inside the branches, Qan."

"Yes. Perfect. We'll rest there. We may have to wait until dark to cross into Gorn," the wyzard advised. He appeared tired and old to them. His eyes lolled in hollow sockets. He suddenly stopped and froze, slackjaw, staring off into nothingness as though he just realized something very important. Before anyone could speak to him, he snapped out of it, shaking his befuddled head. "Blast these infernal Gharnians! Carry on! I'm going below to take a nap!"

"We can't wait too long," Jasmine told them. "The enemy is thickening like flies around here. And I feel something else. We are still being tracked..." She cut off in midsentence. They knew of what she was speaking. "It is not too far behind us."

The day passed slowly, but eventually night came. Heavy clouds obscured what might have been a bright midnight sunrise that night, for which they were grateful. After Ott had returned from scouting the countryside feeling optimistic, the crew of Stardeer prepared to depart and cross the wide river that separated two vast countries, Galgariah and Gorn. "As a bandit thief of some repute once said to me, 'it's time to fly or die'," Commander Binder said.

Dedlin Dane rose from below deck, rested and in better spirits than earlier that day. He asked everyone for news, and then made his way to Jasmine, greeting her with one of his wizened, disarming smiles.

"Good morning," she patronized. "I see you've braided your beard."

"Damn thing keeps getting in the way," he said. "Wind

always blowing it up into my face. I'm tempted to get rid of it altogether. I'm just afraid of what I'll look like underneath, all withered up like an old gray prune..."

Jasmine smiled at him.

"Do you have a minute?"

"Of course," she said, taking him by the elbow.

"It's time for us to talk. Are you ready for the last leg of this race, my dear?" he asked her. "Now it comes to it. We draw nigh. The enemy is closing in on this location from all sides. We are nearing the finish line, and with them simultaneously."

"I can feel it," she said. "I can feel many things, Dedlin. I feel as though things are awakening in me, and I'm frightened by it. Especially when I am alone at night."

"Yes, yes, I'm sure you are. Don't fear it. Embrace it, my dear," he said to her. "It is your destiny."

"I am starting to see things," she told him. "Visions, I think."

"Yes?" The wyzard seemed concerned but more pleased, which comforted her.

"But nothing I can use. Fleeting colors. Fleeting emotions. Like I saw in the sinkhole mirror..."

"You may yet have use for such visions, and very soon, if you allow this skill to develop. Allow your visions to solidify and focus. It is a blessing for you. You will see. That is why I must speak to you now, for we are drawing close to that which we seek, and I must prepare you for it," he said. "You must listen closely and remember what I tell you."

"Yes," she said. "I am ready."

Stardeer moved, easing slowly back out of the tree. The small blue moon, known as Duan, appeared pale lavender in the cold northern skies between the branches above them. It was still pitch dark, except for a pale glow on the eastern horizon.

"Once we have crossed the river, we will head nor'east toward the narrow shoulders of the dark Aasar Mountains. We will follow the desert edge for a day, no more, then into the scrubs and thorns that cover the Aasar plains, that was once a great sea many ages ago..."

"I've seen that place," she said. "Dirt. Thorns. Fossils. Chalk. I have seen it..."

"Yes, I believe that you will begin to recognize things, the closer you get to the Stone. It will be calling you, because it is, in essence, part of you. It will pull you to itself, if you hearken its call, past the dreary marshes and dead sea. There is an oasis there, hidden and protected," he said. "An old forest, beautiful and mystical, like an island in the harsh plains of the Aasar wastelands. It is not a large forest, nor is it small. It has no discernable boundaries and it cannot be mapped. No human has set foot in the place, nor laid eyes upon it, not since your legendary forefather, the first Great Day, walked away from there so long ago. Now, the Stone awaits you in that place, cradled safely within a small, wondrous cave, surrounded by its own magick."

"You are acting strangely, Dedlin. You give me this information as if you will not be there with me..."

"You are an observant girl. An amazing girl."

"What is wrong, Dedlin? What aren't you telling me?"

He sighed and smiled at her. "You are not the only one with visions. I still have some gift of foresight, and I see a new path rising before me very soon, leading me in another direction. I am needed elsewhere, and so I will not be with you much longer on this quest, Jasmine Day. I am sorry."

"Dedlin..."

"I have led you as far as I should and could. As far as I needed to. That is why you must heed my words, now. You must be prepared to finish this undertaking on your own if it comes to that..."

She faced the night before her as Stardeer crept into the sky without lights and accelerated toward the vale before the river. "On my own? What about Gaebryl?"

"You must trust me, child, and heed my words now," the wyzard said coldly. "You have proven yourself the most courageous of our fellowship, and should no longer have any doubts of your power and capabilities. I see a wall arising before us. A dividing obstacle leaping up before our very feet. Beyond that wall, all our paths separate. I know not who goes together, or where. Therefore, you must be prepared to now finish what you have started. Alone, should it come down to that. Do you understand?"

"I'm listening," she said, resolved and resolute. "Tell me what I must do, Dedlin, and I will do it."

"When you reach the cave, Jasmine Day, and turn the key that releases the Stone, you must recite the simple ancient scripture to break your great-great-great grandfather's splendid spell: 'In peace I enter Szan Tu Xaq.' Remember the words. This is very important."

"I... I will remember. Thank you, Dedlin."

"You'll remember? 'In peace I enter Szan Tu Xaq.' It's a crazy bunch of words."

"Yes," she simply said. "In peace I enter Szan Tu Xaq."

The wyzard nodded, seemingly pleased with himself. "Practice it as often as you are able." He looked up. Stardeer was low and moving fast toward the banks of the dark Gornian River, as black as pitch. "Ah. The river. Not a good stretch of water even without Gharnian patrols. Keep an eye out."

Stardeer shot out over the lazy, sluggish water from the tree lined bank, staying low to the surface. The warriors manned their weapons on all sides of the small fightercraft, expecting any kind of ambush. They watched the banks on both sides. Downstream about a mile, they could see an ancient plasteel bridge of enormous size, stretched across the river from bank to bank, constructed in a series of rusty triangular arches. It was covered at both ends with dark, strangling vines and ivy. It was a perfect spot for the Gharnians to hide and wait, but if they were there, the crew did not see them.

"Looks good," Binder said. "We're halfway across. Maybe we got here before they could get organized."

"I sure could go for a fresh fish dinner," Ott replied stiffly, peering over the rail into the water with his sharp feline eyes. "They're probably so close to the surface, and I'm famished."

"Me, too," Drer replied. "But we can't lower nets and disturb this water. If the Gharnians don't see us, the riverdragons might. I saw their tracks all over the banks when I scouted earlier this evening."

Binder slipped another shovel of algaestone gravel and dust into the fuel separator. "Just to let you know, we're running low on fuel, gentlemen," he forewarned, closing the algaestone storage bin. "Very low. We'll need to find more soon."

"Next village," Dedlin said. "Now keep a look out."

On the eastern banks, remnants of ancient buildings and temples, set in broken square foundations, were layered up the hillsides. They were inhabited only by denizens of the barren desert border now: lizards, snakes, and scorpions, warming themselves on the flat rocks, still warm from the days suns. A pair of gray coyotes. Stardeer reached the bank without incident, and keeping low, they headed inland at the same brisk speed, following the craggy walls of a narrow canyon.

"Look!" Gaebryl said to them, pointing back toward Galgariah. "We only just made it."

"Gharnian warships!" several crewmembers stated at the same time.

Four great ships came easing over the trees on the horizon, cutting across the river at a diagonal slant, heading toward the great bridge they had spotted. A fleet of fightercraft ensued behind them, perhaps thirty in all, like hungry fish following great ocean predators for scraps. After a few frightening seconds, all had disappeared behind them.

"Keep an eagle's eye," Dedlin advised. "No rest tonight!"

The morning came with a chill in the air, but, the suns were not veiled by clouds, and as morning turned to midday, the temperature being rising rapidly. The ground below was now cracked and brown, dry and barren, blowing with dust and sand. The gnarled, weather beaten trees were dwarfed and twisted, with little but dry cones and long brown needles hanging lifelessly from their limbs. Tufts of brown grasses appeared to have been planted like the barrier walls of a magnificent, complex maze. Occasionally they could discern remnants of walls made from half buried, upright stones that, too, fit the strange design of some giant maze crisscrossing the countryside for miles.

Jasmine climbed to the front bow of the skycraft, the wind pressing past her face, blowing her suns blonde hair back and forth before her eyes. Her arms and legs were outspread, to steady her, like a frail human spider. There were a few wisps of clouds in the west, just thin lines of white, chalky dust, rippled across the azure blue. A flock of tiny white beetlebirds whipped past, clicking. They spun up and down in a synchronized spiral, catching flying insects in their tiny, webbed feet.

She peered out into the clear distance, across the brown lands of Gorn. The familiarity was unnerving to her. Not familiar to her eyes, but to her heart, and to some buried memory. She felt it. Familiarity. Synchronization.

Belonging. Destiny. Danger.

The Stone was out there. It was calling her. She felt it, and it was a warm feeling of reunion.

As night came, Dedlin, Gaebryl and Jasmine Day stood side by side at the helm, while Perce flew. The air was cool enough to chill. Jasmine held onto the arms of the two men standing pensively and protectively beside her, and they stared out the window at the coming gloom of night, wondering what the next day would bring. Jasmine felt, but did not say, that the worst was still yet to come.

In silent fellowship they flew, until fatigue overcame her, and she retired to her cot below for the night.

60

The next morning, they woke with a start. Stardeer was accelerating quickly.

"Let's go!" Ott cried out, growling as he crossed the deck. "Battle stations! We've been spotted!"

Gaebryl sprang from his bunk, dashed up the ladderstairs, and joined Dedlin Dane at the flank of the ship. Several hundred yards behind them, a large black warship, silver battlements glistening in the bright morning suns, rose from a lower position as it angled its flight path directly in behind Stardeer. As the ship advanced upon them, vivid red lettering could be seen as fiery lights, announcing 'Caasar III' in sharp, jagged, Gharnian script.

"I suppose this was inevitable," Dedlin told the prince. "It almost certainly had to come to this at some point."

"It will be hard to lose them this time."

"Nigh on impossible. The word is surely out. This pack of wolferines have focused in on one in the herd -- us."

Jasmine and Drer Fregoode joined Gaebryl and the wyzard at the rail. "By the gods," the minstrel swore. There was a creaking sound of hydraulic metal raking against metal. From the bow of the Caasar III, a rift appeared and began opening with an ear splitting squeal. It looked like the maw of a great black beetle, opening horizontally, revealing the barrels of five large blastguns. The hole was large enough to exhume Stardeer whole.

"They're getting awfully close," Gaebryl said. "And they

are brandishing weapons. We should prepare to-"

Suddenly, blasterfire exploded past them, barely missing the main lower rudder. The startled crew held on tight as Perce enacted evasive maneuvers.

"They're firing on us!" Binder retorted. "Take cover!"

Gaebryl seized Jasmine by her shoulders and rushed her toward the stairs to the lower hold. "Take cover!" he commanded. "Let us fight for you now!"

She hesitated, but another blast found its target just then, on deck, destroying one of the two remaining mounted blastguns. The impact of the explosion reflected out over the port side of the ship, and, amazingly, no one was hurt. Jasmine seceded, and went below, sealing the door behind her.

"Binder!" the wyzard cried. "There's a skycraft charger in the rear hold! Can you manage it?"

"I'll try!"

Another blazing blastfire shot past them, brushing by the port wing with a scrape. It exploded into the woods a hundred yards ahead of them. Fires engulfed the trees almost instantly.

"Surrender," a resonating voice boomed from a speaker behind them. "Take your craft to the ground or you will be forced."

Suddenly, an explosion flashed behind them this time, a direct hit denting the foremost hull of the Caasar III. Lake Tobias, the timid castleranger of Tungulin, stood wide eyed, clenching the blastgun handles with white knuckled fists, amazed at the power of the weapon he had just fired.

"Good job!" Commander Benjyn Binder called to him as he readied Dedlin's large charger. This gun was heavy, usually mounted, but Binder intended to do what damage he could with the weapon while holding it in his muscled arms. "Now, watch this!"

With the pull of the trigger, an electric surge like a ball of copper lightning fired from the bulbous tip, and it struck the hull of the fifty man Caasar III with a loud, searing rip. The air about the crew was filled with blue static electricity.

Perce cut hard to the right, ducking below another series of blaster explosives that screamed past. Then, he came up, hard to the left, slicing between the broken off trunks of two great trees. Despite its size, the Caasar III followed behind them with remarkable dexterity and agility.

Now in range, Ott took the opportunity to fire an arrowjet. It made a direct hit on the dorsal fin of the Gharnian warship, causing a goodsized, fiery crater. He loaded another one and prepared to fire.

"Surrender," the voice repeated from the Caasar III. "Surrender now or you will be destroyed."

"To hell with you!" Gaebryl cried, throwing a small pack over his shoulder. "Make every shot count!," he called out to the crew. "Fire! Fire now! I've got a package to deliver!"

He had unfastened a small, one man skysled from the cabin hold and was running with it toward the rear of Stardeer. He turned it on, seized the guidestick, and leaped off the stern as he straddled it. He fell but for a second before the skysled righted itself, spinning and bobbing right into the path of the mighty oncoming warship.

The Caasar III suffered three more shots simultaneously: Lake with the blastgun, Ott with an arrowjet, and Binder with the charger.

Dedlin cried out, "No more! You'll strike the prince! Give him a chance now!"

As the huge warship banked past him, Gaebryl shot an latchkey anchor bolt at it. It hit the hull and caught on the edge of a bent hull plate. He swung around hard as the ship took up the slack in the wire, and he crashed hard into the side, nearly dislodging him from his precarious seat. He clung there, out of

sight of any Gharnian windows, repeatedly slamming into the side
of the hull.

61

"Where is he?" Binder cried. "What happened to him?"

"He missed the opening," Lake replied. "He's gone!"

"Nonsense," the wyzard replied. "He wasn't trying to fly
into the body of the ship. That would've been foolish indeed! He's
hanging there on the side. Careful now! Don't fire again until he's
found footing!"

Three more rapid shots fired past them, dangerously close,
but Perce was able to dive below them, the keel of Stardeer raking
a trough in the hardened dirt below. One of the missiles had
singed Dedlin's beard; another had missed Qan by mere inches.

The landscape around them changed as they rode the rim
of a shallow canyon. Hills of sandy, rocky earth rose in flattened
mounds, nearly deplete of any vegetative growth. They were
bordering the deadly Gornian desert, small in comparison to the
Bursian desert, but many times more perilous. It was a barrier
between the Aasar mountain range and the Gornian River, the
geographical home of the most dangerous sands in the kingdom,
reputedly uninhabitable by any living creature. The perilous sands
were intensely reflective, and the tiny grains were as sharp and
ruthless as shards of ground glass. But the dunes were as beautiful
as they were deadly. Spectacular mountains of crystal gold sand
dunes opened up before them and to their right, stretching
endlessly over the southern horizon.

Perce angled Stardeer right and left, dodging Gharnian
missile sights. For a moment, he thought he heard rattling in the
turbines at his feet, as if there were some damage there, causing
him to fret with concern. He did not need any malfunction. He
must remain an elusive target. The guidestick began trembling
slightly in his hand. He took Stardeer down low, sometimes only
inches from the rocks jutting up from the sand. The shadow of the
Gharnian warship covered them from above.

Meanwhile, Gaebryl had found footing on the side of the warship, and had climbed to the edge of a small ventilation plate. Hoping to find a weakness in the soaring structure, he opened a hole in the side of the engineering station of the Caasar III with several shots from his blaster. He began firing repeatedly into the great ship, wreaking whatever havoc he could to the drive and propulsion gear. Then, he took the pack from his shoulder and stuffed it into the smoking hole.

The Gharnians fired again. Perce pulled back hard, barely soaring above the passing missiles. An exploding boulder pummeled Stardeer's undercarriage with meteoric shrapnel, lifting the ship several feet in the air. The crew flew in every direction.

"Those imbecilic Gharnians!" Dedlin cried. He looked out over the rail at the dark windows of the Caasar III and shook his fist at them. "If you destroy us, you'll never find the Stone you seek! Fools!"

"And neither will we," Drer added, setting down another crate of munitions. "Use these, if you can!"

Commander Binder could see two dark silhouetted figures, moving like shadows behind the wide front bay windows, shielded by a thin veiled deflector. It was the warship's cockpit, they were the pilots, and they were foolishly close. "Ott!" he shouted, an idea forming in his mind. He set the charger aside, and picked up an old gladiator's shield. "Otthagorus! Come over here! I need you!"

Dedlin stepped up onto the rear mooring, arms and legs spread wide. He began waving his walking stick out vertically before him like a baton, in a figure eight 'lying on its side' motion. His eyes were closed and his mouth moved, chanting some words that no one could hear. Then, the front bow of the Caasar III began to obey Dedlin's strange commands. It began to bow and rise, following Dedlin's lead. Right and left, up and down, in greater and greater increments. This magick taxed the wyzard, though; his face grew red, and sweat poured from him.

Binder took a few steps back, as if preparing to charge. He turned and ran across the deck. "Now, Otthagorus!" he cried as he leaped off the back of Stardeer at the Caasar III..

Ott fired an arrowjet at the warship's bay window. It exploded, rendering the Gharnian's deflector temporarily useless; the thick glass cracked with spreading spider webs. Binder tucked himself behind the gladiator's shield that was strapped to his arm and shoulder, and burst through the enemy's front window, rolling into the cockpit like a huge human cannonball. Blasterfire lit the galley almost immediately.

"I bet they weren't expecting *that*," Ott said.

Gaebryl came crawling across the top of the Caasar III and scaled down toward the busted bay window. As soon as he was in range, he fired his blaster at the enemy inside, calling frantically for Commander Binder to retreat with him.

The Caasar III had not fired upon Stardeer for some time. In fact, it had begun to slow a bit, veering off to the right. From inside came a sudden explosion.

Dedlin cheered. "Bless him! Gaebryl set off a sunbomb!" Flames and white light were erupting from the massive hole in the side.

"There's Commander Binder," Drer said. "Look!"

The crew could see Gaebryl pulling Binder from the window. He was injured, and his military jacket sleeve was in flames. Gaebryl helped him pull it off while they scaled the warship toward the top.

Behind them, four Gharnian warriors emerged from the smoke as well, all of them also in flames. Their purple capes whipped viciously in the hot wind. The foremost, a large, fierce looking General, drew his blaster and began firing at Gaebryl and Binder.

A sudden arrowjet explosion dislodged two of the Gharnians. General Moon Jakarad had a good grip on an exhaust duct and did not fall; the other soldier was holding desperately onto the General. Ott growled, loading another arrowjet.

To the crew's dismay and horror, another Gharnian ship, a five hundred man commandship, the largest skycraft ever constructed, came racing over the western horizon like an upside down flying mountain. It flew for them with great fury, darkening the sky.

Stardeer choked and stuttered, as if she were dragging some heavy weight behind her. She coughed, rode on steadily for a bit, and then sputtered again. Perce held onto the guidestick tightly. Suddenly, they began to lose altitude and control. "Something's wrong!" he cried. "Not now! Not now!"

"We've been hit!" Ott said. "We're falling!"

"Brace yourselves!" Drer shouted.

"We're not hit!" Perce exclaimed fearfully, looking frantically at his gauges. He suddenly realized the real problem. "We're out of fuel!"

Dedlin had already diagnosed the problem. Just as his Stardeer began falling toward the desert floor like a stone, the wyzard tossed the last three chunks of algaestone into the pressure bin and slammed it shut. "Expand, damn you!" he frantically ordered, wishing there were magick in those words.

The textured dunes rose nearer and nearer.

"Hold on!" Perce cried out.

Gaebryl had secured the skysled once again, and hoisted it up by the anchor wire to the top of the Caasar III. He set Binder on the seat and turned it on. The skysled whirred to life and began to slide backwards off the smoking warship. Gaebryl ran unsteadily down the quivering spine of the Caasar III after it, firing over his shoulder at the pursuing Gharnians. Just as the sled slid off into space, Gaebryl leaped onto Binder's hunched back, and they disappeared into the billowing clouds of blue and black smoke.

General Moon Jakarad reached the apex, firing blindly into the swirling clouds, hoping to hit the two escaping saboteurs.

Several others joined him there, firing a rapid volley of blaster shots into the thick greasy smoke, although they were unable to see any sign of their targets anymore.

Just breaching the crest of a dune, Stardeer began falling into a wide valley, hovering just a few feet above the sloping bank. Suddenly, her turbines roared to life as the expanded fuel ignited. Unfortunately, it had happened too late. As she lurched to life, Perce pulled the guidestick back as far as it would go, but the next dune rose up too high to miss. With a sudden sandy burst, a cloud of gold erupted as Stardeer's nose plunged deep into the crest. The skycraft spun up and over, backwards, rolling wildly through the air, hitting another dune, then stood up upon its side as the gyroscopes struggled to interpret her correct position. Stardeer righted herself clumsily as she slid slowly backwards down the hillside, hovering just inches above the flaming Gornian sands, and stalled at the bottom, motionless.

Perce had somehow kept his grip on the guidestick. He turned Stardeer around and slowly accelerated up and out of the valley bed. With a clank and a tumble, Gaebryl and Commander Binder fell aboard the wrecked fightercraft, rolling onto the floor. Perce increased his speed, scanning the east. With a stuttering roar, Stardeer obeyed the mahekian's demanding commands and shot off from the desert floor like a comet.

62

The Caasar III could not keep up. It lurched off toward the mountains, its bow tilted and leaning, ploughing through the sand beneath it.

The giant black commandship, however, drew ever nearer. The intense heat rising from the surface of the sand caused the oncoming ship to quiver hideously.

"We can't fight that," Gaebryl replied, holding a wounded shoulder with his hand. Blood squeezed from his sand encrusted fingers. "We can't fight that."

"Are you shot?" Drer asked, coming with bandages.

"See to Commander Binder first," Gaebryl replied. "He's cut up pretty bad."

"I'm fine," Binder said, coming up beside them at the rail. "But I am burned."

"I'll see to it," Drer told them.

For some reason, the huge commandship did not immediately follow them. Instead, it slowed as it reached the crippled Caasar III, then pulled up and turned, directly over it, like a mother seeing to an injured child. It hovered there. Then, suddenly, it fired down upon the smoking warship with repeated blastfire, knocking it to the desert floor like a jackhammer with each pounding blow. The great warship Caasar III flattened from the blows, burst into flame and fell to the sand with a monumental roar that echoed ominously across the desert wasteland.

"Gharnians do not accept failure well, do they?" Gaebryl said, grimacing.

"I wonder," said the wyzard. "It was foolish to be firing upon the Stonebearer. I don't think the General of the Caasar III was following orders, and paid the price. Anyway, Mr. Perce, stay low. Head southwest for a time and get us away from this infernal desert before we become breakfast to a baerloth. Hopefully, we can lose this big ship, too, if we don't dally."

Jasmine had come from below, and joined the crewmembers at the helm, showing her concern. Drer was already busy playing doctor, and she volunteered to aid him. She, herself, had a bump on her head the size of a walnut.

Qan was sweeping sand off the deck. "What a mess!" he moaned. "We lost everything that wasn't attached. All three blasters are gone now, and Commander Binder's charger. We have no major weapons left."

Gaebryl was looking about at the damage. "Yes, yes, we lost the tent storage box, and the extra munitions as well. Wait," he said, scowling. "Something else, too. Something else is missing."

They looked around. "Not something," Dedlin said. "*Someone.*"

"Lake?" Qan called. His face went pale. "Lake Tobias, where are you?"

"He was standing right beside me when we hit the dune," Drer said. "Firing the blaster." The blaster was gone, also, broken off at the mount. The rail and cracked wooden mooring were badly damaged from the impact.

Qan ran to the back rail, peering out into the wavering distance for his lost friend. "Lake!" he cried. "We have to go get him! We can't just leave him out there like this! What will he do?"

The flaming hull of the Caasar III was hardly discernable. Two more warships had joined the commandship, descending to scavenge. Somewhere back there, in the heated rage of the Gornian desert sand, Lake Tobias from castlecity Tungulin had fallen from the ship, and now, alive or dead, the Tungulinian was lost to the forces of the deadly Gornian desert. All of them knew that a rescue attempt would be futile, and would jeopardize their entire quest. They had to think of the greater good, which did nothing to relieve the pain and sadness.

Qan Methalard, Lake's longtime friend, went below with a bottle of wine to be alone and to grieve. They could hear his woeful sobbing.

"Head west," Dedlin advised Masterpilot Perce. "They'll be coming after us again soon, so we'll circle back northward tonight and try to get in behind them. Hopefully, we won't find the entire Gharnian army waiting for us there."

63

Night came without any signs of Gharnian ships. The crew of the battered and failing Stardeer were exhausted and weary. The water supply was dwindling, as was the fuel for the ship, and the golden crystal desert below them offered no reprieve.

However, the boundary of the desert was drawing close. Withered shrubs and hard, twisted trees sprouted up here and there, and the bony shoulders of the dark Aasar Mountains loomed in the distant eastern skies.

Damage and injuries were abundant. It was a miracle that Stardeer remained aloft at all. There were squeaks and hissing noises coming from everywhere. Nothing appeared to have gone unaffected by the events of the last few days. Gaebryl and Binder suffered the worst injuries; however, neither was incapacitated. Under Drer and Dedlin's care and supervision, ample recovery ensued.

Stardeer drew to a stop over the first water hole they came across. The ship was refilled, as were all canteens and the bellies of the thankful crew. They searched, but no fuel could be found in the desolate hills. They made camp and a quiet night without the comfort of a campfire slowly passed.

As Stardeer hesitantly took to the sky the next morning, Dedlin called everyone to the helm, where Otthagorus was now navigating.

"As some of you have noticed, we are not one but two short, leaving our crew now seven in all," he stated coarsely. "Voluntarily, Masterpilot Perce left us during the night to attempt to find and aid our good but unfortunate castleranger companion Lake Tobias, if he can. He is adept in the wilds, and can manage if anyone can."

"I would have gone with him!" Qan cried, bursting into tears.

"As would I," Commander Binder said. "I feel responsible for Lake's accident. I had noted that the fuel was low, but didn't do anything about it. Besides, I'm Lake's commander. I should have been given the chance..."

Dedlin held up his hands. "What's done is done," he said. "I'm sure we all would have gone after him, given the chance. But all of us cannot. Perce insisted, because he had been the pilot at the time of the mishap, and so, ultimately, the fuel status of the ship was his responsibility. After all were bedded down last night, he came to Jasmine, Prince Gaebryl and myself, and we discussed it briefly. Sending one back seemed prudent and conscientious. Any more than that could jeopardize this mission, so we concurred, and so he quietly departed on one of the sleds. If Lake is yet alive, and not found sometime this very morning, he will not last the day in that pitiless desert without aid and rescue."

"I would've liked to say goodbye to him," Otthagorus said. "I did like him. He was becoming an adequate pilot in his own right."

"No one better than a mahekian to travel this desert," Gaebryl said. "I do wish them both the best."

"They are missed," Jasmine said, looking at the western sky, where the night had now melted away. Losing Perce, the mahekian, was hard for her to bear. "Farewell, my friends. May our paths cross again, someday."

64

Fuel reconnaissance turned up just enough scraps to keep them aloft, but each trip to the ground was risky and dangerous. As the day passed, it was evident that Stardeer was mortally wounded and would not carry them much further. Gaebryl found a motherlode of algaestone along the cliffs of a dried riverbed, but even when the tanks were filled, Stardeer coughed and sputtered as she pulled herself from the ground once again. It was as if, despite their pleads and prodding, she did not have the will to fight gravity any longer. Still, she persevered as best as she could, though she slowed with each hour until she was unable to maintain a speed much faster than a running horse.

"Still better than going on by foot," Drer, ever the optimist, had said.

They plodded on through the following night, but no one slept well, if at all. At any moment, they half expected their loyal skycraft to die suddenly in midair and fall, plummeting to the ground.

Jasmine tried to find a moment's sleep, but she was unable. She stared out broken windows at distant stars, when a vision, like a memory, filled her waking sight like ink filling a crystal pool. She smelled rotten apples, and felt mist upon her skin, before realizing that she was witnessing one of the visions from the sinkhole mirror again. She sat up and glared into the darkness. In the vision, Lake was not among them. She remembered it clearly now. She cursed herself for not remembering it earlier. Why had it come back to her now, now that it was too late to do anything about it?

She looked out the window at the lands sliding slowly past. Below, gray rocks and shadowy trees crept steadily past. A cold chill rode up and down her spine like the keys of a bony flute. She thought she saw something down there, a form following steadily behind, a shadow darker than all other shadows it passed through, beneath the cover of the shadowy gray boughs. She knew what it was.

She was not surprised to find herself weeping.

65

"Good morning, all," Dedlin said. "Despite everything, good morning. What is today?"

"Ever the cheerful one," Binder moaned.

Gaebryl was hungover from a night spent with a gallon of potent apple wine. "The second day of Greenwithe," he replied, massaging his own neck with his right hand. "That makes it Meriday, I believe."

Dedlin nodded, catching himself from falling as Stardeer stuttered.

"I fear that your Stardeer has seen her last sunrise, wyzard," Binder told him. "She is dying. We must make new arrangements."

"We've seen quite a few warships this day,"

Otthagorus advised. "The skies are thick with them this morning."

Dedlin squinted at the Aasar cliff walls, lit with morning's lavender light. Jasmine was quiet, staring off in the same direction.

"We could stop for a new ship," Commander Binder suggested. "We're but a few day's journey from the tricity of Corinth, Attrosen and Corbin..."

"No, we cannot risk that," Dedlin said, frowning. "It could be invaded and overrun. We have a better chance out here in the wilds."

"This ship won't hold out much longer, I assure you."

"No, she won't," the wyzard agreed. "But we're getting close. Very close. And there's good tree cover from here to the mountains."

"What are you suggesting?"

Drer Fregoode's eyes widened. "This isn't the most hospitable land," he said emphatically. "Besides thorns and desolation, there are thorns, snakes, ugres, uusyrapi, dhoellums, quicksand, scyropirates..."

Stardeer nearly stopped in midflight, chugging and coughing. The crew tumbled forward. The turbines blew out black ash, then with a painful whine, she continued slowly onward.

"Gather up your belongings, my friends, and only the bearable essentials," Dedlin told them. "Stardeer, my gracious girl, will not last out this day."

They doused Stardeer with flammable liquid and set a timed explosive under the main turbine. Once everyone was safely aground, Binder set a predetermined course for her, straight toward the mountains in a different direction that they were taking, and leaped over the rail to the rocks below. Stardeer slowly rose, coughing sadly, and disappeared, spinning, over the tops of the trees.

"Let's make haste," the wyzard said solemnly, reaching his hand into a pouch that hung from his shoulder. "I have koffik beans for you to chew on. They are not nourishing, but they will help to make us go farther faster."

Some of their belongings had been secured to the last remaining skysled; Gaebryl pulled it along behind them with a rope, like a reluctant beast of burden. Traveling by foot over that rocky ground was tough and quickly wearisome. There was no path to follow, and plenty of thorn bushes with quills long and sharp enough to pierce through leather boots. Often, spiny trees grew together so dense that their limbs seemed to be knotted together to intentionally thwart the grounded travelers from passing. Commander Binder led the way swinging an axe at the larger brambles; Drer and Ott followed close behind with their machetes.

Within the hour, an echo of an explosion rang throughout the hills. No one uttered a word, but there were a few thoughtful sighs. Dedlin's Stardeer was gone.

They were forced to clamber up rocky embankments to keep their course, or to squeeze through cracks and cross deep ravines. Loose rocks and boulders prattled noisily down the steep slopes around their feet, echoing ominously. There were deep fissures in the earth, as if formed by recent earthquakes. Never had any of them remembered seeing so many snakes and spiders. Something slithered or scrambled away from them with every few steps they took.

They marched all day and night, stopping only to eat in a patch of shade, although they enjoyed no feast. Near dawn they found a cave that could bear them all, and they slept through the morning and midday, taking turns at watch. Before dusk, they warily headed back out again.

The thorn bushes grew further apart on their second night of foot travel, allowing them easier passage. The ground beneath the trees was sandy and dusty, with little or no undergrowth. Jasmine walked second in line, only after Dedlin. Often she would pause and close her eyes as the Stone called to her, and she would guide them this way or that, though most of the time she was not exactly sure. Dedlin encouraged and supported her slightest whim, and marched onward determinedly wherever she set their course.

"I've seen this place, Dedlin," she whispered, as they wound up an embankment toward a grove of gray locusts. "The weird trees with the dry gray leaves rustling against one another in this warm breeze. The choking dust that we stir up as we walk. The leafless bushes, the dry weeds, the burs, the thorns."

"Is this vision important?" the wyzard asked.

A hundred yards to the south, a Gharnian fightership shot past at a great speed toward the mountains. The crew paused in the shadows of the steep incline until they were sure it was gone and that none followed.

"I believe that it is," she answered. "There's something out there. Something hungry..."

"I don't like this place," Commander Binder said. He spoke for the lot of them. "It's unclean. Not black magick, but uncomfortable, nonetheless. Sir Otthagorus, my friend, what can you see with your feline eyes?"

Ott's pupils were wide open, deep and gold. "I see nothing," he said.

"Mind your feet," Drer Fregoode warned them.

The night deepened around them. There were no moons or stars to light their way, and the crew refused to risk any light. They were famished and their provisions were all but depleted, save a few final scraps. Ott had eaten a lizard that he had caught. It had a sour taste, he had said, and it later turned his stomach. Drer advised against eating the occasional brown mushrooms that they saw on the rotting stumps that they passed. "Nothing growing in this place is healthy. It is better to abstain until we have found greener woods."

The night was blind dark. The desert oaks, only an arm's

length away on either side, were indiscernible. Dedlin had trouble guiding them, and they crept at a turtle's pace, so he eventually decided to use the crystal of his cane in spurts now and then, just a little bit, to light the way before his tired and weary feet.

At one point, as the glow dimly intensified, barely illuminating the clearing before them, Jasmine stopped them in their tracks, holding the wyzard back with an outstretched arm. "Wait," she warned. "Hold on. Don't go any further. This is it."

"What is it?" Dedlin whispered. "What do you see?"

The trees, stripped of bark from the ground to the height of a man, thinned on all sides of them, and there were small gray mounds of earth, covered with weeds and dry scrub, throughout the clearing ahead. The wind hissed across the dry reeds, and the clicking of some insects was most unsettling.

"It looks like death mounds of a graveyard," Ott replied.

"I don't know for sure," she said. "I saw this place in a vision, in the magick sinkhole mirror. There are things out there. All around us. Large, deep holes, I think."

Dedlin heeded her warning, looking around them. They were too far in now to try turning back. "Ahh. We should rope ourselves together," he said to the rest of them. "We'll cross this plain, tied to one another. Be careful, now. Make a circle..."

"Nomires," Drer said, nodding. "There's nomires here. I told you to mind your feet."

"I believe so," Dedlin responded. "So we should use precautions, just to be sure."

"They're old, by the growth around them," Gaebryl said. "They were dug a long time ago. And where there are nomires, there are certainly gogres..."

"Let's not frighten anyone just yet," Dedlin said quickly. "We should be fine as long as we hold onto one another. The pits could be vacant. They might be abandoned."

"Nomires? Gogres?" Qan inquired. "I don't see a thing..."

"Pits," Drer answered. "Cleverly disguised pits."

"Disguised?" Jasmine asked. "Disguised by who?"

"Not *who*," Drer whispered. "By *what*."

They knitted themselves together into a circle with their ropes, then slowly, carefully, they continued their way across the clearing. It was awkward going at first, pulling and pushing in the dark. Dedlin set a slow pace for them. He held his cane near the ground before his feet, poking this way and that way to seek any anomaly in the dust and dirt. "Feel for softness," he told them. "Feel with your feet. Don't be fooled by what you see with your eyes."

They walked silently, with only the sound of the rustling gray locust leaves and the clicking beetles around them. They passed a number of the mounds without any cause for alarm.

Then, there was a yelp, and a tug on the rope that nearly pulled them all over. Drer Fregoode was the first to slip into a nomire hole, nearly dragging Gaebryl and Qan Methalard in with him. "It just gave way beneath me!" he said, his head still above ground. He scrambled to pull himself free, but the sides of the pit were slick and slimy with mucus. The hole had been invisible to them in that dim light, covered over with flimsy, dusty, transparent web of film, and masterfully camouflaged on top with leaves, dirt, sticks and pebbles. Beneath, the hole was wet, bubbly and muddy, with no roots, rocks or footholds to climb by.

"Pull him out!" the wyzard said. "Quickly, now!"

"There's something down in there," Qan said as he helped Drer to his feet. "I heard it. There's movement, and a sucking sound."

"They are gogres," Dedlin told them. "Gogres make these nomires. They live in them, rarely leaving them, and they're filthy down there, as you can imagine. They live in their own lifetime of filth."

"They're nasty scavengers," Drer continued, shaking the slime from his hands. "Hunters. Carnivorous type of, I don't know, a spider or an eight legged piglike arachnid kind of creature. Horrible things. Large tusks. Big jaws. Spines. Flat on the top, round on the bottom. Quite deadly if they get a hold of you."

"Spider pigs?" Jasmine asked.

"Good on a barbecue spit," Gaebryl added jovially.

"What is that sound?" Jasmine asked. "I... I hear a crunching sound..."

Gaebryl answered her. "They're chewing on the bones of past victims..."

Suddenly, the ground beneath Jasmine's feet gave way and she slipped into another hole, spinning upside down. The ropes went taut. She shrieked as she dangled, trying desperately to pull her feet back down beneath her. She felt something move against her cheek, licking her neck with a hairy, wet tongue. She squealed and frantically thrashed at it as the men quickly heaved her up and out.

"Let's be careful now," Gaebryl said to them. "Some gogres are bigger than others..."

As they crossed the nomire field, only Dedlin and Binder managed not to blunder into a hole. Jasmine slipped twice, and Drer had the unfortunate distinction of falling in three times. Still, they crossed the gogre clearing getting filthy, but fairly unscathed. Fortunately, gogres were basically lazy creatures by nature, since their prey usually plummeted directly in upon them, without any chance of escape. There, they could inject them with their paralyzing poison and toy with them until their insides liquefied, to be devoured at their own lethargic pace. The crew had awoken quite a few of them, leaving them all hungry and upset, with much work to do on the broken camouflage coverings of their nomire lids.

When the unnerved fellowship entered the dark trees on

the far side of the nomire pits, where the thorny thickets and rocky earth returned underfoot, they felt safe enough to remove their ropes from one another. They shared their meager water reserves, and continued their pace through the waning hours of the night, grateful to get past the slimy holes and a possible tragedy there.

To the north, between the dark, dull leaves of the trees, above the hilly crags at the mountain's feet, a fleet of Gharnian warships idled silently, joined together with catwalk cylinders, as if they were convening there. The crew turned their faces away from that direction and picked up their speed in the direction that Jasmine led them, toward the south, where Uran, the soft, rose colored moon dove into the failing trees on the horizon.

They slept uneasily through the next day against a wall of dead trees that appeared to have been formed from some great deluge in a canyon base. Drer alone had gone hunting, and brought back two small squirrels, some onions, and tubers, and a bag full of bitter, barely edible greens, which he put into a stew. It did not taste good, but it was important that they ate something, to keep their energy level up.

There was no cloud covering that evening, so they remained hidden until the suns had fully set. Commander Binder gently shook Jasmine's shoulder as they made preparations to depart. "We're moving," he said softly.

"What? Oh, Binder," she said, obviously startled from a dream. "Oh, it's you..."

"Your Highness?"

"I just had another dream," she said to him, as she sat up, rubbing her eyes and nose. She had leaves and dust stuck to her face and in her hair. "Or a vision, or whatever. It concerns you, Benjyn, so let me tell you about it now before it fades away."

"Go ahead," the Commander said.

She focused. "You are running... You are with Otthagorus, and others, but I cannot say exactly who, in a cave, I think. You are running from something. Actually, you are running away from many things, Binder. They are chasing you."

"And you?" he asked. "You are not there with us?"

"I am not there. Dedlin and Gaebryl are not there, either," she said, squinting into space. The vision was fading away quickly. "In this vision, and it is very brief, you will find yourselves in the fork of a cave, and will have to make a decision on which way to go. One way, to the right, leads down into a dark tunnel. The other way, directly before you, runs uphill a short distance toward what appears to be a dead end."

"This vision... Is it a precognition of things to come?"

"I believe so. I believe that it is an event that is soon upon you, Commander. It may be the deciding point in your life...."

Binder nodded. "A dead end, you say? Perhaps it is a trap then."

Jasmine frowned. "I do not believe that it is a trap, nor even a dead end. Do not take the easy way, the tunnel down to the right, Commander Binder, or you will perish."

"No?"

"Take the path that leads to what appears to end at a rock wall. I know this sounds foolhardy, but it is right. I tell you, run for the dead end, and do not stop when you reach it. Do you understand? Lead them all, and keep going, right through it. At full pace. It is not what it appears to be. This will save your lives."

"I will," he said. "I will do this whenever this time comes."

"It will be soon," she said forebodingly, rising to her feet. She brushed the debris from her clothes, staring into the sleeping vision that faded off into the air like so much smoke. She looked at him with her grim eyes. "It's going to happen tonight."

They were able to follow some sort of trampled footpaths in the brush that night, weaving and crisscrossing the hills haphazardly, whenever the direction suited them. Sometimes they saw fat, webbed footprints in the mires and puddles that appeared to be semihuman, but those who knew who or what made them would not tell the rest until they had safely passed the region by. Occasionally, Jasmine would veer away from their path into tougher brush if the call of the Stone led her, and none questioned her.

"We are crossing the salty rim of the once great Barton Sea," Dedlin ventured to tell them. "Emptied into the outer oceans beyond the mountains through breaches in the earth caused by earthquakes many centuries ago..."

The firmament was rocky and porous, like hard sponge, completely depleted of anything green or wholesome. There was a strange odor that sometimes wafted by, a familiar, yet strange scent that no one could place with certainty. The place was wicked, of that they were sure. Sometimes, the ground beneath their boots crunched like thin flakes of tender glass as they crossed vast lakes of ancient white shells from that salty sea, long dead. The bleached rocks were full of fossils and bones of strange plants and animals, long ago extinct, protruding like markers on great oceanic tombstones. Huge bones and skulls of fish and long lost marine life littered the deepest gullies, and now the ancestors of great mangroves grew there in the salt marshes, and trees with giant spreading roots.

"I don't like this place," Otthagorus said. "It is a massive graveyard and does not like our passing."

"I have the oddest feeling that we are being watched," Drer Fregoode whispered after he could stand it no longer. "I can't see any eyes, but I can feel them."

"Just hush and keep on walking," Dedlin warned. "If we're lucky, and they're not too curious or hungry, they might just leave us alone."

There were movements in the dry reeds to their right, and more rustling directly behind them, followed by airy, croaky whispers. The crew began to detect movement all around them, subtle and secretive, and shapes began forming in the dark between the mangrove clumps, moving along with them on a parallel path.

"W-what are they? Tell me, now," Jasmine needed to know, pulling close to Gaebryl.

"Whatever they are, there's an army of them," Ott said. "We're surrounded. And they're getting braver every second..."

"Just keep your weapons at hand," Dedlin said. "They are getting restless, and contact is now inevitable. But worse than that, my friends, to compound matters even worse, I feel – "

Before Dedlin could finish his sentence, a feeling of fear and cold dread washed over them like an icy wave of water, as if from behind them, something very evil was drawing near.

"Morgoth has come upon us again," Jasmine said aloud, and her words caused a weight of helplessness to fall over the crew. "The hell hound has reached us here. It is coming up that path. Gods help us. It's coming and we're right out here in the open with no place to go..."

"Maybe we should separate and run," Qan suggested, rising panic apparent in his voice.

"No! They would all overcome us immediately," Binder said. "We must stick together at all costs."

The woods around them suddenly sprang to life. Shadows turned into shapes, and bent figures approached from all sides from out of the trees.

"I knew it," Gaebryl muttered. "Cave ugres."

"A very large tribe of them," Dedlin said. "Footprints or no, I would know the smell of their foul stew, full of the most hideous ingredients, anywhere. These dumb, cannibalistic creatures attack on impulse, my friends. Do not startle them or move abruptly. Look for the leader. Kill the leader first if you can.

It may confuse them temporarily..."

Jasmine's heart was leaping. "Gogres and ugres."

Now, flat, bald heads could be seen emerging from the misty shadows, and the glare of dull green bulbous eyes beneath thick, hairy brows, high on their froglike heads. The ugres were small in stature, with long muscular arms, big feet and hands. Many carried clubs.

The crew marched on, staggering and stumbling as they watched the figures in the trees dogging them with certain cruel intentions, each minute seeming like ten.

"They're getting very close," Ott said, growling, claws retracting. "Too close! I'm tired of them. I'm ready for whatever they've got. Enough of this! Let's hit them now with everything we've got..."

From all sides, the ugres suddenly advanced in upon them, barbed spears withdrawn, forcing the crew to stop in their tracks and form a tight circle, back to back. They were awful creatures to look at, part men, part frogs, moist mottled greenish brown skin with hairy patches on their shoulders and torsos. They wore no clothes. They had broad, flat noses, and wide, lipless mouths, and no foreheads. Their bulbous glistening yellow/green eyes nearly on their heads were cold and dull, devoid of intelligence or apathy.

"We're trapped," Binder said. "We have to make our stand right here, right now."

"There are hundreds of them!" Ott growled.

"I don't care about them," Qan blurted, his voice riddled with terror. "What... What about... What about the..."

"How very kind of you to remember me, young Qan Methalard," said a voice from behind and above them, a voice so innately evil that the crew instantly wavered in bonemarrow fear.

Drer Fregoode and Commander Binder crumbled

helplessly to their knees. Qan fell to the ground as though he were a dropped marionette, nearly unconscious.

"And to lead us here, to the doorstep of the Great Stone." The great black dog came lumbering slowly up the hill behind them, red eyes glowing in the void of his smoky mass. Thick foamy slime hung from its lips. The oblivious ugres parted for it as it drew nearer, then closed back in behind it. "We are so close now, aren't we, *Your Highness*?"

Gaebryl turned to the skysled, knocking all the gear off of it to the ground with his forearm. "Jasmine!" he said, seizing her by the wrist. "You must go now!"

Morgoth snarled, its eyes blazing like red flames. "I am here for the key and the Stone," it said. From behind it, two great glistening Gharnian commandships, even larger than the one that had mercilessly shot down the Caasar III in the desert, drew in close and stopped, hovering above the dead trees behind their immense demonic pet, blocking out all heavenly lights. "Will you oblige me willingly, or die? One breath from my mouth, and you will evaporate into nothingness, from which you came. Surrender instead, and your remaining days may live out in purest agony..."

The crew scrambled to gather their wits. Dedlin began chanting. He was summoning all the powers at his disposal, and was passing the benefits of every good spell he could muster to the trembling crew about him. They could hear the hydraulic opening of doors from the commandships above them.

The ugre king began shouting orders from his perch on a nearby caravan. They were preparing an attack.

"Go, now!" shouted the prince, ripping the entrusted key from around his neck and shoving it into Jasmine's trembling hand. "Here!" he said, handing her one of the boxes that had fallen to the ground. "This is your only chance now, Jasmine." Gaebryl grabbed the guidestick as the shrieking ugres charged them from all sides. "Go!"

"Don't be stupid!" the great dog said. "You cannot escape!"

"Surrender, King Day," boomed a voice from the warship. They were still looking for a man. The great dog wailed. "Find the young king!"

Jasmine took Gaebryl's face in her hands. She looked deeply into his fearful eyes. "I love you," she said, and kissed him on the mouth.

Gaebryl shifted the sled forward, and with a push on the accelerator bar, it went spinning off upward toward the trees, Jasmine clinging desperately on. He watched her sail helplessly away and he feared for her life, for he could help her no more. She was left to finish her quest on her own.

Then, strangely enough, at this ending of all things, his mind went to Princess Amber Leigh, his betrothed, and he suddenly felt totally selfish and alone. He had lived his whole life a fool, and must die now full of regret and shame. He turned to face his enemies and he drew his sword and his blaster. "If this is truly the end of all things, then what an end it shall be!" he cried to his fellows.

"Fools!" Morgoth howled with an ear splitting, gut wrenching shriek. It leapt for Jasmine, nearly flying across the clearing in one supernatural bound, its drooling mouth agape. Suddenly, before its eyes, Jasmine was instantly gone. The skysled sailed up and over the trees with nothing on it except for a small wooden box sitting squarely in the seat.

"Where is she?" it wailed, poised to strike. It turned its wrath back toward the small crew, gathered just a few yards away. Around its shadowy edges, flames ran and flickered. "What kind of magick is this? Where have you hidden her, wyzard!?"

"There now!" Dedlin cried, lighting up the entire clearing with a million dazzling fireballs.

The dog cringed from the bright light, but it noticed then, two small hands emerging from the wyzard's passage box, clinging tightly onto the seat of the retreating skysled. It was a simple magician's trick! She was hidden in the small wooden box!

Morgoth sprung like an explosion from the earth, its mouth unnaturally wide to take in the sled and rider in one monstrous bite. But Jasmine had just passed out of its reach in its current form, and morgoth missed by mere inches, crashing into the trees and thorns below her with a raging howl. The forest exploded into red flame.

Shrieking and croaking, the snarling, biting ugres attacked from all sides. Commander Binder, spinning back and forth, threw them like burlap seed bags into the thorns, although they continued to clamber back upon him in greater and greater numbers.

Troops of Gharnian soldiers flew down lines and ladders to the ground as chaotic blasterfire began to echo madly throughout the valley. Dedlin lit the trees with a fire of glorious white and gold. The small troop of six put their backs together to make this one last stand so valorous that it would go down in the annals of all time as the most courageous and heroic battle ever fought in the great Kingdom Continent of Day.

"Never surrender!' Dedlin cried, and a blue flame shot from his cane, engulfing a wave of attacking ugres.

"For Tungulin!" Binder decreed, swinging his axe right and left, hewing off ugre heads so that they piled at his feet. "Come die before my blade!"

Gaebryl swung his sword and fired repeatedly with his blaster. "For Bursia!" he cried, as Gharnians began pouring into the clearing, hauling great black nets. "And Isaial Dindiane, my father, the king! Come, enemy! I await you!"

Ott pounced, ripping everything in sight to pieces with his fangs and claws. "For Mead!" he bellowed ferociously. There was nothing civilized left in the Thordian. He had reverted in nature to the wild animal that lay suppressed inside of him, furious, feral, and deadly. His thunderous growl shook the ground and caused the hair to stand up on the back of the neck.

Drer and Qan stood back to back, using swords and blastguns. The fearsome and tenacious ugres were piling up at their feet. "For Tungulin!" they cried. "And King Tital Vantoo!"

Dedlin Dane was at his most glorious. He seemed to be clothed in white fire. His wrath was great and unfathomable to the mindless ugres that came after him to their deaths. Never had the Gornian cave ugres or Gharnians seen such fury. "For the Kingdom!" was Dedlin's solitary battle cry. Ugres spontaneously burst into flame all around him. He attacked like a whirlwind berserk.

The Gharnians continued to come, most allowing the ugres to do the fighting for them while they prepared their own final assault. The army of ugres seemed endless in numbers. They poured in like ranks of ants over their fallen comrades. They were fearless, perhaps from mere stupidity, or perhaps inspired by the strength and power of the morgothyon of Gheelgahar flaring behind them.

The crew fought fiercely, but they were weary and grossly outnumbered. As the battle unfolded, the air was soon filled with a confusing cloud where no one could discern friend from foe. Voices cried, swords clanged together, blasterfire exploded. The forest was going up in flames around them. Smoke engulfed them all.

The giant black hound of Gharne did not stay to fight. It was already off, hot on the trail of Jasmine Day and her key, and eventually, the great Stone of Power. The great Stone of Destruction was so near now, beckoning them both.

67

Jasmine lifted Dedlin's magick box up over her head and tossed it into the treetops below. It had certainly saved her life. Those last few seconds of confusion had surely allowed her to escape the hell hound's jaws of death. There were tears in her eyes. She had just deserted her friends to a fate and peril inescapable.

"Hey, there you are," said a voice in the air, startling her. "Follow me!"

Jasmine had the guidestick pressed forward as hard as she could. It was nearly bent from the effort, and her arms ached with fatigue. "Who is that?" she said. "Who's there?"

"It's me. Venni," said the crow. "I know the layout of this land pretty well. I'll get you away from here. Just follow me! We must hurry!"

She could not see him in the dark. "I need a place to hide, Venni. The fuel is low. This sled won't stay airborne much longer..."

"Can you make it across the Great Gorge Canyon? It's seven or eight miles across from side to side, 'as the crow flies', as it were. Nothing will be able to trail you on foot..."

"How far?"

"Two miles ahead of us."

"I...I think so," she answered. "We shall try. But I can't see you, Venni. It's too dark."

"Follow my voice!"

"I don't know if I can!"

A few seconds passed. "Follow the path of the whip on the thordian warrior constellation," he said to her. "Do you know it?"

She squinted into the heavens with wet eyes. Stars twinkled on the dark horizon before her. "I see it. I see it!"

"It's directly east. Just follow the path of the warrior's whip. Can you do that?"

"Yes," she said. "How did you find us? How did you find me?"

"That was easy," the crow answered. "Morgoth followed you. I followed morgoth. Pray it cannot quickly sprout wings!"

Twelve

SZAN TU XAQ

68

The contrast of the trees within the small canyon was intriguing. The birch, lark, and hemlock were remarkably tall and as straight as arrows, bare trunked for thirty feet from the ground, but thick with seasonal greenery at the tops. The junipers and mimosa were bent and twisted, some growing out from the side walls of the canyon, creating hidden hollows and winding trails that led through and across the fertile woodland hills. There were other dwarfed shrubs that Jasmine had never seen before along the path, with fat, flat stubby dark green needles and long, fragrant yellow cones, often housing an array of woodland birds and playful chipmunks.

The skysled had run out of fuel hours ago, so Jasmine had gone on by foot, with Venni riding noisily upon her shoulder. The ground was soft as a cushion beneath her feet, a mixture of earth and moss, creating a most comfortable earthen carpet, which made the long walk much easier for her to bear. The air was cool and refreshing, and the scents ranged from the fragrant mimosa blooms and juniper to occasional honeysuckle and sweet pine.

"What was it that the old wyzard told you to say?" Venni asked.

"In peace I enter Szan Tu Xaq," she answered for the third time that hour. "Please don't ask me again."

The crow squawked, somewhat offended. "I just want to make sure you don't forget," he said. "What is this Sand To Zack, anyway? That's a crazy bunch of words."

"That's exactly what Dedlin said," she said, faintly smiling. She missed the old man dearly. "The secret name of the cave, I suppose, Venni."

"Maybe they're magick words."

"Maybe they are."

There was such a strange comfort here, something Jasmine had not felt since the day before she left Mead. The scenic canyon was not deep, but it made her feel oddly secure. Beyond the trees she saw the red/gray rock walls on both sides of her, keeping her course steadily eastward. After a long, gradual slope down a hillside, her path crossed a featureless dry creek bed, one of many she had crossed that day. The incline on the next rise was not steep, but the strange comfort she had been experiencing began to falter as she climbed the hill, and so she stopped at the crest, questioning her course.

"What's wrong? Why'd you stop?" Venni asked.

"This isn't right," she answered. "This isn't the right way. We've got to go back."

"Are you sure?" he asked, his head spinning.

"I can feel it. We... we passed it."

Jasmine headed back down into the ravine and paused at the dry creek bed at the bottom.

"Here," she replied. "We leave the path and go downstream from here. We follow this trail."

"Are you sure you're sure?"

She left the footpath and followed the course of the dry creek bed, her feet crunching the fragile black, red, and blue shale with every step. There were ferns and mushrooms sprouting from the trees and stumps on both sides of her. Moss covered rocks and pools, filled with minnows and fat tadpoles, made the path before her zigzag.

"Are you sure you know where you're going?" the crow asked. "Oh, never mind. I'm just along for the ride."

"This is the right direction," she confirmed. "I know it is."

As miles passed behind her, the forest grew deeper, darker, much older, and more mysterious. The trees were very old, dark, and protective. Their strong, heavy roots grew long and twisted. Mushrooms were everywhere. From the trees, red ones grew in layers, stacked like cupboard shelves. From dead fallen logs, orange and white spiraled mushrooms shot up like miniature castles with numerous freckled towers. The long stemmed ferns covered the shaded hillsides between the mossy stones and fallen logs. Here and there, fat toads of various sizes and colors passively sat on the tops of rocks and stumps, curiously watching her pass them by, their throats ballooning with croaking song. Jasmine saw an old owl hooting from his doorstep, way up in a hollow tree. The crickets were loud, almost as if they were trying to compete with the noisy green and brown spotted frogs that croaked from the banks of the shallow pools she passed. Strange songbirds topped it all off, orating melodiously from the topmost branches of the old willow trees.

"Maybe you should check things out again, Venni," Jasmine suggested.

"Whatever," he croaked, flapping his wings. "Do this, Venni. Do that, Venni."

He launched from her shoulder, fluttering up through the trees. Jasmine saw him circling through the distant forest, then disappearing. A few minutes later, he returned with a swooshing flutter. "As I expected, nothing as far as I can see."

"Good," Jasmine replied, holding the key in her pocket tight within her fist. "We'll keep following this creek bed southeast, keeping a mile or so from those foothills."

"If you say so. You're the boss, Boss."

The rough path was pleasant and easy enough to follow. Raspberries grew abundantly, but most of them were still flowering and weren't quite ripe yet. Jasmine's stomach rumbled. It had been a long time since she had had a decent meal. She wondered when she would sit at a full table again. One of Drer's breakfasts sounded awfully good.

"Venni, can I ask you something?" she said in a shy, inquisitive tone as she bounded from stone to stone over a pool, trying to keep her feet dry.

"Um, if you, uh, well, if there's no..."

"Do you remember the one traveling with us named Gaebryl?"

The bird hopped from one shoulder to the other. "Sure," he said, then finished with, "No, not really."

"The tall, handsome one?"

"The wyzard?" he inquired. "Did have a beautiful beard thing."

"No!" she said. "The younger one with dark hair and green eyes."

"Oh, yes. Him. Sure," Venni said. "He frightened me."

"Frightened you? How?"

"All thordians frighten me. I'm a bird, and they're cats," Venni piped. "Big cats. I thought he was going to eat me at any second! But you're right, he was handsome."

"That was Otthagorus," she said, frustrated. "I mean the human, the prince. Never mind. Obviously, you have no taste."

Venni squawked. "I beg your pardon, Your Highness," he said, rebuking her, "but indeed I do have taste. In fact, to prove it, there's some wild strawberries just ahead, some breadfruit just next to that, and a spring with fresh water to wash it all down. I can tell you one thing. *That* tastes good."

"I *am* hungry," she said. "Let's have some."

Jasmine knelt near the spring, picking two full handfuls of large, juicy strawberries with one ambitious grasp. Venni perched among the berries, pecking diligently at one particularly large one. The breadfruit was ripe, and the water was remarkably refreshing. They ate until they could eat no more.

"So, what is it?" Venni finally asked her. "You love this Gaebryl?"

Jasmine looked at the crow and nearly blushed. She shrugged. "I don't know... Maybe. Is it that obvious?"

The crow cocked his head. "Can't say for sure," he said. "I was only guessing, since you brought it up, but wouldn't say why."

"Oh," she said, reflecting and analyzing herself.

"That, and the way you look at him all the time."

"Oh!"

"It's all right if you do. I mean, it happens to all of us. I've been in love a time or two myself."

"Have you?"

"Well," he trilled modestly, "to be honest with you, actually about twenty seven times, but who's counting, right?"

Jasmine smiled at her little shiny feathered friend. "You're certainly a free spirit, Venni. I didn't realize you were so prolific with the ladies. Are you saying that there are other intelligent, talking crows out there somewhere?"

"Other intelligent, talking crows? Ha! I'm the dimmest one you'll probably ever come across!" he told her. "The rest are too smart to let themselves be known! I come from a long line of great birds from the great reaches of Eaoph. The annulara, we are known. I am surprised you have never heard of us! Renowned we are in the world of the wise. I, myself, am a great annularan chieftain..." He looked at her sidelong, to see if she was falling for his feign.

"Come on, let's go, chief," she said with a chuckle. "I don't want to get caught dawdling here in a berry patch."

69

Jasmine strolled the afternoon away with hardly a negative thought. The peaceful woods had absorbed her, easing her into a state of tranquility, and she felt as if no harm could possibly befall her there. Sometimes the pull of the Stone was strong; sometimes she could feel nothing of it at all. She knew the direction, and remained steadfast. Evening was now upon them; the sky was red and gold beyond the fissure of the valley, the billowy clouds silver/blue along the dark eastern fringes of arriving twilight.

As evening drew on, she thought a lot about the rest of the crew. She was alone again, and her crew was gone again as well, each relinquished off to the shifting, tossling hands of fate. "I hope they're all right," she said aloud.

Venni had been dozing. "W-what?" he stuttered, wings flapping. "Oh. Yeah, sure they are. Don't worry about them." A moment later, "Who?" and then he dozed off again.

She thought about poor Lake lost in the desert, and brave Perce who had volunteered to go back after him. That desert had looked so uninviting and deadly. She thought about King Tital Vantoo and wondered how he was faring far away in Tungulin without Binder and Drer there at his side. She thought fondly of her Meadian home and her many friends there. How anxious they must be to hear from her. Had the Gharnians reached that fair island yet? She feared so. But hoped not. And where was that Habad? She shivered at the thought of that devious, soulless assassin. She was nearly sure that she was not done with him yet.

Her heart went out to Kadazaat and to his family. She had made a vow to him that she meant to someday fulfill. But somehow, she felt as though they would never cross paths again, not in this lifetime, anyway.

Dedlin Dane had certainly proved his worth, she thought, smiling. And so had the others, brave and true; Drer always cleaning and cooking without complaint. Steadfast Binder and his whining and overprotectiveness. Perce's coolheadedness and masterful navigational skills. Ott's sixth sense when it came to sniffing out Gharnians. Even Lake and Qan, who had been pulled up by the roots and drug off across the continent had proven themselves courageous and pure of heart. She would never forget any of them.

But mostly, she thought of Gaebryl. She longed for him to be there, strolling along with her at her side, talking, laughing and making sure she was always okay. She hoped more than anything that he was okay himself, and that he was on his way even then, searching diligently for her, coming quickly to guide and protect her against whatever dangers still lie ahead. That was her one wish, but that possibility seemed unlikely to her now. Her instincts told her that if Gaebryl were indeed still alive, he was now far, even farther, away.

"Will I ever see any of them again, Venni?" she asked.

There was no response from the bird this time. He was fast asleep with his beak tucked beneath a wing, bouncing with each step she took. The scenery of the forest changed very little with the passing miles, although a few small springs she passed along the way, trickling down into the creek bed, had caused a bit of a stream to run. There was a cool mist about her, cloaking the distant trees. Time felt as though it were standing still. She felt as though she had been walking there for days, or weeks, and when she turned around to look behind her, it was as if the path and trees had moved, magically and protectively covering her passing.

Darkness began to fall, and for once, the coming night was comforting. It was like a warm, protective bed and blanket to sleep within. The trees scattered up along the hillsides were small, yet dense and concealing. The limbs seemed to be intertwined and hugging, like long netted arms and fingers. As she stared at them through the mists, the trees resembled little old men with gray faces, bearded with brown, leafy whiskers, hiding her within their world with outstretched arms, and holding the cruel outside world at bay.

Colorful fireflies began dancing to the night songs, playing about among the branches of the trees. Sometimes they would come at her, flying circles around her head like a halo of gold.

70

Venni grunted, looking up with a start. "We still lost?" he mumbled, half-asleep.

"I don't know," she admitted, ducking beneath a moss covered log that crossed her path. "And I don't really care. Isn't that odd?"

"Then someone needs to say it. I say we're lost," he said. "Look, I can't keep my eyes open any longer. Let's have us a sleep for a bit, what do you say? I can't take any more of this bouncing about. We're safe enough here, aren't we? We can start again in the morning. You know, a fresh start and all that."

"I'm sleepy, too," she said, yawning. "It's hard for me to keep my eyes open as well. Strange. I hope we're not bewitched."

"We both need some sleep. I can't get any decent rest bobbing up and down on your shoulder all night. I've nearly plummeted to my death twice! It's torture!"

Jasmine climbed up the bank to a flat ridge and found a seat in a soft bed of dry ferns and mosses. Venni perched comfortably on a nearby limb, falling back into sleep at once. "Good night, then," he mumbled.

"Never seen him so quiet," Jasmine said, watching the bird. She laid back and folded her arms to keep out the chill, and watched the stars through the canopy above. They were especially bright that night. Cold and twinkling, but friendly.

She fell asleep.

71

Harsh reddened eyes searched in all directions. A nasty,

dripping nose scoured the ground and trees for a scent. For some reason, the trail was dim and confusing, and the scent seemed faint and old, although the morgothyon dog knew it was fresh. It was this *place*. It was hiding her; that's what it was doing. The paths moved at will, as did the rocks and trees, guiding it away from her trail time and time again. It wanted to take a new shape. A shape with wings, to help speed it on its way. But that would take too long. And the trees would hide her from above even more. There was no time for that. There was no more time for anything now but haste.

Nonetheless, it had discovered the empty skysled earlier, and the half eaten raspberries, strawberries, and breadfruit sometime later. She couldn't be too much further ahead. Night had come, and, unlike the morgothyon, she would have to sleep. Night was the morgoth's greatest ally.

It dashed down the dry creek bed, crashing over bushes and small trees.

It drooled in the anticipation of tasting her. One snap, a few seconds to relish her between its teeth and lapping tongue, then gobbling her down into the swelling rot of its belly, still alive, but barely. How delightfully tasteful she must be. How soft her young bones.

The Gharnians could then burn this whole infernal forest, take it apart piece by piece. The Stone was close by. Very close by.

Yes, the morgothyon dog of Gheelgahar could feel the Stone, now, too. It repelling it away. Which made it an easy beacon to now seek out.

72

For no apparent reason, Jasmine Day awoke. The night sky was as black as pitch, for deep clouds now shrouded the stars. Venni still slept soundly on his perch. She looked around for whatever it was that had awakened her, but she saw or heard nothing. There was just the forest blackness, lit with playful fireflies, dancing to the woodland concerto.

Then, one firefly, brighter than all the others, came forward, dancing to and fro before her face. Jasmine noted immediately that the color of this firefly was different from the rest. It was bright pink instead of yellow.

"You're not a firefly at all," she exclaimed, bewildered.

To her astonishment, there, before her eyes, was a beautiful, tiny, winged imp, a fairy maiden, with dragonfly wings and a sparkling pink gown made of shimmering, sparkling light. She was very tiny and fragile, but so beautiful that she took Jasmine's breath away.

The fairy beckoned Jasmine to follow her with the wave of her tiny hand.

"I'm...I'm being summoned," she said. "Venni! Come on!"

The bird did not flinch, as if Jasmine had not said anything at all.

Jasmine quickly stood and followed the racing light. "Venni! I've got to go, or I shan't keep up! Venni!" she cried over her shoulder, running through the woods after the fairy. "Wait for me here then! I'll be back as soon as I can!"

The pixie weaved through the trees with ease, gliding as gracefully as a dancer on the night air. Jasmine crashed through the underbrush below her, hopping from one small clearing to the next, high stepping through impossible thickets in every effort to keep up. It was like she was running through a surrealistic dream.

The pink light was joined by a delicate blue light, and then one of gold. They were all fairies, but with butterfly wings and glowing antennae. Then came a green one and a lavender one with the slower flutter of iridescent moth wings, all beckoning her to hurry faster. Jasmine followed the cluster of silent fairies with all her strength, far into the thick of the woods, stumbling sometimes over roots and fallen logs, but never slowing for fear of getting left behind or lost.

The trees began to thin a little and the heavy underbrush eased. All three moons came out from behind wispy clouds, illuminating a tripod of focusing light, onto a cool white path that fell before her feet. Jasmine ran on, watching as the tiny fairy maidens flew further and further away into the distant trees.

"Don't speed up!" she cried. "Please! I can't keep up with you!"

She ran faster, if that was even possible, almost blindly through the woods. Up one hill, down another. "You're losing me! Wait!"

The magickal lights moved farther away, far beyond the farthest trees, until they disappeared completely from her view. Just like that, *poof,* they were gone.

"Wait!" she cried again. "Come back!"

Jasmine slowed to a stumbling walk. She ran a few more steps, then stopped. What was the use? She was completely and utterly lost now, and she had no idea which direction she had just come from. It had gotten very dark once more. There were no sounds in this part of the forest, except for one single, solitary cricket, seeming to serenade the lonely night all by itself, as lonely and forlorn as she now found herself.

She sighed, wondering what to do now. What had just happened? Was it some kind of trick? She tried hard to catch her breath.

At least the air was cool and fragrant there, she was thinking, so sweet, so delicious. What was that aroma? She knew it...

It was jasmine blossoms!

The solitary cricket went as silent as the rest of the night.

Jasmine took in her breath and held it. She felt an

anticipatory tingle from the roots of her hair to the tips of her toes.

"I... I *found* it," she joyously exclaimed, her voice but a whisper.

Just then, a thousand beautiful lights of every magnificent color shone all around, so incredibly bright and vibrant that she could barely keep her eyes open. She was knee deep in jasmine flowers, standing upon a small shelf on the bank of a magickal pond that was surrounded on the other three sides by a rough rock wall, covered in roots and vines.

Thousands of illuminated fairies swirled all around her, and then they dove away across the water, their bright lights casting glorious reflections upon the still, glistening surface. Somehow, fountains burst from the pond, lit from beneath with magnificent lights and colors, and there was music in the air, magickal music and natural singing beyond compare. The voices of nature and magick had come to delight and warm Jasmine's wearyworn heart. The sound of harps and cymbals and the fanfare of brassy horns chased away all of her doubt and fear.

"It's the most beautiful and wondrous thing I've ever seen in my entire life!" she said, tears rolling from her joy filled eyes.

A stone walkway rose from the depths of the spraying waters, presenting a path at her feet, leading across the blue/green pond of pink, aquamarine, and turquoise lights, to a small architectural cave in the rocks on the opposite shore.

The cave was lit from within with light from crystals as white and pure as the light from the suns. The entrance was covered with ivy plants, flowering ferns, and trailing moss hanglets, which opened for her like a welcoming curtain. She had heard rumors of this place for years, and had traveled so far to seek it out, but nothing had prepared her for the natural, pure splendor and regal greatness she witnessed. It was an absolute wonder for her to behold.

Jasmine gathered her wits and stepped out upon the sturdy walkway. Curious golden fish lined the sides of the walkway as she crossed to the other side. Then other animals began appearing on the shores to watch, lining the banks of the pond: deer, rabbits, birds, a unicorn, squirrels, a fox, a bear, and many others.

The fairies crowned Jasmine with sparkling stardust and clothed her with a fiery robe. Even above the sound of thousands of buzzing wings and fairy voices, Jasmine could hear her own heart pounding in her ears.

She stepped into the cave. The walls were carved with statues of grim men and women, looking down with a righteous, caring and comforting demeanor. There was a crystal pedestal in the center of the room. In its clutches was a small, nearly round stone, the size of an apricot, that shone with magnificent fury and angelic brightness.

"The Stone," she whispered, stepping up before it. The Stone of her great-great-great grandfather, the first Day.

Jasmine reverently took the small stone key from her pocket and gently slid it within the small lock at the edge of the pedestal. It was a perfect, soundless fit.

She swallowed.

As she gently turned the key, she recited the magickal words that Dedlin had instructed her. "In peace I enter Szan Tu Xaq."

The key tingled in her fingers, like soft electricity.

The four claws that had held the Stone in place for centuries opened slowly and gracefully with a click.

Jasmine Day, one of the five heirs to the throne of Day, reached out and took it up in her trembling hand.

She was instantly filled with white light and power, more intense than she was humanly capable of acknowledging. It took her breath away.

All good hearted people across the miles were instantly filled with a sense of determination, courage and hope. All evil biding men and creatures slithered quickly into shadows as feelings of fear, paranoia, and doom overcame them. Many Gharnians went suddenly mad with confusion, and began fighting among themselves. Lord Gheelgahar the Black, standing in his dark tower nearly a continent away, shrieked as his heart froze, and his right hand withered, permanently useless.

And across the small pond, two red eyes suddenly knew the true meaning of absolute fear. The evil morgoth of Gheelgahar had arrived just minutes too late. It sensed its own doom, and howled, leaping across the pond toward the cave, mouth drawn open wide. Instantly, the howl became a pitiful squeal as it became as ash, empty and without form or substance. As a gentle wind took it, it fell powerlessly across the water and into the nearby woods to become the shadow of the old guardian trees for the rest of eternity, some of it settling beneath the restraint of the roots of the tiny fragile jasmine flowers that thrived around the cave at Szan Tu Xaq.

Jasmine was unconcerned with any of these things. She watched the shining Stone in her hand as its great light began to fade. She did not understand what she was to do with it now, or how to regain and retain the power from it. The Stone of Utter Destruction looked, to her, like an ordinary gray stone.

All the lights faded. The fairy imps fluttered quickly away into the night and the music and magick slowly died all around her. Jasmine pocketed the round Stone of her forefathers and ran back out across the sinking walkway.

Somehow, she knew as if by some magick, that her youngest brother was very close by, and he needed her help.

"Chance," she said, remembering his name. Then in a fleeting glimpse, it all came rushing back to her: she had two brothers and two sisters, and startlingly, they were not quintuplets, as she had first believed when seeing them in the magickal sinkhole mirror. Each one was two years apart from the next, she being the fourth child born to Mikael Nicholias Day. Somehow, Gheelgahar's Curse had faltered this generation, because the Five, although living as strangers spread all across the land, were all alive, and now it was time for them to come together again against this great enemy. The horrible Curse was, somehow, already broken.

She ran up the hillside, feeling elated, invigorated, and strong, to find Venni first, and then on to find Gaebryl, Dedlin, and the rest of her friends.

She was now a Stonebearer, and it was time to fight.

To follow the story complete,
you are invited to read the next installment of the

The Spiritmaster Chronicles

ANIMAL KINGDOM COME

The Extinction Virus

Bucky Montgomery

They're not coming. They're already here.

Animals...

One book to rule them all. One book to find them. One book to bring them all and in the darkness bind them. They're not coming. They're already here. Everywhere. All of them, from top to bottom. Revenge and justice has begun against the guilty. Is it led by God? Or Mother Nature? Or just another natural scientific recurrence due from imbalance?

For some unknown reason, household pets have started going feral, turning viciously on their masters, all around the world. Veterinarians, animal behaviorists, and viral scientists are baffled as they scramble to find some scientific reason. Soon, it gets even worse. It's not just pets and barnyard animals turning against us. Isolated incidents of animal revolution begin happening more frequently all around the world, from stampeding buffalo herds in Wyoming, to whales demolishing whale watching ships off the coast of California. From baboons in the Ugandan rainforests to a revolt at the Louisville Zoo. Humans are now forced to fight back just to survive as the strange viral epidemic escalates and, for whatever reason, the entire animal kingdom, from microbes to whales, is trying to reclaim their earth back from we humans. This is the basic premise of **'ANIMAL KINGDOM COME - The Extinction Virus'**.

Follow William "Buzz" Aldrin as he is forced to leave his home in Key West, Florida with his daughter Dezarae, his dog Max, and a few close friends, to travel back home to Louisville, Kentucky, to rescue and reunite with his lost son Chase. Parental guidance suggested.

☐   Another Amazon paperback and/or Kindle eBook by Bucky Montgomery.

www.ingramcontent.com/pod-product-compliance
Lightning Source LLC
Chambersburg PA
CBHW070403260626
47161CB00001B/259